EXIT THROUGH THE JUNGLE

ESCAPE IN PARADISE (BOOK 1)

ALICIA CROFTON

3DIMPLES
PUBLISHING

Book cover design by Erik Ebeling

Editing by Sarah Pesce

Proofreading by Anne Victory

ISBN 978-1-7352353-3-2 (paperback)

ISBN 978-1-7352353-0-1 (ebook)

To Lana.

she longed
for the ungodly
beast in me
by night,
but a tender
saint by
morning.

— E.CORONA

Mo' money. Mo' problems.

— THE NOTORIOUS B.I.G.

CHAPTER ONE

I t would have been the perfect Instagram shot if it weren't for a naked Santa Claus prancing in the waves. Jolie waited patiently in tree pose as the nude gentleman behind her lumbered his way into the ocean. His dimply butt cheeks clenched with each stride into the icy Pacific.

Jolie's friend stifled her giggle behind the tripod.

"Can you change the angle to get him out of the frame?" Jolie said, her teeth chattering. "It's freaking freezing out here."

"Then why are you topless?" Nora said, readjusting the camera.

"Because this is art," Jolie said with a scoff. "And it'll get me a lot more followers."

"Do you really need more? Aren't you up to a hundred and fifty thousand or something?"

Jolie rolled her eyes. "I guess it's less about getting more followers. I wouldn't mind showing Haiku Swim what they're missing by backing out on me."

Haiku Swim wasn't the only brand that had bailed unexpectedly lately, but that one hurt the most. Jolie had been working with the swimwear company for over a year. For no reason at all, they had canceled their contract. Jolie needed new branding partners soon, or she would be out of business.

Nora fiddled with the tripod. "I can adjust the camera, but we would lose the Golden Gate Bridge."

"Fine, but take it quickly. The lighting is just right, and I need the perfect shot."

Nora cleared her throat. "Um, Jolie? Your nipple is showing."

"Crap." Jolie repositioned her arms, her hands in prayer position in front of her sternum.

Click.

"Got it," Nora said triumphantly.

Jolie came out of the position and jogged to the camera. "Let me see," she said, pressing her Playback button.

The sun had just peeked over the horizon, creating a glow on her golden skin. The calming lavender sky hung behind decadent hills of green and crimson. The water sparkled under the newly born sun.

Jolie let out a soft breath of air. "Oh my God, it's perfect. I think this picture might have just saved my blog."

"Oh, come on." Nora gave her a nudge. "It can't be that bad."

Jolie shimmied into her sports bra, then pulled on her T-shirt and fleece jacket, grateful for the residual warmth that lingered inside the fabric. "My agent hasn't booked me a modeling gig in months. *Months.* I've had two brands end their contracts without renewing. I'm telling you, I'm washed up. I'm old."

Nora perched her knuckles on her hips. "Thirty-two is not old."

"Maybe I'm not old, but I must be losing my edge." Jolie

unclicked the camera from the tripod. "I need a new angle. Something to attract new followers."

Nora shielded her face with her hand as the sun peeked over the Golden Gate Bridge, and she pointed to the burly Santa still skipping in the waves. "You mean adjusting your angle to add Sir Naked Frolics-a-Lot to your shot?"

Jolie squinted at the jiggling belly. The man was splashing in the waves like a child. "Something tells me he wouldn't mind, but that's not what I'm talking about. I need something fresh in my newsfeed. Something that can compete with the waiflike twentysomething Instagram princesses with their perky boobs and pouty lips."

Nora chuckled. "You've got perky boobs and pouty lips, you brat."

Jolie rolled up her yoga mat and tucked it under her arm. "Maybe people are tired of my shtick."

"Your shtick?"

"Yeah, my shtick. My tattooed-badass-yogi-in-San-Francisco shtick."

Nora shrugged. "For what it's worth, I still think you're cool."

Jolie put her arm around Nora's shoulders and squeezed her tight. "Thanks, Nora, but no offense, next to you, anyone can look cool."

"Hey!" Nora elbowed Jolie in the ribs.

"Ow. You know I'm just kidding," Jolie said, squeezing Nora closer to her chest and planting a big sloppy kiss on her cheek. "Seriously though. Thanks for helping me with the pictures today. You're a lifesaver."

"My pleasure," Nora said, wrapping her arm around Jolie's neck. "Nothing like a perky peep show before I head to the office."

Jolie laughed at that. Nora was definitely the more

conservative one of the two. Thankfully, she never turned her nose up or made Jolie feel bad about her racy blog posts or imposed conditions or judgment. She was the best of friends.

Together, they shuffled through the cold sand, stepping over sand dollars and seaweed.

"I don't know how you do it," Jolie said.

"Do what?" Nora said, trying to fix her bangs despite the wind blowing them out of place.

"I don't know how you go into an office every day. You're an editor and a writer. You can work wherever you want."

Nora shrugged. "I like my office. I can get so much more work done there than at home."

Jolie stuck out her tongue. "Yuck." She couldn't imagine anything worse, tied to an office desk like a caged animal only to be released at dinnertime. "I'd rather chew off my right arm than work a nine-to-five job."

"Then it's a good thing you don't have to."

They reached the pavement of the parking lot, and Jolie felt the coarse gravel under her feet. Slipping on her flip-flop sandals, she scuffled back to her car.

Two eyes stared at her from underneath the front tire. A black kitten appeared, maybe less than a year old.

"Who's this little one?" Jolie cooed. "Nora, look."

Nora threw her bag in her car and shuffled over to see. "Oh my gosh, of course a stray cat would be under *your* car. You're like a magnet for homeless animals."

"It's so cute!" Jolie reached out to it. "No collar. No tags." The cat sniffed Jolie's fingertip and rubbed its cheek against it. "He likes me."

"Of course it likes you. Every stray animal in the city seems to like you. You've got a reputation."

Jolie chuckled. Petting the black fur of the kitten, she wondered if he was homeless or if he was just lost. "Maybe

I'll take him home with me for now and see if I can connect him to his owner."

"Sucker." Nora smiled.

She was right. Jolie was a sucker for animals, especially ones without a proper home. Jolie needed to help him find one, or she would keep him herself.

The cat jumped into Jolie's lap, purring in her arms. His tiny little claws poked through her yoga pants. Her heart swelled with joy, and she clutched the sweet little creature in her arms. "It's settled then. I'll take it to the vet on my way home."

"Don't you have a business to save?"

"Yes, but this is an emergency," Jolie said, letting the kitten sniff her nose. His scratchy tongue licked the tip of her chin. "That tickles, little guy."

"You and your animals," Nora said, shaking her head.

She decided to call him Franklin. The vet couldn't find a chip, but Franklin appeared to be healthy and safe for her to bring home after a few immunizations. Jolie posted a picture of Franklin on her neighborhood app with "Lost kitty needs his owner" and hoped she could reunite them before it was too late. She was already starting to fall in love.

Jolie tossed her camera bag over her shoulder and scooped Franklin up in her arms. "You're going to like it here," Jolie said, walking up the stoop. The jangling of her keys sent the inside of her apartment into a frenzy. Barks and yips emerged from behind the door.

"Hey, guys! Look who I've brought home." Franklin clawed up her shirt, scratching at her neck. "Don't be scared, Franklin. Let me introduce you to the clan."

Jolie stepped over the yipping dogs and through the hallway. "This is Frido," Jolie said, pointing to the shih tzu, who was yipping the loudest. Jolie reached into the bowl on the counter and grabbed a bone-shaped dog treat. "Frido is the feistiest one."

Franklin still gripped her neck. His back arched. "It's okay, honey," she said, petting his fur.

"And this is Sneeker. The one with the snaggly teeth." Jolie handed a dog treat to the white-haired Chihuahua, who scurried to the corner of the living room. He never liked to share.

"This is Duchess," Jolie said, giving the corgi-dachshund mix a slightly larger bone treat. "She's the mother of the troop." Duchess was more interested in Franklin than the dog treat, wagging her tail as if she were a puppy again.

After a while, Franklin relaxed, lying on Jolie's chest in the crook of her neck.

"There you go. Just get comfortable. I'll introduce you to Samuel the tabby cat later. He's probably asleep on my pillow."

It took several rounds of sniffing, each dog taking their turn, smelling Franklin's nose and then his butt, until finally Franklin began to purr. He leaped onto the top of the couch and settled into a perched position as the dogs went about their normal business. Frido and Sneeker fought over a rope toy while Duchess plopped her thick tummy onto the floor near the balcony window.

All was settled for now. Time to get back to work. Jolie pulled out her camera and plugged it into her laptop. Sitting cross-legged on her couch, she petted Franklin while the pictures loaded. "Let's see if we got what we needed."

Jolie opened her uploaded pictures and clicked through.

Nope. That one didn't have the right composition. *Next.*

Absolutely not. The camera added ten pounds to the

picture. Her cheeks looked like she was gathering nuts for winter. *Next.*

The next wouldn't work either. *Next.*

Jolie squinted at the image on her laptop screen. *Too blurry. Next.*

The golden image of her in tree pose appeared. *There it is. That's the one.* The one that would most definitely get her noticed. The photo radiated with color and contrast. The tattoo along her collarbone was on full display, her forearms covering her breasts just enough to pass the Instagram guards. The turquoise ocean and dewy Marin Hills glittered in the background.

It was perfect. The sound of Franklin's purr led Jolie to believe he agreed.

Jolie could almost hear the sound of her agent's raspy voice now. *I'm so sorry I've been MIA, but I saw your latest post, and it's gorgeous! I booked you a photo shoot at* Vogue. *Pack your bags, sweetheart, you're flying to New York.*

A flutter in her stomach appeared as she uploaded the photo to Instagram. *This was it.* The photo that would put her back on the map.

She set the caption:

Just another day at the office. #SanFranciscoyogi #yogabuff #jolieboulardyoga #model #bakerbeach #tattooedforlife

Pleased with herself, she popped up from her couch and fixed a green smoothie. Kale, frozen bananas, blueberries, almond butter, and soy milk. She resisted the urge to look at her post to see how many likes she had received in the first couple of minutes.

She chewed on her straw, negotiating with herself to wait at least ten minutes.

Jolie poked at the kale bits lodged between her two front teeth with her tongue, then a tap-tap-tap peeled her away from her own thoughts. The dogs went into a frenzy, yipping and barking, alerting her that an intruder was at the door.

Who could it be? It was too early for the mailman, and the mailman never came upstairs.

Jolie peered through the peephole and cocked her head to the side.

"Gregg?" Jolie said, opening the door for her landlord. "What brings you here?"

Gregg had hunched shoulders and a thin frame. He would have been taller than Jolie if he stood up straight, but instead he avoided eye contact and looked down at her feet. "I… uh…" He swallowed. His Adam's apple bobbed so low she thought it would fall to his stomach.

He held a check in his hand, and Jolie recognized her signature.

"I'm sorry to bother you, Ms. Boulard, but your check didn't go through this month."

"Didn't go through? That's so weird." Jolie grabbed the check from his tremoring hand and scanned it.

"The bank charged me thirty dollars for trying to cash it," Gregg said, his voice more dry than when he first spoke. "Insufficient funds, they said."

Jolie looked up through her eyelashes. His balding head had formed little beads of sweat on the verge of sliding down his pasty skin.

"I'm so sorry about that. I can write you another check."

"You may want to call your bank first. I don't want to be charged again."

Jolie's brow furrowed. "Of course. I'll call them right now and get this whole thing figured out."

"Thank you," Gregg said, cowering away.

"I'll also pay the extra thirty dollars for the trouble," Jolie said.

"It's no problem," he mumbled, not turning to look at

Jolie. Pit stains seeped from his armpits, nearly connecting with the sweat stain on his back.

Poor guy. He had always been nervous, but today he was particularly anxious.

Jolie shut her front door softly and stared at her check. It was impossible to think she didn't have any money in her bank account. Being an heiress to a jewelry company had its perks. Money had never been an issue before. Her father had financially supported her for years—well, that is, until she'd cut him off about two years ago.

Tired of her father's vise grip on her life, she had told her father she wanted to live on her own, to support herself with her own income. She needed to prove her independence so she could free herself from the wrath that came down with every bikini post online.

It was her life. Not her father's. If he didn't approve of how she chose to support herself, then he could keep his money. Her freedom was more important anyway.

Jolie pried her laptop open and strained her memory for her bank's username and password. Why hadn't she saved them on her computer? When was the last time she checked her account? She couldn't even remember which email address she used.

Her pulse quickened at the thought there might be an actual problem. She lurched toward her phone and dialed her father's assistant. Cindy handled all of Jolie's and her father's accounts.

"Hi, Cindy?" Jolie said. "I can't remember my username and password to my bank account. Do you have it?"

"Give me one minute and I'll find it for you, dear."

Jolie put the trumpet jazz music on speaker while she unsteadily walked toward the kitchen to grab her smoothie. Her teeth ground down on the straw between sips.

Franklin was exploring the kitchen countertop, and Jolie shooed him away. "Not on the counter please."

The phone clicked on, and Jolie twitched.

"Jolie, you there?" Cindy's sixty-year-old voice quivered.

"Yes, I'm here."

"I've pulled up your account, and it looks like you've got a balance of one thousand and eight hundred dollars."

Jolie couldn't have heard that right. "I'm sorry, you said one *hundred* thousand and eight, right?"

"No, I said one *thousand*."

Jolie's vision darkened around the edges, like she was watching a vintage film of her own life. Cindy was saying something through the speaker, but Jolie could only hear "one *thousand*" playing over and over in her head.

One thousand and eight hundred dollars wasn't enough to cover her next month's rent. She was out of money.

"Jolie, did you hear me?" Cindy asked.

Jolie snapped back to real time. "No, I'm sorry. What did you say?"

"Have you been depositing your income into another account, dear?"

"Income?" Jolie cupped her hand over her mouth. *Her brand partners.* They had all pulled out. The money she was receiving from her blog advertisements must not have been enough to cover her expenses. She knew it had been on the decline, but...

"Jolie?"

"I... um..."

"Oh, Jolie." Cindy's grandma-like tone pierced through Jolie's heart. Cindy knew it too. She was broke.

"It shows you have a pending payment of two thousand dollars. Maybe you can still cancel it before it's too late."

A sour film crept around the sides of her tongue, the same taste she would get just before she threw up.

That money was for her mother, who flitted into Jolie's life whenever she was desperate for money and right back out again when she had gotten her check. Jolie never would have thought a couple thousand dollars here and there would put her in jeopardy.

"I can't cancel that."

"Well, honey, I don't know what to say."

The kale in her stomach churned. "Please don't tell my dad," Jolie said, her voice cracking. "I will tell him myself."

Her head was swirling. Her chest burned. Her fingers trembled as they hovered over the phone.

"Your secret is safe with me."

"Thanks," Jolie said weakly.

"Maybe the two of you can go out to dinner tonight. I can reschedule his conference meeting with China. Would you like me to do that?"

Jolie squeezed her eyes shut. She didn't want to see her father. Not like this. He would call her irresponsible and immature. He was always looking for an excuse to tell her how much of a disappointment she was for not coming to work for him.

But she didn't have a choice. She was desperate.

Jolie swallowed. "Yes, please. Tonight works."

"I'll send you over the details shortly. Good luck, honey."

Jolie clicked the Speaker button and flopped back on her couch. She sank into the sofa and wallowed in despair.

Her father would make her feel every ounce of disgrace that he could pour out. It would be a bloodbath of shame and fatherly advice.

Taking a deep breath, she stood up and floated to her kitchenette, pulling out a bottle of Jim Beam. Perhaps a little whiskey would soften the blows she was about to endure.

Jolie poured herself a full glass and sipped away the hours, planning how to ask her dad for money without sounding desperate. She didn't need to give him another opportunity to control her any more than he already was.

The restaurant was like her father, pretentious and dripping with money. Silicon Valley business people hunched over tiny plates, tea lights reflecting off their trendy square-shaped eyeglasses.

Jolie drifted down the aisle, bobbing through hushed tones and clinking glasses, her head still in a whiskey fog. Her knees were like jelly as she followed the stiff-spined hostess to the booth in the far back.

Jolie's father was studying the wine list through wire-rimmed spectacles when he looked up. "I see you forgot your cardigan again."

Jolie looked down at her tattoos and let out a muted puff of air.

Great, he was already in a bad mood. Normally, this would be the moment she would snap back with a comment about how nobody cared what she looked like. She was an adult, and she could wear whatever she wanted. But she held her tongue.

"Good to see you too, Dad."

He returned to his wine list with his brows pinched together. "You know how I feel about the"—he waved his plastic menu at her cleavage, shaking his head—"in front of all these people."

It wasn't *that* much cleavage.

Jolie looked down. Maybe it was a *little* cleavage.

Jolie picked up her menu as a shield from her father's icy glare. Staring at the fuzzy swirl of French words, she blinked a few times until they came into focus.

The waiter arrived, slicing through the tension and began

listing their specials for the evening. The amount of effort and care the server put into each syllable of the *poulet vallée d'auge* was kind of sweet. Jolie gave him an encouraging smile as he went on.

"Can we please get a bottle of the 2009 *Chateau Leoville Poyferre*?" her father said, cutting the waiter off before he could finish the last syllable of *boeuf bourguignon*. "She'll have the steak tartar, and I'll have the filet mignon, medium rare, *s'il vous plaît.*"

Jolie glowered at her father. She hated when he was rude to the staff and hated it even more when he ordered her dinner for her as if she were a child.

Her dad ignored Jolie's glare and cleared his throat. "I have good news."

Jolie handed the waiter her menu and gave him an apologetic smile for her father's rude behavior.

"We have an opening in our marketing department. It's a communications role focused on social media. It's basically what you do now, but without your"—he waved at her chest again, still unable to say the word "chest" or "boobs"—"without your... *girl parts* on display for everyone to see."

Jolie summoned all her self-control to not roll her eyes. "About that," she said, breathing in sharply. "I was thinking of a new angle for my website."

Her father frowned. "Did you hear what I just said?"

"I did. I get that you want me to work for you, but I don't want to work for a jewelry company. I'm sorry. I want to do my own thing."

"By prancing around in your bikini all over town, with your tattoos and your..."

"They're called boobs, Dad."

The waiter was setting down their wineglasses, and his eyes widened.

"Sorry," Jolie said under her breath.

The waiter let out a small cough, pulling out a wine opener and pretending like he hadn't just cut into an awkward debate. Jolie and her father stared at each other while the server poured their wine.

"I think you're lost, Jolie," her father said. "You need direction and structure."

The back of Jolie's neck warmed, and she waited for the end of the glugging sound of wine before speaking up again. "Dad, I appreciate you trying to help me, but what you're offering me is a life sentence. I can't work there."

"I'm offering you a respectable job. One that will give you a steady wage. Insurance. Security."

"But I don't want those things. I want freedom. To come and go as I please. To work on my own terms. To create content that inspires people."

Jolie's father closed his eyes, taking a sip from his wine as if he was blocking out her words. "It's time to start acting like an adult. You're thirty-two years old."

Jolie sipped from her ice water, watching her father swish the wine around in his mouth. After one wine tasting class, he had to make a big show of it every time they were out. She tempered her irritation by focusing on the ice crunching between her teeth.

Her plans of asking her father for money faded away with every passing moment. How could she reject her father's job proposal in one breath, then ask for money in the next?

She needed to negotiate. Speak his language. Find a way his loan would benefit *him*.

Taking a sip of wine, she let the charcoal-like aftertaste sit on her tongue as an idea formed in her head. "What if we could make a deal?" Jolie said slowly.

His eyebrow rose.

Jolie picked a piece of bread from the table and placed it

in her mouth. "I want to give my business one last try. I need something to recharge my online presence to attract new brands."

Her father narrowed his eyes on her.

"If I fail, I'll come work for you. I'll put on a long-sleeved blouse and slacks if I have to."

"What's the catch?" her father asked, swirling around the wine in his glass.

As if he didn't know—he knew what the catch was, or so it seemed as he taunted her with the smug look he got when he had the upper hand. And he always had the upper hand.

Jolie swallowed, bracing herself for what she was about to propose. "I just need a loan to update my image. To rebrand."

Her father sat stiffly in his chair. "How much cash are we talking about?"

Jolie bit her lip. "A hundred grand?" Although she wasn't quite sure. Managing money hadn't really been her forte. It seemed like a lot though.

Her father sucked in his breath and narrowed his eyes.

"You want me to give you one hundred thousand to help you populate your social media? What about all the money I've given you over the years? Where did it go?"

Jolie tore away from her father's glare and focused on the tiny wooden grooves of the restaurant table. The truth was too difficult to say out loud.

"I lost some of my big branding partners recently, and my agent hasn't booked any modeling gigs in a long while."

"That's a lot of money you pissed down the drain, Jolie."

"I know."

She couldn't look him in the eye and took another sip of cold water to help distract her from the shame of begging for money.

Her father set down his wineglass and crossed his arms.

He shook his head at her, the way he did when she was young and in trouble. "How much has your mother taken?"

"What?"

"Your mother. How much has she been taking from you?"

Jolie froze. She had no idea he even knew that was happening. Could her mother have said something to him? No, that's impossible. She wouldn't have wasted a single breath talking to this man.

"She has nothing to do with it," Jolie said, ignoring the fact that wasn't entirely true. "I'll admit I've made mistakes with how I've managed that money, but I've learned from them. I want to give my business one more shot."

"Let's say I loan you the one hundred thousand from your inheritance. Then what? How much time will you need to determine if you are able to live on your own without coming to me, begging for my money again?"

Jolie's jaw dropped. "I'm not begging." Okay, maybe she was a little bit. "Give me six months to turn my business around. If I'm not making enough money to cover my expenses in six months, then I'll shut it down and come work for you. I'll file papers or work in the mail room if I have to. Whatever job is available."

Her father pursed his lips. "Do I have your word?"

It was like making a business deal with the devil. "Yes."

"Then I'll have Cindy draw up the paperwork tomorrow morning."

Jolie shot back in surprise. "Paperwork? What paperwork?"

"A contract."

Jolie hit the table with her hands. "You don't trust me?" Her voice rose an octave.

She eventually realized her plate of steak tartar was hovering by her arm, waiting for her to release the grip on the tablecloth. She apologized to the stunned waiter, again, and placed the white napkin in her lap.

"I want this in writing," he said tersely. "And if you don't come through your end of the bargain, your inheritance will be on the line."

Jolie froze. "My inheritance?" The millions of dollars that came with being an heiress to an international jewelry company? *That inheritance?*

"You heard me," he said with finality.

Jolie took a sip of water to soothe her dry mouth. The stakes were raised beyond Jolie's imaginings. "I have to give this one last shot."

"Six months then?"

Jolie nodded.

Her father picked up his steak knife. "Deal."

Jolie exhaled, both relieved and anxious at the same time.

"So what's your new angle? How are you planning on rebranding yourself?"

"I'm not sure yet. My seven-day challenges seem to be popular. I might focus on something like that."

Her father grunted. "It doesn't involve you being half-naked, does it?"

Jolie rolled her eyes. "I'm still figuring it out, but maybe I could extend my seven-day challenges into something different. Something more… meaningful. I want to figure out a way to do something that could make this world a better place."

Her father raised his eyebrows at that. "What do you mean?"

Jolie shrugged her shoulders, looking down at the plate of raw meat. She stared at the juicy pieces of cow as if they might have the answer.

Then it hit her. "Maybe I could try to become vegan or something like that. For the animals."

Her father laughed. "Vegan?" He slapped his knee. "Now that's funny. You could never be a vegan." He took a bite from his severed piece of filet mignon and placed it on his tongue. "My daughter likes her meat too much."

Jolie narrowed her eyes at her father. His skepticism lit a fire in her belly. Pushing the plate of steak tartar away, she looked him square in the eyes. "I may like meat, but that doesn't mean I can't do it."

"You'll never make it."

Jolie placed her napkin on the table. "Challenge accepted."

CHAPTER TWO

There was a break in the rain. The clouds parted, and the Costa Rican heat barged into the funeral like an unwanted guest. A small crowd, possibly twenty people or so, stood around the hole in the ground.

Kai put his arm around his mother's limp shoulders while the casket descended into the earth. The time had come to say their last goodbye.

His father's death came as no surprise. His failing health had been at his side for years, like a loyal pet that never strayed far. Late nights, smoking cigars, drinking brandy, and hard days building his coffee roastery from the ground up had taken their toll.

He squeezed his mother tight, knowing how much his death was ripping her apart. His parents had been the perfect couple ever since Kai could remember, dancing in the kitchen, sneaking in kisses after dessert. A once-in-a-lifetime kind of love that most people only experienced in movies or books. Kai feared his mother would never be the same after losing the love of her life.

"He was a good man." The words reverberated in Kai's

head, repeated by almost every neighbor or employee who attended the funeral that day.

"I assume you'll be taking over the family business?" an older gentleman asked in Spanish, firmly shaking Kai's hand. Kai recognized him. One of many friends his father had made while living in Costa Rica.

"Raffi, my brother, will take over," Kai replied in Spanish, acknowledging his older brother standing next to him. "But I'll stay back and help for a little while."

Raffi shifted on his feet and shook the man's hand. "The smart one here is taking a break from his big-shot finance gig and is going to help me until we hire an office manager." Raffi grabbed Kai's shoulders, giving him a shake. "I've got some big ideas for the business. We'll see if little brother tells me if I can afford them."

A smile appeared on the man's face. "I see the business will be in good hands. I'm sorry about your father."

Kai leveled his eyes at Raffi as the man walked off. "What ideas?" Kai said, switching back to English. "Did Pop know about them?"

"Don't you worry that pretty little face." Raffi grabbed Kai's cheek between his fingers. "I'll run them by you later."

Kai brushed off Raffi's hand. "Don't patronize me. I'm only here to help."

"And we're all so glad you can take the time out of your perfect life to make sure I don't mess everything up." Raffi gave one more solid pat on Kai's back before turning on his heel.

Kai let hot air out through his nose as he watched Raffi walk toward a group of Ma's friends, greeting them with his arms open wide.

Kai narrowed his eyes on him. Wrangling down Raffi's crazy plans for their father's business was going to be a challenge, but he would have to worry about that later. His mother and his younger brother were still standing by the coffin together, clutching each other in their arms.

"Are you doing okay?" Kai asked, putting his arm around Noah's broad shoulders.

Noah gave Kai a tight-lipped smile, never taking his eyes off the casket covered in flowers. His eyes glistened with unshed tears while Ma clutched his waist tightly, sniffing into a tissue.

"I was just telling Ma that I've decided to stay back and help with the business," Noah said.

"You can't do that, Noah. You've been putting college off too long now. It's your time to do what's right for you," Kai said, his eyebrows pinching together.

"I know, but Ma needs me to stay."

Ma looked up at Kai with her puffy round eyes. "I tried to tell him, but he wouldn't listen," she said, her thick German accent muffled by the tightness in her throat.

"You don't need to be a hero anymore. You've done your part, helping Pop and his business for what... five years now?" Kai said.

Noah nodded.

"Don't worry. My boss approved my sabbatical, so I'll be here for a while. Raffi will be here too. We've got it taken care of."

"You're okay with Raffi running the business on his own?" Noah whispered, looking over his shoulder.

"He'll do just fine," Kai said, following Noah's gaze to their older brother, who was shaking hands with a neighbor.

Who was Kai kidding? Raffi was a wild card. He always had been unpredictable.

Kai wasn't sure Raffi could run the business on his own, but he would soon find out. He had taken a few months of leave to help stabilize the business.

"Pop put everything they had into starting up that

company," Noah said. "If it fails, Ma won't have a retirement plan."

Kai gripped the lighter in his pocket. "Is that true? Ma?"

Ma nodded, blowing her nose into her tissue. "He put all our savings in that business. It's why he worked so hard all the time."

"Dammit," Kai said, promptly getting a swat to the chest.

"Language!" Ma hissed.

The business was in worse shape than he thought. He only had a few months before he would need to get back to his job and his life in San José. Uncertainty seeped into his racing thoughts. Would he be able to salvage the business before his brother ran it into the ground?

"You see? I can't go now," Noah said. "Maybe I'll reapply next year. I just want to make sure the business runs smoothly. For Ma's sake."

Kai pulled out the lighter in his hands and flicked it on. He stared at the flame as if it could give him the confidence that everything would turn out all right, just like his father used to do.

Two weeks later...

The stack of papers in his father's inbox mocked him. A physical inbox. Kai knew nothing of the inner workings of his father's business, and to make matters worse, the man had never trusted the computer. Everything was written by hand.

His accounting and balance sheets and receipts for all his investments were hidden in unorganized piles everywhere. There was no logical method or pattern to his ledgers. It would take weeks to decode the mess his father left behind.

A splitting headache grew from the back of his head and around his skull.

The rattle of the garage door shook the walls, and Kai looked through the window of the main office. The warehouse was packed with coffee beans in burlap bags ready to be roasted. Raffi pulled up in their company van and parked next to Kai's truck.

Raffi stepped out of the van, his face twisted, shadowed by the overhanging light. He looked at Kai but didn't seem to see him.

"Raff, are you okay?" Kai said.

Raffi's lip quivered, his hands shaking at his sides. He didn't answer.

"Raffi?" Kai padded toward him cautiously. "You look like you've seen a ghost. What's going on?"

Raff's mouth opened and shut, but nothing came out.

Kai had never seen Raffi so distraught. He stood there, paralyzed and shaking, as if he were in shock.

Kai clamped his hands on Raffi's shoulders and tried catching his gaze. "Look at me."

Raffi's eyes shifted, returning to focus.

"Say something."

"I...," he stammered. "I..."

"Let's go sit down," Kai said, sliding his hand to the back of Raffi's shoulder. He began to lead him toward the office when Victor, one of their employees, approached the van, Noah following behind.

Raffi tore himself from Kai's arm and yelled in Spanish, "Get out of there!"

Kai shot back in surprise. Victor froze, slinging back his hands away from the van as if it were on fire.

"Raff, what the hell, man? Victor is only trying to help."

"Get him out of here," Raffi growled in English. "All of them, including Noah."

Kai looked at Victor and Noah's stunned faces as Raffi's words echoed off the warehouse walls.

"Um," Kai said, shrugging his shoulders. He looked at the clock on the wall, and it was near closing time. "Victor, feel free to take off early," he said in Spanish. "I'll clock out for you at six."

Victor nodded, scurrying out the warehouse, occasionally looking over his shoulder toward Raffi, who was still standing there, trembling.

"I'm not going anywhere," Noah said, stalking over. "What the hell is going on?"

"Is anyone else here?" Raffi said.

Kai shook his head. "Franco left an hour ago, and you sure as hell scared the crap out of Victor. What's the matter with you?"

Raffi rubbed his cheeks with his hands. "I need to sit down," he said. Slumping into one of the chairs in their break room area, he rested his head into his hands.

Kai and Noah exchanged worried glances. Noah was probably thinking what Kai was thinking. What did Raffi get into now?

Raffi was always into trouble as a kid. His harebrained ideas never seemed to work out, including his most recent one: eloping with a stripper. It didn't take long for him to figure out that was a disaster of a decision when she had to go back to work after their honeymoon. The Greene men were known to be the jealous type. Luckily, Kai was able to convince Raffi to annul their marriage before Trixie could get pregnant and Ma could throw a baby shower among Costa Rica's finest strip-dancing crew.

"Shut the garage," Raffi barked.

Noah did as he was told, and he and Kai both took a seat around the folding table.

"I'm in deep shit," Raffi said. "I didn't know where to go."

"What happened?" Kai said.

Raffi dropped his hands from his face. His eyes looked more bloodshot than they did when he'd stepped out of the van. His hands shook as they fell into his lap. "I picked up a side gig. You know, to make a little extra cash."

Kai cocked his head. That didn't seem like such a big deal.

"I didn't really know what I had signed up for exactly," Raffi continued, "although I had my suspicions."

"What are you talking about, Raff? Get to the point," Noah said.

Raffi glared at Noah. "I was working for a guy that needed help with getting stuff delivered from one side of town to the other. It was a don't-ask-don't-tell kind of situation. Every now and then, I'd get a call from this guy Ricky. He'd give me a pickup and a drop-off location. It was easy to fit in our normal coffee deliveries, and the pay was really good."

Kai felt his blood pressure rise. A sharp pain scratched at the inside of his stomach. He was sure it was an ulcer forming.

"Raffi," Kai said through clenched teeth, "what did you get yourself into?"

"You don't even know the half of it," Raffi said, his face growing blotchier by the second. "I got a call last night, you know? No big deal. I picked up whatever loot they were stuffing in the van and took it to a warehouse on the north side of town. When I got there, I swear to God, it was a bloodbath."

"Jesus Christ," Noah said, running his hand through his wavy hair.

Kai's ears were ringing. He watched as his older brother fell apart before his eyes. "There was blood everywhere," Raffi said, taking a moment to swallow. "I didn't know what to do, so I called Ricky, my guy, thinking he could help me, but it just rang and rang. No answer. That guy never went anywhere without his phone. Ever."

"Do you think he's dead too?" Kai said.

"I don't know what to think," Raffi said. "I don't even know what's in the van."

"So you're telling me that you got yourself involved in something obviously illegal, and you brought that crap here?" Kai said. "Are these killers going to be looking for you too?"

Raffi shook his head. "I don't know," he said, his voice constricted. "I'm so sorry. I really fucked up."

"Yeah, Raffi, I would say so," Kai said curtly. "How could you be so reckless?"

Raffi shut his eyes. "I said I was sorry! What more do you want from me?"

"I want you to think, Raffi. For once! Think before you act. You're supposed to be taking over Pop's business, for God's sake. It's time to grow up," Kai said, storming toward the van.

"What are you doing?" Raffi said.

"I'm going to see what's in the van so I know what to tell the police," Kai said.

"No. Kai. Please." Raffi shot up from his chair.

Kai ignored his brother as he gripped the back handle and swung the door open. Stacks of green coffee bags were piled from floor to ceiling. Grabbing one of the bags from the top, he plopped it to the floor.

Noah and Raffi gathered around while Kai ripped the seam of the burlap sack. Green coffee beans spilled from the top, tumbling onto the cement floor at their feet. Kai pushed his hand through the beans until his fingertips landed on something smooth and firm.

The little boutique shop in Noe Valley was bustling with women flipping through racks of sale items. Jolie pulled out a floral maxi skirt and held it up next to the tank top. "Don't these look great together?" She held the hanger up to her chin in front of the mirror. She knitted her eyebrows together and pulled out the tags. "Is this expensive?" Jolie asked, holding out the white tag to Nora.

"It depends on what your budget is."

Jolie let out a sigh. She had never had a budget for clothing before. With one hundred thousand in the bank, she wasn't really sure how long it would last.

"What's wrong?" Nora asked.

"What do you mean?"

"You're chewing on the string of your hoodie."

"Am I?" Jolie spit out the soggy cord. It flopped down to her chest like a wet noodle.

"You haven't gnawed at something like that since our final semester at Berkeley," Nora said, putting her hands on Jolie's shoulders. "What's going on?"

Jolie admired the beautiful ensemble in her hands one last time and then hung it back on the rack. Times were different. She couldn't shop the way she used to anymore.

"I think I just need a coffee or something. You want to head across the street?"

"Sure," Nora said.

Jolie marched toward the exit, waving goodbye to the owner of the store. She stopped to admire the teardrop necklace that would have gone perfectly with the outfit she left behind but then shook off her instinct to pull out her credit card and marched across the street to the coffee shop like a good girl.

Jolie took a seat at the round table by the window while Nora finished placing her order at the counter. The sunshine seeped through the window and warmed Jolie's face. People with shopping bags walked down the busy street. Dogs on leashes waited, tails wagging, for their owners to finish their brunch.

"Okay, something must be up," Nora said, placing her foamy cappuccino on the table. "You never walk away from that store empty-handed."

Jolie placed her coffee stir stick next to her cup, resisting the urge to put it between her teeth.

"You know how I told you my business is in a slump?" Jolie said, taking a sip of her soy milk coffee. "It turns out it's much worse than I thought."

"How so?"

Jolie released a large sigh, resting her head in her hands. She couldn't make eye contact while she said it. "I'm out of money."

Nora gasped. "No way! How did that happen? I thought your dad was giving you money."

Jolie shook her head. "I cut him off years ago. I was tired of him telling me what to do all the time. I was doing fine on my own."

Nora quietly took a sip of her cappuccino.

"I feel like such an idiot, you know?" Heat rose on Jolie's face. "Like the rug was pulled out from under me and I've fallen on my ass."

"You are not an idiot," Nora said loyally. "You're just in a rough patch."

Jolie gazed out the window, wondering if this really was just a rough patch or if her plan at rebranding could actually work.

"Not to mention," Nora continued, "you've been exceedingly generous with your money."

"Nah," Jolie said.

"Jolie." Nora voice grew stern. "Half my wardrobe are gifts from you. Think about the money you spent as my maid of honor. Remember? The wedding shower? That trip to Bali? You paid for all that."

Jolie hung her head low.

"And don't get me started on the animals," Nora added. "How many animals have you taken in now? Ten? Fifteen? The veterinary expenses alone would result in bankruptcy."

"I only have five, thank you very much."

"Either way," Nora said. "What I'm saying is that you're too generous. You've done so much for the population of San Francisco's homeless animals, including myself."

"You were not a homeless animal."

"I sure was." Nora smiled. "You helped me get on my feet then, Jolie. Now I want to help you."

"I can't take your money, Nora."

"I insist."

"Nora, stop," Jolie said, more firmly than she intended. Her nerves were sizzling. "I got myself into this mess. I'll get myself out."

Nora looked away, settling her gaze outside as if she were trying to think of a solution. Her finger tapped on her lower lip.

"I already asked my dad for a loan on my inheritance."

"You didn't." Nora's head snapped back to face Jolie. Concern pooled in her eyes.

"I did," Jolie said. "We made a deal."

"What deal?"

"A contract, actually. He had me come into the office and sign freaking legal papers and everything." Jolie looked into the creamy swirl of her coffee and found herself nibbling on that damn coffee stir stick. "If I can't create a sustainable income in six months, then I'll give it up and work for him."

"No." Nora's mouth fell open. "Like, a real desk job?"

Jolie gave a nod.

"But you hate—"

"He's giving me one last shot at working for myself. For that, I'm grateful. It just comes at a hefty price if I renege on our deal."

"What happens then?" Nora's eyes grew round.

"If I don't adhere to our agreement, he's taking me out of the will."

"He *wouldn't*."

"Oh yes, he would. It's in writing. If I bail on our deal, the inheritance goes somewhere else."

Nora cupped her hand over her gaping mouth.

"It's a risk I'm willing to take." Jolie brought the stir stick to her teeth again and bit down hard. "I've got to try one more time to make it on my own. I can't stomach working for someone else—especially my father."

"So how are you going to do it? How are you going to turn your business around in six months?"

Jolie took a sip of her coffee. "I'm going to rebrand."

"What do you mean *rebrand*? Like, change what you post about?"

"Yeah. I'm going vegan."

Nora's eyes bulged, and she tilted her head back for a hearty laugh. "You're joking, right?"

Jolie narrowed her eyes on Nora. "I'm not joking. I'm totally serious. Why does no one believe I can do it? Don't you remember that meatless challenge I did in college? Thirty days without meat. It was a cinch."

"Oh yeah. I remember. Those were dark days, my friend." Nora's eyes twinkled. "By day five, you had become an überbitch."

"Hey!" Jolie said, throwing a crumpled napkin at Nora's face. "I was not a bitch."

Nora giggled into her cappuccino. "Yeah, you were."

"Whatever. Things are different now. I'm doing it for the animals. I was up all night watching vegan documentaries. I can't even stomach the idea of eating meat or dairy now."

"I've seen you get after meat before. It would make all the vegans in the world shudder."

"That's not helpful, Nora."

"Sorry. I don't mean to be unsupportive," Nora said. "I know you'll be able to do whatever you put your mind to."

Jolie relaxed in her chair. "Thanks."

"So, you think that will work?" Nora said. "Going vegan?" She made air quotes with her hands as if it weren't a real thing. "Isn't that a bit disingenuous?"

"Listen, this is a business. I was doing a little research with my social media tool, and the analytics all point toward this being a good strategy. Vegan brands are on the rise. More and more people are talking about it. It's becoming an increasing trend with no signs of slowing down anytime soon."

Nora's brows shot up, wrinkling her forehead. "Wow. You have analytics that tell you all that?"

"Oh yeah. Clicks. Shares. Video watches. The data doesn't lie. I also found there's a huge overlap between the yoga and vegan followers, so I won't be alienating too many of my current followers by doing the switch."

"I'm impressed that you know all that, but are you being your authentic self?"

"Sure I am. I can be vegan. I mean, I love animals. It's a win-win. I'm a little disappointed in myself for not thinking of it earlier."

"Well, whatever you do, make sure to slip in your sexy near-nude photos from time to time. You don't want to alienate the creepy men who follow you for your… *physique*." Nora winked, taking another sip from her cup.

"I've thought of that too. I will definitely need to keep up the bikini shots."

"Vegan bikini shots?"

"I'm not sure that's a thing, but I'll look into it," Jolie said. "Anyway, I was thinking about changing my location. Somewhere that's warm all the time."

Nora tilted an accusatory brow. "Aren't you on a budget?"

"Yeah. So it has to be somewhere cheap."

"Hm," Nora said. "The desert?"

"Not a bad idea," Jolie said. "Palm Desert could work, but I think I would get sick of the desert vibe thing."

"How about Mexico?"

"Maybe… like Cabo San Lucas? That could work," Jolie said, taking a mental note.

"Oh, I know! It's been there in front of me the whole time. How about Costa Rica?" Nora said, pointing to the poster behind Jolie's head. It was an advertisement for a Costa Rican coffee blend with a colorful toucan featured in the center. "I've always wanted to go there. They've got rainforests, beaches, sloths. It seems like it would be right up your alley."

"Oooh," Jolie cooed, "I just love sloths."

"They're so cute, right?"

"It's perfect."

"There you go," Nora said. "I'm glad I could help."

"You want to come with me?"

"I wish I could, but I promised Kellen I'd stay home with him for a while. The last book tour was way too long."

"All right. I'll go by myself then."

"Is it safe for you to go alone?"

"I'm sure it'll be fine."

"Sounds like you've got a plan now."

Jolie held her coffee up to her friend. "To new beginnings."

Nora clinked her cup with hers. "To new beginnings."

CHAPTER THREE

Kai's fingers pressed against the smooth surface of the object in the coffee bag until his hand was able to grip it. Pulling it out, several more green coffee beans spilled to the floor.

The plastic-wrapped brick stuck to his sweaty palms as he examined it. "This is cocaine," Kai said, holding it up for Raffi and Noah to see, his eyes blazing at his brother. "You just brought a van full of cocaine into our warehouse."

Raffi cursed under his breath and kicked at the van's tire.

"This is bad," Noah said. "Really bad."

"How could you have been so stupid?" Kai hissed. Kai watched Raffi as he continued to kick the tire over and over again.

"Raff, are you sure no one saw you when you got to the drop-off location? Could someone be following you?"

Raffi froze, his eyes swimming in worry. "I don't know." He swallowed. "I didn't see anyone."

"We need to call the police. This is too dangerous," Kai said.

"No!" Raffi shouted. "If we call the police, they'll ask how I was involved. They'll put me in jail."

Kai drew in a deep, calming breath. A part of him knew Raffi deserved to be in jail. He was endangering them all with his carelessness. A few months in jail might actually do him good.

Raffi leaped to Kai, gripping the sleeves of his shirt. "Please," he begged. "I know I made a mistake, Kai. And I'm so sorry. I should have known what I was getting myself into. I didn't mean any harm. Please. I can't go to jail. Whoever these drug dealers are, they'll find me and kill me. Especially if I go to the police. They'll know I snitched. Please, Kai." His voice wavered as he dropped to his knees. "I don't want to die. Please. Don't call the police."

Raffi dropped his head into his hands and sobbed. It was the first time Kai could ever remember seeing his older brother cry. Raff had always been the tough one growing up. Lord knew if five-year-old Kai had ever been caught crying, Raffi would've torn him apart and called him names.

Noah looked just as surprised as Kai felt.

"If we call the police and tell them what's going on, they will be able to protect you. More than we can protect you right now," Kai said, imagining the worst. His eyes glanced at the door leading to outside. The drug cartel, or whoever they were, could be out there now.

"You don't know that," Raffi said, sniffing against the back of his hand. "You don't know what can happen when people go to the police. The police can try to help, but these people could have connections on the inside. If we call the police now, it would be a death sentence. I can almost promise you that."

Kai dropped his head, wishing his brother didn't have a point. Kai wouldn't be able to live with himself if something happened to Raffi in jail. His ulcer throbbed at the sight of his brother, blotchy-faced and blubbering like a little child.

"What are we supposed to do then, Raff? We can't keep the cocaine here. I want it gone," Kai said.

"Can't we just dump it in the ocean?" Noah asked.

"No," Raffi said. "If these people show up, we need to be able to give it to them immediately as a peace offering. It's our only way to survive."

Kai's tongue dried out as his mouth hung agape. "Did you just say *we* need to? It's *our* only way to survive?"

Raffi blinked away his tears. "I'm so sorry," he said shakily. "I don't think anyone saw me, but if they did, they would have seen our logo on the van."

Kai's eyes landed on the Greene Coffee Roastery logo plastered on the passenger door. It was clear as day and could be recognized from a good distance.

"I'm so sorry I've gotten you in this mess too," Raffi said.

Kai clenched his fists, stepping away from his brothers. He paced with his hands on his hips, growling under his breath as he tried to comprehend how his life had come to this. It wasn't just Raffi's problem now. It was all of their problem.

"You know what I think?" Noah said, stalking over to the front door. He peered outside. "If they had seen Raffi or the van, they would have been here by now." Noah unlocked the back door, poking his head outside. The sun shone on his eternal optimism. He looked left and right. "See?" His head popped back in. "No one is here."

Maybe Raffi had gotten away with it. Maybe the cartel wouldn't be able to trace the stash after all. Even though Kai wanted to believe there was a chance that they weren't in real danger, he knew he needed to make a plan.

"Noah's right. It's possible they didn't see the van, but we can't keep the stuff here. I say we dump it and call the police anonymously so they can take care of it."

"Wait. Hear me out," Raffi said. "If these guys do show up, we can't tell them it's with the police. They'll shoot us on the spot. Let's just give it a few days. Okay? Just a few days, and if they don't come, then we can go along with your plan."

Kai found himself toying with his lighter, flicking the flame on and off to soothe his mind. The orange glow calmed his nerves, but he felt his jawline tighten at the idea of keeping the cocaine. They would need to hide the stuff until it was time to dump it for good.

"How much cocaine are we dealing with here?" Kai said, assessing the bags. "Are any of these bags ours?"

Raffi stood up, shaking his head. "The van was empty when I went for the pickup."

"All right," Kai said, looking around. "Let's take the cocaine out and hide it somewhere the employees won't find it. Three days, *max*. You understand?"

Raffi nodded.

The three brothers stood in front of the van, Noah's hands in his hair, Raffi's palm over his mouth, Kai's hands on his hips.

"Noah, grab a few cardboard boxes and some duct tape," Kai directed. "Raffi, grab some extra burlap sacks." Kai pulled out a sack from the van, tearing it open at the top. The brothers created an assembly line. Kai dumped the beans. Raffi held the bag, and Noah grabbed the bricks of cocaine and placed them into the boxes.

They worked until Kai's forearms burned and his biceps ached. He had been counting the bricks in his head but lost count at around one hundred and fifty, all the while cursing himself for wanting to protect his brother despite what he'd done.

Kai had never seen so many drugs in his life. There was

that one time at a college party when he knew the guys in the back room were snorting the stuff, but Kai had never bothered with it. His friends would tease him for being a prude, but Kai didn't care. Getting drunk and high never interested him much. He couldn't see the appeal, maybe because he saw what drinking and smoking had done to his father's health over time.

"Why take the risk?" Kai would ask, with no reasonable response in return. "You're too practical for your own good," they would say. "Live a little." But Kai avoided danger at all costs. He had spent a lifetime watching his reckless older brother make mistake after mistake. Break bone after bone.

Kai didn't want to end up like Raffi, and yet here he was. Shoveling out what seemed like two hundred kilos of narcotics out of the family-owned van.

"How many is that?" Kai said, shaking out the last bag.

"Two hundred and ten," Noah said, wiping the sweat from his forehead. He finished stacking the last brick in a box.

"This has got to be worth millions," Raffi said, his gaze raking over the opened boxes.

"Don't you dare get any ideas." Kai scowled. "You've gotten us in enough trouble."

"We could sell one and—"

"No!" Kai snapped. "Get that out of your head now. It's not for us to sell."

"Yeah, I guess you're right. The cartel might be pretty pissed if they knew one was missing."

Kai knew Raffi couldn't help himself. His older brother was born with bad ideas running through his veins, feeding his organs and poisoning his mind.

Noah was shaking his head. He must be thinking the same thing.

The last thing that made sense was to continue to allow

Raffi to run the business. Kai had known it deep down all along, but he didn't want to believe it. Raff was unfit to run the company, which meant Kai would need to step in and walk away from the life he had built for himself in San José. The life he had worked so hard for. The dream job. The studio apartment with an amazing view. He could kiss it all goodbye because there was no way he could go back now.

Just then, something caught Kai's eye. A dark figure appeared from the front door under the exit sign's red light. Kai jumped, his heart skipping a beat as a man with coal-black hair entered the warehouse. He held a phone up, blocking his face, but Kai knew who it was. The snakeskin cowboy boots and the pack of cigars sticking out of his shirt pocket gave him away.

It was *him*.

Kai's worst nightmare.

CHAPTER FOUR

A sticky heat swept over Jolie as she stepped onto the Jetway. Her muscles were stiff and achy from the long flight, and her stomach grumbled.

Passing through the airport, she came across a burger restaurant. Fumes from the grill lured her in like Pepé Le Pew to his next object of desire.

Her mouth salivated. It had been weeks since she had eaten meat products of any kind. She thought it would have gotten easier by now, but Smashburger called out to her like a long-lost friend. She had hoped that being in Costa Rica, she could avoid the rich aroma of charbroiled burgers and salty fries, but alas.

She shook off the temptation, determined to take her new vegan life seriously. She carried on, eventually finding herself in line for a cab just as the sun was setting. Jolie soaked in the warmth of the Caribbean air, watching the tourists jovially hop onto giant tour buses and resort shuttles.

By the time her cab arrived, the sun was shining directly into her eyes. Jolie plopped into the back seat and fumbled through her bag, grabbing her sunglasses to shield herself from the sun's peek-a-boo game at the edge of the skyline. The cab drove off toward the streaks of hot pink and purple across the turquoise sky.

Jolie rolled her window down and breathed in the salty air. Her hair whipped in the wind, tickling her face. She stretched her arm out the window, letting the cooling breeze roll over her arms like a built-in massage.

This was heaven.

The cab pulled off the highway onto a gravel path leading into a jungle of shaded trees. Jolie could hear the ocean waves nearby, despite being surrounded by swaying palms and cackling birds. The soft glow of the Yogi Garden Resort's front lights came into view.

After Jolie checked in, she carried her luggage to the small hut down the stone path, just across from an outdoor gazebo where a late-night yoga class was in session.

The room was warm, adorned with wood panels from floor to ceiling, the full-size bed draped in fresh white linens. A single pink hibiscus rested on a folded towel. A vibrant rug with turquoise blues, pinks, and oranges rested on the floor, and a bamboo ceiling fan above circulated the air, creating a soft breeze.

It was the ideal scene for her first post as a born-again vegan. She could set up her photo shoot right in front of her bed.

Although sleep beckoned, she pulled out her tripod and positioned her camera to face her bed. Slipping into a silk nightgown, Jolie rubbed a pink stick on her cheeks and her lips, blending with her finger until she reached the perfect amount of natural blush. Then she pulled her wild hair up into a messy bun. Not too messy but messy enough to make it look like she'd just woken up.

Jolie pressed the timer button on her camera and leaped onto the bed. Crossing her legs like a lady, she stretched her arms high into the air, and shut her eyes tight.

Click.

She checked her camera and repeated the process six more times until she was happy with her image. Just a couple of edits to the contrast and it would be the perfect post to kick off her adventure in Costa Rica.

Her eyelids felt heavy as she tweaked her image on her computer and sent it to the cloud. Slipping under the bedcovers, she thought of what her caption should be for her first official vegan post.

This meat lover is giving up the meats. Follow me on a vegan trip around Costa Rica.

A vegan sunrise in paradise.

Jolie tapped her finger on her lower lip as she scraped her brain for another idea.

Woke up a vegan in a jungle paradise. Follow me on my new adventure!

Jolie stared at her phone screen. The text blurred, and her brain felt like mush. Maybe if she slept on it, she'd think of an enticing hook in the morning. She turned off her phone and snuggled under the covers, listening to the soothing sounds of tropical birds and raindrops against the trees.

She would wake up in her new life as a vegan entrepreneur. A businesswoman who finally had a handle on her finances. A daughter who could prove she could live life on her own terms.

Kai's nostrils flared at the man stepping into the yellow overhead light. The man lowered the phone, revealing a twisted smile. Marco Venega's black eyes sparkled above his potholed, aging face.

Kai's pulse switched on like a jackhammer in a construction site. "What are you doing here, Marco?"

"I came here to give my condolences," Marco said in Spanish. "But it appears I've stumbled across something more interesting." His voice oozed like black tar, hot and thick.

"You didn't catch shit," Raffi spat out, throwing the burlap sack on the ground.

"Ah, ah, ah," Marco said teasingly, placing the phone in his back pocket. "I think this little video tells a different story."

Kai cursed under his breath. This day couldn't get any worse.

"You don't have anything on us," Raffi said, puffing his chest.

"I beg to differ. It looks like you and your brothers' true colors are showing. I always knew your father was raising a bunch of thugs."

"You son of a bitch!" Raffi lunged at Marco. Kai shot out toward Raffi, wrapping his arms around him, pulling him back. Raffi fought against Kai's grip.

"Raffi, calm down," Kai said.

"You piece of shit!" Raffi spat at Marco's feet. "Delete that video, motherfucker."

Marco's lip curled into a sinister grin, watching Kai struggle to get control of Raffi's flailing arms.

"Get your shit together, Raff," Noah said, helping Kai get a solid grasp on their brother. Raffi thrashed and pulled, tugging against Kai's fatigued arms. Noah's strength was enough to subdue Raffi's attempt to pounce on Marco.

"What do you want?" Kai growled. "What's it going to take for you to delete that video?"

Marco rubbed his chin as his eyes fluttered around the warehouse.

"I want this," he said, his hands outstretched, waving around him. "I want this warehouse, to expand my business."

Kai should have known. Marco's motorcycle dealership across the street had been busting at the seams with bikes. He had attempted to buy out their father's company once or twice before, Kai recalled, only to end in a screaming match that had made people's ears ring for miles.

"The warehouse is not for sale," Raffi hissed, giving up the fight. His hands settled to his sides.

"Raffi is right," Kai said. "I never understood why you and our father had so much contempt for each other, but he would turn over in his grave if we sold our warehouse to you."

Marco chuckled, pulling out a cigar from his front pocket. "I'm sure he would."

"Have a heart, man. Our father just passed away, and this is not what it looks like," Kai said, pointing to the boxes. "This isn't our stuff, and we intend to turn it over to the cops."

Marco raised his eyebrows. "Sure you do." He took a step back as if he were about to leave. Kai felt Raffi's body relax under Kai's grip until Marco lit his cigar, pulling in small puffs of air. Smoke billowed from his mouth. "You do have a lot going on, indeed. It would be a pity if the police were to get a tip that there are drugs in the Greene Coffee Roastery."

Raffi's body tensed again. He yanked himself free from Kai and Noah's arms. "Piss off," Raffi spat out.

Marco smiled. "I will enjoy watching your family rot in jail. Including your mother." He turned on his heel, leaving a trail of white smoke in his place. Marco pulled the door open to leave.

Visions of Ma in a jumpsuit and handcuffs around her

wrists flashed across Kai's mind. He hadn't even thought about Ma and how she could get roped into this disaster. Kai blurted out, "How much?" without another thought.

Marco paused with one foot out the door. Kai silently begged for him not to leave.

"What was that?" Marco cupped his hand around his ear.

"How much for the video?" Kai sucked in his breath.

Marco had a reputation for being a tough negotiator. His business was thriving because of it, which was probably why he needed more space.

"Five hundred grand. US Dollars," Marco said without blinking.

"You're out of your mind!" Raffi yelled.

"Quiet." Kai scolded Raffi. "And you," Kai said, looking into Marco's beady eyes, "come with me."

Kai's heart was beating so fast he was shocked his voice stayed as steady as it did. He led Marco into the office and took a seat in his father's chair.

Marco strolled in as if he owned the place. "I see you're going through some of your father's paperwork."

"Sit," Kai said coolly. "Your tiff is not with me and my brothers. I don't want to maintain this stupid war you had with my father. Okay?"

Marco sat in the cushioned chair across from the desk and leaned back, folding his arms with a smug grin across his face. "This isn't about your father. This is about business. I need this lot to expand."

Lacing his fingers, Kai stiffly placed his hands on the desk. "Like I told you before, this business is not for sale, and it certainly isn't even close to being worth five hundred thousand."

"Didn't your father teach you anything about business? Let me teach you something, boy. Rule number one: never show your cards or tell your opponent what something is worth."

Kai gritted his back teeth.

"Rule number two: start the negotiations first. You asked me what I wanted for the video. Now I have control."

Kai let the hissing sound of breath through his nose be the only sound in the room while he subdued his rising temper.

"All right then. Ten grand," Kai said, knowing full well that he would be able to cover that expense with his own money.

"Four hundred thousand."

"Impossible."

"Then give me your lot."

"Never."

"Then we are at an impasse," Marco said, his hands rotated up toward the ceiling. A flick of cigar ash fell to the floor.

Kai growled under his breath. He wasn't yet sure how much his father had in cash, but he guessed it wasn't much. "One hundred thousand," Kai said. "That's more than we have. We would need time to gather it."

Marco didn't blink as he released a large cloud of smoke from his mouth. It floated into the air between them, coating Kai's lungs.

"Two hundred thousand and that's my final offer," Marco said, staring at Kai. Taunting him.

Kai looked up through the office window to see Raffi and Noah having an argument. Raffi shoved Noah, trying to make his way toward Marco, only to be stopped by Noah's grasp.

Two hundred thousand was more than the three of them could pitch in. He was sure of it. He would have to take out a loan if the company didn't have enough assets. Kai stared at the paperwork on the desk, wishing he knew where his father's latest balance sheet was.

Maybe it was possible to pay it, but then their mother wouldn't have a dollar to her name.

"One hundred fifty thousand," Kai said, taking the chance. "I'm not even sure I can get that much money, but I am sure it's the highest I will go."

Marco stood from his seat and started walking out the door.

"Where are you going?" Kai said.

Marco paused at the door, turning his neck slightly back toward Kai. "You've got ten days to bring me one hundred fifty thousand. Have the money in cash, or this video gets released to the police."

Kai followed Marco out as he strolled past Kai's brothers, blowing smoke into Raffi's irate face.

"Pleasure doing business with you, boys. I'll check in on you in a few days." He took one step out the warehouse door when he turned back, his cigar hanging out of his mouth. "And again, my sincerest condolences for the loss of your father." Marco erupted in a deep throaty laughter, coarse and wicked.

"Asshole," Raffi said. "What did you just agree to?"

Kai pulled out the lighter from his pocket, flicking the metal ridges of the flint wheel.

"One hundred fifty thousand US dollars," Kai said.

"One hundred and fifty what?" Raffi said, pushing Noah off.

"Holy shit, that's a lot of money," Noah said.

"I know," Kai said. "It was either that or we give him the warehouse."

"We can't," Raffi said.

"Since you got us in this mess, you need to start coughing

up some of that money you've been pocketing during your cocaine deliveries." Kai pointed to Raffi's chest.

Raffi huffed, kicking the nearest stack of bagged coffee beans with his boot repeatedly until the pointy toe punctured the bag and hundreds of green coffee beans scattered across the warehouse floor.

CHAPTER FIVE

K ai and his brothers hunched over their mother's tiny kitchen table like three giants at a little girl's tea party. Without their father around, Ma refused to set the dining table anymore.

The three brothers complied, not daring to protest despite knocking knees under the table. Elbows were thrown when Ma wasn't looking.

The local news blasted in from the living room—a new development since their father passed. It was as if Ma were filling the void in her broken heart with blaring advertisements for kitchen gadgets and local news stories.

Kai could barely hear himself think. They had only five days left to pay Marco's debt, and no one had yet come looking for the van of cocaine. Kai agreed to keep the boxes hidden under the stacks of paperwork in the office until they could settle their debt with Marco. Kai's ulcer grew more bothersome with each passing day.

Paranoia had settled in. The doors were always locked. The warehouse was never open, despite the suffocating heat. They had spent the past few days baking from the inside out, sweating over any stranger that crossed their path.

"I'm stuffed," Kai said, rubbing his stomach, hoping it appeared as though he was stroking a full belly and not the ache in his gut. "Dinner was delicious, Ma."

"Do you want to take some of the leftovers back to your apartment, Raffi?" Ma asked, holding out an empty Tupperware.

"No, thanks, Ma," Raffi said. "Kai and I have some things to take care of at the office tonight. We won't be home for a while."

"Don't put that away yet," Noah said, spearing another bratwurst from the center of the table. "I'm still eating."

"You're always still eating," Raffi said, shoving Noah nearly off his chair.

"Boys, stop it. I swear it's like the three of you never grew out of your teenage years."

"Sorry," Raffi said, looking down at his hands. As soon as Ma turned her back again, Noah gave Raffi a solid punch to the arm.

"Oof," Raffi muttered, elbowing Noah back, knocking the fork out of his hand. It clanked against the ceramic plate, and Ma whipped around.

"Boys!"

"Kai and I are leaving." Raffi pointed to his watch, giving Kai the signal it was time to go.

"Thanks for dinner, Ma," Kai said, standing up.

Ma wiped her wet hands with a towel and reached her arms out wide. Kai wrapped her up in a hug, letting her head rest on his chest for a brief moment.

"I know it's not the same without your father," she said, still holding him close, "but I appreciate you still making time for Sunday dinners." She peeled herself off Kai and grabbed Raffi by the neck, pulling him in for a hug. "You boys make me so proud, working late hours, keeping your father's business afloat. I know he's smiling down from heaven." Ma squeezed both their cheeks.

"I'll be back when we're done," Kai said, freeing himself from her vise grip.

"Can I go with you guys tonight?" Noah perked up from the table. "I want to help."

"Uh, I don't think that's a good idea, Noah," Kai said.

"I put off college to help you guys with the business, so let me help."

Kai exchanged a glance with Raffi. "How about some other time, okay, kid?" Raffi said, clamping both his hands on Noah's shoulders, pushing him back down in his chair.

"I'm not a kid anymore." Noah jabbed Raffi's lower back.

"Ow," Raffi said. Raffi hooked his arm around Noah's neck as if he were going to wrestle him to the floor. "You're only twenty-two. You *are* still a kid."

"Boys!" Ma screeched.

"Come on, Raff, we gotta go," Kai said, yanking Raffi's arm. "Bye, Ma. See you later, Noah."

Noah and Ma followed them through the living room. Noah put a foot in Raffi's path, and Raffi tripped, stumbling toward the front door.

"Dickhead," Raffi said, swinging his hand at Noah's head.

"Language!"

"Sorry, Ma," Raffi said, giving Noah a stare down in the I'm-going-to-beat-you-up-but-I-love-you kind of way.

Kai shook his head. Those two were always at it.

"Good night," Kai said, letting the door shut behind them, closing out the megaphone of the local news station. He took a deep breath in, the fresh air filling his lungs. Bugs chirped. Palm trees rustled in the breeze. His eyes checked the street up and down for anything that might look out of the ordinary.

"You're being paranoid," Raffi said, hitting Kai in the chest. "If someone was looking for that cocaine, they would have tracked it down by now."

Kai let out a sigh. The more time that went by, the more it felt they were in the clear from being the cartel's next target. It should have made Kai feel better, but it didn't. Kai stiffened his jaw and stepped into the driver's side of the truck.

"What's wrong with you?" Raffi said.

"I'm worried, that's all."

Raffi nodded in silence, gripping the handle of the truck until his knuckles turned white. "I am too."

"We still have a lot more money to find and less than a week to find it. I can chip in the rest of my savings, but it's not much." Kai backed out of the driveway. As he shifted the truck into forward gear, Noah appeared in the headlights with his hands up.

"What the—?" Kai slammed on the brakes.

Noah opened the passenger door and jumped in.

"I'm coming with you whether you like it or not," Noah said, catching his breath.

"What the heck were you thinking?" Kai said. "I almost ran you over."

"You both need to stop treating me like a little kid. We're in this together, and if you recall, I'm in that damn video too. I should have a part in getting us out of this mess."

Kai looked up at Raffi.

"All right, he can come," Raffi said. "He might come in handy."

Kai sighed and drove out of their mother's neighborhood.

Under the streetlamps, Kai could see Raffi's eyes shifting from side to side. "You've got that look on your face like you're cooking up an idea," Kai said.

"Something like that," Raffi said, rolling down the window.

Kai didn't want to entertain the ideas running through Raffi's head, so he drove in silence until he pulled up to the warehouse.

Kai flicked the office lights on, and the men crowded around the desk while Kai read over his notes.

"We've got sixty-five thousand in cash on hand," Kai said, sitting back in his chair, his head in his hands. "I've got about ten grand in my savings account, so that's seventy-five thousand. That's only halfway there."

"You can take the five thousand I had set aside for college," Noah said.

"Absolutely not," Kai said. "That's your future."

"So is your savings account," Noah said.

"You see, this is why I didn't want you helping us out," Kai said, shaking his head. "You can't throw your life away over this blackmail."

"I'll take a second job and make it back in time for next year," Noah said.

Kai grunted. It was no use changing Noah's mind. He was just as stubborn as the rest of the family. "What about you, Raff?"

Raffi held out one finger, signaling them to wait while he rushed out of the office. He dug through the back of his truck and came out with a pillowcase, proudly dumping heaps of cash on the floor.

"What's this?" Kai said, staring at the money. A sick feeling irritated his ulcer.

Raffi laughed as Kai took handfuls of it and gaped.

"Raffi, where the hell did this come from?"

"Most of it is from the money I was making on the side. The rest is from the convenience store."

"What?" Kai said.

"The convenience store down the street. You know the one with the old man who's always grumbling about football? He never even saw me do it. He was out for a smoke break, and the register was left unattended."

Kai's mouth fell open. "You *stole* it?"

"This is bad. This is very bad," Noah said, pacing around the room. "I don't feel good about this at all."

"Raffi, you have to give the money back," Kai said urgently. "We can't take it."

"I only took one, maybe two thousand dollars. The rest is money I earned."

"You mean, the *drug* money?" Kai felt his blood pressure rising.

"Come on. You just counted the money we have, and we're not even close to paying Marco's debt. Either we take this money now, or we all end up in jail."

Kai's veins were about to burst. "You just can't go stealing from convenience stores though. It's wrong!"

"But what if we could pay off the debt tomorrow?" Raffi said, his arms crossed over his chest. "We can 'borrow' it from a few local shops and give it back later."

"It's stealing," Kai snapped.

"It's *borrowing*. We'll pay it back eventually," Raffi said.

"But we're not criminals," Kai said, his arms folded tightly across his chest.

"Right," Noah chimed in.

"Come on, guys. The problem right now is that we don't have time. Think of this as buying us some time. We can always pay it back later with interest," Raffi said.

Kai bit his lip. "It's too risky, and it's wrong. Very wrong."

"What do you suggest we do here, Kai? Our only other option is to sell. And by sell, I mean give our father's company away and all Ma's retirement plan with it."

Kai looked up at Noah. "This is crazy, right?"

"Definitely crazy," Noah said, crossing his arms.

"What if we just ask for an extension," Kai said. "We can

give Marco what we have now and give him the rest later," Kai said. "He won't turn down the chance to get more money."

"You're willing to take that chance?" Raffi said.

Kai let out a sigh. "Either we end up in jail for something we do, or we end up in jail for something we didn't do. Which is worse?"

"Come on, Kai. Give my idea a chance. We'll be super-careful, and we'll give back the money over time. The businesses we borrow from will get reimbursed by their insurance companies, and then they'll get their money back from us later. We can drop off little bags of money like we're Robin Hood or some shit like that. It's actually a bonus for the businesses we choose. They'll come out of it ahead."

Kai pulled out his lighter and flicked it with his thumb. It was a habit he had formed years ago when his father had stashed them around everywhere. At some point Kai discovered the little gadgets helped calm his nerves, so he always had one on hand even though he didn't smoke.

He watched the small flame twitch, soothing his racing mind. Could there be any sense to Raffi's idea?

"It's ludicrous," Kai said, staring into the small blue center of the flame. "We're not robbing convenience stores to pay off our blackmail."

"Who said anything about convenience stores?" Raffi said with a dark twinkle in his eye. "This is chump change. I bet we could get way more money taking on something bigger. What about a bank?"

"Okay, now you're talking crazy again," Noah said.

"It's these types of ideas that are getting you, and us, in trouble," Kai said. "We're not robbing anyone or anything. Ever."

Raffi looked at Kai, but it was as if he were looking right through him.

"Raffi? You hear me?" Kai asked.

Raffi paused. "Yeah," he said finally. "I hear you."

"Let's try to get a loan tomorrow. Okay? Enough with this nonsense," Kai said.

Raffi quietly collected his money, avoiding Kai's or Noah's eye contact.

"Okay, Raff?" Kai repeated himself.

"Yeah, okay. Okay. I get it," Raffi said, convincing no one in the room.

Jolie's yoga class started in five minutes. She pulled on a pair of loose white yoga pants that bloomed around her thighs and tapered at her ankle, then wrapped a multicolored scarf around her hair in lieu of taking a shower. Slipping on flip-flops, she raced out the door.

The path to the gazebo was surrounded with lush tropical palms and colorful birds that squawked and whistled. The roar of ocean waves grew louder as she approached the large outdoor gazebo at the east end of the resort.

Several people were already folded in child's pose, their chests lying on their bent knees. The instructor was an older woman with curly gray hair that fell to her shoulders. She pointed at an open mat, and Jolie tiptoed her way between the folded bodies and followed along with the class warm-up.

Stretching and strengthening her limbs, Jolie immersed herself in the exquisite torture of arm binds and twists, flowing from one move to the next. Just beyond the bushy hill, Jolie could glimpse the sparkling ocean.

She was in paradise.

Jolie leaned into an open leg stretch, placing her forehead on her mat with her legs stretched out to her sides. She breathed into the tightness of her hips and let go of all the stress that had been building up in her body.

Would her plan to rebrand her image really work? Would the vegan thing attract more followers? Would she have enough income to avoid working for her father?

She needed to let go of her thoughts, so she forced her mind to relax; the worries fluttered like little birds out of her head.

I am calm. The mantra wrapped around her like a warm blanket. She was at peace by herself. Enveloped in the quietness of her breath.

By the time she woke from her dreamy Savasana, lying on the floor with her arms and legs relaxed and splayed out on the mat, she realized that two women from the class had been waiting for her.

A girl with dreadlocks and a nose ring approached. "Hi. Sorry to bother you. Are you Jolie Boulard?"

Jolie looked her over curiously. She didn't recognize her. "I am. Do we know each other?"

"No, actually. My friend Sarah and I follow your blog." She motioned to her friend who stood behind her. Sarah's makeup-free face was rosy from the heat. Her hair was cut short, buzzed on one side, with one single feather earring that hung from her ear.

"We just love your posts, and I must say, you are so much more beautiful in person," Sarah said shyly.

"Oh, thank you," Jolie said.

"I'm Shanti."

Jolie shook her hand. "Wow, I've never met any of my followers so far from home like this. What a small world."

"Would you mind if we take a photo with you?" Shanti asked. "I know I'd regret it if I didn't ask."

"Of course." Jolie smiled politely and huddled between the two girls while Shanti held her phone with her long arm.

"Thanks," Shanti said. "I hope you don't mind if I post this on Instagram."

"Go for it. You'll be doing me a favor actually. I'm rebooting my website. I could use all the publicity I can get," Jolie said.

"Oh yeah? How so?" Shanti asked.

"Well, for one, I've started eating vegan now," Jolie said. "And I'd like to focus more on that."

"Very cool," Shanti said. "Sarah and I are both vegan, so you have our support."

"That's awesome," Jolie said.

"Will we see you here tomorrow?" Sarah asked.

"Definitely," Jolie said, spraying down her yoga mat. "It was nice meeting you."

The girls scampered out onto the jungle path leading them back to the casitas.

They seemed nice, Jolie thought. Her stomach growled in response.

Time for breakfast.

The restaurant was a few yards from Jolie's room. One of the walls had large sliding doors that overlooked the Caribbean. Jolie sat at a small table tucked in the back. Echoes from the waves crashing onto the shore penetrated through the trees.

The place was truly remarkable. She wondered what it would be like to live there. Not at the resort, but in this country where she could be surrounded by rainforests and the ocean every day. Just think of the amazing photographs she could get from there.

Jolie looked over the menu of vegan options and went with her server's recommendation. Within moments, several small plates of colorful vegetables and fruits displayed on green and purple decorative leaves were spread in front of her. It almost looked too pretty to eat.

She reached for her bag to grab her phone and took a picture.

The chomping of raw carrots and jicama was comforting, but it felt like gravel in her stomach. She drank her black coffee and relaxed in her chair.

Jolie floated around the resort over the next few days, setting up photo shoots in the meditation room and on the beach. She would occasionally find a helpful stranger to take her photo, but the composition was always off. Sarah and Shanti would take photos of her in yoga class, but the lighting was never quite right.

Most of her day was spent setting up her tripod, taking and retaking photos, and plotting out the stream of Instagram and blog posts for the next few weeks.

By the fourth day, Jolie was eating lunch with her new friends, Sarah and Shanti. It was their last day at the resort, and their luggage was packed and tucked under the table.

"It was such a pleasure hanging out with you," Shanti said, bringing Jolie in for a hug.

"Thanks for all your help with the photo shoots," Jolie said. "I hope you guys have a safe trip home. Let's stay in touch please."

"You bet. Good luck with revamping your image. We'll be sure to share your stuff," Sarah said.

"Thanks so much." Jolie waved goodbye as they both got into a cab.

Sweet girls.

She was done with lunch, but her stomach still ached for something more. The vegan diet wasn't fulfilling the taunting craving for a gooey cheeseburger. She had a hankering for the saltiness of meat. The melty goodness of cheese. The richness of fat, in all its glory, dripping down her fingers as she took a bite.

She wouldn't cheat of course. But a girl could dream. And

she did need a break from the resort's tiny portions. Perhaps she would venture out to Limón. Jolie jotted down a few ideas in her phone as she planned her trip into the city:

How to eat vegan in a foreign city

How to eat vegan among a sea of empanadas

This little vegan eater goes to the market

Exotic fruits—the good, the bad, and the ugly

While she was there, she could shop and practice her self-control. After all, she was on a budget.

If she could make it to the city without eating meat and without buying something for herself, then she could do anything—including saving her business.

CHAPTER SIX

Raffi hadn't shown up to work that morning. He wasn't answering his phone either. The day before, Kai and Raffi had gone to the bank and tried to apply for a loan, but it was denied. Apparently, Pop had too many recent credit inquiries, but Kai couldn't figure out why.

They were shit out of luck with only a few days left to pay Marco's debt, and Kai was starting to suspect Raffi was up to something.

Not showing up to work was unlike him. Despite his crazy ideas and constant ploys getting him into trouble, he always made it to work on time.

Kai drove to his apartment to check in on him, terrified what he might find. Maybe the drug dealers had found Raffi after all. His hands shook as he turned the knob to the front door. Raffi's apartment was about as messy as it normally was. Magazines and trash littered the countertops. Sock nests in every corner.

No blood, Kai thought with relief.

He crept down the hallway until he approached the bedroom. The son of a gun was in bed. Beer bottles were strewn around the room, and the blue light from his computer screen glowed over his half-naked body.

Kai was relieved to see his brother alive, but now he would have to kick his ass for ditching work. "Get up," Kai said, pulling the sheet off the bed. "It's ten o'clock. I was worried sick about you."

Raffi groaned, pulling his pillow over his head.

"You can't just not show up to work, Raff. We're counting on you to be there."

"Get out," Raffi said, his voice muffled by the pillow.

"No, you get out and get your butt back to work."

Raffi threw the pillow at Kai. The stench of stale beer and drool slapped him in the face. Kai grimaced and threw it back. "I don't even want to think about the last time you washed your sheets." Kai looked at the beer bottles in disgust. "What the heck were you doing anyway? Trying to drink yourself to death? There's like twenty bottles of beer in here."

Raffi grunted, shoving his head deeper underneath the pillow.

Kai reached over to grab the bottles from his desk when his hand nudged the computer mouse. A bright white screen flicked on. The Boulard Jewelers website was front and center.

Kai furrowed his brow, studying the page. Why would he be so interested in jewelry at a time like this? He had only just gotten his marriage annulled a few months ago. He didn't have a new girlfriend, at least as far as Kai knew.

"What were you doing last night, Raff?" Kai said, clicking on the next open webpage. Google Maps appeared with directions from his apartment to the Boulard Jewelers store in downtown Limón.

Raffi stirred in bed, kicking off the sheets to the floor. He arose like a mummy coming out of its tomb, his hair disheveled in every way imaginable. His breath smelled like something had died in his mouth overnight.

"While you two sissies were sleeping like little babies in Ma's house, I was doing real man's work." Raffi shouldered Kai out of the way, passing through the doorway as he shuffled toward the bathroom.

"What are you talking about?"

Raffi squeezed toothpaste on his frayed toothbrush as Kai held his hands up, suspended in the air, waiting for Raffi to give him a hint.

"I was researching where I can get the money to pay off Marco's debt," Raffi said between brush strokes. His mouth filled with a foamy paste.

"And how do you propose to do that?"

"It's simple," Raffi said. "I'm going to go into a store that has expensive shit, and I'm going to take it."

Kai's eyes grew wide. "We've already talked about this, Raff. We're not criminals. There will be no stealing of any kind."

Raffi finished scrubbing the inside of his mouth and spit out the white froth into the sink. "That's where you're wrong, brother." He rinsed his toothbrush and set it back on the bathroom counter. "I'm going to get the money because I'm the one who got us in this mess in the first place."

"You can't be serious," Kai shot back, watching his brother rinse his face with water. "You must be joking. Our father didn't raise you to be a criminal."

Raffi got up in Kai's face, water dripping from his nose and chin. "He didn't raise us to be pansies either, but look how you and Noah turned out."

Kai glared into his brother's darkened eyes. There was something different in their depths. Something Kai didn't recognize anymore.

"You can either sit back like the priss you are, or you can

help me," Raffi said, grabbing a towel from the rack and wiping his face. "It's your choice."

"I'm not helping you," Kai growled.

"Suit yourself," Raffi said, pushing past Kai again, only this time his shoulder knocked Kai back into the wall. Kai held the shooting pain in his arm as he watched his brother stalk toward his room. Raffi pulled on a T-shirt like it was just any other day, acting as if he wasn't talking like a crazy person and about to rob a jewelry store.

"Think about the consequences if you get caught," Kai said. "It would kill Ma."

"Think about the consequences if I don't get the money," Raffi said, slipping on his jeans. "I'm doing it for *us*, to make up for my mistakes."

"Don't give me that self-righteous crap. There's another way."

"And what's that, smart guy?"

"We call the cops, like I've been saying the whole time. The drug dealers haven't found you, which tells me they don't know you're involved. You'd be in the clear. You can tell them you didn't know about the cocaine, which is true, sort of. Although you should've known better."

"I'm not calling the cops," Raffi said. "I've got it all figured out." Raffi brushed past Kai again down the hall as he entered his kitchen. He pulled open his fridge and grabbed a beer. Prying off the top with his can opener, he took a long drink.

"What are you doing? It's ten a.m. and you need to get to work."

"I'm devising my plan."

"What plan? You have no plan. You just have terrible ideas floating around in that head of yours."

"I'm going to start small and work my way up to a bank."

Kai gasped. "No. No way. You can't pull that off."

Raffi took another pull from his beer. "You bet I can. And

I will." He belched so loud Kai felt the vibrations in his own throat. Then, setting the beer bottle down, Raffi grabbed his car keys and headed toward the front door.

"Where are you going?"

"I'm going to work, and then I'm going to rob a jewelry store. Where are you going?"

Kai threw his hands in the air. "What? You can't just… Do you always drink before you go to work? And a jewelry store? Raffi, be reasonable. Please. You don't have to do this."

Raffi nodded toward his front door. "You comin'?"

"No! I mean, yes, to work. I'm going to work. But we are going to talk about this more."

"Sure," Raffi said, closing the door behind Kai. "We can talk all you want. But my mind is made up."

Kai closed his eyes while Raffi's feet clanged against the metal steps, echoing off the concrete walls.

His brother was going to rob a jewelry store today, and there was nothing Kai could do to stop him.

Jolie walked through the Parque Vargas in the city of Limón, admiring the large sculptures set in front of the turquoise Caribbean Sea. A line of palm trees swayed in the breeze. She carried her camera, snapping photos of colorful buildings and tiny markets, occasionally jotting down ideas for her blog. Papayas, guava, and bananas filled her SD card; ideas for vegan recipes filled her notepad.

Just as the sun began to set, reflecting bright flashes of light against the building windows, her stomach growled. She needed to eat. Even though she was craving things that would make a vegan squeal in horror, she trudged on through the city streets, looking for a restaurant that might have vegan options.

Jolie passed a boutique featuring brightly colored dresses and sun hats. It beckoned her to come inside.

Just one look, she thought as she stepped through the front door. Her eyes landed on a bright red maxi dress with splashes of yellow and green tie-dye. If only she had the budget for clothes.

She stepped away and came across a glass case of jewelry. Large hoop earrings that would go perfectly with the tie-dye maxi dress *if* she could afford it.

But she *was* trying to rebrand her business, and her business *did* require pictures of her. Surely she would need a brightly colored outfit to go with the brightly colored fruits and vegetables and backdrops she had spent all day photographing.

Jolie walked back to the dress, ignoring the little voice in her head that told her she should be saving her money for promoting her business instead.

The price tag was marked at nine thousand colóns, which was about sixteen US dollars. A freaking bargain. She had to buy it. For the business.

The gold hoop earrings and sunhat were also necessary.

The little sequined coin purse wasn't, but it would be a gift for Nora. She couldn't possibly come home from Costa Rica without a souvenir for her best friend. She was watching all her pets after all.

Jolie strolled happily down the sidewalk with her new sun hat perched upon her head, occasionally taking selfies in front of Costa Rican street corners.

The pang in her stomach would have to wait until the warm glow of the setting sun was gone. She couldn't waste a single second of the perfect lighting.

Across the street, Jolie recognized the sign for a Boulard Jewelers store, nestled between a watch repair shop and cigar store. She didn't know her father's business had a location in

Costa Rica. The sun had just set over the buildings, but perhaps she could snap one more selfie.

Jolie jogged across the street, holding her sunhat to the top of her head. The lights were out, and the sign on the door said Cerrado. She positioned herself in front of the storefront sign and took the picture, quickly adding it to her Instagram story.

Look what I came across in Costa Rica, she typed. She added a sticker of a jaguar, just because it was cute.

She hit Send and took a deep breath in. *All right. Time to eat.*

Jolie took one step on the sidewalk when something caught her eye. Through the glass of the jewelry store, she could see a man hunched over the cash register.

They must have just closed, Jolie thought. The store clerk was probably locking up for the night.

It was odd the lights were out though. Jolie squinted to see the man's face when she saw the pantyhose pressing against his features.

Jolie blinked a few times. Her hands froze, and she dropped her phone. It clattered against the cement.

She needed to call the police. As she steadied herself to grab her phone, her camera strap slipped off her shoulder and clanked against the plexiglass, startling her and the man inside.

He looked up, and Jolie gasped.

She grabbed her phone from the sidewalk and lunged forward. Her sandals flopped against the soles of her feet as she took off down the street. Her new sun hat flew off her head, landing somewhere in her wake.

Jolie hadn't gone more than a hundred yards when the alarm bells screamed behind her. She turned around.

The burglar stepped out the front door. Jolie felt the color drain from her cheeks. He ran toward her, and Jolie nearly tripped over her own feet. She ran faster, her heart pumping so hard it burned her chest.

Jolie turned onto a side street, hoping she would come across people for help. The city street was dark and silent except for the huffing of her breath and the flopping of her sandals.

Jolie needed to run just a little farther to get to a busy intersection ahead. The pounding of weighted footsteps echoed through the alley. Cars and people were within her reach if she could just get there fast enough.

Her lungs heaved for air. Her shins ached. The footsteps behind her were getting closer, but she was almost there. The flashing car lights were her ticket to safety.

She made it to the sidewalk, scanning the street for people. A couple was strolling along on the opposite side. Jolie called out for help just as a van peeled around the corner and screeched to a stop in front of her, blocking Jolie from the couple across the street.

The side door swung open, and she was shoved forward. Thick hands lifted her up and threw her into the van. Her head hit the opposite window, and then everything went black.

CHAPTER SEVEN

M *oments earlier...*
Kai nervously tapped his hands on the steering wheel while Raffi ransacked the diamond store.

"You sure this is a good idea?" Noah asked from the passenger seat.

Kai sighed. "No, I'm not, but if something goes wrong, we need to know about it and get him out of there if we can."

"Doesn't that make us the getaway drivers?"

Kai gripped the steering wheel. "No, it makes us plan B. Assuming Raffi's plan fails—and it always does—we'll try to get him out of there before he spends the rest of his life in jail."

"I still think that makes us getaway drivers."

Kai huffed. Noah was right of course, but Kai had been trying to convince himself otherwise. Raffi didn't even know they were there. The stubborn ass had left work that day without even saying anything. Kai and Noah had to hightail it out of there to catch up with him. Luckily, Kai had seen the Boulard Jewelers website on Raffi's computer, which had brought them here. Parked in a hot van kitty-corner to the jewelry store where their older brother had gotten in somehow.

A pretty girl in a sun hat strolled down the street.

"Whoa," Noah said under his breath. "Do you see that?"

Kai squinted to get a better look. Killer body. Trim waist. Big, pouty lips. Silky, olive skin on long, thin limbs. Tattoos delicately placed across her chest and forearms.

She was gorgeous but way out of Kai's league.

"Now *that* is a woman," Noah said. "I'm going to go talk to her."

"Settle down, Casanova. We've got to be on the lookout."

"Yeah, but that chick is hot."

"That girl is like eight or ten years older than you. Can't you ever find a girl your age?"

Noah smiled, raising his eyebrows a few times. "Guilty as charged and proud of it." He had always been the charming one of the three brothers, with a sullied reputation of sleeping with women up to twice his age, namely tourists who went to the bars, looking for a good time.

"We need to focus," Kai said, unable to keep his eyes off her. "She's a distraction." The prettiest distraction he had ever laid eyes on. More beautiful than the cute girl in accounting he had been planning on asking out before his life had turned upside down.

They watched her closely while she glided down the street, happily taking pictures of random objects, street corners, and the little food market that had just closed. All of a sudden, she seemed to take an interest in the jewelry store.

Kai's butt clenched as he watched her skip across the street, holding her hat on her head. She looked inside.

"Uh-oh," Noah muttered.

Oh God. "Get out of there," Kai whispered under his breath, his heart pounding in his chest.

"Here's my chance to distract her," Noah said, gripping the handle of the door.

"Stop," Kai said. "Wait." He held his breath.

Was she taking a selfie in front of the building now? Oh, that's just great. "For crying out loud, get out of there," Kai muttered.

The streetlight glowed around the girl as she stood there, texting on her phone.

"Get off your phone and walk away," Kai said, fidgeting with his hands. He felt helpless sitting in the van.

"Let me go talk to her. I can distract her." Noah opened the van door when the girl put her phone away and started to walk forward. A wave of relief washed over Kai.

"I think we're in the clear," Kai said. "Get back in the van."

But then she stopped, facing the window.

"No, no, no. Keep walking," Kai begged.

Her phone dropped.

"Oh God no." Did she spot him?

She leaned forward to grab her phone and froze. Her hand shook. She must have seen something.

Get out of there! Get out of there!

The girl took off, her hat catching the air behind her.

"Get in the van now!"

Noah hopped back in and slammed the door as Kai turned the keys in the ignition. They watched her run down the street. She would have to turn down the alleyway to get to a main road.

Then the alarm bell rang.

Crap.

Raffi popped out the front door and took off after the girl.

"We need to get him out of there," Kai said, putting the vehicle in gear. He pulled forward when he realized the van couldn't get through the alleyway. "Shit." He reversed and slammed his foot on the gas pedal to come around the other side.

Kai jerked the steering wheel, peeling around the corner, his veins pulsing in his neck. The city lights were a blur as he sped around the block.

"There! Right there!" Noah yelled, pointing toward the other side of the alley.

Kai slammed the brakes, and the van came to a screeching halt just before the girl ran into it.

Noah pushed the back-passenger door open as Raffi barreled up to the girl and threw her into the van. A swirl of brown wavy hair thudded against the interior.

"What the hell are you doing?" Kai roared. "Get the girl out of here!"

"Go!" Raffi screamed, sliding the door shut.

Horns honked behind them, sending Kai forward, forcing him to blend into traffic. He checked his rearview mirrors for any sign of cops.

Kai's blood simmered. "We can't kidnap a girl," Kai said. "We need to drop her off."

"She'll call the police," Raffi snapped.

Kai looked over his shoulder. The girl was still passed out, bumping along with the van.

"Is she breathing?" Kai asked.

Noah reached over from his seat. "It looks like she is."

"Dude, what were you thinking?" Kai slammed his palm on the steering wheel. "We need to drop her off somewhere now." He turned onto a side street, hoping he could stop where there weren't a lot of people, but the nightlife in Limón was ramping up. Bars were blaring Latin dance music out into the streets.

There were people everywhere. How on earth did she pick the one alleyway in the entire city where there weren't any people?

Kai pulled a U-turn and drove back toward the jewelry store. Maybe they could drop her off where they found her.

"I think she might have seen my face," Raffi said between gasps. "She'll be able to identify me in a lineup."

"How could she see your face?" Noah said. "You had Ma's stocking on your head. Gross, by the way."

"I couldn't see very well running after her with that thing over my eyes."

"Why were you running after her in the first place?" Kai hissed.

"I don't know; I panicked."

This is a shit show. Raffi had one bad idea after another. When Kai pulled up to the jewelry store, there were now several people swarming the streets, dressed for drinking and dancing. Of course there were people there *now*.

"Crap," Kai said. "I don't know where to drop her off."

"Let's just take her to the warehouse," Raffi said. "We can explain everything."

"You think apologizing for kidnapping her and taking her out of downtown is going to help smooth things over? Are you insane?" Kai said.

"We'll let Noah unleash his charm on her. He can flirt the pants off anyone, including a kidnap victim," Raffi said.

"I kind of like that idea," Noah said, scratching his neck.

"You both have completely lost it. This is so messed up," Kai said, shaking his head. He continued to scour the streets for a pocket where they could drop her off inconspicuously, but he kept coming up short. He was losing time. She would wake up any second.

"Who is she? Can you check her bag?" Noah asked.

Raffi clambered at her purse, pulling out a pink wallet.

"She's American. Jolie Boulard," Raffi read from her driver's license. "Oh hey, she's your age, bro." He nudged Kai's arm. "And her driver's license picture is smoking hot."

"For God's sake. Did you just say Jolie *Boulard* as in *Boulard* Jewelers? The very same jewelry store you just robbed?" Kai said. "No. No. No. No." Kai hit the wheel over and over again.

This was a disaster. A complete nightmare. Kai's ulcer was flaring up again.

Pulling up to the coffee warehouse, he parked next to the truck. "This is just great. Just great. We have an obscene amount of narcotics in the office and a kidnap victim in our garage." Kai stepped out of the van, his blood boiling hot. He kicked the tires for good measure. "Stupid. Stupid. Stupid."

"Maybe we could use her as ransom," Raffi suggested, stepping out of the van.

"Are you out of your mind? Absolutely not!" Kai snapped. "That would never work. We need to apologize to her for the misunderstanding, take her home, then lie low for a while."

"If you recall, we still have a shitload of money we need to make. I'm just trying to think ahead here," Raffi said.

"Think ahead?" Kai laughed sardonically. "That's cute. Real cute."

"What do you suggest we do? We've got Marco breathing down our necks. Maybe she could come in handy," Raffi said.

"I obviously can't reason with you. You've gone insane," Kai said, throwing his hands in the air.

"Well then, we'll have to just kill her," Raffi said.

Kai and Noah both gasped. He couldn't be serious. That would be too far even for Raffi. He might be a criminal, but he was no killer. Right?

"I'm just kidding, guys. You're the smart ones. Think of something."

The van jostled, and the brothers snapped their heads up and looked inside. The girl was wide-eyed, frantically looking around. "Where am I?" she screamed. "What are you doing with me?" Jolie's voice was muffled through the truck window.

"This is the worst thing that could have ever happened," Kai said.

Raffi handed Kai the girl's bag and marched to the side of the van.

"I'm going to need you to be quiet while we figure out what to do with you," Raffi said.

"Please, just let me go. I won't tell anyone what I saw. I won't say anything if you let me go right now."

"I said I need you to be quiet," Raffi said. "Can you just sit here until I—"

Jolie spit in his face.

"What the hell?" Raffi lunged at Jolie, and the van bobbed up and down in their struggle.

Kai ran to the truck, grabbed Raffi by the shirt, and tugged him off the girl, who was kicking and scratching.

Raffi snapped his right hand to his chest, cupping it with his left. "She just fucking *bit* me!"

"Serves you right for grabbing at her. Jesus, man. Get ahold of yourself," Kai said. "Miss, I'm sorry about my— oomph!" A sharp kick to the groin had him keeled over in pain, and he fell to the ground. Jolie's flip-flops came into view as she took off.

Raffi lunged at her again, but she wiggled free from his grasp.

"Don't let her get away!" Raffi growled.

Noah blocked her from escaping, wrapping his long arms around her and holding her tight as she thrashed against him.

"Calm down. I'm not going to hurt you. I just want to talk," Noah gritted through his teeth. She stomped on his foot, but he didn't flinch. She writhed under his clutched arms, almost breaking free. "Damn, you're strong for a lady."

Raffi stormed over to Noah when Jolie chomped on Noah's arm.

"Ow!" Noah screamed, letting the girl loose.

Kai was still in too much pain to get up from the ground. Struggling to find the air, he panted out the words, "Just. Let. Her. Go."

Jolie took off toward the office door when Raffi caught up to her and grabbed her arms, pinning them down to her sides.

She wiggled and squirmed. "Help! Help me!" she cried just before Raffi duct-taped her mouth shut.

"Stop," Kai cried out. "Leave her alone." He got to his knees, crawling over to Raffi, who continued to strap her down with long strips of tape. Jolie was still putting up a fight, kicking and flailing. Her eyes were wild, like a frightened animal. Kai gathered the strength to stand and push Raffi out of the way.

"Stop this now. This has gone too far. We need to let her go."

Raffi scoffed, ignoring Kai. He tied her wrists behind her while Noah stood behind him with his hands in his hair. Then Raffi tied her ankles to the chair legs. "This devil woman isn't going anywhere. She's seen our faces now. She's in too deep."

Jolie slumped in her chair, tears streaming down her reddened face. She took quick jagged breaths through her nose before sobbing into the tape.

Kai pushed Raffi out of the way and got right up in his face. "Get out of here for just one second and let me talk with her, okay?"

"Don't you dare untie her," Raffi said, backing away. "You can talk to her, but I'm not going anywhere."

Kai shoved him farther away and pointed to Noah. "Get me a glass of water and a wet towel."

Noah nodded and shuffled out the door.

Jolie's face had turned a bright pink, nearly purple.

Kai knelt down in front of her. "Jolie, I'm going to take the duct tape off you if you promise not to scream, okay?"

Jolie's head nodded vigorously.

Kai took the corner of the tape and slowly peeled it back. Her face winced in pain.

"I'm so sorry," he whispered. "Everything is going to be okay if you can just stay calm."

He pulled the last bit of tape off her lips, and she took a deep breath in, whimpering on her exhale. "Please don't hurt me."

Noah came back with a glass of water and a washcloth and handed both to Kai.

"This has been a horrible misunderstanding," Kai said softly. "We did not mean to take you with us, but my dimwit brother here wasn't using his head." Kai sneered at Raffi, who was standing in the corner with his arms crossed.

"Can I offer you some water?" Kai asked, holding out the glass. The girl shook her head. "How about a towel?"

Jolie glared at him. "Please just let me go," she begged. The caramel color of her skin had begun to normalize, apart from the red rims around her eyes.

"Let's just calm down first," Kai said softly. "Can you do that for me, Jolie?"

Jolie nodded her head. "How do you know my name?"

"I'm sorry, but we looked at your driver's license. As a precaution. Okay?"

Jolie huffed at that. "So you know who I am. You know who my family is."

Kai sighed. "Yes."

"My father will ruin you for this if you don't let me go right now."

A pounding on the warehouse door made them both

jump. The boys looked toward the door and exchanged nervous glances. Somebody was trying to get in.

"Help! Help me!" Jolie screamed.

"Shhh!" Kai hushed her, placing the duct tape back over her mouth. "Be quiet!"

"You've got to be kidding me," Raffi said. "It's Marco. He already saw me." Raffi peered through the glass door.

"Great. Now *this* is officially the worst thing that could happen. Get him out of here!"

Raffi walked out of the warehouse, closing the door behind him. Maybe Marco didn't hear Jolie's scream after all.

"Come and help me move her to the office," Kai whispered to Noah. He crouched down in front of her, gripping the bottom slats of the chair when a loud thwack knocked him back on his butt. His head buzzed in a dizzy spell as he started to realize he had been hit in the head.

"Damn, she just headbutted you and won," Noah said.

Kai shook off the stars and got back to his feet, ignoring the black spots that appeared in his vision.

Jolie glared at him, a triumphant glint in her eye.

"I deserved that," Kai said to her. "But we need to move you."

Kai and Noah braced the chair from behind her and dragged her across the cement floor. Jolie's muffled cries were probably not loud enough for Marco to hear, but he brought his finger to his mouth to quiet her. "Please don't make a noise. The man out there will not be able to help you. He'll only make your life miserable, just as he has made mine."

They dragged her to the office and shut the door behind them.

"We need to act natural in case Marco walks in," Kai said. "You go pretend like you're fixing the roaster. I'll clean up the break area."

Kai and Noah scattered. The sound of Kai's own heart-beat was just loud enough to drown out the strained grunts from behind the office door. He turned on the sink faucet for good measure. His hands shook as he placed the sponge under the tepid water, waiting for the inevitable clicking sound of the door.

"I want a word with you," Marco said in Spanish, his voice booming from the warehouse entrance.

You've got to be kidding me.

Raffi followed Marco into the warehouse, a defeated look on his face.

"You couldn't hold the fort?" Kai said, his hands in the air.

Raffi shrugged. "I couldn't reason with him. He wanted to talk to you."

Kai shook his head, placing his wet hands on his hips.

"What do you want, Marco?" Kai said, flipping to Spanish.

"I saw you boys drive in and wanted to check in on my *investment*." Marco's lip snarled. "And to see if you would consider giving me your warehouse instead."

"We're not selling," Raffi said through gritted teeth.

"I wasn't talking to you," Marco snapped. "I was talking to the reasonable one."

Kai took a deep breath in, the sink faucet whooshing behind him. He could faintly hear the rattling of the chair in the office. He imagined Jolie was thrashing about as wildly as she could.

Selling the warehouse seemed like their only way out. They didn't have the money to pay Marco off, and no one wanted to go to jail. Maybe this was what it came down to. Giving up. Sometimes giving up on something you've been holding on to was the only way to be free. If his father were alive, he would understand Kai needed to make a tough deci-sion. And if his father knew how badly Raffi had screwed up, he would have never left the company in his hands in the first place.

Just as Kai was about to open his mouth, Raffi brushed past him.

"Come on, Kai, we can't leave the water running," Raffi said, turning off the faucet.

"No!" Kai growled, but it was too late. The water stopped, and the warehouse grew quiet. All but the sounds of muffled screaming in the office could be heard.

Dammit, Raff.

Marco tilted his head toward the office door. "Did you hear that?"

"It's nothing," Kai said, giving Raffi a death glare. "But I want to consider your offer about selling the warehouse."

"No, he doesn't," Raffi said.

"Yes. I. Do," Kai said. "And I'd be happy to talk through the details tomorrow if you could just—"

"What's in there?" Marco said, stepping one foot toward the door.

A large thud shook the office door. And then another. Jolie must have shifted her chair, thumping the door with her head.

This can't be happening.

Kai shut his eyes in despair. There was no explaining that. He darted in front of Marco again, pressing against his chest. "That is nothing of your concern, Marco. Like I said, I'm willing to consider selling the warehouse, but we need to reconvene. This is not a good time."

Marco pushed Kai away, reaching for the door handle.

No.

Kai tried to stop him, but Marco brushed him away. His meaty hand clasped the doorknob, and it dawned on Kai that his life as he knew it was officially over.

CHAPTER EIGHT

Marco pushed the door open, and Jolie cried out in pain, despite her mouth being taped shut. Marco opened the door all the way, and Kai felt the walls of the room close in on him.

As if his life couldn't get any worse. Marco found a freaking kidnap victim in the office, surrounded by boxes full of cocaine.

Marco's eyebrows darted up in surprise.

"This doesn't concern you," Kai said.

"Oh, I believe it does," Marco said, looking over his shoulder.

"It's not what you think," Kai lied. "We're just…" He struggled to come up with some sensical reason why a girl would be tied up in a chair, but he stammered. "We're just playing a game." It sounded ridiculous the moment it left his mouth.

"Is that right?" Marco asked, folding his arms. "That's one sick game you have here." He bent down, peering at Jolie's face, squinting his eyes. "Are you all right, dear?" he asked in Spanish.

Jolie looked at him blankly.

"Are you all right?" Marco asked again in English. She shook her head violently, screaming through her tape.

It was over. They were doomed.

Marco ripped off the tape, and Jolie belted out a howl. "Help me, please. They kidnapped me. I just want to go home!"

Marco turned around to give Kai and Raffi a mocking stare.

Noah stepped in between Kai and Raffi. "Oh shit," he muttered.

Marco tilted his head back and cackled like a hyena. "Oh shit is right," Marco said. He turned back to Jolie. "However did a pretty girl like you get in this predicament?"

Jolie looked up at Kai, assessing him, clearly trying to decide what to tell Marco. "They were robbing a jewelry store. My family's jewelry store."

The pit of Kai's stomach curdled.

So, she went with telling him everything.

Marco twisted his neck to look back at the brothers in a delighted surprise.

"I saw them, and they chased me," Jolie continued. "Please, you've got to help me. I didn't do anything." Jolie's voice quivered.

"My, my, my. This is very interesting indeed." Marco straightened and turned on his heel. "Robbing stores? Kidnapping women? I see you boys have gotten into far more trouble since I last saw you."

"It was all a misunderstanding," Kai said. "We were just about to let her—"

"I believe your debt has just increased in value," Marco said, interrupting Kai. Marco turned back to the girl. "What's your name, sweetheart?"

She leveled her eyes at him and cocked her head, as if she just realized he wasn't going to help her after all.

"Leave her alone," Kai growled.

Marco shoved Kai back and ambled to Jolie and crouched down; his thick finger tilted Jolie's chin up. "What's your name?"

Jolie breathed through her nose, clenching her lips tight.

"How much is your freedom worth?" Marco asked.

In one swift movement, Jolie bit Marco's finger, hard, her jaw gripping on his thick appendage.

"Ow!" Marco yelled, and he kicked her in the shin with his snakeskin boot.

A guttural cry escaped Jolie's throat.

Kai flinched. As if this girl hadn't been through enough, now she has a giant mark to remember them by. "Leave the girl out of this," Kai said.

"Shit," Marco said, shaking off his finger. "That really hurt."

Serves you right.

"Oh yeah, watch out. She bites," Raffi said, chuckling at the spectacle.

"What do you want, Marco?" Kai said, switching to Spanish. "You want more money? Is that it?"

"We're having a hard time coming up with what we already owe you," Raffi said.

Marco wiped his hand on his shirt and backed away from Jolie slowly. He leaned in toward Kai, his smoky breath grazing Kai's ear as he began to whisper in Spanish. "How about you idiots find out how much this girl is willing to pay for her freedom so you can come up with the money?"

Kai closed his eyes, wishing he hadn't planted that seed in Raffi's head. But it was too late. Raffi's eyes grew round as if he were calculating how much he could get out of this poor innocent girl. The *heiress* to Boulard Jewelers.

"You've got three days to get me two hundred thousand."

"That's more than we bargained," Kai said. "I want to discuss selling the warehouse."

"No," Raffi said. "We're not selling."

"Raffi, stop. Enough is enough. We can't pay him."

"Yes, we can." Raffi's eyes flicked over to Jolie, who looked stunned and confused, seemingly oblivious to their conversation in Spanish.

"Boys, boys. We can settle this in a couple of days," Marco said, strolling toward the exit door. "But you know what'll happen if you don't come through."

Kai turned to face Raffi and scowled. "This is the last straw."

Jolie blinked, forcing back the tears that threatened to spill over. Her hands and ankles were bound tight. Her shin throbbed. The duct tape around her wrists pulled at her little hairs every time she moved.

Two of the three men began arguing over Lord knows what in Spanish. As far as Jolie could tell, they were brothers. The two oldest had the same coarse dark hair, and all three of them had the same strong jawlines and square shoulders.

The nice one seemed the most reasonable of the crew. He stood calmly with his hands on his hips, yelling something about *la camioneta*. If Jolie's high school Spanish wasn't failing her, they were talking about a van, but she couldn't be sure.

Jolie's heart almost stopped. *Are they going to put her in a van?*

She watched carefully as the scary one started kicking a bag of coffee beans. *Why is everyone kicking everything around here?* It felt like she was living in a Three Stooges film.

The mean one was the one she was scared of the most. He

had that evil look in his eyes that gave Jolie a really bad feeling. She was usually really good at reading people, and she could tell he was a bad seed.

The one who looked like the youngest had freckles all over his skin and wavy sun-kissed hair. He approached her cautiously and knelt down. "These two are always at it," he said. She picked up on a unique accent, not quite British or American, with a tinge of Spanish, a strange blend of all three. The freckled one ran his hands through his locks. "But I'm sure we'll figure something out in no time." A lazy grin spread across his face. "Do you come to Costa Rica often?"

"Knock it off, Noah," the nice one said in English. He gave Jolie an apologetic look and swiped the top of Noah's head with his palm.

"What?" Noah shrugged.

"I say we hand over the warehouse," the nice one continued, but in English this time, with that same distinct accent that Jolie couldn't place.

The scary one seemed to have calmed down from his kicking fit. "I say we take Marco's advice," he said. "We borrow a little money from the girl and save the business. We can give it all back. I swear."

"We're not taking her money," the nice one said heatedly.

"What the hell else are we going to do with her?" the scary one said.

Noah said something in Spanish, resulting in a whack to his chest. "Oof," he muttered. "What was that for, Kai?"

So the nice one's name was Kai.

"Get that out of your mind," Kai said.

Jolie's heart pounded. She could see they needed money, but for what? She still had one hundred thousand in the bank. She had used her credit card to pay for her trip. If money was what they needed, then they could have it. All of it. She just needed to get the hell out of there.

"How much?" Jolie croaked.

The men snapped their heads to her.

"How much for my freedom?"

"One million dollars," the scary one said. Noah punched him in the arm. "Ouch. Okay, okay. Not a million," the scary one said, rubbing his arm. "But I can't remember. How much money have we gathered so far?"

Kai stormed in his office and pulled out a notepad. "I can't even believe I'm entertaining the idea," he muttered as he scanned his notes. "We were able to raise almost a hundred grand, which means we need a hundred grand more."

You've got to be kidding me. Of course they would need every last penny that she had. It technically wasn't even her money; it was on loan from her inheritance. An inheritance she wasn't even sure she would get anymore.

Kai shook his head. "That's a lot of money to pay back."

"But we can pay it back," the scary one said. "We will."

Jolie watched the brothers argue some more as her life flashed before her eyes. Her dreams of working for herself were vanishing with every fleeting moment. She wouldn't have the money to advertise her rebranded efforts. Her new business idea was dead on arrival. But what else could she do? Her alternative was looking much more grim.

The scary one would kill her if she didn't pay up. She knew that for sure. She had no other choice.

"I'll pay it," Jolie said. "If you promise to let me go. I can write you a check right now. I just want to go home."

"Yes!" the scary one shouted. "Problem solved." He nudged Kai in the chest. "See? Can't you see this was fate?"

Jolie looked up at Kai. One hand cradled his forehead as he paced. The other flicked at a pocket lighter as if it were a nervous tic.

"Please," Jolie whispered. "Let me go."

"Excuse us for just a moment," Kai said to Jolie, turning on his heel. He led the other men to the back-office room. Through the window, Jolie could see the men congregate around the desk. Kai sat down, his fists clenched, occasionally looking back up to Jolie.

The low murmur of their voices penetrated the walls, but Jolie couldn't hear what they were discussing, and even if she could, she was sure they had switched back to Spanish.

They didn't seem like the types of people who would be plotting out her murder, but the scary one made her nervous. Even if she did give them the money, she would be tempted to call the police on them all, exposing whatever sick operation they had going on there.

The warehouse was full of coffee beans, but was it a front? Could they be involved in some form of international black market? They obviously weren't from Costa Rica.

Would they let her think she was free until the money went through, only to later chop her up in a barrel full of coffee beans and put her in a van?

Please, God. Help me get out of this. I've been so selfish. This trip was a mistake. I should have just taken my father's job offer.

Kai stood up, and the men filed out of the office. They approached her cautiously as if they had decided her fate.

"Jolie." Kai cleared his throat. "I realize this is really crappy, and I'm sorry about all this."

Jolie held her breath, waiting for the ultimate decision that would change the course of her life forever.

"My brothers and I are in a bit of a dilemma with that man who just came through here. It would help us out very much if we could borrow some money. We would pay you back at some point, but it might take a while."

"Borrow?"

"Although it might have seemed like my brother was

robbing the jewelry store, he was only intending to take what he could eventually give back. Right, Raffi?"

Raffi nodded solemnly.

"You see, we're on a bit of a time crunch with Marco, and now we're out of options."

Jolie swallowed. "So you'll *borrow* my money and let me go?"

"We will have to keep you here until the money goes through," Kai said apologetically. "I hope you can understand."

Jolie's mouth went dry. "I have to stay here?"

"Think of it as waiting here until everything clears up."

Jolie nodded. "As long as I can go free tomorrow. Unharmed." She looked up at Raffi.

His face scrunched up in a scowl.

"Of course you'll be unharmed," Kai said. "We would never hurt you."

Tell that to your brother.

"How do I know you're not going to just kill me after the money goes through?"

"Because we're not killers, Jolie. You'll have to trust us, and we'll have to trust you too. We can't involve the police in our little... mishap."

Jolie nearly choked on her laugh. *Mishap? Is that what he's calling it?* How dare he downplay the single most trauma-tizing day of her life. They were worried about her going to the police? Well, they should be. Of course she would go to the police. She had been kidnapped and taken as a hostage, and they were going to take literally all her money from her bank account.

But she needed them to trust her, to think she would just let everything go the moment she walked out of the warehouse.

"Of course," Jolie lied. "I just want to put this whole thing behind us."

Kai waited a beat before saying, "Good."

"And you'll pay me back, right?"

"It might take a couple of years, but we'll pay, with interest. I promise."

Yeah, right. Jolie nodded. "Okay."

"Now that that's settled, we'll have you write a check in the morning. When Raffi gives me the signal that the money's gone through at the bank, I'll take you home."

Jolie nodded, frustrated she would have to endure at least another twelve hours as a hostage.

"Are you hungry?" Kai asked.

Hungry? Was he offering her food? What kind of hostage situation was this?

"Noah and Raffi are going to pick up some food."

Jolie shook her head as she watched the two men walk out of the warehouse. The truth was, she *was* really hungry, but eating at a time like this didn't feel right.

"Hey, Raff, can you bring back a few blankets and something for us to eat tomorrow morning?" Kai called.

"What is this, a bed-and-breakfast?" Raffi said, his arms in the air.

"Just do it."

Raffi closed the door behind him, and Jolie became acutely aware that she was alone with Kai.

He pulled out the lighter from his pocket again, flicking the flame on and off. On and off. Kai paced the floor, deep in thought.

In some small way, Jolie felt bad for the guy. He had been trying to stop this whole thing from the beginning. He was clearly out of sorts.

Kai eventually quit pacing and walked over to Jolie.

"I am so, so sorry for this," he said.

Jolie looked up at him through her eyelashes. Was he

really apologizing?

She wanted to be mad at him. She had to if she was going to keep her wits. But he had an innocent face. It was beautiful in a way, with thick black eyelashes and full lips and that manly jawline that would have normally made her knees weak. Stubble had formed on his skin. He had the broad-shouldered build of an athlete.

In any other circumstance, she might have found him attractive. For now, he was the enemy.

"You don't seem like the type of guy who would kidnap an innocent girl," Jolie said.

His eyes shot up. "I'm not."

"You also don't seem like someone who would rob a jewelry store."

"I'm not. I mean… I didn't. I was just—"

"The getaway driver?"

Kai gritted his teeth. "I've let my brother make some bad decisions," he said, "but I guess I'm guilty by association, yes."

"You don't seem like someone who would kill another person either." Jolie let her words hang in the air. She watched as his face morphed into alarm. "Will you let yourself be guilty by association when your brother decides to kill me?"

Kai froze in place. "That's not the plan."

"Maybe it's not *your* plan," Jolie said. "But I can see it on your brother's face. He's not going to let me go after he gets the money."

"But he wouldn't—"

"Really? Are you sure about that?" Jolie watched Kai pace some more, rubbing the stubble on his face with his hands. "You seem like a nice guy. You can prevent him from doing something really stupid."

Kai stopped.

"Let me go now before it's too late."

Kai seemed to be contemplating the idea for a second but went back to pacing.

"You can end this vicious cycle you're in now. Help me. Please," Jolie begged.

"Stop, just… let me think."

He was clearly scared. Whatever kind of trouble he was in must be clouding his better judgment.

"I promise I won't tell anyone if you let me go right now," Jolie said. "You don't even have to drive me home. I can find a way back. Please, Kai, do the right thing." Tears welled in her eyes, spilling onto her lap.

"Please. Please don't cry," Kai said. He jogged over to the sink and came back with a tissue. He crouched down in front of her, holding the tissue up. "You promise not to bite me?"

Jolie couldn't help but snort a laugh. He was scared of *her*.

"I promise."

He blotted her eyes and her cheeks softly, as if he were taking care of a porcelain doll. He smelled of coffee and chocolate and a hint of smoke. As he got closer, she could see a little freckle underneath the corner of his left eye.

"I just need to think," Kai said, his eyes glossy with worry.

Jolie nodded.

Kai paused, wiping her face. "How do I know you won't call the cops?"

Jolie swallowed the truth. She had to save her life. One day he and his brothers would pay for what they'd done, but she needed to get out first. "If you let me go, I promise you will never hear from me again."

Kai bit his lip, studying her expression.

"Raffi saw your driver's license. He knows your name. Your address."

"What are you saying, that he would come find me and kill me if I escape?"

"No, but…," Kai said. "I can't predict what he's going to

do. I don't even know myself anymore."

"Well, I won't be living at that address. I'm moving out." More like getting kicked out, but he didn't need to know that detail.

Kai's eyes locked on her wrists, like he was actually considering setting her free. He was thinking about it at least. Jolie's heart thudded in her chest.

"Please. Let me go now before they come back. I need that money for my business."

Kai tilted his head slightly, like a dog hearing a high-pitched noise.

"Just because my father is rich doesn't make me rich."

"You've got one hundred thousand to spare, and you think you're not rich?"

Jolie let out a sigh. "It's complicated."

Kai nodded his head.

"How's your leg?" he said, letting her plea go unanswered.

"It really hurts."

"Would it hurt too much to run away on your own?"

Jolie swallowed. Her pulse quickened again. Was he seriously contemplating letting her go? "I'm sure I can manage." She was so close to being free.

"I'll grab you some ice," Kai said, getting up from his chair.

"I don't need ice. I need to leave *now*."

Kai ignored her, disappearing for a while until he came back with a baggie full of ice.

"May I?" Kai asked, more polite than was necessary. Jolie blew out a frustrated sigh.

Kai lifted her skirt just high enough to expose the baseball-size bump that had formed on the middle of her shin. A small trickle of blood had dried where Marco's boot punctured her.

He placed the ice bag on it, and its biting cold made her

flinch.

"Does that hurt?"

"Yes. A lot."

"I'm really sorry Marco kicked you."

"He had it coming. He's an asshole."

"You're telling me."

At least they had one thing in common. That man was a devil in snakeskin boots. Jolie wasn't sure how, but she would make sure Marco went down with all of them. He was guilty of something.

"Why do you guys owe him money?"

"It's a long story… one that you'd probably be safer not knowing." Kai held the ice pack in place for a while.

Jolie was trying to come up with something else to say, hoping she might be able to charm him into letting her go. An idea sparked.

"Can you do me a favor and get this hair out of my face? It's driving me crazy." A strand had been draped over her eye.

Kai pulled the lock out of her face and placed it behind her ear. The gesture was innocent, but his touch was so delicate. A strange jolt of energy rushed through her. She shook it off but found herself staring into his deep pools of umber.

"You can trust me," she said, more softly this time. She could almost see the gears turning in his head.

Kai's hands floated over to her wrist. He was going to let her go.

Thank God. He was finally going to do it.

Just then the door swung open and Raffi appeared with a large pizza box in his hands.

"Honey, we're home!" Raffi sang from the open door.

"I brought sheets and blankets," Noah chimed in. "For the record, Raff wasn't going to do it."

"Shut up, Noah, I was busy getting rope," Raffi snapped.

Kai shot up, leaving her hands tied where they were.

CHAPTER NINE

Jolie strained her neck to watch the brothers hover around a table in the kitchenette. Pizza fumes drifted to her nose, taunting her. Despite being tied up and kidnapped, she was starving but too proud to say so.

"You sure you don't want some pizza?" Kai asked, holding out a slice on a paper plate.

Jolie shook her head no.

"You sure?" he asked again.

Jolie nodded her head, ignoring the pang in her gut.

"Please, you need to eat." Kai walked over to her, a concerned look on his face. He held the pizza in front of her. Pepperoni and mushrooms, two feet from her mouth. Her traitorous tongue salivated.

"I realize you're in an awkward situation with your hands tied up and everything, but I'd never forgive myself if I knew you were hungry and I didn't feed you."

It was oddly sweet, but Jolie shrugged it off. "I'm not hungry," Jolie lied. "I'm a vegan anyway." She averted her eyes, hoping he couldn't see right through her.

"Oh," Kai said, jerking the pizza away. "Sorry." He walked back to his snickering brothers.

Little did he know she had been eating pepperoni less than two weeks ago. She missed it almost as much as she missed cheeseburgers.

"Way to go, moron." Raffi chortled.

Kai shoved Raffi's shoulder before sitting back down. He looked back one more time, locking eyes on Jolie for a split second before he turned back to the table.

Was he still thinking of letting her go? Was that look his way of communicating to wait until his brothers were gone?

Jolie held on to hope.

She waited while the men spoke in hushed tones, occasionally talking about the van as if it had something to do with their trouble.

Stolen? Maybe. Jolie couldn't be sure.

A cell phone buzzed on the table, and all the boys jumped, eyeing Kai as he fumbled with it in his hands. The phone screen flashed a lime green light, and he flipped it open. What was this, the nineties? She hadn't seen a phone like that since middle school.

"It's Ma," Kai said, pressing his Call button.

Both Raffi and Noah shot up from their chairs, nearly tipping over the table.

"Hey, Ma. Everything okay?" Kai said into the phone.

"Is she all right?" Noah asked.

Kai put his finger to his lips, shaking his head. "Oh no."

Their bodies tensed. Muscles flexed, ready to go into battle.

Jolie found her own body tensing for some reason too.

It was peculiar to watch this band of criminals concerned about their mother like any other normal family. They acted like they didn't have a kidnap victim in their midst.

"Okay, we'll be right there. Just hang tight."

Kai clicked the phone off, putting it back in his pocket. "Ma fell on the steps. She thinks she sprained her ankle."

Noah let out a sigh. "I thought that call was going to be much worse."

"Me too," Kai said, slumping back in his chair.

"She'll probably need ice and some help getting around. You guys head over there, and we'll stick with the original plan," Kai said.

"You sure I can't just talk to her for a little bit?" Noah asked, nodding at Jolie.

"Get out of here, Casanova." Kai gave him a shove.

"See you in the morning then?" Noah asked, bringing their handshake into a bro hug. "See you later, Jolie. Sorry about the whole kidnapping thing."

"It's not kidnapping," Raffi said.

"What is it then?" Noah said.

"It's a hostel," Raffi said. "A hostile hostel." He elbowed Noah in the side. "Get it?"

"You're a buffoon," Kai said, pushing Raff toward the door.

"Hope you can get some sleep with Kai's horrendous snoring," Raffi said, giving Kai a fake punch in the stomach.

"Get out." Kai pushed Raffi with his palms.

Raffi and Noah walked out the door in the far corner while Kai locked it behind them.

"You guys always act like that?" Jolie asked.

"Like complete goons?" Kai said, walking back to her. "Yeah, I guess so."

Jolie couldn't wait any longer to ask. She had to know if he was going to help her or not. "So what's the plan?"

"We'll go to the bank in the morning, and then I'll take you wherever you want to go. I recommend going straight to the airport if you can."

"But… but…," Jolie stammered. "I thought you were going

to help me. I thought you were going to let me go before I give away all my money."

"I said we'd pay you back. Six percent interest."

"But I need the money *now*, or my life is over." The tape tied around her wrists dug at her skin. "Maybe that's an exaggeration, but my business would definitely be over."

Even if she did explain to her father she had to use the money for ransom, he wouldn't give her another chance. A contract was a contract.

Kai's eyes softened. "I can't."

"Your brother is going to kill me."

"My brother is a lot of things," Kai said, "but he's not a killer." He paused, letting his words linger in the air. "Plus that's not the plan. We agreed on the plan. We will let you go, and you will be the first person we pay back."

Jolie shook her head. The lump in her throat made it hard to swallow. Kai was wrong. Or he was lying. Either way, Jolie knew her fate. Her lip trembled in fear.

"It's late. We should probably get some rest," Kai said. "Let me make you a bed so you have something to sleep on."

Kai busied himself with a makeshift bed while Jolie tried keeping her wits, looking around for something large and hard to club him on the head with.

Kai piled bags of coffee beans on top of each other as a mattress, then layered on the blankets that Noah brought. He stood back, proudly overseeing his handiwork like he deserved a damned trophy. "There you go. Hopefully this is comfortable for you."

Jolie's natural inclination was to say thank you, but she suppressed the urge. He was a criminal after all. Even though he seemed to have a good heart, he still allowed this to happen, and he wasn't letting her go. A part of her hated him, and she would never forgive him or his brothers for what they'd put her through.

Kai crouched down and cut the tape that was still attached to her legs and wrists. Using the rope that Raffi had brought back, he wrapped it around her wrists and secured it tightly to a pipe nearby. "It's just a precaution. I hope you can understand," he said. "This will all be over before you know it."

Jolie tugged on the rope. He had given her plenty of slack.

She tried to stand, but the pain in her shin was too much to bear. She hunched over. Any idea of escaping in the middle of the night was squashed by the fact she wouldn't be able to run.

"Here, let me help you," Kai said, placing his arm around her. His body was warm and strong, and he carried her with so much ease she felt like she was floating.

The coffee beans crinkled beneath her as she rested on the bed.

"He got your shin bone pretty bad, didn't he?" Kai said. "Hold on one second."

Kai darted toward the break area and came back with a bandage. He placed it delicately on her skin and assessed his workmanship before standing up. "Can I get you anything else?" Kai asked.

"An escape route?" Jolie quipped.

"Anything but that, sorry," Kai said, a subtle smile forming on his lips. "Do you need another blanket? More water?"

"You're really not good at this hostage thing, are you?"

"I'd prefer to think of you as a temporary guest."

"If you're not going to help me escape, then I'd like to be left alone," Jolie said, lying down while Kai pulled a cotton sheet over her shoulders.

"I understand. Good night."

Again, Jolie almost reflexively said good night, but she pressed her lips firmly together.

Kai stood up from the bed and got in the van. It shifted

back and forth a little bit as he adjusted his weight. He leaned the driver's seat back, and then he was out of view.

Jolie yanked on the rope and wriggled her wrists until a raw patch of skin formed, stinging with every twitch of her hand. It was no use. She was stuck.

Kidnapped.

About to lose everything.

Including her life.

Kai tossed in the driver's seat of the van, readjusting his head against the seat without finding an angle that was comfortable. He willed himself to sleep, but the nagging voice in the back of his mind was calling to him.

Save the girl. Let her go.

There was something about Jolie that he couldn't get out of his head. It tugged at his heart, forcing his thoughts to drift over her fiery eyes and olive skin.

Raffi said he would let Jolie go after tomorrow, but Kai couldn't push down the sick feeling that Raffi would go against the plan. Raffi was rash. Unpredictable. His wild ideas were never fully thought through. Could he go as far as killing her?

No.

Impossible.

But was it?

Kai wasn't sure he knew his brother anymore. One minute he was the same guy he'd grown up with, joking, teasing, and wrestling around. The next minute he was on the brink of complete self-destruction.

Maybe Raffi wouldn't kill her with his own hands, but would he find someone else to do it? Possibly. He had said repeatedly over pizza that she couldn't be trusted.

If Kai helped Jolie escape tonight, then it would all be over. They'd have to give away his father's business. Raffi would be out of a job. Ma would have to sell her home and move in with Kai in the city in his one-bedroom apartment.

He tossed again. The crick in his neck forced him to roll over. He squeezed his eyes shut, trying to block out the noise in his head until he couldn't take it anymore.

Giving Marco the business was the only way out. They could even leave the cocaine behind and let Marco be the one to handle the drug dealers.

Raffi would never be convinced it was the best option. He was too blinded by his need to run the business. *And look what a fine job he'd done so far.*

It was inevitable. His brother would have run the company into the ground with or without the cartel on their trail or Marco's blackmail.

If Kai was going to save Jolie, he would have to act quickly. He tossed his blanket to the side and let the night air cool his skin.

He sat up, focusing on his breath. His heart raced a mile a minute. He had to save Jolie. He had to put an end to this horrible nightmare. There was no other solution.

Peeling himself off the car seat, he poked his head out the van window. Jolie was awake, staring at the ceiling with those big brown eyes.

Kai darted out of the van and ran to her.

"What are you doing?" Jolie grumbled.

He quickly untied the rope around her wrist. "I'm taking you home, wherever that is."

"To San Francisco?"

"No, to your hotel. You'll need to take the first flight home though. Do you understand?"

Jolie's eyes sparkled with hope, and she nodded feverishly.

Kai pulled her off the bed and tried helping her stand, but she couldn't put any pressure on her leg.

"Lean on me. Let's get you in the van."

Jolie obeyed, wrapping her arm around his waist. The nearness of her stirred something deep in his belly. Kai threaded his hand under her shoulder, helping her hobble across the floor.

Kai scooped her into his arms and placed her gently in the passenger seat.

He scurried over to the driver's side and put the van into drive.

It's now or never.

He clicked the garage door open and rolled out of the warehouse and into the parking lot.

"Where am I headed?" Kai said, looking down at her beautiful, scared eyes.

"I'm staying at the Yogi Garden Resort. It's south of here, down the coast," Jolie said.

"You sure you don't want me to just take you directly to the airport?"

Jolie shook her head. "All my stuff is in my room. My computer. My clothes. My passport."

As he drove forward, a parked vehicle across the street came into view.

The hairs on his neck stood on end. Were these the people looking for the cocaine? Kai's hands shook on the steering wheel as he waited for men with guns to jump out.

The car door opened, and Noah stepped out.

Kai had been caught, by his own brother.

CHAPTER TEN

The headlights washed out Noah's face. He covered his eyes with his arms as he walked toward them.

Kai rolled the window down. "Are you spying on me?"

"Raffi asked me to stand guard. Sorry. Needed to make sure the girl stayed here. What the hell are you doing?" Noah looked through the open window at Jolie and gave her a wink before turning back to Kai. "You're not bailing on us, are you?"

Kai rested his head on the steering wheel and let out a long sigh.

"Listen to me. I'm ending this whole thing, here and now."

"But—"

"You've got to admit things have gotten completely out of control."

"Yes, but we had an out! We can keep the business if Jolie lends us the money. She can go home after that."

"Don't you see? Raff isn't going to let her go that easily. She's a liability. As is Raffi. Who knows what he might do at this point?"

"He wouldn't do anything..." Noah's words trailed off into the night.

They both looked at Jolie. The streetlight illuminated her bright eyes swirling with fear.

"We've done enough damage by taking her against her will. Let's not ruin her life," Kai said.

"She's the heiress to Boulard Jewelers. One hundred thousand dollars is chump change to her."

"Actually," Jolie said, "it's all I have left."

"Oh," Noah said, taking a step back, his hands raking his hair. "I didn't realize."

"Giving up the business is the only option. Okay?" Kai said. "If you want to do what's best for you and everyone in our family, I suggest you go home and stay with Ma until I come back."

"But..."

"Just do it!"

"I can't let you go. Raff is going to kill me if he finds out."

"Then come with me," Kai said. "Get in."

Noah stared at the door handle as if it were on fire.

"We're running out of time, Noah. Get in or go home."

Noah's face contorted into a frown. "I can't just leave. Raffi will think we ditched him."

"Fine," Kai said. "Then tell him my plan. I don't care. Just give me a head start so I can drop her off, okay?"

Noah stiffened his jaw, then nodded. He stepped back, and Kai gunned it out of the parking lot.

Stars brightened overhead with each passing mile out of the city and down the coast. The silver ocean shimmered under the moonlight. Jolie caught Kai looking out to the sea, stealing long glimpses between settling his eyes back on the road.

Their path curved farther and deeper into the rainforest. Croaking frogs and chirping nightingales serenaded them through the window. Droplets of rain tickled Jolie's nose until Kai rolled the windows up.

The thumping rain against the windshield lulled Jolie to sleep until a bump in the road shook her out of her slumber. With one eye open, she watched Kai through her lashes as he gripped the steering wheel. The moonlight kissed his face so beautifully she became entranced with his profile—the soft curve of his nose, the perfect shape of his lips.

The van rolled to a stop, and Kai jumped out. He opened the passenger door and slipped his arm behind her as she wrapped her arms around his neck, holding as tight as she could.

"Through the little path over there. Room sixteen," Jolie said.

"Do you have your room key?"

"It's in my bag."

He carried her in his arms, the ground crunching underneath his feet.

After fumbling through her purse to find the key, she unlocked the door. Her stuff was right where she'd left it. Her phone charger on the bed. All signs that she had been returned to normalcy. She had made it out alive. Tears started streaming down her cheeks.

"Jolie, I am so sorry for everything. I hope you can forgive me and my brothers for what we've done. I want to make it up to you." His eyes pleaded with her, begging her for forgiveness.

She stared at him for a moment. *He wants to ensure I don't call the cops.*

Jolie chewed on her lip, unsure of her decision. For now, he just needed to hear what he wanted to hear.

"Let's just say we can let bygones be bygones," Jolie said, plastering on a smile.

Kai visibly relaxed and smiled back. He held her gaze for a moment, then stood up to leave.

"For what it's worth, you're a horrible kidnapper," Jolie said.

Kai grinned, shrugging his shoulders.

"I can tell you're a good guy. I just don't understand how you got caught up in all this."

Kai shook his head. "To be honest, I don't either. I wasn't thinking straight. I was just trying to protect my family."

Jolie thought back to how the brothers had reacted to their mother's phone call. They all seemed to care so much about each other. They didn't have enough money to pay off their problems—unlike her father who had plenty of money but no family to care for him. Jolie could barely stand to be around him.

"What are you going to do now, if you don't mind me asking?"

Kai stared out the window for a while with his hands in his pockets. "I'm going to give our business to Marco to pay off our debt. Then I'm going to go back to the city and start saving up enough money to help pay for my mother's retirement."

Jolie sat up on the bed, careful not to move her leg too much. She found herself wanting to know more about him even though she knew it would be better if she didn't. "What do you do? In the city?"

"I'm in finance. It's what my father did before he started the coffee roastery."

Jolie laughed at the irony. "You must suck at finance if you're robbing jewelry stores."

Kai chuckled. "I guess it would seem that way, but I just finished paying off my student loans. And for the record, I wasn't the one robbing. I was just making sure my brother didn't get caught."

"You suck at that too."

His face brightened as he laughed at her jab, and Jolie found herself lost in his smile until she blinked away her daze.

"I guess I can't poke too much fun. Turns out I don't know how to manage my own finances at all either."

Kai cocked his head to the side. "You just happened to have one hundred thousand in your bank account to hand over for your freedom?"

Jolie sank into her pillows, pulling one over her face to cover the shame. She eventually came up for air. "It's literally all I have."

"Here. In case you want some crappy finance advice," Kai said, handing her his business card. "It's the least I can do for the trouble. And if you were planning on calling the police, I'll just go ahead and make it easier for them to find me."

Jolie laughed nervously, letting the sharp corners of the card poke at her fingertips as she studied the embossed name. KAI GREENE. Running her thumb over his phone number, she felt like he was giving her something more than just an offer to help her financially. When she looked up at him, she noticed how his face had changed. He was blushing, looking at her as if they had just met for the first time.

His phone buzzed and it jolted them both out of the moment. He pulled out his flip phone, and Jolie shook her head. "Seriously, what is with you and this phone? It's ancient."

"What's wrong with this? It still works," Kai said, holding it up. "Pardon me for one second."

Jolie rested her head back on the bed. Despite it being in

the middle of the night, Jolie was wide-awake. She watched Kai curiously and, for some inexplicable reason, had a tiny pang of sadness that he was about to leave. She must be experiencing Stockholm syndrome or something. There was no other logical reason she would want to continue talking to the man who held her hostage just moments ago.

"Are you serious?" Kai hissed into the phone. "Okay, thanks for the call." He flipped his phone closed and tucked it in his pocket. A grave frown spread across his face.

"What's wrong?" Jolie asked. The tiny little hairs on her skin stood on end.

"I have to take you to the airport now. Noah thinks Raffi is on his way here."

"What? How?"

"Noah said Raffi looked you up online. There was a picture of you at this resort."

Jolie's world came crashing down. *Her posts.* How could that be? She hadn't tagged the resort in any of her pictures. It was her protocol to wait until after she left somewhere to tag her location. There had been too many weirdos in her past that would show up out of nowhere.

Then it dawned on her. Jolie's eyes grew wide. The picture with Shanti and Sarah came to mind. One of them must have tagged the resort.

Anyone could know where she was this very moment, including Raffi.

Her throat closed up, and her breath got stuck in her throat.

"Come on, grab what you can quickly. We need to leave now."

"You got everything?" Kai said.

Jolie nodded, slipping her tennis shoes on her bare feet. She tried to grab the handle of her suitcase, but Kai held it firmly in his hand.

"I got it," Kai said. He might have started out as her kidnapper, but he wouldn't let that taint his chivalry. He took the suitcase and rolled it to the front door. The moment he touched the knob, his phone buzzed again.

"Hold on a second," Kai said, pulling out the phone.

It was Raffi.

Kai's heart raced. He placed his finger against his mouth, hushing Jolie.

"Raff," Kai said, placing the phone on his ear.

"Kai, I know what you're doing," Raffi said.

"Where are you?"

"I'm at the resort. I just want to talk."

He was already there? Kai let go of the suitcase and peeked out the window. The moonlight shone on the trail that led to the lobby. Leaves swayed in the night breeze. Birds and monkey calls were about all he could hear besides the beating of his own heart.

"Will you come out and talk to me? I'd hate to make a scene."

"Raffi, you need to leave. Don't make me call the cops."

Raffi's laugh burned through the phone. "Wouldn't that be a fun little twist? You think I wouldn't take you down with me?"

Kai clenched his jaw. "Go home, Raff. We can talk in the morning."

"I'm not going anywhere, and neither are you."

"What is that supposed to mean?"

"It means you've got a couple of holes in your tires, and you're not leaving here unless it's with me."

Kai's eyes grew wide, and he looked at Jolie, who was holding her suitcase like a crutch.

"You slashed my tires?" Kai hissed into the phone. "What the hell?"

"You're going to ruin *everything*. You can't let her go. We need her money."

"Where are you?"

"I'm in the lobby."

"Stay where you are. I'll meet you there."

Kai snapped his flip phone closed. His chest heaved, and the rage boiled inside him. He whipped around to find Jolie digging through her bag. Her hand trembled as she lifted her phone.

She looked up apologetically. "I'm sorry, but I'm calling the cops."

CHAPTER ELEVEN

"Please, Jolie. If you call the cops, I'll end up in jail too."

Jolie gripped her phone. The green Call button beckoned her to push it. Nine-one-one had already been pressed, waiting for her to hit Send. She had been waiting for this moment ever since she'd been thrown into the van.

When she looked up at Kai's tormented face, her body froze. She balanced on her good leg while her thumb hovered over the screen.

"I'm only trying to help you. Let me get you out of here."

Jolie's lip quivered as the man in front of her begged.

"I would get life in prison."

"How are we going to get out of here if your tires are slashed? I didn't rent a car."

"We can call a cab. I have a plan, but you have to trust me. Put the phone down." Kai's hands hung in the air as if he had surrendered himself to her.

He was her prisoner now. With one small tap of a button, his life would be over.

Call the cops.

No, save him.

Call the cops.

No, spare him.

"We can call a cab. I'll go and talk to Raffi to distract him, and you can slip away. Okay? But you have to do it now. We have to find you a car."

Jolie stared into Kai's determined eyes.

"Raff thinks I'm heading to the lobby now. I can help you sneak out the back window and into a cab."

Maybe she was crazy. Or maybe she just saw the good in Kai and felt the need to protect him as much as he had been trying to protect her. He reminded her somehow of one of the homeless puppies that needed saving.

She pressed the Cancel button and found the number for a cab company instead.

Kai's shoulders hunched as he thanked her under his breath. He stood up and took the luggage from Jolie's firm grip. Just as Jolie got off the phone with the taxi company, Kai stuck his head out the front door.

"I don't see him," Kai said. "I'll head out first. Give me about two minutes to reach the lobby, then you can go. I suggest walking toward the road that leads to the parking lot. See if you can catch the cab before it gets anywhere near the lobby."

Jolie gave him a nervous nod. She took the luggage handle back, but she wasn't sure she would be able to pull it up the street with her injured leg. She would have to leave the suitcase behind to be sure she could get out.

"You ready?" Kai said.

Jolie studied Kai's face. She would never see him again, and for some odd reason it pained her as if she was losing a friend.

She really must have lost her mind.

"Ready," Jolie lied.

Kai gave her a curt nod and then slipped out the front door. He closed it softly, and her heart raced. She was alone.

The stillness and quiet of her room scared her more than her plan to escape.

One, one thousand, two, one thousand.

Jolie counted until she was sure she had reached two minutes. The cab driver would be there soon.

Balancing on one foot, she hopped over the threshold. Jolie cut between two casitas, letting the tall grass tickle her one good leg.

As she reached the clearing, she saw the warm glow of headlights coming down the path. It was the cab.

She was saved.

She hobbled faster, putting a little weight on her bum leg and bit through the pain.

The cab made its way toward the parking lot, and Jolie waved her arms wildly, hoping she could divert him from driving up to the lobby. Its lights flashed directly on her, but it turned away, making its slow crawl on the gravel road.

"Over here!" Jolie yelled, but it was too late. The cab pulled up to the lobby, just as Kai came running out through the front doors.

Kai appeared to look in the cab long enough to realize Jolie wasn't in it, and then he darted toward the casitas.

Raffi tore through the front doors after him. "Stop!" Raffi yelled.

And then Kai saw her and shifted his direction, sprinting toward her.

Jolie didn't know if she should run or hide. Before she could make a decision, he was only inches away.

"We need to go," Kai said. He slid his arms, lifting her up off the ground. Kai whisked her away, in the opposite direction of the cab driver.

"Where are you taking me?" Jolie said, as her body jostled around in his arms.

"Away from him," Kai said between breaths. "We need to get out of here."

Raffi had gained speed, tearing across the lot. "Stop!" he yelled again.

They tore into the leafy bushes. It grew darker with each step. Palms scratched at her skin and whipped her face until she could no longer see. A black cloak coated her vision as they slashed through the leaves, deeper into the jungle.

Sharp leaves raked at Jolie's back as Kai raced forward. His breath was heavy and loud in her ear. There hadn't been any sign of Raffi for a while, but Kai continued to trudge into the thick black night.

"I think we're in the clear," Jolie said softly.

Kai slowed his pace to a walk. His chest surged for air. He continued to walk with her in his arms for a little while longer, taking her farther into darkening trees. Raindrops bounced off the leaves above. The jungle calls swirled around them in the absence of light.

"What happened back there?" Jolie said as he set her down. Grass and dead leaves crunched underneath her sneakers.

"Raffi was furious that I had left you alone," Kai said. "He had that wild look in his eye. I thought he was going to do something stupid. Then the cab showed up. He started to head out of the lobby to grab you. He was going to stop you from getting in the cab, so I shoved him and ran."

"You did?" Jolie said. *That is oddly gallant.* "Can we start heading back now?"

"He'll be waiting for us there."

Jolie's hand searched the inside of her bag for her phone, and she pulled it out. She had one missed call from the taxi service and no bars. Even if she wanted to call the police, she'd have to wait until she got back to the resort.

"So what's the plan? We obviously can't stay in the jungle," Jolie said.

The blue light glow from her phone illuminated Kai's frown and cast a dark shadow under his eyes.

"I was going to take you to the highway and catch you a cab from there. The problem is, we should have hit the highway by now," Kai said.

"We're not lost, are we?"

"No, but it's impossible to tell exactly which way we're headed. I don't know if we veered off course, but the highway should definitely be right here."

Jolie stilled, hoping to hear the rushing sound of a car or truck on cement ground. Instead, they were cocooned in a swarm of grating murmurs and chirping crickets. Monkeys whooped and howled in the distance.

"Could my compass help?" Jolie asked, pulling up her app.

"Your phone has a compass?" Kai asked in surprise.

"Most people's phones in this century do." Jolie rolled her eyes.

Kai held her phone up, the bright light illuminating his face. He twisted a little to the right. "Okay, I was going the right way. I'm not sure why we haven't hit the highway yet."

An owl hooted overhead, and Jolie ducked. "What was that?"

"It was just an owl."

"I'm really scared, Kai. I want to go back."

"We can't go back now. It's not safe. I'm afraid we'd get lost trying to find our way back, and even if we did make it, I'm worried what Raff would do."

Jolie looked around, but only the faint swaying of leaves

could be seen among the kiss of moonlight. Visibility had vanished just as quickly as it arrived as black clouds swirled above.

"Should we just wait?" Jolie said shakily. "So we don't get any more lost in the dark?"

"Waiting for the sun to come up is probably a good idea."

Kai interlaced his fingers through Jolie's hand and pulled out his lighter with the other. The orange glow flickered, illuminating a few fallen trees a couple yards away. "Let's rest here. The sun should be coming up in about an hour."

Jolie limped toward the patch of dead leaves, Kai's supportive grip keeping her steady. She sat down, leaning her back against the thick trunk.

Kai flicked off his lighter. Tickling antennae crawled all over Jolie's skin and buzzed around her ears. Big thick bugs bumped into her face, and she swatted them away.

"Yuck!"

"I can try to make a fire. It might help with the bugs," Kai said.

"Is that safe?"

"It is if you know what you're doing," Kai said, shifting his weight away from the trunk. "Luckily I know a few things. My father would take us out into the forests when we were kids. No matter where we lived, he would always find a way to get us outdoors."

"Did you live in a lot of places?" Jolie said.

"We lived everywhere," Kai said as he gathered up sticks and leaves. She could hardly make out his movements with her eyes, but she could hear twigs breaking and the scraping of leaves near her feet. "Berlin. Prague. Madrid. Montana. Sacramento. You name it."

"That explains your funny accent."

Kai chuckled. The flash of his lighter sparked, and he held it to a small bundle of twigs.

"Me and my brothers get that a lot."

"You sound kind of American, but not quite. There's a hint of British and Spanish in there. Maybe a little German?"

"Ah." Kai laughed. "I'm surprised you picked up on that. My mother is German."

"How… eclectic," Jolie mused.

"The darn thing won't light. It's too damp," Kai muttered under his breath. He flicked off the lighter and rustled with something in his pocket.

"Do you smoke? Jolie asked. "Or do you just happen to carry a lighter around?"

"My father used to ask me to get a lighter for his cigars all the time. Eventually I got sick of running all over the place to find one, so I just kept one in my pocket."

Kai flicked the lighter back on and held it in front of a receipt, setting it aflame. He tossed the burning paper into his small pile and blew gently. Soon the light took shape and danced along Kai's brow as the flames grew into a small campfire.

"Your dad used to, but not anymore?"

"He passed away a couple of weeks ago," Kai said.

"Oh," Jolie said, watching the flickering of the fire in his eyes. "I'm so sorry."

Kai poked at the fire, offering her a polite smile.

"Were you close?"

"Yeah, we were close," Kai said, letting the rest of his answer fade into the darkness.

He sat down next to Jolie, his arm brushing up against her, unassuming, just there. But the small patch of cotton fabric that rubbed against Jolie's bare shoulder was oddly comforting.

She resisted the urge to pry any further about his father, although she wanted to know more. She wondered if his father's death had anything to do with the trouble he was in.

Jolie let her unanswered questions shrivel among the embers in the fire and wondered why she found herself feeling sad for her kidnapper.

Could this whole thing be an act? A ploy for sympathy to keep her from calling the police once they were out of the jungle? It was working if that was his plan.

"How about you? I take it your father is still around since you threatened he would ruin my life if he found out you had been kidnapped," Kai said.

"He is," Jolie said, contemplating how much she should tell him. "He's in San Francisco, where I grew up and never left. He made sure I stayed in the city my whole life."

"I sense there's tension between you two."

"Yeah, you could call it that."

"I see," Kai said. "But a wildcat like you can't be contained."

Jolie looked up at his playful smile. "Wildcat?"

"Yeah." He smiled. "You know, with all the biting and scratching you do. Don't get me wrong, we deserved it all."

Jolie narrowed her eyes. "You certainly did."

"That headbutt though," Kai said, rubbing his forehead. "It was impressive. I mean, the sheer force behind it was staggering. I'll have this knot for a month."

Jolie giggled. "Serves you right."

"How did you learn to fight like that?"

"Instinct, I guess." Jolie shrugged. She hadn't taken a self-defense class before. Popping him in the head with her forehead *had* hurt like hell, but he didn't need to know that. She was just doing whatever she could to fight them off at the time.

It was silly to think she went from fighting Kai for her life to being nestled close to him by a small campfire in the rainforest, acutely aware of his arm pressing more firmly against hers than when he first sat down.

"Wildcat instincts," Kai mused. "Sounds like a band name."

Jolie smiled. "An eighties metal band."

"Yeah."

Jolie smiled through her yawn. The night had finally caught up to her, and her eyelids drooped over her tired eyes.

As if on cue, Kai shifted his weight. "You can lean on me if you want to while you get some rest."

Jolie looked at his broad chest, inviting her in like a warm, snuggly pillow. His eyes crinkled at the edges in a tired, welcoming grin.

"I promise I won't bite. Unlike you, I'm more of the cuddly kitten type," Kai said.

Jolie snorted. "Yeah, right." But she believed him. He really did seem harmless. And in that moment, his chest looked like the most comfortable place on earth.

Scooting herself closer, she rested her ear above his thumping heart. His muscles were smooth and hard under his shirt.

"Are you cold?" Kai whispered in her hair.

"Just a little, but I'm fine," Jolie said, aware of her bare shoulders catching the cool night air.

Kai wrapped his arm around her. The weight of it gave her warmth, and she felt safe, despite the cacophony of howling beasts in the distance.

"Try to get some rest. Before you know it, you'll be getting into a cab and on your way to the airport. You'll be able to leave this horrible nightmare behind you."

A small part of Jolie wondered why this didn't feel like the nightmare he described. It was more like two friends camping around a fire. The fear of being caught by Kai's brother had completely left her system somehow.

Jolie let her heavy eyelids shut as a small twinge of guilt crept its way into her chest.

A tree branch snapped only a few yards away. Jolie's head

shot up from Kai's chest as they both looked in the direction of the rustling bushes.

Jolie's heart pounded. "What was that?" she whispered.

Kai brought his finger to his lips, hushing her while his eyes fixated on the moving object in the dark.

CHAPTER TWELVE

The leaves parted just enough for Kai to see a black eye reflecting the light from the campfire. Its mole-like head appeared in the dim glow, and Kai realized their intruder was nothing but a capybara. A giant, hundred-pound guinea-pig-looking thing.

Kai relaxed when he realized the scary monster was just a harmless rodent, but Jolie's hands gripped at Kai's shirt, tugging at his collar.

"Do we run?" Jolie's voice shook. "Is it going to eat us?"

"You've never seen a capybara before?" Kai asked.

"A what?" Jolie said, still yanking on his shirt.

Kai put his hand on hers. "Relax. It won't hurt us."

Jolie let go of his shirt, and he stood up to shoo the animal away before sitting back down on the damp ground.

"That really scared me," Jolie said, holding her hand over her heart. "I thought it was one of those r-o-u-s's."

"R-o-u what?"

"*Princess Bride*? Rodents of unusual size?"

Kai scrunched up his nose. "Never heard of it. Although

there is some truth to the name. That rodent is unusually big."

"How have you never seen *Princess Bride*? It's a classic movie."

Kai shrugged. "I lived in a house full of boys. I can't say anything with 'princess' in the title made it on our list of things to watch."

Kai opened his arm for her, welcoming her to lay her head back down on his chest. When she obliged, Kai felt a glimmer of happiness. There was something soothing about holding her close. A wave of calm rolled through him.

Her hair smelled like jasmine in an ocean breeze. As she nestled closer, he draped his arm over hers to keep her warm. The softness of her skin sent electric currents through his body. He caught himself holding his breath.

"Your heart is pounding," Jolie whispered.

"It is?" Kai asked, homing in on his pulse.

"Seems like you were more scared of that r-o-u-s than you were letting on."

Kai bit back his smile. "Perhaps," he said.

It was a raindrop that woke Kai from his sleep. Another one forced his eyes open. Sunlight seeped in through the trees. The rich green leaves had come alive after the blackness of night. The jungle was awake, and the swarming trill of crickets and birds enveloped them.

Jolie's head was pressed against his chest. Her shoulders rose and fell with a steady sleeping breath. She had the soft, sweet purr of a kitten, but the soul of a tigress.

Warmth spread in his chest, yearning for this girl in his arms, as if he had grown feelings for her overnight.

Was he mad? It would be foolish to fall for someone like

Jolie. A woman this beautiful and wealthy was way out of his league. He was sure of it. And it didn't help that their first encounter was so dramatic. It was not the best of first impressions.

But she had certainly made an impression on Kai. He smiled at the memory of her nearly biting Marco's finger off. She had gumption, a spark fierier than the flick of his lighter.

Even though it was ridiculous, he closed his eyes and relished in her closeness, finding peace in holding her before he had to send her back to her life in the States.

She would eventually forget about him, and maybe someday he would be able to forget about her too, although the thought of it irked him.

Jolie stirred awake under his arm. She blushed as she peeled herself off him.

"Sorry I fell asleep on you."

"You don't need to be sorry." If only she knew how much he enjoyed it.

"Shall we go?" Jolie asked.

"Yes." Kai helped her up, brushing off the fallen leaves from her hair.

"Which way?"

"Can I see your phone's compass again?"

Jolie dug through her purse and switched on the phone. "Still no bars and hardly any battery left." Bringing up the compass, she turned her body until she was facing the opposite way they had been heading. "That way is north."

"Impossible," Kai said.

"See for yourself," Jolie said, handing him the phone.

Sure enough, the dial pointed in the direction they had come from. "Are you sure this is accurate?"

Jolie shrugged. "I don't know. I've never had to use it before."

Kai scratched his head, looking around. He knew the

highway was north of the resort and they were heading north when they escaped. The compass was now directing them to backtrack. It didn't make sense.

"I dropped my phone in front of the jewelry store," Jolie said. "I wonder if something broke."

Kai handed it back and looked up toward the sky. A canopy of trees made it hard to tell where the sun was rising, but his gut told him to keep walking the direction they were headed.

"Let's head this way," Kai said. "Can you walk?"

Jolie tested the weight on her leg and grimaced a little. "I think so." She hobbled toward him.

Kai held out his hand, and she accepted it with a soft smile.

An hour went by. Kai was starting to doubt his sense of direction. He stopped and looked up toward the sky, but the shift in sunlight was too hard to track.

The damp heat imposed on his lungs. He assumed Jolie was struggling too. She had sweated through her tank top, and her cheeks were bright red.

"Do you need a break?" Kai asked.

"I can go a little farther." Jolie huffed. "It seems like we should have hit the highway by now, right?"

Kai swallowed the panic that had begun to rise, burning the back of his throat.

"It should be just a few yards farther."

It wasn't.

Another hour and Kai finally had tracked the sun. They had been traveling west, deeper into the jungle. He wasn't sure how or when he had gotten off track.

Rain plopped against the tops of their heads, trickling down their faces and soaking their clothes.

"Catch what you can," Kai said. "I'm not sure we're going to find a water source to drink from until we get out of here."

Kai tilted his neck back, opening his mouth. He let the raindrops fall onto his tongue. The rain tasted sweet, soothing his dry, hot mouth.

Jolie did the same. "This rain tastes like heaven."

Kai laughed. "It really does." He stuck out his tongue again.

Kai determined that watching Jolie catch raindrops on her tongue might be the single most adorable thing he had ever witnessed in his life. Like a kid in a candy store, she lapped up every droplet she could muster. She ran between two leafy trees where water rushed down in big splashes.

When the rain stopped, they continued forward through the brush.

"We're lost, aren't we?" Jolie said.

Kai froze, wondering how lost they actually were. They had walked for miles without any sign of hope. "We might have gotten off track, but we're going the right way now."

"But you're not sure. I can tell."

"How?"

"You've been fidgeting with that lighter for the past hour."

Kai looked down at his hand. The skin on his thumb pad was red and raw.

He sighed. "I'm a little worried we are lost, yes."

"Shit!" Jolie hissed, dropping her bag at her feet. She rifled through it to pull out her phone. "Still no bars either."

"I'm really sorry. I'm trying to do my best here."

"This has been the worst twenty-four hours of my life."

Kai frowned. Of course it was the worst day of her life. Any logical person could see that. So why did that statement bother him so much? Maybe because it was all his fault.

Kai gingerly walked over to her, picking up her purse. "Can I carry this for you?"

Jolie glared at him. "Stop being so nice. I'm trying to be mad at you right now."

Kai backed away, his hands in surrender. "I'm sorry, truly. Be mad at me all you want." *Just don't call the cops when I get you back to the hotel.*

Jolie picked up her bag with a grunt. "Just get me out of this damn jungle."

"Okay," Kai said, trailing behind her. "I didn't realize you had such a potty mouth."

"Don't even get me fucking started," Jolie hissed.

Kai blanched.

He had poked the wildcat.

Jolie had been limping for hours. Her feet hurt. Her shin pulsated like it had its own heartbeat. Her mouth was dry, and the heat was suffocating. She could have wrung Kai's neck for getting them lost in the jungle even if it was an accident.

Jolie huffed through the rainforest, occasionally looking back at Kai, who looked like an ashamed puppy with a tail between his legs.

It's not like he could have asked for directions, but still! They were *lost*. In the Costa Rican jungle. She hadn't eaten since her vegan lunch the day before. Her stomach screamed for food.

She tried to think of anything else. The patterns of the leaves, the colorful birds in the trees, the monkeys that perched on tree limbs, cackling down at them. The jungle was beautiful in a way—if it weren't about to kill them.

Limping through the jungle, Jolie felt the weight of her bag lifted from her shoulder. Kai tried hoisting it up, indicating with his eyes that he could take it for her.

"Thanks but no, thanks," Jolie said flatly. "I can carry my own stuff."

Kai gently released the bag, letting the weight of her wallet and her camera bear down on her shoulder.

"You sure?" Kai said.

It *had* felt nice without all that weight even if it was for the briefest second.

She stopped in her tracks, and Kai nearly walked right into her. Then she stared up into his sappy eyes, contemplating his offer.

"I'm just trying to help," he said.

Jolie pursed her lips. He was just trying to butter her up. His fate was in her hands after all. Regardless, she could use the break. Jolie reached in her bag and grabbed her cell phone.

A knowing smile etched at the corner of his mouth as he took her purse again.

It felt amazing to be free from the extra load. "Thank you," Jolie said softly.

Kai marched on in the direction they were headed, and Jolie's shoulders relaxed.

It really was hard to stay mad at the guy.

"So what's with the van?" Jolie said. "We're lost in the jungle, and we've got nothing but time now. Why don't you tell me what all the fuss was about?"

Kai took several steps, avoiding her gaze. "You picked up on that? I thought you didn't know Spanish."

"I don't, really. I studied it in high school, and for some reason *camioneta* stayed with me."

Kai chuckled to himself. "Of course that was the one thing you understood." He shook his head in dismay. "I think it's safer if you don't know."

"It's not like I've got anyone to tell at the moment."

"It's when we get back that worries me."

"Listen, you're going to need to trust me," Jolie said, "or this whole escape bit is for nothing."

Kai sighed. "I suppose you're in pretty deep already," he said, running his fingers through his hair. Sweat had seeped down his shirt, clinging to his skin. She found herself hypnotized by the curvature of his chest.

"Raffi got involved with some bad people."

Jolie snapped out of her trance. "Well, that's the least surprising news of the century," Jolie said. "I could tell there was something wrong with that guy the moment I laid eyes on him."

"Raff's not usually like that. He's a bit crazy, and he's always getting himself into trouble, but I think you saw him at his worst."

Jolie rolled her eyes. "I don't believe that, but keep talking."

"The nitwit took a side job being a delivery guy for drug dealers, and one day he shows up with a van full of cocaine and nobody to deliver it to. They were all dead."

Jolie gasped. "Holy shit."

"No kidding," Kai said. He flinched before moving on. "I don't know who killed whom, and if someone is looking for that van, but if they are, we are in big trouble."

"Why?"

"Because the cocaine is currently sitting in my warehouse."

Jolie stopped limping for a second, covering her open mouth with her hands. "You've got to be kidding."

"I wish I was. You were sitting among boxes full of the stuff in my office."

"Oh my God. How much is it?"

"It's hard to say exactly. About two hundred kilos or so."

"*Two hundred kilos?* That's like... millions of dollars' worth of drugs. Why the hell is it in your warehouse? Couldn't you dump it? Call the police?"

"I wanted to call the police, but Raffi begged me not to.

He was afraid of going to jail and getting killed by men from the inside. I couldn't do that to him. I wanted to dump the stuff too, but he convinced me to hold on to it in case the cartel showed up. Which they didn't, but Marco Venega did and saw the whole thing."

"He's the guy I bit?"

"Among the three men you bit yesterday, yes," Kai said with a wry grin.

"He saw the cocaine in your warehouse and then what?"

"He had a video of us sorting through the stuff. He threatened to send it to the cops unless we paid up. The rest is history, I guess. One bad choice after another led us here."

"So Raffi was stealing from the jewelry store to pay Marco's debt?"

"You pick up quick," Kai said.

Jolie felt the air escape her lungs. "I had no idea how bad of a situation you were in."

"It's pretty bad." Kai held out his hand to help her over a fallen tree. She placed her hand in his, and his fingers closed around hers. With a firm grip, he hoisted her over the log.

"Why don't you guys just leave? Go back to one of those places you've lived before? Montana has got to be safer for you."

Kai smiled. "It might come down to that, but not yet. Costa Rica is my home now. I've lived here for over ten years. My father put everything he had into his business. My mother's retirement depends on it. Although, now that I don't see a way around giving up the business to pay off our debt, we may not be tied here anymore. Except for one thing."

"What's that?"

"I have a job waiting for me back in San José. A really good one."

"Couldn't you just get a really good job somewhere else?"

"I guess you're right." Kai rubbed his chin. "I'd have to take my mother with me though. She'll need to be supported somehow. But leaving Costa Rica would break her heart. She loves it here. As do I. There's something special about it, unlike any other place we've lived. The people here aren't in a rush to get to tomorrow. They live in the moment. They're happy."

"Were people not happy in Prague or Berlin?"

"Not like here," Kai said. "Maybe it's the Caribbean air. The tropical scenery. The music. I don't know. I can't tell for sure, but it feels like island life with all the benefits of being on the mainland. Every day is like a vacation."

Jolie pondered that for a moment. *Every day is like a vacation.* It's exactly what she wanted for herself. She wanted her business to thrive so she could live like she wasn't working. She wanted to call her own shots because she hated deadlines and schedules.

"What's going on in that head of yours?" Kai said. "You look deep in thought."

"I guess something you said really resonated with me," Jolie said. "I'd love to be able to live every day like a vacation. It's why I want to work for myself."

"What do you do?"

"I have a blog and an Instagram account. I make money through endorsements and advertising. I guess I should say I *made* money. My business fell off a cliff recently. I'm still not even sure I understand what happened. One day I had more endorsement deals than I knew how to manage. The next, I was losing brand partners left and right."

Kai's eyes narrowed. "Hm, that's strange."

"I guess I just lost my edge. I wasn't coming up with anything new or fresh. Companies are probably upgrading to newer, younger versions of me."

"Really, you think so?"

"It's the only thing that makes sense. The data showed that my followers have been every bit as engaged as they used to be, but that didn't seem to matter to my partners."

"What are you going to do now?" Kai said, swatting at a bug circling his head.

"Thanks to you, I'll be able to keep my money and rebrand. I'm going to target a slightly different following."

Kai ducked under the eight-ball-sized bug that continued to attack him. "This little guy really doesn't like me."

Jolie chuckled. "He sure doesn't."

Kai swatted at the air until the bug flew away. "Thank God. So what kind of people are you targeting?" Kai said.

"Vegans."

"Ah. That explains why you turned down the pizza last night."

Jolie looked down at her hands. Her stomach ached for food, and a part of her regretted not eating when she had the chance. "The truth is, I've only recently become vegan to prove to my father that I can do it. He didn't think I could."

"What kind of father would tell that to their daughter?"

"Mine would," Jolie said. "My father would also be willing to wager that I would fail at successfully rebranding my business."

"That's horrible. I can't imagine my father being like that."

"He has his reasons, I guess. He hates what I do, and he wants to control every little thing, including what I do for a living."

"Why do you suppose he's like that?"

Jolie pursed her lips as she thought about it. "It probably has a lot to do with my mother and how she left him. He was controlling with her too, but not nearly as bad as he is now. When she left, he became a monster version of himself. His money became his source of power, especially over me. He convinced me to stay in the Bay Area for college with a huge sum of money. And he was able to keep me in San Francisco by supplementing my income—that is, until I cut him off.

"I was tired of him telling me what to do. Patronizing me for the lifestyle I had chosen for myself. Shaming me for my Instagram photos. I had enough. Little did I know that I would end up broke and desperate to save my business."

"But you have one hundred thousand in your bank account."

"Oh yes," Jolie said. "The bargain money. He loaned it to me under the condition that if I fail, I have to work for him, or I can kiss the rest of my inheritance goodbye."

Kai shifted her purse on his shoulder as his face scrunched up. "Seriously? If you fail, you have to work for him?"

"Yeah," Jolie said. "It's a life sentence."

Kai tilted his head. "Now wait a minute, that actually doesn't seem all that bad. I mean, I'm assuming he'd offer you a steady job?"

"Yes, but you don't understand. I'm not wired the way most people are. I don't have this need to have a security blanket. I don't want a routine. I work hard enough on my own terms. I can't have someone else telling me how I should run my day."

"Have you told your father that? Maybe he would be willing to allow for a flexible schedule. As long as you're getting the work done, it shouldn't matter if you're in the office or working remote, right?"

"Companies aren't like that though, are they? I mean, every business is all about productivity and employee engagement, blah, blah, blah. Even the flexible tech companies in the Bay Area still expect people to be working eighty hours a week. I can't stand that type of restriction on my life. Besides, he would never go for it. My father's too traditional."

"People can change with a little influence," Kai said.

"Not my father. He's the most stubborn man I've ever met."

"You don't think he can change?"

"Absolutely not."

"Not even the slightest bit?"

"I said no already. He's set in his ways, and that's that."

"Are you sure?"

Jolie looked over her shoulder at Kai and noticed a mischievous smile on his face. "What are you really asking me, Kai?"

"I just wanted to see if you were as stubborn as your father."

Jolie raised her eyebrow, daring him to tell her the verdict. "And?"

His eyes twinkled. "It seems to me like your father isn't the only one set in his ways."

Jolie's mouth formed an O. Did he really just compare her to her father? If he hadn't had that adorable grin on his face, she would have unleashed her fury. Instead, she went with a playful whack to his shoulder.

"Ow," Kai said, pretending to be hurt. He rubbed his arm as if she had stabbed him. "You are very violent."

Jolie pushed back the smile that threatened the corners of her mouth.

"And stubborn," Kai added. "What about a different job? Can't you find an employer that can give you the kind of flexibility you need? I mean, there's got to be some company out there that gives employees autonomy to work when they want to and all the other high-maintenance demands you require."

"High maintenance?" Jolie nudged his rib cage with her elbow.

He recoiled under the jab. "Hey, that tickles."

She never considered herself high maintenance, and she hated that he had a point. Maybe there were businesses out there that wouldn't crush her soul. She made a mental note to do more research when she got back home.

Jolie poked at his ribs again, relishing in his squeals. "You sound like a pig!" Jolie teased. Then he darted away from her behind a tree.

"Come back here," Jolie said. "I'm not done with you."

It was silent apart from the shuffling noises of leaves behind the large tree trunk.

"Kai, get back here. We have unfinished business."

When she received nothing back in response, Jolie's face fell. Her pulse quickened. Was something wrong? "Kai?"

"Jolie," Kai said.

"Yeah?"

"Come over here. You're going to want to see this."

CHAPTER THIRTEEN

Jolie hopped around the trunk to find Kai staring through the trees. She followed his gaze toward the sunlight reflecting off of a turquoise body of water in the distance.

"What is that? A mirage?" Jolie said. "Are we that dehydrated already?"

Kai shielded his eyes from the sun with his hand and squinted. "I think it's a lagoon. You want to check it out?"

Jolie's heart quickened. "Can we drink from it? I'm dying."

"It might not be safe," Kai said. "But maybe we can stick our feet in it for a minute. I could use a break."

Jolie agreed. Her body ached all over. She imagined this might be what marathoners feel like after a race. She gladly accepted Kai's hand as he led her toward the pool in the middle of the rainforest.

Trees and mossy rocks surrounded the twinkling lagoon. Storks with twig-like beaks shuffled along the edge, sticking their pointed noses in and out. It looked a page right out of *National Geographic*.

"Wow," Jolie said. "It's stunning."

"This country never ceases to amaze me," Kai said, taking a deep breath.

Jolie reached for her purse, slipping it off Kai's shoulder. She pulled out her camera, grateful that it still worked and had enough batteries. "It would be a pity to pass up the opportunity to take a picture. This is social media gold."

Kai placed his hands on his hips, looking over her shoulder as she adjusted the exposure settings.

Jolie took another picture and checked the digital screen. The photograph was beautiful, but it would never capture the true magnificence of this place.

"You seem like you have a knack for photography," Kai said, looking over her shoulder at the screen.

Jolie shrugged. "Eh, I'm okay. Lord knows I've had a lot of practice. I should be better than I am."

"I don't know how you do all that, messing with those settings until you get the perfect picture. That takes skill."

Jolie's cheeks warmed as she held her camera up. Only this time she pointed at Kai's face.

He looked away, holding out his hand to block her shot. "You don't want a picture of me."

Jolie was ready for the shot, but he refused to turn around.

"Come on. Just one?"

"No way." He held his hand steady.

Jolie put the camera on her shoulder. He probably didn't want his picture taken if he thought there was still a chance she'd call the police. She couldn't blame him, although she was sure now that if she were to call the police, it would only be to put his evil brother in jail. Not Kai.

"All right, relax. No picture." Jolie pouted. "Could I ask you to take one of me?"

"Sure," he said, taking the camera, "but we should probably get going soon. We need to get out of this jungle before we shrivel up like prunes. We need drinkable water."

He pulled the camera up to his eye and clicked.

"Hold on. Let me get ready." Jolie tugged at her damp tank top.

"What are you doing?"

"I'm getting ready for the shot," Jolie said. "Do you mind turning around for a second?"

"But why?"

"I'm getting in the water, silly. I can't just take a plain picture of me in front of the most beautiful lagoon I've ever seen in my life. I need to seize the moment. This is what Instagram dreams are made of."

Kai turned around obediently. "I still don't understand why you need to be in the water. It's probably not safe to be in there. Think of the parasites. And the—"

"You're thinking too much," Jolie said.

She stripped out of her clothes and laid them on the boulders along the edge of the pool. "I'll be careful not to get any water in my mouth. I've just got something in mind, similar to a perfume ad I saw once."

She dipped a toe into the cool blue. "The water feels amazing."

"Can I turn around now?"

"One second," Jolie said, making her way into the water. "As I was saying, I need the perfect picture to attract new brands. A smiling girl in front of a pretty landscape is not enough to get attention. I like to be doing something in my images. I want the person looking at my photographs wondering what I'm about to do next."

"You sound like an artist."

"Hm," Jolie hummed, fully immersing herself in the water. The cool water soothed the sunburns she had accumulated on her shoulders and arms. "I guess I never considered myself an artist. To me, it's just business—my way of selling something."

"I guess there is a fine line between art and business," Kai said. "Not so much in the finance world though. I don't think I've got a creative bone in my body."

"Oh, I'm sure you do somewhere."

"Can I turn around now?"

Jolie held her breath and squeezed her eyes tight before dipping her head below the water's surface. She reemerged, wringing her hair out with her hands. "Now, Mr. Polite. I'm ready. How do I look?"

Kai turned around, catching her gaze from the center of the pool. "You look… beautiful," he said breathlessly, holding his stare.

Jolie felt the rush of heat to the tips of her ears. She had been called beautiful many times, but not like this. Somehow it was different. It didn't feel like he was talking about her face or her eyes. It felt like he was seeing through the superficial layer. Unless she was imagining it, which was also possible. She *had* thought the lagoon was a mirage.

"Let's take this picture, and we can go," Jolie said. She pinched her cheeks to help add color that had drained from exhaustion.

Kai held the camera up to his face. "Like this?" he said, snapping a photo.

"Come a little closer, and zoom in. I want my face to take up most of the frame and the waterline to be in there too."

Kai twisted the lens. "I don't know what I'm doing."

"Just click. I can photoshop the rest."

Jolie homed in on the lens. She stared at the camera as if she had naughty plans for the future. Pouting her lips ever so slightly, she gathered the courage to rise out of the water, just enough to feel the water line above her nipples. She heard the click of the camera, but Kai stood frozen in his spot.

"A few more?" Jolie called out.

"Uh, yeah," Kai croaked.

Jolie suppressed her giggle and posed for the next shot. Raising her arms with her hands behind her head, she stared deeply into the camera.

Click.

She turned to an angle, looked up through her lashes and let a faint smile reach her lips. She pretended like she had a secret, although it was close to the truth. If she was being honest with herself, this photo shoot wasn't just about business and seeking attention from new brands.

Click.

It probably wasn't wise to seduce Kai through the camera, but she couldn't stop herself. There was something between them. Something electric. Could he feel it too?

The camera clicked again, shaking Jolie from her thoughts. "Thanks, Kai. Can I see?"

Kai stood still, as if the camera had been glued to his face.

"Kai?"

"Right, yes. Of course." He held out the camera and looked away, covering his eyes with his hands. The edges of his ears were bubblegum pink.

"Are you blushing?" Jolie asked, swimming to the edge of the water.

"No," Kai said, "but you should know your chest was nearly out of the water."

That was the point, she thought, biting back her mischievous smile. Her tactic must have worked because he was squirming like a teenage boy in a porn shop.

She swam to the edge of the water and grabbed the camera from his outstretched hand.

"How'd I do?" Kai asked.

Jolie flipped through the pictures. He had taken a lot, a

few decent ones too. "The composition of these are really good. Nice job."

"Thanks," Kai said. "Can't say I've taken any pictures like *that* before."

"You've never taken a nude picture of someone?"

Kai shook his head, his eyes sparkling.

How could a man so devilishly handsome be so innocent? "Have you ever skinny-dipped?"

Kai averted his eyes, shaking his head. "I can't say I have."

Really. His purity was so... intriguing. Her inner siren had been summoned. Compelled to take her seduction efforts one step further, she set the camera on her purse and swam back to the center of the pool.

"What are you doing?" Kai said. "We really need to go."

"Come in," Jolie said. "We can take a break a little longer. I'm tired of walking, and the water feels good."

Kai shoved his hands in his pockets, kicking a small rock into the lagoon. "I don't know. We probably shouldn't stay here."

Jolie silently beckoned him from the water with her pointer finger. *Come hither.*

Kai held her stare for a moment, then reached for the back of his shirt and pulled it over his head.

Jolie smiled victoriously as she watched him toss his shirt to the side.

When Jolie's eyes landed on his broad chest, her mouth fell open. She had figured he was trim and muscular, but she was not expecting the rock-solid body stripping down in front of her and the shadows casting below his pecs and the tiny ridges of his stomach. He had a slim waist that dipped into his jeans, resting loosely below his hip bones, and his arms—*my God, his arms*—were perfection in all their manly, rippling glory.

Jolie felt her breath hitch in her throat. "You're pretty fit for a finance guy," Jolie said, gathering her faculties.

Kai laughed, and his smile did a funny thing to her insides. He took off his sneakers and then his socks, placing them in the sun. When he reached for his jeans, he looked up. He wagged his finger at her, denying her the show she so desperately wanted to watch.

"Your turn to turn around," he said.

Jolie scoffed, peeling her eyes from his chiseled body. "I was just about to, sheesh."

Reluctantly she turned her back to him, but as soon as she heard the swooshing sound of water ripple near the edge, she whipped her head. "Is it safe?"

"It's safe."

Kai had dunked his head in the water, and little droplets clung to his facial stubble. He couldn't have looked more like a Ralph Lauren Blue model if he had tried.

"I'm surprised you got in," Jolie said. "A nice guy like you doesn't seem to take many risks."

"I don't," Kai said, swimming closer. "But apparently when it comes to you, I'm a downright scoundrel."

"You mean a thief and kidnapper, right?"

"You can now add flasher to that list," Kai said with a lopsided smile.

"Who uses the word *scoundrel* anymore anyway?"

"I do," Kai said, bobbing in the water. "I am a scofflaw now after all."

"You are not." Jolie splashed his face. "You're not even a *real* kidnapper."

Water dripped down Kai's nose. "Oh, now you say so!" he said through a smile. Kai retaliated, splashing back gently enough that it didn't reach her face. "I do, however, have a large sum of narcotics in my warehouse. I believe the police would quite literally consider me an outlaw."

Sunlight reflections shimmered in his eyes. There was a playfulness at the surface but a real fear in their depths. The burden of his brother's mistakes must be taking a toll on someone who was so good. So pure.

Kai couldn't even hurt the baseball-sized fly that was buzzing around his head earlier.

She attempted to splash him again, but Kai caught her arm.

"We're in a pool of water that probably has enough parasites to take down an elephant. We should probably stop splashing water in each other's mouths."

"You started it." Jolie teased him, sticking her tongue out.

"No, I believe you started it," he said, grabbing her other wrist. "And we need to get out of here now."

Jolie squirmed but didn't put up much of a fight. She let him pin her arms to her sides, where he was dangerously close to brushing up against her naked body.

"Are you always this childish?" he whispered. His breath tickled her nose.

"Are you always the party pooper?" she whispered back.

Jolie's cells came alive as he smiled down at her. The little crow's feet around his eyes deepened as he inched closer. His lips were merely a lick away, parted and ready for the kill.

She held steady, challenging him in a game of who-will-go-first.

His eyes were ablaze. A subtle smirk tugged at the corner of his mouth. "Is this what you call 'seizing the moment'?" he said.

"Only if you seize it," Jolie said breathlessly.

Kai released her arms, looking her square in the eyes. "I can't kiss the hostage. What kind of gentleman would I be?"

"I'm not your hostage anymore."

Her lips softly brushed his in a tease, not quite giving him a kiss she knew they both wanted. But in her attempt at seducing him, she ignited the fire within herself. A need that grew strong and fast like an untamed mustang. It took every ounce of self-restraint to not wrap her legs around him.

"You can't be both a scoundrel and a gentleman," she said, hovering over his full lips, daring him to take the plunge. "You have to choose one."

The peaks of her breasts grazed his skin, shooting bolts of lightning to her core. If she hadn't been in the water, she would have gone up in flames.

Kiss me, dammit, she thought. Her body shimmered, waiting for him.

In a blink, Kai slipped his arm around her waist and began guiding her toward the edge.

Jolie looked up at him in surprise. *That's it? No kiss?*

"We have to go," Kai said, tugging her farther. "We can't stay here."

He wasn't bluffing, she thought, stunned by his rejection. She had never been turned down for a kiss before. Her heated body turned ice cold as she was dragged through the water to its rocky edge.

Jolie studied Kai's face: the tightened jawline, the lowered brow, the spark in his eyes that had cooled into lumps of coal. What happened back there? How could he have resisted? Was he really that much of a gentleman that he couldn't bring himself to kiss her because she was his captive?

How does someone possess such restraint? Such self-control?

She tried putting herself in his frame of mind. He was probably thinking a platonic relationship was less risky. Less volatile. Something he could control when the time came to say goodbye. It was the only explanation that made sense for a guy like him.

She couldn't have been imagining his attraction to her. Their connection was palpable.

Or was it not? She was dehydrated, exhausted, and frail. Their trek through the jungle could have been taking its toll on her psyche. Maybe she was imagining the desire she saw in his eyes. He could be playing into her little game to appease her, to prevent her from doing the one thing that could destroy his and his brother's lives—calling the police.

She had the power and control that could break him. It would be in his best interest to keep Jolie happy but at arm's length. Even if she wasn't fabricating their connection, the truth was that he was the practical type, someone who would choose reason over impulse.

Jolie should respect the space he was trying to protect.

She should.

But then again, she always enjoyed a challenge.

"You go first," Kai said, turning his back, giving Jolie privacy to get out of the lagoon. She pulled herself over the mossy ledge and sat down next to her clothes.

She was not finished with him. Not yet.

Her clothes had dried some but were still damp in spots. She lamented putting them back on.

A rustling in the trees caught her attention, and her eyes snapped to the offending leaves.

"What was that?" Jolie whispered.

The palms parted, and a giant jaguar adorned with black and brown spots sauntered toward the pool. Its muscular body moved in smooth, fluid strokes as he prowled toward the water.

It was majestic in a way. A beautiful wildcat in real life. She was in awe of it, and yet its claws could shred her into tiny little pieces.

Jolie's scream caught in her throat.

CHAPTER FOURTEEN

Jolie held her breath until it felt like needles pricked the insides of her rib cage. The jaguar leaned in toward the lagoon and lapped up water with its tongue.

"Don't run, and don't make eye contact," Kai whispered. "Come back in the water."

With shaky legs, she took a step backward, focusing her eyes away from the jaguar yet keeping it in her peripheral vision, her heart skyrocketing up into her throat.

She took a hop with her good leg and waited a beat. The jaguar didn't seem to notice her yet, or so she hoped. She took another step, feeling the water hit her toes. Her muscles shook as she lowered her body, crouching on her hands and knees, dragging herself back into the water.

The jaguar looked up in her direction, and Jolie stilled.

"Relax," Kai whispered right behind her.

Jolie moved her neck as if it were stuck in concrete and strained to see his outstretched hand. She could feel the jaguar's eyes on her, paralyzing her from moving any farther.

"Slowly," he mouthed with his lips. She locked eyes with Kai, pulling the strength from his sense of calm and moved her hand and knee closer to Kai at a snail's pace. The rough edges of rocks scraped her knees and palms as she crept back into the lagoon. After what felt like an hour later, she was finally submerged in the water.

"Is it still there?" Jolie whispered, unable to find the courage to look.

Kai held her gaze and gave a slight nod.

With shaky hands, Jolie clutched Kai's arms. He pulled her deeper into the water like a floating submarine. The swarming jungle sirens of birds and bugs were drowned out by her jagged breath.

"It's. Going. To be. Okay," Kai mouthed.

Jolie imagined the jaguar leaping into the lagoon any moment, its sharp claws tearing apart her flesh. This would be the end of her, naked and afraid, quaking in Kai's arms.

Jolie wrapped her arms around his rib cage and pulled herself closer, her chest pressed up against his, seeking his touch. Her safe place.

His chest rose and fell in steady breaths as they bobbed in the water, bracing themselves for an attack that neither of them could survive.

Fear jumbled in the back of her throat as she choked down her cry. She imagined the worst. Limbs tearing off her body. Muscles shredding from the bone. Blood everywhere.

And there was nothing they could do but hope it didn't like to swim.

Did jaguars swim? She had no idea. All she knew was that she wasn't ready to die.

She cranked her neck to catch the jaguar in the corner of her vision. It stood silently. Still. Unmoving.

Jolie trembled in Kai's arms, and he squeezed her tight.

"Shh," he whispered, caressing her spine underwater with his callused hands. She found her calm under his soothing strokes. Her breathing slowed to a steady rhythm as she awaited her fate.

Closing her eyes, she imagined a place that she would teleport them to if she could. She pictured Baker Beach. The Golden Gate Bridge arched behind them. A happy naked Santa frolicking in the waves. It would be an unusually sunny afternoon, the sand hot, the breeze cool.

They'd have a picnic on a blanket like honeymooners do. Drink wine and eat cheese and—wait—no cheese. She had to remain a vegan even in her fantasy.

Jolie squeezed her eyes tighter, bringing herself back to her imagination.

They'd regale each other with tales of their childhood and their most beloved teachers in school. Kai would tease her for her sailor's mouth, and she would retaliate with a frenzy of kisses.

A crackling branch snapped Jolie out of her dream, and she gripped Kai with all her might, bracing herself for the impact.

"Look," Kai whispered.

Jolie opened her eyes just in time to see the flick of the jaguar's tail. Within seconds, it had vanished into the trees.

It was gone.

"Thank God." Jolie let out the breath she had been holding in.

Kai was still clutching her, their naked bodies pressed tightly together.

Peeling her cheek off his chest, she looked up into his gaze. The fire was back, encircling his irises. Perhaps she hadn't just been imagining it there before after all.

When his eyes drifted to her lips, she couldn't take the wait anymore. She reached around his neck, pulled herself up to his mouth, and pressed her lips to his. Kai kissed her back and grabbed her legs as she wrapped them around his waist.

Kai's hands roamed her back and gripped her behind, like a real scoundrel. His hands no longer played the gentlemanly role as he squeezed her buttocks, pushing the center of her legs against his skin.

She took his bottom lip between her teeth and bit down gently, just enough to make him groan into her mouth.

"Easy, wildcat," he said between kisses to her neck.

"That nickname," she said, arching her neck, "has a whole new meaning now. I thought we were goners."

Kai pulled away from her, leaving behind the ghost of his mouth on her skin. "You're right. That was too close."

Something had changed in him. His eyes had darkened. His lips clamped shut.

"We need to get out of this jungle." Kai pressed forward, slicing through the water like the US Coast Guard on a deep-sea mission, with Jolie still wrapped around his waist.

He had that determined look on his face as if nothing would stop him from getting out now. Not even a hot and needy naked chick clinging to his body.

When he approached the edge of the pool, he grabbed her waist and hoisted her body onto the nearest rock, not bothering to look away this time.

"Did you leave the gentleman back there in the lagoon?" Jolie teased when she caught him eyeing her breasts.

Kai darted his eyes away. "Sorry. I didn't mean to stare."

"It's okay. I kind of like your naughty side."

Kai was quiet while Jolie dressed. *Too quiet.*

"Did I lose you? What's wrong?"

"I shouldn't have kissed you like that. I'm sorry."

Jolie's face fell. "Don't apologize. I liked it."

"I was taking advantage of the situation."

"What situation?"

"This! This situation," Kai said, circling his hands in the air. His back was still turned to Jolie, but she pictured the frown that swept over his face.

"Oh, you mean the whole kidnapping thing? I thought we went over that. I'm not your hostage."

"No, but if it weren't for my brothers and me, you'd be safe, without the threat of death around every corner. It's not safe here, and I need to get you home now. No more messing around."

"But—"

"But nothing. Our situation is complicated enough."

"We were just blowing off a little steam," Jolie said. "We could have been mauled by a jaguar, for God's sake."

"We can't do that again."

Jolie huffed at the back of his head. Can't do that again? How can he say such a thing after a kiss like that? And he thought *she* was stubborn?

Jolie slipped on her underwear and yanked her shirt over her head.

Of all the men she'd ever kissed in her life, he was the only one who'd denied her. Ever.

He was right of course. They did need to get out of the jungle and soon, but a little kissing never hurt anyone, did it?

Kai was reasonable and gentlemanly by nature, that was clear. But Jolie had gotten a taste of his impulsive side. The side of him that spoke her language, and she wanted more. She *needed* more.

She wasn't finished with him. Not yet.

If I ever get out of this godforsaken rainforest, I'll get a taste of him again.

There had to be some sort of Nobel Prize for being able to turn Jolie Boulard down for the sake of her safety. He deserved extra points for shutting it down while she was naked and writhing around his waist.

They could have been eaten by the jaguar. They could have *died*. They should have been living life to its fullest, grabbing the bull by the horns. It was the single hottest moment of his life. And yet somehow God had bestowed upon him the pious gift of practicality. The Incredible Hulk-sized power of reason. The gift that felt more like a burden, yet it kept on giving.

If only he could live like normal men who followed their peckers to the ends of the Earth. He certainly would be happier. Sexually gratified. And definitely, most likely, more pleasant to be around.

He let the cooling waters settle down his nether regions while Jolie dressed. From the amount of sighing going on behind him, he surmised she was just as frustrated as he.

One day, when they were safely out of the jungle and the threats that awaited him had been resolved, he would find a way for them to be together. She'd forgive him for what he did back there. She'd thank him for his mutant level of restraint because it had saved their lives.

So he told himself.

"We should get going," Kai said. "Hopefully we'll find our way back soon."

Just then he noticed the tiny fish swimming around the edge of the water.

"Look at these," Kai said. "They're minnows."

"Oh yeah?" Jolie said flatly.

Kai cupped his hands in the water, capturing one for her to see.

He showed it to Jolie proudly, but she hardly looked up.

"Let's grab several of these little guys in case we need to cook up some food later."

Jolie gasped. "Are you crazy? I can't eat minnows."

"What's wrong with minnows?"

"I'm a vegan, remember?"

You've got to be kidding me. "This is hardly the time to be following a strict diet plan. You need food. You need protein. You need your strength to keep walking. I don't know how long we're going to be out here."

Jolie snapped her lips shut and became instantly enthralled by the dirt under her fingernails as if it mattered.

"What about bugs? Is that vegan?" Kai said.

Jolie grimaced. "Yuck. No. Eating bugs is definitely not vegan."

"How can that be? I heard they don't feel any pain."

"I'm not eating bugs," Jolie said, rinsing her fingertips in the water.

"Well, you'll need to eat something. I can't promise that we'll find fruit or fresh water. I will catch these as a backup plan to keep us alive."

Jolie grunted and resumed her busy work of tending to her nails.

Kai returned to the minnows. The little suckers slipped through his fingers every time he attempted to lift them out of the water.

"This is harder than it looks," Kai said, trying again. He finally caught one and threw it on the rocky ground. "Got one."

"It's going to take you an hour to get enough minnows to eat," Jolie said.

"I know. I would use my shirt, but I need something to wear. I wish I had a net or something," Kai said, scooping up his hands and coming up short.

Jolie stood up from the rocks and wobbled to her purse.

She yanked a bundle of fabric out of her bag and tossed it to him. "Here," she said, "you can use this."

"What is it?"

"It's a dress I bought in Limón," Jolie said, her hands on her hips. "You can make it into a net if you think that'll help."

Kai held out the brightly colored dress, imagining her wearing it. "You sure I can use this?"

"We don't have all day," Jolie said, holding her chin high. "Like you said, we need to get going." She resumed cleaning out her nails, but Kai could sense that something was off.

"What's wrong?" he asked. "Is it the dress?"

Jolie rolled her eyes. "No, it's not the dress."

"Is it the other thing?" Kai said, pointing toward the middle of the lagoon. "Back there?"

Jolie looked upon the water, squinting her eyes as if she were studying it or trying to forget it ever happened. Kai couldn't be sure which.

"Do you want to talk about it?" Kai asked.

Jolie shook her head and hugged her arms at her stomach, staring out into the water.

It bothered Kai that she was upset, but he needed to finish his task so they could move on. He'd get to the bottom of it soon enough.

Kai tied the end of the skirt into a knot, pulling it tight until his palms burned under his grasp. Then he grabbed the makeshift sack and scooped the water around him. When he lifted it out of the water, sopping fabric came alive with flopping minnows inside. "It works," he said, showing it to Jolie.

Jolie peeled her eyes away from the lagoon. They glimmered with unshed tears.

"Hey," Kai said, wading toward her. "What's wrong?"

"Nothing. I'm just… scared. That's all," Jolie said, wiping a lone tear from under her eye. "I thought we were going to die, you know? And in that moment, everything became clear. For the first time, I figured out the most important thing in my life."

Kai tilted his head to the side. "And what was that?"

"That's just the thing," Jolie said, sniffing into the back of her hand. "It wasn't my business or the money raking in from new brand endorsements. It wasn't being able to afford my fancy apartment in the marina. It was none of the stuff that I thought was important to me before."

Kai searched her eyes for what she was not telling him. He waited silently for her to proceed, but instead, she found a pebble and tossed it into the lagoon.

"What is it then? What is more important to you now?"

Jolie smiled, but it didn't reach her eyes. Instead of responding, she shook her head back and forth. "I can't say. I'm not ready to admit it to myself."

Kai was intrigued by her sudden existential reflection. Although he deeply wanted to know and understand what was going on in her head, he wanted to respect her wishes to keep it to her herself. For now.

"Do you need a hug?"

Jolie smiled and nodded; blotches of red surfaced her cheeks and nose.

Kai reached up to give her a hug, when he felt the draft between his legs.

"Oops," he said, sloshing back down into the water with a splash. "Apparently I forgot I was naked. But as soon as I'm finished gathering these minnows, I owe you that hug."

Jolie giggled, sniffing back her tears. "Thanks. I needed a laugh."

"You're welcome. Although I hope you're not laughing at what you may or may not have seen just then."

Jolie didn't give him the satisfaction of a reply. Instead, she offered him an impish grin and came to her feet. "I'm going to look for coconuts while you fish for minnows."

Kai surveyed the trees. "All right, but stay close. I don't have a knife to crack one open, but we may be able to use that noggin of yours. You can headbutt the thing until it splits in two." Kai smiled his biggest, toothiest grin.

Jolie's face softened as she laughed. "I did knock you pretty hard, didn't I?"

"Now *that*," he emphasized, "is the understatement of the year."

They continued their trek through the jungle, poking and teasing each other as they had grown fond of doing. It was easy to forget they were lost, hungry, and thirsty when they were having more fun than they probably should have, given the circumstances.

"There!" Jolie pointed. "Look! It's a coconut. A whole bunch of them." The hairy cluster of fruit was tucked under wide, leafy palms, and Jolie could almost taste its sweet nectar.

Kai set down his wet sack of minnows and barreled toward the tree. He hugged the width of it but couldn't quite get his arms around. Taking a few steps back, he looked up and crouched down as if he were going to leap into the air.

"It's too high," Jolie said. "You'll never reach it."

The twinkle in his eye gave away he was up for the challenge.

Jolie crossed her arms as she watched him launch himself from the ground and smack into the trunk of the tree, clawing his way down until he crumpled into a pile of dead leaves.

"Are you okay?" Jolie rushed over to check on him.

"I'm fine," Kai said, scrambling to his feet. He brushed off the dirt from his knees and looked up again. "Do you think you could stand on my shoulders and reach them?"

Jolie scrunched her nose. The coconuts seemed too high, but perhaps if she could find a stick, she could knock one down to the ground.

"It's worth a try," Jolie said, searching the ground floor. When she spotted a long branch, she held it up like a warrior going into battle. "Let's do this."

Kai knelt down in front of the tree, and Jolie placed a foot on his shoulder. She grasped his hands, gripping them tight as she squeezed her thigh and stomach muscles to lift herself up. Her good leg shook, carrying all her weight, while her injured leg dangled in the air. Kai's hands kept her steady as she balanced her way up, lightly placing her other foot on his shoulder.

"Are you okay down there?" Jolie asked.

"Yeah," Kai said. "Can you reach?"

Jolie looked up at the coconuts. They were just beyond her reach. "Hand me the stick."

Kai released her hand, grabbing the branch at the foot of the trunk and slowly raised it up to her.

Jolie released her other hand and gripped her fingertips on the tree to keep her steady. Sharp streaks of pain shot through her right leg as she tried balancing equally across both Kai's shoulders. "I need to put less weight on my right leg," Jolie said. "Can you handle that?"

"Go for it," Kai bit out. "Just tell me if you're going to fall, and I'll catch you."

Shifting more weight onto her leg, she was able to fight through the pain, slowly raising the tree branch until it towered over her head.

"This brings a whole new advanced level to tree pose," Jolie grumbled under her breath. The tip of the branch only tickled the coconuts. She reached and she prodded, but the wiry bastards wouldn't budge.

"They're not even moving," Jolie said. "The branch is too pliable."

"Did you try the other end of it?" Kai groaned.

Jolie lowered her arm, loosening her grip so that her hand could slide toward the other end. She felt the end hit something below.

"Ow," Kai said. "You bonked my head."

"Sorry," Jolie said. Looking down made her lose her concentration. Her balancing leg wobbled violently. She tightened her stomach muscles until she regained her balance. Twisting her wrist, she raised the branch once more, this time with the thicker end up top. The coconut actually moved this time.

"It's working," Jolie said, prodding once more. "It's actually budging."

"Get that sucker down before you crush my shoulder."

Jolie reached a little farther before cranking her elbow back for a big whack. Just as she was about to ram the branch into the coconut, the weight of it tipped behind her. She swayed back to hold on to her stick when her foot slipped from underneath her.

She reached for the trunk, but her fingertips grabbed at air.

She was going down and going down fast.

CHAPTER FIFTEEN

Jolie's foot jabbed Kai's collarbone as her ankle broke free from his grasp, and Kai cast his arms like a net, attempting to catch her. Her backside came down first, slamming against his cheekbone, and taking him down with her.

Kai yanked her hips forward to break her fall, when her head crashed against his skull. A flash of light followed by a sheet of darkness draped over his eyes as he crumpled to the ground.

When he blinked his eyes open again, he didn't see Jolie. A throbbing pain radiated from the top of his head, and he gingerly pressed his fingers into his hair to assess the damage. He was fully expecting a giant, gaping hole but instead came across a golf-ball-sized knot.

How long had he been lying on the ground? And where was Jolie?

Kai propped himself up on his forearms and looked around, his eyes sensitive to the light.

"Oh, thank God," he heard Jolie say from behind a tree,

followed by the swishing of bushes. "Are you okay? You had me worried sick."

She appeared in his line of sight as an angel with a halo around her head. The sun shone from directly behind her, shadowing her face. She didn't look real. Was any of this real?

He needed to touch her, to make sure he wasn't dreaming, to know he hadn't died and gone to purgatory. Jolie crouched beside him, her shimmering eyes in full view.

When he reached his hand toward her face, she took it in hers and pressed it against her cheek. "I'm here. I'm so sorry. I'm here."

"Did we bonk heads again?" Kai said, wincing through his migraine.

"Yeah," Jolie said. "That hurt like hell, but you broke my fall. I could have snapped into pieces if you hadn't caught me the way you did."

"I did?" Kai breathed. "I didn't think I had you."

Jolie touched the tip of his forehead, gliding her fingertips along his hairline and down his jaw. "You did have me." She looked up at him through her lashes.

"How did you come out unscathed after our heads collided? Do you have a metal plate in there or something?"

Jolie shrugged. "I must just have a hard head."

Kai chuckled, when he felt the stabbing pain in his rib. "Ow, okay, now *that* really hurts." He lifted his shirt but found no sign of damage.

"You could have cracked a rib," Jolie said. "I fell on you pretty hard."

Her fingers grazed his abdomen, caressing the ridges of his rib cage with just a hint of pressure.

"Does this hurt?" she asked.

Kai shook his head. He was practically purring under her touch. "It's over here," he said, pointing to the offending spot.

Jolie swept her finger over his rib. It was tender to the touch. Kai jolted at the slightest bit of pressure.

"I can't tell if it's broken or bruised," Jolie said. "We'll need to keep an eye on it. No more carrying my stuff for me either." Her eyes continued to drift over his body for a long while before she tugged at the hem of his shirt until he was covered.

"I'm so sorry. It's all my fault. We should have never pulled a stunt like that."

Kai shifted his body weight and stared at her. "It's not your fault. That was all me. I'm just glad I was able to break your fall."

"It only cost you a concussion and a broken rib," Jolie said, crossing her arms. A crease between her eyebrows deepened as she scanned his body. "Is there anything else that hurts?"

"I'm fine," Kai grunted, pulling himself up to his feet with his good side. "We need to keep moving though. We need to find water."

"Which way is north?" Jolie said.

Kai looked up at the sky and behind his shoulder at the moss on the trees. He pointed in the direction he hoped and prayed was north. They needed to get out of this jungle.

The pair of them slogged like zombies, limping and grunting with each step. Kai's mouth had dried up, and his tongue felt like a lump of cotton.

He prayed for rain, as it was the safest form of water for them to drink, but nothing came.

"I was thinking about something you said," Kai said. "About your parents."

"Yeah?" Jolie said. "What's that?"

"You mentioned your mother left your father," he said. "How old were you when that happened?"

"I was thirteen. Old enough to understand that my mother was being a selfish brat." She paused.

"Is she still around?"

"She's around when she needs cash," Jolie said ruefully.

Kai reached for Jolie's hand and squeezed it. "I'm sorry."

Jolie waved him off. "It's fine. Although I've never told anyone about it before. Not even my best friend, Nora. I guess I was always kind of embarrassed by the whole thing. Your parents are supposed to be the adults in the relationship, right? I mean, my mother should have been taking care of me. Not the other way around. My relationship with my mom is solely based on guilt. She feels guilty for walking out during my teenage years. I feel guilty for not going with her even though it was for the best." Jolie snapped a twig from a nearby tree and examined it for a while before gnawing on the end of it.

"Why couldn't you be with your mom if your father made you so miserable?"

"Mom just flitted her way around California from boyfriend to boyfriend. She couldn't be tied down anywhere for too long. And even though she asked me to come with her a thousand times, I knew that she really didn't want me to. She just wanted to be free."

"Do you think you got a little bit of that from her? The need to be free?" Kai asked.

Jolie scowled.

Mayday. Mayday. Kai was clearly in dangerous territory. "I mean, do you think you got your independent spirit from her?"

Jolie's face softened a touch, but Kai wasn't quite sure he could relax just yet. He watched her as she looked out into the wilderness ahead.

"I seek my independence, but I still want to work hard. My mom expects everything to be given to her."

"Do you love her?"

Jolie bit her lip as she seemed to think about her answer. "I pity her," she said finally. "I feel sad for her because she had everything she wanted when she was married to Dad. A life of luxury, fancy restaurants, designer clothes. She just couldn't handle my father's overbearing control. When she left him, she left all that behind. My father had an airtight prenup, so my mother was left with nothing, and yet she still feels entitled to the life she once had. She doesn't call me for money to survive. She calls me for the stuff she can't afford in between boyfriends."

"What kind of things?"

Jolie shrugged. "A bikini wax. A new dress. Eyelash extensions."

"I don't understand why you do it though. Can't you just tell her no?"

"According to my mom, I abandoned *her*. That woman can lay on the guilt, and it's thick. Money hasn't been an issue for me until recently. If my mom's eyelashes made her feel good, and it made up for me ditching her at thirteen, then it was a no-brainer."

"Is she still asking you for money?"

Jolie averted his eyes. "Yes," she muttered under her breath.

"But you've had to ask your dad for a loan recently, correct?"

"Yes." Her voice had grown small.

"Maybe it's time you have a little heart-to-heart with your mother." Or give her a swift kick to the pants, but that wasn't any of Kai's business. He never had to deal with a mother like hers.

Then again, there was Raff.

"You know what, I think your mother and my brother might have a few things in common," Kai said.

"Oh yeah? How so?"

"Well, like your mother, we all used to live a life of luxury." Kai wavered on the description. "Not quite luxury, but an upper-middle-class life. When my father was in finance, we could afford almost anything we wanted, assuming our mother would let us have it.

"We lived comfortably, you know? My mother laid out fine china for special occasions. We went out to eat all the time. My parents would bring back gifts from their travels from all over the world. But then one day my father decided to quit it all and live a simpler life. It was during his brief stint at the San José branch in Costa Rica when he realized he wanted to do his own thing. So he put all his savings into starting up his own business but struggled to make a profit for years. We went from eating lobster on the Parque Vargas to eating beans and rice like most people."

"Did that bother you?" Jolie asked. The twig had made its way back between her teeth.

"You know, I never thought it did, but now that I think about it, it probably had something to do with why I went into finance, to get back to the lifestyle I used to have. And my guess is that it probably is the reason Raffi was so eager to take the extra money from that side job. Like getting a ticket back to the good life."

"Little did he know…," Jolie said, letting the words trail.

"It would lead to the mess we're in," Kai said, finishing her sentence.

Jolie spit out the twig from her mouth and threw it back behind her. "He deserves to be in jail for what he did." She looked up at Kai as if she were searching for his reaction.

Kai tugged her to a stop and held her arms steady. "You're not going to call the cops, are you? I thought we had a deal."

Jolie looked away, biting her lower lip. "I don't plan on turning you or Noah in," she said, "but Raffi is the one who pushed me in the van. Raffi was the one who tied me to the chair and tried to take all my money. Raffi deserves to pay the consequences of his actions."

Kai swallowed hard. "You do realize that if you call the cops on my brother, they will find the cocaine in the warehouse, in my *father's* office. The office that I currently occupy. My brother won't be the only one going down for what he did. I will too."

"It's not fair," Jolie growled, breaking free of Kai's grasp. "He doesn't deserve to be walking free. He's a bad seed."

Kai's mouth fell open.

Her hatred for his brother was stronger than he had thought. She had that wild look in her eyes, the same one he'd seen right before she bit Marco's fat finger.

If he didn't play his cards right, she could turn on him too. Before he knew it, his whole family would end up in jail among men who would be happy to see them dead.

The sun had fallen behind the tops of the trees. It was getting late, and there was still no highway in sight.

Jolie regretted telling Kai her plans to call the police. He'd been tiptoeing around her ever since.

She didn't want to get Kai in trouble. Not after everything he'd done for her. If letting Raffi go is what she had to do to protect Kai, then that's what she'd do.

She would have told Kai she had changed her mind about calling the cops, but she was out of breath and too tired to keep up any more conversation.

Jolie continued to press on through the forest, but she noticed the skin around her wound starting to fester. It had become red and raised around the cut. Every step shot daggers up and down her leg. The more she limped, the more her opposite hip strained to bear the weight.

"Stop." Jolie choked out a hoarse whisper. "I need to rest." She slumped down on a fallen tree and put her head in her hands.

Kai backtracked to get to Jolie and crouched down. When she looked through her fingers, she saw the concern on his face. He was staring at her shin.

"How long has it been red like that?" Kai said.

"I don't know. Maybe a couple of hours."

Kai's jaw tensed. "We'll get you out of here, and we'll get that taken care of, okay? It's going to be okay."

Jolie wobbled her head weakly.

"It's getting dark, and I don't want to walk through the jungle at night. We can set up camp here now," Kai said.

Jolie held back a whimper. She didn't want to spend another night in the wild, but she also didn't want to walk anymore.

Kai put his arm around her shoulders and hugged her close. "We can do this. You stay right here."

Jolie watched Kai grab little twigs and leaves. He squatted over his makeshift campfire, occasionally hissing at the pain in his side.

He attempted to light the bundle with his lighter, but the only thing that lit up were the curse words under his breath.

"I'm almost out of lighter fluid," Kai said as he flicked the switch. "The twigs won't burn."

"Here," Jolie said, pointing to her bag. "I have a notebook in there. You can try to light the paper."

"That would have been nice to know," he said through a smile.

Jolie shrugged. "Sorry, my head is fuzzy. I'm not thinking clearly."

Kai pulled out her pink notebook and flipped through it. "You've got a lot of notes in here."

"They're just random ideas."

Kai stopped on a page. "Animal rescue?"

Jolie shook her head. "Oh, I have a soft spot for animals. I was trying to think of ways to weave them in my business, but I couldn't really get it to work."

Kai looked up at her with an intrigued smile. "You are full of surprises, wildcat," he said.

Jolie smiled on the inside, although she was sure it didn't reach her lips. Her face muscles were too tired to accommodate the action.

Kai got back to the notebook and ripped out several pieces of blank paper. He held out his lighter until the corner started to smoke. Kai tended to the burning kindle until a small fire flickered in front of them.

Jolie sat down on the ground and relaxed into the dead leaves, succumbing to the darkness that fell among them and their small campfire. They sat quietly for a while, apart from the howling monkeys setting the tone to what felt like a failed day.

The fire flickered against Kai's strong jawline, smeared with mud and sweat. He poked at the embers with a stick while his face morphed into a frown.

"I'm sorry we couldn't find anything else to eat. It'll have to be the minnows," Kai said.

Jolie rocked her head from side to side. "Don't be sorry. We did everything we could."

Kai rested his hand on hers and squeezed. "I know you were trying to prove to your father you could do it, but don't take this as a sign of failure, all right? Take this as a sign of strength."

"Strength?" Jolie balked. She'd hardly call it that. "It certainly doesn't feel that way."

"Hear me out," Kai said. "You weren't just proving to your father that you could live your life without meat or dairy. You were proving to him that you could survive on your own."

"Yes, but on *my* terms." Jolie brushed the spider that had crawled up her ankle. "The vegan thing is more than a diet to me. It's symbolic. If I can't survive on my terms, then I've lost. Don't you see?"

Kai gawked. "Your stubbornness never ceases to amaze me."

Jolie scoffed. "I'm not stubborn. I'm…" Jolie flicked another unidentifiable bug from her shoulder while she thought of the right word. "I'm *steadfast*. There's a difference."

"Whatever you want to call it," he said, pulling out the handful of minnows from the sack. "Just don't think for a second that you've lost. You hear me? You haven't lost anything."

Jolie chewed the bottom of her lip as she watched him stick the eel-looking things on a branch limb. They certainly weren't appetizing. If she was going to cheat on being vegan, it was the last thing she would have chosen to eat.

But like Kai said, she was surviving. And if she wanted to prove to her father she could live on her own, she needed to start with keeping herself alive. As if her stomach were excited to share the news that she had a change of heart, it chose that moment to growl violently.

Kai looked up. A smile slowly spread across his face. "Does that mean you've changed your mind?"

Jolie didn't dignify his question with a response. He knew the answer.

"I'm glad you're making the rational choice," Kai said. "It would have been a pity to put all this time and energy into saving you if I couldn't keep you alive."

Kai smiled triumphantly into the fire, rotating the branch

of fish until they turned a dusty charcoal color. He pulled the branch from the fire and blew on the fins that had charred.

"You want to do the honors and try one first?" Kai asked.

Jolie shook her head. "You go first."

Kai popped one in his mouth and chewed. He frowned as he gnawed on the minnow between his teeth. "It's not bad, really. You should have one."

"You're a liar."

Kai pulled another minnow off the branch, cooling it with his breath before he handed it to Jolie. Within a flash, a little furry creature swooped in and grabbed the fish from Kai's hand.

"What was that?" Jolie screeched.

A rustling in the tree came from above. Light from the fire flickered in a little monkey's eyes. It was eating the fish, letting its tail hang down playfully.

"It's a monkey," Jolie said with wonder. "A monkey who just stole my dinner!"

"Well, I'll be."

The monkey cocked its head to the side, chewing the fish with the same frowned expression that Kai had.

"Looks like he doesn't like the fish either." Jolie laughed.

And then she saw a scar that draped along the side of the monkey's head, across what used to be a right ear, a deformed little stub in its place.

"What happened to you, little buddy?" Jolie asked, leaning forward. "You've got a gnarly scar for a tiny little monkey."

"Ouch, that looks nasty," Kai said. "Wonder if he got in a fight or something."

"You think so?"

"Here you go, little fella." Jolie grabbed a minnow from the branch and held it out. The monkey stared at Jolie's hand for a while and climbed down the tree, approaching her cautiously. He sat less than a yard away from her, eyeing the fish but watching intently.

Jolie held out the burnt minnow with her right hand and reached in her purse with her left, pulling out her phone.

"I'm sorry, but I just have to take a picture of our little friend here," Jolie whispered. She powered up her phone.

Still no bars. Battery life 1 percent.

"Here you go, friend." Jolie held out the fish even farther, snapping pictures with her other hand as the monkey approached.

The monkey snagged the fish and scurried to a rock a few yards away from the campfire. Satisfied with one of the photos, she powered the phone down again and slipped it back into her bag.

"I think we should name him," Jolie said, watching the monkey munch away on her dinner.

"Thief?" Kai said.

"Now isn't that the pot calling the kettle black?"

Kai glowered at her. "Here," Kai said, handing her a minnow. "Eat this before you give our new friend the rest of our dinner."

Jolie looked down at the blackened fish in her palm. She looked back up at her new friend who looked at her expectantly.

"How many more do we have?" Jolie asked.

"About a dozen," Kai said with his mouth full.

Jolie held out the fish for the monkey. He crawled up to her and took it from her hand with his little monkey fingers.

"I think I'm going to call you Buddy," Jolie said happily. This time the monkey didn't return to the rock. It sat in front of her, eating the fish. Jolie studied the gruesome scars across its neck and down the back.

"Where's your family, Buddy?" Jolie asked.

It blinked back.

"Eat," Kai said, sternly this time. "You have to feed yourself."

Jolie let out a long sigh. She grabbed the fish from his hands and placed it in her mouth. It tasted like ash and fire. The insides were bland, like an unseasoned sliver of tuna. She swallowed. "Mmm, failure tastes about as I expected."

Kai chuckled.

"I wonder why he's so comfortable around us. I would think he would be afraid to get close to humans," Jolie said pensively as she pulled another charred minnow from the branch.

Jolie watched Buddy carefully, imagining what kind of trauma he went through to get that scar. It broke Jolie's heart to think of how helpless the animals could be.

Rustling leaves in the distance caught Buddy's attention, and he ran in the opposite direction and out of sight into the darkness.

"What was that?" Jolie asked.

Kai stood up and looked around. It was quiet for a long while, and then he sat back down next to Jolie. "It doesn't seem to be anything to worry about, but let's finish these up so we don't attract any other animals looking for fish."

Jolie swallowed the rest of her dinner like a good girl. It was just enough food to ease the pain in her stomach, but it left her thirstier than she was before.

The temperature plummeted once the forest had settled into complete darkness. Jolie caught a cool breeze at her back, soothing the sunburns on her skin. She shivered before scooching closer to the fire.

Kai snapped the branch he used as a skewer in two and tossed it into the burning heap. A croaking frog nearby serenaded them under the moonlight.

Croak.

Croooaaak.

Jolie and Kai looked at each other and giggled.

"Dinner *and* music. My kind of date," Kai said with a wide grin.

Jolie arched her brow in response. "Was this a date? I would have spruced myself up had I known."

Kai laughed. "You're beautiful just as you are."

Jolie blushed. She knew her hair was in knots. She had mud on her sun-burned face. Her clothes were browned and sweaty. She probably smelled like a capybara. Despite all that, Kai made her feel beautiful anyway by the look in his eyes.

"So what does Kai Greene usually do after a date?" Jolie asked, unable to contain the mischievous smile on her lips.

Kai looked up, locking on her gaze. There was a flicker of heat in his eyes, but it vanished as quickly as it arrived. "I… I guess I don't know. I don't go on many dates," he said, returning his attention to the fire.

Jolie watched Kai rubbing his hands together, his biceps nearly bursting from his shirt sleeve. Mentally she wrapped herself into his arms, craving his touch.

Kai leaned back on the tree trunk and opened his arms. She inched forward, scooting toward him, when a slithering object caught her eye.

A green snake with scales edged in black glided among the dead leaves. Its underside was a soft yellow, and it had beady little black eyes. Picking up speed, it prowled forward, heading straight toward Kai's outstretched legs.

Jolie gasped. "Kai, look out!"

CHAPTER SIXTEEN

Kai's eyes widened as the snake approached him. Before Kai could react, the snake opened its mouth wide, the inside of its throat milky white. It launched itself at Kai's feet before he could pull them back.

Kai flinched, kicking his legs wildly before he scooted back into the brush. Had he been bitten? He couldn't tell. Perhaps the snake's fangs were too small and sharp to feel anything. The venom could be seeping into his skin this very moment.

Just as he was about to panic, he heard Jolie moan in disgust.

"Eww!" Jolie pointed toward the offender.

Kai found the slippery devil, its mouth wrapped around a twitching frog. Frog legs hung out of the snake's mouth as it made its slow descent into the depths of the snake's belly.

"Whoa, that's awesome," Kai said.

Jolie cupped her hand over her mouth. "It's gross."

"So much for our musical accompaniment," Kai said. "I had grown fond of Kermit's vocals."

"Ugh. I don't understand how that frog can fit inside that little snake's gullet. Yuck."

Kai walked over to a trunk on the other side of the campfire and sat down. The ground was wet and damp, already soaking through his shorts. Too late now; he had committed to the spot. The temperature had dropped, which meant he had a solid case to be even closer to Jolie. He had been waiting for this moment all throughout "dinner": a night under the stars with Jolie.

"It's going to be a cooler night, I think," Kai said. "We should probably huddle close… for warmth, you know. I'd hate for you to catch a cold."

The corner of Jolie's mouth turned in. "You're full of shit," she said, kneeling down beside him, a knowing smile on her lips.

Kai shrugged and pulled her into his side, wrapping his arms around her. She didn't protest. Instead, she made little circles on his chest with her delicate finger, sending ripples of pleasure throughout his body.

"You're killing me, woman."

"Exactly the point."

Kai fluttered his eyes shut, allowing himself this moment, her touch, and nothing more.

Pushing down his carnal desire, he sank into the ground with Jolie on top of him, letting the crickets hum around their heads until they both fell into a deep, sticky sleep.

Jolie fluttered her eyes open. Her skin shimmered in a dreamlike state. She looked down at her black tank top and paused. Was she dreaming? She didn't remember wearing black.

Wait.

Her top wasn't black at all. She was covered in ants.

They were everywhere. On her clothes, her arms, her legs. She felt tiny little movements on her lips, and she spat them out. She screamed, waking Kai up, and frantically brushed off ants from her face.

"What the hell?" Kai's groggy voice was muffled by Jolie's screaming.

"Get them off! Get them off!"

Kai's hands swarmed her body, brushing off the tiny little enemies, plucking them from her hair and her shoulders. His hands ran the length of her arms as he tried holding back his laugh.

"It's not funny!" Jolie pouted.

"It kind of is."

"Help me get them off!"

"I am! I am!"

There were so many of them.

"How come I'm the only one with ants?" Jolie said, lifting up her hair. Kai's finger ran down her neck in soft caresses.

"Probably because your skin is so sweet."

"You are such a cheeseball."

Kai grinned, sweeping the length of her back in long, fluid strokes.

Jolie stilled, closing her eyes. It was silly to enjoy it as much as she did, but her body came alive under his strong hands. He swiped the ants at her hips and down her legs until he reached her ankles.

She pulled her skirt up, brushing off straggler ants from the top of her thighs when Kai looked up, a devilish grin on his face. Her underwear was less than an inch from his mouth, and he knew it.

Jolie let out a puff of air when his eyes dropped to her underwear.

"You have a few enemies trying to breech the gate over

here," he said. He visibly swallowed. "Shall I extinguish them?" he asked, his finger hovering over her panties.

Jolie let out a raspy yes. She closed her eyes as his finger trailed over the cotton fabric. He seemed to be taking his time, sweeping away ants that Jolie wasn't even sure were there anymore. He traced the hem of her panties with his finger, and Jolie's knees nearly buckled underneath her.

"There's a rogue soldier," Kai said wryly.

Jolie shook her head. "Just get it off. I hate ants."

A coy smile met Kai's lips before he blew a cool stream of air through the fabric of her underthings, sending a ripple of pleasure to her core.

Oh my God.

If he didn't touch her again, she would surely combust. She reached for his chin, tilting him up to see the wicked look in his eyes.

"Do that again," Jolie said, daring him to tease her, to ease the ache that yearned for him.

But in a flash, the molten lava cooled, and he blinked away the desire in his eyes and rose to his feet. "I'm sorry. I lost control down there."

"But I want you to lose control," Jolie said breathlessly. "Stop thinking so much."

"You seem to keep bringing out a side of me that I don't even know." Kai scratched the back of his head. "I need to focus on getting you out of here."

And just like that he shut her out. Again.

This was war.

"You are the most frustrating and stubborn man," Jolie said, flicking at a persistent ant on her wrist.

"You," Kai said, looking squarely in her eyes, "are a wildcat. We need to be practical. We need to get you out of here and get you back safely to the States. Now is not the time for romping in the woods."

Jolie scoffed. *"Romping?* This is hardly romping. We're trying to survive! Who uses words like that anyway? You are the most old-fashioned person I know. You can't deny there's something between us."

Kai's jaw clenched shut, and he leveled his eyes at her. "This is serious, Jolie. We need to get the hell out of here."

Jolie huffed, breaking away from his glare. "Fine," she said, stalking into the woods.

"Where are you going?"

"I'm going to take a piss." Jolie hissed. She ducked under a large leafy bush and limped past a few trees until she found a clearing. Each step was almost too painful to bear. She would not be able to make it much farther like this. The cut on her shin had festered into a round lump, pink and hot to the touch.

If Kai was going to play games, she wanted nothing to do with it. She was tired of the tease.

If he really wanted her, he could have had her. But that ship had sailed. She could get any guy she wanted. Why would she wait around for him when he clearly wasn't man enough to step up? *He can keep his chivalry and shove it up his ass.*

She hobbled forward, resting her weight on her good leg until she could safely crouch behind a tree. It was nearly impossible to squat with an injured leg, but her years of yoga training had prepared her for this very moment: peeing in the woods, with only one foot on the ground.

A gurgling sound continued even after she was done. Jolie held her breath to listen.

"Kai! Come over here! I think there's a stream!"

The rustling sound of leaves and branches grew near as Kai bounded to her. "Where?"

"Listen," Jolie said, pointing to where she heard the noise.

Kai's head poked in through the bushes. He looked like he

was wearing a mane of green leaves. "That sound? Oh man, I thought that was you peeing this whole time."

"Ha ha. Let's follow it. It might lead us to people."

Kai held out his hand. Jolie stared at it as if he were handing her a poison apple, but when she tried putting her weight on her leg, she nearly collapsed from the pain.

"Your leg," he said. "It's getting worse."

Without hesitating, Kai scooped Jolie into his arms and carried her through the trees.

"Kai, slow down," Jolie said, her teeth suddenly chattering as she bobbed up and down in his arms.

"We need to get you out of here *now*. I can't have you dying of sepsis on me."

"*Sepsis?* I could get sepsis?" Jolie clutched Kai's neck.

There was no exit sign leading them out of the rainforest. They could be there for days with no medical help. She felt silly now, throwing herself at Kai when she should have been hauling ass out of the jungle.

No wonder Kai had turned her down. She had been acting like a foolish child.

Jolie's cheeks burned with shame as she bounced in his arms, hoping her infection didn't spread before they could find help.

Kai marched for hours, occasionally taking breaks to put Jolie down. His back strained, and his legs shook. The pain in his ribs had subsided at least, but his arms were being torn from their sockets.

"Still with me, wildcat?" Kai panted.

Jolie's heavy eyelids fluttered open, and she nodded weakly. "You need to put me down now. You've carried me enough."

"Absolutely not."

Heat radiated from her body. A fever? He had to get her to a doctor, now. No more breaks or Jolie wouldn't make it. If it wasn't the sepsis that'd kill her, it would be the dehydration.

"You are so stubborn," Jolie said. "Let me walk."

"No," Kai said, ignoring her exaggerated eye roll.

Each step was more arduous than the last. His muscles seized and fought against each forward movement. Sweat dripped down his chin, landing somewhere in Jolie's hair. She looked up at him through her lashes and muttered hazily, "You're sweating on me."

Kai puffed out a burst of air as another droplet fell on her chest. "Sorry," he said through gritted teeth. At least she was talking to him now. That was a good sign.

"I don't mind," Jolie said, readjusting her arms around his neck. "But you should really take a break."

"I will," he said, looking down at her shin. It was red and angry. Adrenaline surged him forward. He had to get her out of there before it was too late.

It had been another hour, maybe two. Kai couldn't keep track anymore. He had only taken a couple of breaks, but he could feel his body giving up.

The sky darkened, and the sunburn on his neck found relief in the shade.

Crackling thunder rumbled overhead, and Kai slowed to a halt. His body tingled as a change in the air gave him hope. He looked up to the sky.

Please, he begged to the clouds.

He waited.

"Is that rain?" Jolie's faint whisper was barely audible.

Then, a deep whoosh rolled in from the distance like an ocean wave, and the first drop of water hit Kai's forehead.

Setting Jolie down on the ground, he tore a giant leaf from a tree and handed it to her. "Here, take this."

Jolie pinched her eyebrows together. "What for?"

"Wait for it." He tugged at the plant and snapped another leaf for himself, cupping it into a funnel.

The second drop hit Kai's cheek, like a kiss from heaven. The third drop was even more divine. And then it poured. Glorious liquid fell from the sky, stinging the cuts and scrapes on his skin. Kai held the leaf out by his mouth, catching the deluge of water. It trickled onto his dry tongue, and the sweetness ran down his throat.

Jolie did the same, and the rain poured, washing away the grime from their hair and clothes, soaking them from head to toe.

"I've never tasted anything so delicious in my entire life," Kai said between swallows, then realized he was wrong: he had tasted Jolie's lips, and God knew how much he wished he could have her again.

Jolie didn't respond, too busy drinking what little water she could catch with her makeshift cup.

"I think this rainfall just saved our butts." Kai tried again, hoping Jolie would say something. Anything.

"*Save our butts?* You sound like a *Leave It to Beaver* episode," Jolie said sarcastically. She eyed him before returning to her leaf.

Her sass was back, which probably meant she was feeling better and also still pissed from earlier.

One day she would understand why he was so adamant to get her out of the jungle. She needed to think more with her head than her heart. There was a time and place for hooking up. A near-death situation was not it. This wasn't a movie.

The downpour tapered off to a light drizzle, and Kai remained kneeling in front of Jolie. He wondered how someone drenched in rain and mud and covered in ant bites could be so beautiful.

Water droplets had collected in her lashes. Her cheeks were flushed, and her lips dewy. Strands of damp hair stuck to her face. She took his breath away.

"Feel better?" Kai said.

"Yes, but I'm still mad at you."

"I can tell. You don't hide it well."

Jolie narrowed her eyes.

"You're cute when you're mad though," Kai said.

"Bite me."

"Maybe I will when we're out of here."

Jolie sucked in a breath. The wild look in her eyes was back as she dropped her gaze to his mouth. She was casting her spell, he was sure, if the fire igniting deep in his belly was any indication.

She was tempting him again—only this time he was too weak to resist.

Inching forward, he could feel her breath on his lips. His heart pounded in his chest.

Maybe just one kiss. A little taste to ease the suffering from denying himself what he really wanted. As he leaned in closer, Jolie turned her cheek.

"Ah, ah, ah," Jolie said. "No *romping* in the rainforest. We need to go."

I deserved that. Hell, he was mad at himself for denying her before. She was the single most beautiful and tempting thing on earth, and she had been turned on by *him*. *Why him*, he would never understand.

Kai cursed himself for blowing the chance and stood, offering his hand to Jolie. She took it, struggling to get to her feet when a shrieking howl startled them both. Kai and Jolie looked up.

A monkey hung from a tree limb, grunting furiously. His fangs on display.

"Is that… Buddy?" Jolie asked.

"It can't be." Kai stood up to get a closer look when he saw Buddy's gnarly scar. "Holy crap, it is." Kai gasped. "He must have been following us the whole time."

"Buddy! It's so good to see you. I'm sorry we don't have any food."

Buddy howled, swinging himself up on the tree. He shook his body and jumped, his screams getting louder. Then he jumped to another limb.

"That's peculiar," Jolie said. "Do you think he's mad that we don't have anything to eat?"

"Maybe he's pissed that he didn't get a kiss either," Kai said sardonically.

Buddy stopped and howled again, jumping up and down.

"It's almost as if he wants to be followed," Jolie said.

"Hold on there, Dr. Doolittle. This isn't one of those Lifetime movies with a trained monkey on set. He's probably rabid."

"He followed us for hours. He's got to be trying to tell us something. Let's go."

Kai arched his brow at her, but Jolie crossed her arms, making it clear she wasn't going to budge.

"Okay. If you want to follow the monkey, then we'll follow the gosh-darn monkey."

Jolie beamed, a triumphant smile reaching her lips. She tried stepping forward, but she recoiled. "Ow."

"I'll carry you. But just for a little bit," Kai said. "I don't want to stray too far from the stream."

Buddy hooted, shaking the tree limb.

"We get it, Buddy. We're comin'."

Kai scooped Jolie up. *This better be worth it*, he thought as he ducked under a branch.

Buddy swung to another tree, then the next. Whenever Kai fell too far behind, Buddy would screech at the top of his lungs.

"Feisty little fella, isn't he?" Kai said.

Jolie smiled.

Buddy was taking them south, the opposite direction Kai thought they should be headed.

"I don't know about this," Kai said, looking around his shoulder. "I feel like he's taking us deeper into the jungle."

"You're right. We should stop. Your sense of direction has been impeccable so far."

Kai fought back his smile. "You've got a mouth on you."

"Follow that monkey."

Grudgingly Kai trudged forward.

Buddy stopped at a tree and gave a high-pitched trill, piercing Kai's ears.

"Come on, man. I'm right here," Kai said.

Buddy clambered up the tree and back down again, shaking the leaves and branches as he shrieked.

"I think he's gone mad," Kai said.

"Where are you taking us, Buddy?" Jolie said gently, but the monkey only quickened his pace.

"Let's go back. I don't think I can take his screaming anymore," Kai said.

"Wait a minute. Do you hear that?"

Kai stilled, trying to listen beyond the monkey calls.

There was a voice, muffled by the trees, echoing through the jungle. Then there was another.

"Is that…?" Jolie asked.

Kai's heart quickened. Gripping Jolie tighter, he glided through the trees toward the sound. The voices grew louder.

"*Ayuda!*" Kai cried in Spanish, panting heavily. "Help!" His lungs burned and his legs quaked as he tore through the bushes toward the echo.

"Help!" Jolie cried.

Kai slowed his pace through the leaves to see if he could hear a response.

"*Hola?*" a man's voice echoed back in Spanish. "Who's there?"

Kai picked up the pace.

"We're coming!" Kai yelled. "Where are you?"

"Here!" more voices called back.

Kai stumbled through the brush until he came over a hill and saw a sea of ponchos, a glorious swarm of teenagers in bright red plastic garments with white ARS logos across the front. They looked up from their hiking path and gaped.

Kai dropped to his knees, Jolie almost tumbling out of his arms. "We made it." He sighed.

Jolie squeezed his neck. "We did it," she choked out, her voice quivering. "We survived."

"Are you two okay?" a Costa Rican man said, running up the hill.

Jolie burst into tears.

"Do you speak English?" Kai said.

"Yes."

"We need a doctor," Kai said, switching to English so Jolie could understand. "For her leg."

"What are you two doing out here?" the man said, approaching them, his face scrunched up in confusion.

"We've been lost," Jolie said between sobs.

"Well, come on then. Let's get you out of here," the guy said, taking Jolie from Kai's arms.

Kai found himself surrounded by a bunch of small hands. Three young girls, about fifteen years old, raised him to his feet.

With shaky steps, Kai and Jolie staggered toward the group.

CHAPTER SEVENTEEN

"I'm Trip," the leader said, steadying Jolie on her feet. He looked about thirty years old and had kind chocolate-brown eyes and a lopsided smile. He had more accessories than Jolie would wear on a normal day; a headband pulling back his curly black hair, a cluster of bracelets around both wrists, and a puka shell necklace that fit snugly around the base of his neck.

"I'm Jolie," she said, sniffing back her tears. "And this is Kai."

"What happened to your leg?" Trip asked.

"She's got an infection." Kai jumped in. "You got anything for that?"

"Do you feel feverish at all?" Trip asked.

"No, well, yes. Maybe. I have no idea," Jolie said, shaking. She had been so overcome with joy, seeing Trip and his little band of poncho-wearing high schoolers, Jolie had forgotten all about her leg.

Trip pulled out a water canteen and held it out. Jolie looked at it with wide eyes, clutching it with her hands as if it was the nicest thing anyone could have ever offered her. She looked back at Kai and held it out to him.

"You go first," Kai said, ushering her to take a drink.

"He can have mine," one of the high school girls said, handing Kai her canteen. She batted her eyes up at Kai as if she were looking up at a movie star.

Jolie giggled, opening the canteen. In that moment, Kai did look like a movie hero, straight out of an adventure scene, with his shirt sopping wet and translucent, contouring against his sculpted chest. His skin was tanned and riddled with bug bites and sunburns.

He had been through hell for her, carrying her for miles in the heat. A true hero, despite the whole kidnapping thing.

The smitten girl didn't seem to mind as Kai downed the rest of her water. She watched Kai with stars in her eyes, her friends snickering behind them. Jolie couldn't blame the young girl for having a crush. Jolie was sure she had one too.

Trip pulled off his backpack and unzipped the side pocket. He pulled out a round tin. "Here. Let's put this on your leg for now. It's a salve a buddy of mine made with tea tree oil. It's a natural antibacterial ointment. It'll help until you see a doctor."

Jolie nodded and thanked him, letting him goop out the jellylike stuff and dab it on her shin.

Jolie looked back at Kai, who was boring a hole through Trip's forehead. His nose flared when Trip touched her leg.

Trip held out his hands for Jolie. "All right then, let's get you home. Can you walk?"

Jolie shook her head. "Barely."

"I've got her," Kai said sharply, slipping his hand under Jolie's arm.

Jolie put her hand on his. "Kai, you need a break," she said softly. "You've carried me all day."

"I can keep going," Kai said.

"Dude," Trip interjected. "We're about a mile and a half out. You look like you need a break. I've got her. You chillax."

Kai balled his fists, not letting go of Jolie.

"It's okay," Jolie pleaded. "Like he said, just… *chillax*." The corner of Jolie's mouth curled into a playful smile.

Kai softened as he met Jolie's gaze. An unsaid understanding settled between them. Kai had no reason to be threatened by Trip. It would only be a matter of time before they could hold each other again. The thought of it gave Jolie strength to let go of his hand.

Trip put on his gear and slipped his arm under Jolie's legs. He strained to hoist her up, holding his breath and grunting until she rested in the crook of his arms.

He stepped forward, huffing hot breath out of his mouth that smelled like honey-nut granola and flaxseed. After several wobbly steps, he put her back down.

"Sorry, I guess I don't have it in me today," Trip wheezed. "Maybe you can lean your body weight on me while you hop."

"That works," Jolie said, slipping her arm around his thin waist. He seemed frail compared to Kai, his hip bones digging into her forearms.

Jolie looked behind her shoulder to find Kai stifling his laugh.

"Stop. It," Jolie mouthed.

"So, what happened?" Trip asked. "How did you two end up lost in the rainforest?"

"We were at the Yogi Garden Resort," Jolie said, not even considering telling him the truth. It was her turn to protect Kai. "We went on a hike and got lost."

Kai mouthed the words "Thank you."

"Ah. Another honeymooners' hike gone wrong." Trip shook his head.

"Something like that," Jolie said, giving Kai a playful smile. "But we're not married."

"It's easy to get lost when you stray from the path," Trip said. "How long were you lost for?"

"Two days. Two nights," Jolie said.

"Without water or anything?"

"Nothing but the rain and the shirts on our backs," Jolie said. "And my purse that may or may not be soaking inside."

"Wow. You're lucky you found us."

Jolie gripped Trip tighter as he helped her over a rocky patch. The crinkling of his poncho ruffled in her ear.

"We're lucky, all right. We made a friend in the jungle," Jolie said, thinking of Buddy. She looked up into the trees to see if he might be following them, but no monkeys were in sight. She gave a silent thank-you to the little creature that saved their lives and returned her attention to Trip.

"Technically, you were in the rainforest."

"Is that not the same thing?"

"A jungle is denser, much harder to pass through. This part of the woods is considered a rainforest by the amount of rainfall. We usually get a lot of rain."

"Oh, so we picked the two days it doesn't rain much. We nearly died of dehydration back there."

"You shouldn't ever go hiking without a canteen of water or a purifier of some kind."

"Noted," Jolie said. "So what is this group? ARS? Is this a high school?"

"ARS is the Animal Rescue Sanctuary," Trip said. "*My* rescue center." He cleared his throat. "I was taking these kids on a field trip to learn more about what we do."

"Oh!" Jolie said. "I'm just realizing now that we totally interrupted."

Trip laughed. "I think getting you two to safety takes priority." He turned to ask the kids something in Spanish.

"Sí!" they all shouted.

"They agree," Trip said.

"Well, don't let us stop the learning process," Jolie said.

"All right then. Let me catch you up. ARS is a shelter for animals who need medical attention before they can go back into the wild."

"What kind of animals?"

"All kinds. We have monkeys, birds, sloths. Whatever comes our way, really."

"How do they get hurt?"

"Various ways. Sometimes it's as simple as an animal fight in the wild. Sometimes we take in animals that were accidentally electrocuted."

"Electrocuted?" Jolie gasped. "How does that even happen?"

"Animals can get electrocuted by transformers or electrical lines that aren't insulated."

"God, that's awful," Jolie said. "Can't you just insulate them?"

Trip rubbed his neck. "That's exactly what we're trying to do, but it's expensive."

"Wow," Jolie said, heartbroken. "What do you do with the animals when they are healthy? You just set them free in the jungle?"

"Yep. We'll usually drop them off not too far from where we found you. I was telling the troop, just the other day, we were dropping off Sylvester the monkey, and on our way back we found Coco the sloth. He had a large gash in his head, probably from a fight with something out here. He was in pretty bad shape."

"Poor Coco," Jolie said.

"He'll be fine. It took a couple of stitches. The vets got him stabilized. He'll be able to return to the wild in no time at all. It's funny, it seems like every time I go into the jungle, I find something—or *someone*—that needs to be saved."

"Did you hear that, Kai? They have a sloth named Coco!" Jolie beamed at Kai. "Oh, I so want to meet Coco."

"Once you're patched up and healthy again, you should swing by the shelter. We'd love to give you a tour," Trip said. "Ah, here we go. The trailhead is just down here. We'll be on the road in no time."

He wasn't jealous, Kai kept telling himself, but by the time they reached the school bus, Jolie had asked a million questions about the ARS. Trip was happy to oblige of course.

Seeing Trip's scrawny arm around Jolie did something to Kai's insides though. Call it jealousy, or whatever it was, Kai didn't like it.

Jolie was in her element, learning about the ARS and what Trip did for a living. She absorbed it like a sponge. It was as if she came alive before his very eyes, excited and bubbly.

And there Trip was, with his stupid headband and his stupid friendship bracelets and his stupid cargo shorts, basking in Jolie's enthusiasm.

Occasionally Jolie would look back to see if Kai was all right. He'd smile, giving her a thumbs-up, only to sink into a worried frown when she turned back around.

They were alive. It was all that mattered, but Kai wondered if this was the end. Would he ever see her again? The thought of her walking out of his life forever was unbearable now after what they'd been through and how he felt about her.

It had been his plan all along to get her to safety. She would need to hop on a plane and get as far from Costa Rica as she possibly could, away from Raffi and his twisted schemes. She wasn't safe there, and there was nothing Kai could do about it.

When they reached the school bus, the kids cheered, hopping on excitedly to claim their spots. Lucia, the fifteen-year-old with braces who had given him her canteen and had been clinging to his arm, offered him a spot next to her on the bus.

"I think I'll sit next to Jolie if that's okay with you," Kai said gently.

The girl dropped her head and nodded as if she understood, but her long face said otherwise.

Kai helped pull Jolie up the school bus steps. The chattering of excited teenagers rang in his ears as he sat on the ripped upholstered seat. Jolie slumped next to him, resting her head on his shoulder.

"We made it," Jolie said, squeezing Kai's arm. Her touch sent ripples of energy through his body, and he placed his hand on her knee in return.

The roar of the engine kicked in, and Kai leaned back into the seat, thumping along with the rickety bus down the gravel path.

"Hey, do either of you need to call someone?" Trip asked.

Jolie shot up from his chest.

What was she doing? Was she going to call the police after everything they'd been through?

He went rigid, watching Jolie take the phone from Trip's hand. His heart raced. He had to trust her now, or he would never be free.

Jolie held the phone in her shaky hand, staring at the numbers as if they were foreign.

Kai's mouth went dry; a solid lump formed in the back of his throat.

Jolie looked up at him, her lip quivering.

This was it. This was the end. She was going to turn him in.

Jolie dropped her gaze back to the phone and dialed.

CHAPTER EIGHTEEN

Jolie only knew one number by heart. She dialed it, letting it ring a few times.

Kai shifted in the seat. His hands fell into his lap, eyes searching Jolie's for an answer.

Why was he nervous? Had he thought she would call the police after all that?

Jolie had plans to torture him in her bedroom later, but not here. She hadn't meant to give him the impression she would call the cops.

Then Nora picked up the phone.

"Nora?" Jolie said, resting her hand on Kai's knee.

Kai's body relaxed, pressing his palms to his eyes. A slow smile spread across his face, melting Jolie's insides. He shook his head before tickling her ribs in retaliation.

"Jolie? Is that you? Whose phone number is this? Is everything okay?"

Jolie clasped her hand onto Kai's shoulder, giving it a tight squeeze.

"Yes, I'm fine. I just wanted to check in with you. I've been off the grid for a couple of days."

"I noticed you hadn't been posting anything. I sent you a text yesterday. I was starting to worry."

Jolie sighed. "Everything is fine. I have a lot to catch you up on when I get home."

"Oh good. I can't wait."

"How are my babies?"

"They are wonderful. You have nothing to worry about. All happy and healthy. Franklin and Samuel are cuddling on the couch. Frido and Sneeker are fighting over their rope, and Duchess is here with me on my lap. I love having them here. I don't want you to take them back."

"You are an angel," Jolie said. "Thank you so much."

"It's my pleasure."

"Okay, I have to go. I'll call you when I'm home." Jolie clicked off the phone.

Kai's mouth was agape. "How could you do that to me? I was about to have a heart attack."

"I didn't mean to make you worry," Jolie said, handing the phone back to Trip.

"You're going to give me another ulcer," Kai said.

"Sorry. I had to call my best friend. I knew she'd be worried about me."

"I see you're feeling better now?"

Jolie sighed. "Yes." She looked down at her shin. It was still red and puffy and painful, but her spirits were lifted. They were out of the jungle, and she was free.

"Uh, Jolie?" Kai said, his elbow resting on the seat in front of him. His eyebrows pinched together.

"Yeah?" Jolie said, a wave of concern washed over her.

"Do you have children?" Kai sucked in a breath.

Jolie giggled. "No. I mean kind of. My pets are kind of like my children."

"Your *pets*," Kai said through a smile, leaning back in the seat. "You hadn't mentioned your babies before."

"I guess I was too busy focusing on the whole survival thing, you know?"

"Can you tell me about them now?"

Several miles down the bumpy path, Jolie told him all about her pets and how she tried finding homes for them all but wasn't too disappointed when she failed. They had become her little family ever since Nora had moved out of her apartment years ago.

Kai listened intently, watching her mouth as she spoke. It wasn't lost on her how much he paid attention to her lips, flicking his eyes back and forth between them and her eyes.

The school bus finally pulled onto the highway. They arrived at an urgent care center before Jolie could tell Kai about the time she found Franklin under her car at the beach.

Jolie and Kai got off the bus, thanking Trip and the high schoolers profusely for saving their lives. The young girl who had been ogling Kai the entire ride tugged on his arm and gave him a big hug.

Trip handed Jolie his business card in case she wanted to come and visit Coco before the end of her trip. "We're just up the street a little ways," Trip said, pointing back toward the highway.

"Thanks for everything," Kai said, shaking Trip's hand.

"Don't go wandering in the rainforest again now, you hear?" Trip said, jumping back up on the steps.

Jolie waved as the school bus pulled away. The kids waved back out the windows, laughing and singing all the way down the road.

"Let's get your leg checked out and take you home," Kai said, letting her rest her weight on his arm as they hobbled into urgent care.

"You think they'll turn us away?" Jolie said, eyeing their

drenched clothing. She took a sniff of her armpit and coughed.

Kai chuckled, pulling a piece of moss out of Jolie's hair. "They might not like us very much, but they won't turn us away."

Jolie smiled, limping through the gliding doors, letting the cool, fresh air-conditioning wash over her.

"My tires aren't slashed at all."

"What?" Jolie gasped, hobbling on one foot, a plastic bag full of antibiotics in her hand.

"Look! They're fine!" Kai said, kicking at his tires in the parking lot. The cab driver pulled away, rustling up dirt into the air, tacking on to their mud-streaked faces. "My brother was lying! He made me think he—"

"Wait a minute." Jolie's hands stretched out into the air. "You're telling me we could have just hopped in your van and drove away from your psychotic brother instead of barreling into the jungle in the middle of the night like two lunatics?"

Kai's mouth fell open. His fingers raked through his hair.

It was all for nothing. The escape. The near-death experience with a jaguar. The dehydration. The ant bites. All of it.

If only they had just checked the tires.

A bubble of laughter formed deep in her throat and came out in hysteric bursts. She blinked away tears, laughing until her stomach muscles hurt.

"How can you possibly be laughing at that?"

Jolie wiped a tear, muffling her chuckle. "How can you not?"

Kai shook his head and smiled. "It is kind of ridiculous," he said, starting to chuckle.

They stood in the parking lot like laughing fools until

raindrops fell overhead, shaking them out of their merriment. Jolie looked at his van and back at Kai.

He was free to go now, and so was she.

Rain sputtered down harder as Jolie tried thinking of what to say to keep him there a little while longer. She wasn't ready for him to leave.

"So…" Jolie swallowed. "What do we do now?"

Kai put his hands on his hips. "I can still take you to the airport if you want."

"Don't you have a giant debt you need to settle?"

"Yes, but I'd rather see you safe before I go take care of all that."

Kai helped her to her casita. They both received strange looks from the outdoor yoga class as they staggered past.

Jolie opened the door to her room and breathed in the floral, salty air. It seemed so clean and welcoming compared to the depths of the jungle. She was afraid to walk in and soil the pristine wooden floor.

Kai froze in the entryway. "You sure I can come in?" Kai said. "I'm very dirty."

"Don't be silly. Of course you can. You can shower too if you want," she said, setting down her bag on a nearby chair. "Come in. Don't be shy."

"I should probably call Noah."

"Sure, let me see if my phone works," Jolie said, pulling out the cord from her luggage. She plugged in her phone and was relieved to see the little green bar with the electric bolt, indicating it was charging. "It's a miracle." The phone had been through hell and back in the rain and in extreme heat.

She unlocked her screen and handed it to him, her fingers brushing against his. Her body tingled in anticipation as their eyes met.

"I need to shower," she said breathlessly.

Kai nodded, never taking her eyes off her as she limped across the room.

Jolie stepped into the bathroom and didn't recognize herself. Her face was smeared with mud, and her hair had matted clumps of moss and dirt. She could only imagine what people must have thought when they saw her.

She needed sleep and food. Catching a plane tonight was out of the question. She would figure that out first thing in the morning.

Slipping out of her wet clothes, she washed away what she could in the shower until the brown water turned clear. Wrapping herself in a white towel, she stepped out of the steamy bathroom.

Kai was standing on the balcony. His hands were clenched into fists. His muscles were taut.

"What's wrong?" Jolie asked.

"Raffi's gone. He refuses to sell the business, so apparently he's trying to rob a bank. At least that's what he told Noah he's going to do."

Jolie clasped her hand over her mouth. "What? Oh no."

Kai tossed the phone on her bed, pacing and sweating like a wild man. "The money is due tomorrow." He ran his hands up his cheeks, scraping at the stubble on his face. "I need to let Marco know we're giving him the warehouse, but I can't do it without Raff. He needs to sign the papers with me."

Kai picked up the notepad from the nightstand and tore off the top sheet. Taking the phone again, he dialed the number from his scribbled handwriting.

"Who are you calling now?"

"Marco," he growled, pacing to the patio and back again, over and over, until his shoulders slumped. He clicked off the phone and set it on the nightstand.

"No luck?" Jolie asked, tightening her towel around her chest.

Kai shook his head.

Jolie walked over to him and touched his shoulder. He stilled at her touch, closing his eyes.

Jolie studied the sliver between his eyebrows.

"It's going to be okay."

Kai grunted. "Raffi is going to get himself caught."

Jolie pursed her lips. He was probably right, but what could she say? "Sorry your brother is an idiot" didn't seem like it would be helpful.

"Why don't you take a shower and relax? You've just been through a lot."

Jolie had plans to make things better. Much better. If she could just get his shirt off.

"A lot?" Kai said incredulously. "I'll say. The debt. The van. My brother. Trip. It's just more than I can handle right now."

"Trip?" Jolie shot back in surprise. "Why's Trip on your list?"

"I didn't like the way he just swooped in and carried you away. Or… tried to carry you away rather. With his stupid puka shell necklace and his stupid cargo pockets everywhere."

Jolie stifled a giggle. "Oh, come on, he was harmless."

"Yeah, I know. It just felt appropriate to add it to my list of grievances."

"I would hardly put your little jealousy with Trip in the same bucket as your kilos of cocaine." Jolie stepped closer, wondering how aware he was that she was naked and dripping wet underneath her white towel.

"Did I say I was jealous? I'm not jealous."

"You seem jealous."

Kai parted his lips. The ghost of a smile appeared.

She waited for his next move. She could see it in his eyes. He wanted her as badly as she wanted him. And they were safe now.

His mouth opened and closed as if he were going to speak, but nothing came out. She could see him restraining himself before her eyes. She needed to coax the wild side out again.

"Say it," she whispered, locking her eyes on the little freckle below his eye.

Kai blinked, pressing his lips together in a hard line. "I really need a shower." He was gone in a flash.

Jolie watched the back of him as he slipped into the bathroom, shutting the door with a frantic thud. Jolie sat on the bed, crossing her legs, sticking her lip out. She hoped he would be quick, but by the look of him, he needed a long shower.

The phone buzzed on the bed, startling Jolie. It was a Costa Rican number she didn't recognize. She wondered if she should tell Kai. Maybe it was Noah calling him back.

Jolie pushed the Call button. "Hello?" Her voice wavered.

"Who is this?"

The low timbre of his Spanish accent gave him away. Marco.

Her hand shook as she started to stumble toward the bathroom.

"Um… Kai tried reaching you. Hold on one second."

"If he doesn't have the money tomorrow, I'm going to release the video to the police."

Her hand was on the bathroom doorknob, frozen.

Kai had mentioned he didn't have enough money and now she knew he wouldn't take hers if she offered it to him. He had just spent two days and two nights in the rainforest, escaping the very thought of taking her money. He wouldn't accept it now, especially after all they'd been through. He was too hell-bent on saving her from everything, including this.

She certainly didn't want to be in the middle of their

negotiations, but she felt she needed to explain. "I believe he had something better to offer, just hold on."

"I'm not interested in another offer. I'm only interested in his money," Marco snapped. "End of discussion."

Jolie's hand trembled. "What about his warehouse? That's what you wanted, isn't it?"

It was silent on the line.

What was she doing? Jolie peeked through the bathroom door. Through the steam, she could only see Kai's tan body blurred behind the shower door.

"I changed my mind. I don't want it," Marco said. "Their warehouse is a liability. I want the money by tomorrow, or the Greene brothers are going down."

Jolie's tongue felt tacky in her mouth. Kai was too stubborn to listen to her. If she told him what Marco said, he would probably still try to give the business to Marco anyway. He'd do anything to keep her out of it, despite himself.

She closed her eyes. She knew what she had to do to save Kai from ruining his life.

"I've got the money," she said.

"How much?"

"One hundred thousand dollars." Her voice cracked. Her forehead perspired. She slipped out on the patio, letting the breeze cool her face.

"They owe me twice that."

Jolie swallowed, about to lose her nerve. She pictured what her father might do in this situation. Poised and unwavering. She gathered up all the confidence she could muster. "Take it or leave it. This is how much I can transfer to you. It's either that or you end up with nothing but hours of police interrogations."

Marco grumbled under his breath; she could hear smoke blowing into the receiver.

"You drive a hard bargain," he said.

"This is my final offer."

Her heart was pounding so fast she could hardly hear him say yes.

Jolie let out the air she had been holding in. "I'll make the arrangements to wire you the money, and you must promise to delete the video and never bother Kai or his brothers again."

"You get me the money, and the boys will never hear from me."

Jolie jotted down his bank account information and clicked off the phone.

The shower was still running, but she didn't have much time. She dialed the number to her father's assistant, her fingers slipping off the phone enough times that she had to redial the number.

Cindy's voice came over the line. "Hello? Jolie?"

"Cindy, it's a bit of an emergency, but it's super important you don't tell my dad."

"What's wrong?"

"Nothing is wrong, but I have a big ask of you. I need you to wire one hundred thousand from my account to someone named Marco Venega."

"Oh my, that's a large amount of—"

"Please. I need it done immediately."

"Okay, well I can get the process started tonight, but it probably won't go through until the morning."

"As long as it gets there by tomorrow." She might have a chance at saving Kai.

"Can I ask what this is about? That is a lot of money, Jolie."

"It's... um... for charity. It'll be the last time I ever ask for favors like this again, I promise."

"You know I don't mind," Cindy said over the phone.

"You're a lifesaver. I'll send over the details in an email now. Please, my dad can't find out."

"You got it, honey."

The shower turned off. Kai would be coming out any second.

Jolie clicked off the call and pulled up an email to Cindy, furiously typing the bank account number with her thumbs. She checked it again and again to make sure it was correct, all while keeping an eye on the bathroom door for Kai to come out. Her pulse pounded in her ears.

She hit Send the moment the bathroom door opened, and Kai came out with a cloud of steam billowing around him. The towel was tied below the deep grooves of his defined waist. Jolie's breath hitched at the sight of him.

His tan was glowing, and his wet hair flopped over his eye in a loose wave. His white teeth shone brightly, sending the butterflies in her stomach in a frenzy.

"I borrowed your toothpaste. I hope you don't mind."

"Feel better?" Jolie asked, clicking off her phone.

"A thousand percent better," he said. "The thought of putting on my dirty clothes kind of bums me out though."

"Are you in a hurry to get back? I mean, we could wash your clothes in the shower and let them air dry."

Kai ran his fingers through his damp hair. "I don't know. Depends on how much of a hurry I should be to stop my big brother from robbing a bank."

Jolie stifled her laugh. "I'm sorry, that sounds funnier than it is."

"My life has turned into a real comedy show," he said glumly.

Jolie sat down on the bed, letting the towel slide up her freshly shaved legs. "Not everything is so doom and gloom, is it?" She ran her hand over the bedspread, patting the place she wanted him to sit down. "Stay with me. Maybe just for a little bit. I decided I'm going to catch a plane tomorrow. I need to rest tonight." Jolie scooched toward the headboard, leaning back against the pillows. "Please," she said, beckoning him with her finger.

She could almost see the thoughts running through his mind. With a soft sigh, he climbed onto the bed next to her. "Just for a little while."

Raindrops hit the roof overhead, and Jolie took a deep breath, relaxing her head on his shoulder. It felt like home after having slept on it for two nights in a row. She breathed in the clean soapy scent mixed with his uniquely smoky musk.

"Remember when that jaguar showed up?" Jolie said.

"How can I forget?"

"I realized there are things more important to me than my business. My silly Instagram account. Everything that I've been fighting for."

Jolie closed her eyes.

"What *is* important you, Jolie? Can you tell me now?"

Jolie swallowed, unable to find the words to describe this feeling she had with him. *This* was important. Just being with someone she cared about—someone who cared about her too—without strings attached.

His hand rested an inch away. Her fingers twitched, yearning to touch it.

When she shifted her body closer, she let her hand graze his. Electric sparks shot up through her arm as the tops of her fingers tickled the back of his hand.

He kept his hand in place, allowing the micromovements to brush against the tiny hairs of his knuckles.

"I guess I realized how much it mattered to have someone in my life to share it with, you know? That had never really been something I cared about before."

"Is that right?" Kai said. In one graceful motion, he

threaded his fingers through hers, clutching her hand, pressing it firmly but sweetly. She waited for his next move, but he held her hand in place.

She wanted more. She needed more. If he wasn't going to make the next move, then she would.

Bringing their clasped hands toward her chest, she pressed the side of his palm against her skin. "Kai," Jolie said, her mouth dry. "I…"

Struggling to find the right words, she paused. She was never good at communicating her feelings. She wasn't sure she'd ever tried. She had always let her body do the talking.

Kai leaned on his side, resting his head in his free hand. Jolie slid down beside him, noting how he did not pull back his hand the way she thought he might, given his gentlemanly tendencies.

She took it as a cue, and with her free hand, she unwrapped the knot in her towel, peeling away the terry fabric from her bare skin. A breeze brushed over her naked body, leaving a sea of tiny little gooseflesh.

Jolie waited patiently as Kai's eyes tracked over her body. It prickled under his gaze. Her breath quickened as he drank her in, and she waited for him to do something. Say something. Anything.

CHAPTER NINETEEN

There had been a handful of beautiful things Kai had seen in his life, but none came close to the majesty of Jolie's body. Her skin, as smooth as satin. Her breasts, round and full. The curve of her hip alone was something to be cherished and admired for days.

He could feel the breakdown of his resolve. Their situation was precarious, to say the least. Although he wanted to touch every inch of her body, she had been his captive just three days ago.

And... what if? What if they did sleep together? What if they fell in love? Would they be able to withstand the challenges ahead? What if she got caught in the middle of a drug bust? What if the drug dealers were outside her door this very minute, waiting to slash and burn everything that Kai cared about?

"You're thinking too much again," Jolie said. "I can see it all over your face."

Kai smiled. She had learned how to read him too well.

"Let it go," Jolie said. "Let go of whatever is holding you back. You can trust me."

Kai licked his lips. He wanted to trust her more than anything. He wanted to be with her, and only her, for the rest of his life if he could.

Just let go, he thought, and he watched his hand move as if it had taken control, tired of waiting for his brain to make the call.

His fingertips gently caressed the outside edge of her knee, then up the length of her leg at a torturous pace.

Jolie closed her eyes, a soft smile on her lips, as he glided up her leg, tracing that beautiful curve of her hip. A small puff of air escaped her mouth as he lingered around her hip bone. Jolie's breath quickened under his touch.

When his finger made it to her rib cage, she twitched.

"That tickles," she said, sweeping a smile across her face.

Unapologetically he continued, tracing the outside of her breast, up to her collarbone and circled her shoulder.

Jolie's breath deepened, growing louder with each circular motion of his wrist, as he traced and retraced her skin. She writhed under his touch, whimpering every time he bypassed her breasts or detoured from the center point between her thighs.

"You are torturing me," she said breathlessly. Her chest rose and fell with shaky spasms.

God, he wanted this. More than anything in the world.

She had the spirit of a wildcat and a heart of gold. She was strong and funny and sweet and the most generous and caring woman he had ever met.

Kai stared into her eyes, his breath picking up speed as his inner fire obliterated all his self-control. He crashed down to her mouth, caressing and exploring with his tongue massaging hers.

Jolie gave him everything in her kiss, pulling him down onto her.

Kai's hands explored the soft mounds of her chest, the

curvature of her rib cage. He was lost in his breath, in her mouth, and the wave of her body as she rolled him over to his back and straddled him.

He gripped her hips and stared into her big brown eyes. Wet strands of her hair dripped on his chest, sending ripples of pleasure throughout his body.

Jolie bit her lower lip as she pulled her hair over to one side of her neck. My God, she had mastered the art of seduction. He would be dreaming about this moment for years. Jolie lowered her mouth on his, nipping at his lips and up his jawline when a boom of thunder outside shook Kai from his trance.

What was he *doing*? He had a brother about to rob a bank, the devil himself waiting for his blackmail money, and hundreds of kilos of cocaine in his warehouse. He had responsibilities.

He grabbed her hips and moved her off of him, setting her gently down on the bed. "I'm sorry," he said, gasping for air. "But I have to go. I can't do this right now."

Jolie's eyebrows pinched together as she gathered the towel around herself. "I don't understand," she said, catching her breath.

"I've got to stop my brother before it's too late."

"Your brother is going to do what he's going to do. Robbing a bank is his choice, not yours."

Kai ran his hands through his hair. "It's not just my brother. I've got a million other things I need to deal with right now. The debt. The cocaine. My life is in complete shambles. You deserve all of me, and I can't give that to you right now."

Jolie's jaw dropped. "Your life doesn't have to be perfect to be with me. It's just sex."

Kai felt the arrow to his heart. "Just sex? Is that all this is to you?"

Jolie's face fell. "No… Kai, wait."

Kai shot up from the bed, pulling his mud-stained jeans up his shaky legs.

Jolie bit her lip, her eyes darting around the room and back again. "I…"

Kai let the unfinished phrase go unanswered and yanked his swampy shirt over his head. He stared at her, watching her grapple with the words that wouldn't leave her mouth.

"You are more than a one-night stand to me." Kai's chest constricted. "If this is *just sex*, then I say we end this now. I don't work that way."

"This was not going to be a one-night stand to me either." Jolie's nostrils flared.

"Then what is it that we're doing here? After sex, then what?" Kai challenged.

Jolie looked away, flicking the tear away from the corner of her eye. "I thought… I thought maybe we could be together."

"You deserve perfection. I want to give you that. But I still have that damn cocaine sitting in my warehouse. Someone is probably looking for it. I can't stand the thought of you getting caught in the middle."

Jolie swallowed and her lip quivered. "But life is full of problems, all the time, Kai. You can't wait for your life to be perfect before you can live."

"My life needs more than fixing right now, and I refuse to drag you down with me while I'm drowning in it."

"You can't drag me down."

"Really? Let's take inventory, shall we?" Kai began counting on his fingers. "Ever since I dropped into your life, you've been kidnapped, held for ransom, threatened, lost in the jungle, and near death. I'm obviously not good for you."

Jolie fell silent. Her eyes glistened. "I don't care about any of that. I just want to help you."

Kai cringed, squeezing his feet into soggy socks. "I have to do this on my own."

Jolie looked away, wiping her eyes with the palm of her hand. "What if your debt was paid off and you could keep your business? Would that be enough for us to be together?" She sniffed, still looking away, avoiding his gaze.

Kai stood beside her, putting a hand on her shoulder. "I wish it would, but no."

Jolie hung her head and her shoulders shook. A sob escaped her throat.

Kai crouched down in front of her. "What's wrong?"

Jolie sniffed. "I thought if I paid Marco—"

"You know I can't take your money," Kai said, smoothing his hands over her arms.

Jolie's red-rimmed eyes looked up at him. The tip of her nose had turned pink. "It's too late," she said.

Kai stared at her in disbelief. "What do you mean it's too late? Too late for what?"

"Marco called while you were in the shower. I was going to give the phone to you, but he was insistent that he didn't want anything other than money. He wouldn't have accepted your warehouse."

"You spoke to Marco?" Kai felt the rush of heat to his face. His heart pounded in his chest. "I was handling it. Why didn't you get me?"

"Because you are so stubborn!" Jolie sent daggers from her eyes. "I knew you wouldn't have taken my money. You would have rather ended up in jail. I needed to save you from yourself."

Kai took a calming breath and leveled his eyes with hers. "What did you do?"

"I bargained your debt down to a hundred grand. The rest is forgotten."

Kai clenched his jaw, breathing heavily through his nose. "Please tell me you didn't give him your money."

"I convinced him that he wouldn't get any more than a hundred grand. He promised me that would cover your debt."

"And you trusted him?"

"What else was I supposed to do? You were in over your head."

Kai covered his face with his hands. "How could you have been so careless?"

"Careless?" Jolie shouted. "I emptied my entire bank account for you. Because I *care*. I *care* about you. I did it for *you*."

"The whole reason I helped you escape was to prevent this very thing from happening!" He was shouting now. "I am trying to protect you from ruining your life."

"I thought," Jolie stuttered, "I thought if I helped you, you would see." Jolie's voice constricted. She swallowed, regaining her composure. "You would see how much I cared about you. I thought I was saving you from yourself."

"This is exactly why we can't be together right now. We are not good for each other. I will not let my screwed-up life affect you any longer."

"What are you going to do?" Jolie gulped. "Are you just going to leave?"

Kai took a deep breath, wishing there was some other way they could be together without him destroying her life. But it was already too late. She had given Marco every last cent of her bank account, kissing her chance at revamping her business goodbye. She would have to work for her father or some other place where she would be miserable. A life sentence, as she called it.

"I can't allow you to suffer anymore because of me," Kai said.

"That's bullshit," Jolie hissed, her lip trembling. "You can't walk out of here and think I'm going to believe you are *that* altruistic. I've been practically throwing myself at you, and for what? You're keeping me at a safe distance on purpose. You're afraid that if something goes wrong, that your little *wildcat* might do something really dumb, like call the police."

"Jolie…"

"Oh, I get it," Jolie said, her features turned stone cold. "You've been nice. Too nice. Nobody is that nice. No man in their right mind would turn down a naked chick like you have. Multiple times! It's inhuman."

"Now hold on… That was the hardest thing I've ever—"

"I don't want to hear it," Jolie said. "You've been buttering me up this whole time to ensure you and your psycho-ass brother don't end up in jail. I saw the change in you the moment I mentioned turning him in. You backed off."

"I was giving you space. I know you're still angry at my brother."

"You've been keeping me just close enough, probably in fear I'm going to snap and turn you both in. You're not shutting me out to 'keep me safe.'" Jolie emphasized with air quotes. "You're shutting me out because you never had feelings for me at all."

Kai sucked in a breath. "Jolie, that's not true. I care about you."

Jolie scoffed.

"You can't imply that I never had feelings for you," Kai growled. "It's obvious I do." Kai stepped right up to her, inches from her face. He was seething, and yet he wanted to rip the towel from her body and punish her with kisses.

"Then prove it," Jolie said. "I've seen the wild side of you before. I know it's in there somewhere. Show it to me again, and I'll believe you." She inched forward, so close Kai could feel the air escape her nose. A blazing fire had set within her eyes, daring him to take the final plunge.

His eyes raked over her full lips and the curvature of her nose. He would have loved to ravage her, but she was trying to provoke him. This wasn't some invitation to love her. This was a challenge to see if he could let go of his scruples.

"That wild side you saw was irresponsible," Kai said, "and almost as reckless as your attempt at saving me with your money. Now I've got to get it back before it's too late."

"Fine," Jolie said, crossing her arms. She sat back down on the bed, turning her back to him. "Go then."

"We're not done talking yet."

"Well, I'm done talking," Jolie said, her words slicing through him. "You got me out of the jungle. Your job is complete, so go."

"But we can be together. Just some other time. When things clear up."

Jolie arched her brow at him. "Listen, Kai. You are way too cautious to take any kind of risk on me. That is not real love."

"Keeping you safe is my way of showing my *love*. Don't you see? I don't have time for arguing right now. I've got too much stuff to deal with."

"Then that's that," Jolie said, flicking her eyes up toward the ceiling, unshed tears pooling at the bottom of her lids. "There will always be an excuse for us not to be together."

"One of us has to be the responsible one!"

"Just go, Kai. Call me when your life is perfect, and maybe, just *maybe*, my old, wrinkly ass will still give a shit."

Kai pursed his lips. "I will come find you, and I will give you your money back."

"Great," Jolie snapped. "I'll be holding my breath."

Kai grunted as he reached for his shoes and stormed out the door, slamming it behind him. A group of yogis in a night class across the path were in some kind of flamingo-looking pose. They craned their necks and stared.

Jolie had to be the most frustrating, stubborn woman he had ever met. And by God, if he never saw her again, it would be the worst thing that could ever happen to him.

CHAPTER TWENTY

Kai drove back to the city with his hands clamped around the steering wheel. By the time he pulled up to Ma's driveway, the tiny muscles in his palm ached.

Jolie had gotten under his skin. How could she not see the urgency of his situation? Not that he would be able to stop his brother from doing something stupid, but it was not the time to be romping in the sheets.

And *romping* was a perfectly acceptable word to use. *Right?*

Kai gripped his chin, rubbing the prickly beard that had formed.

Crap.

He was a fool. A damned fool. He should have taken her when he had the chance.

He pictured her straddling his hips, dripping with seduction. She was perfect. Wet, willing, and waiting for him. Regret seeped into his consciousness somewhere between the highway exit and Avenue Six.

Well, it was too late now. He could only handle one

problem at a time. Raffi wasn't answering his phone, and Noah had told Kai to come to Ma's right away.

Kai stepped through Ma's front door and slipped off his wet shoes. "Hello?" His words drifted into the oddly quiet room.

The news wasn't blaring. Pots and pans weren't clanking. The kitchen sink wasn't running. It was like walking into a *Twilight Zone* version of his mother's house.

He gazed at the picture frames and vases as if he were seeing them for the first time. Potted plants had wilted and browned at the tips, drooping over their edges, too tired to carry their own weight.

Kai poked his head in Noah's room. It was cleaner than normal but no sign of him. Kai went to his room and rummaged through his dresser drawer for a clean shirt and jeans, dropping his muddy clothes in the hamper.

"Hello?" Kai called out. "Ma?"

"We're in here," Noah said from down the hall.

Kai stepped in to his mother's room to find Ma in bed, red-faced and blotting her eyes with a tissue. Crumpled balls of Kleenex were thrown around the room.

"Ma? What's wrong?" Kai said.

"Raffi's in jail! My baby is in jail," she cried.

Kai's mouth fell open. He was too late. His older brother finally got himself caught. It was only a matter of time, but still the news was a blow.

"Was it the bank?" Kai asked.

"You knew about this?" Ma screeched.

Kai's eyes grew wide as he looked at Noah. "You didn't tell her?"

Noah shrugged. "What was I supposed to say?"

"What's going on here?" Ma shoved Noah off the bed, and he thumped to the floor.

"Ow," Noah said, pulling himself up to stand.

Kai gripped the bridge of his nose. He had been trying to protect her from this burden, but he had to say something now. How much should he tell her? The whole truth? Or just the part about Raffi being a greedy asshole?

"I just don't understand why he would do such a thing," Ma said. "I mean, your father's business pays him enough, right?"

What could Kai say? He exchanged a glance with Noah, who shrugged his shoulders as he gingerly sat back down on the bed.

"I'm never going to see him again," she cried. "And I don't know why. I just want to understand why he would rob a bank of all things."

White strands had come loose from her bun. Locks of white silk draped across her face as she buried herself into Noah's chest.

"Ma, it's going to be okay," Noah said, giving Kai a look that said he wasn't so sure.

"What aren't you telling me?" Ma blew into a tissue.

Kai pursed his lips. Without Greene Coffee Roastery, Ma would need to prepare for a life of retirement she had not expected, without the home she'd loved, the paintings she had put on the walls, and the garden she had tended in the backyard. It would all be gone. Ma would need some sort of explanation before he uprooted her life.

He drew in a long breath and defeatedly sat on the bed next to them. "Raffi was stealing to pay off some unexpected debt," Kai said.

"What do you mean debt?" Ma huffed.

"I mean blackmail."

Ma gasped. "For what? By whom?"

"Raffi had taken a side job, not realizing that he was carrying a load of narcotics in one of our vans. Marco Venega caught us on video when we were trying to figure out what to do with it, and he's been threatening to turn us in ever since."

"Drugs…?" Ma's face morphed from confusion to anger in seconds. "Your brother wasn't into drugs."

"No, but he wanted the extra cash, and he was too dumb to realize what he had gotten himself into." Kai hung his head low. "If Marco hadn't caught us, we would have been focused on trying to get the cocaine out of the warehouse, but we weren't sure if someone was going to come looking for it."

"The drugs are still in the warehouse?" Ma said, cupping her mouth with her shaky hands.

"They're hidden for now," Noah said. "We were giving it time before we dumped it."

"Why didn't you tell me?" Ma said. She gripped Kai's arms, shaking them violently. "This is all Marco's fault."

Kai rubbed her back. "I'm sorry, Ma. Marco is only guilty of being a jerk and blackmailing us. He had nothing to do with the drugs."

"But he's… he's awful. Evil. His blackmail is what pushed my poor baby to steal," she said, her lip quivering. "Raffi would never do something as horrible as robbing a bank if it weren't for that scumbag."

Kai exchanged a glance with Noah.

Maybe Raffi wouldn't have robbed a bank, but he sure would have done a lot of other stupid crap.

"I'm going to talk to Marco," Ma said, tightening her fist around the wad of Kleenex. "I'm going to talk him out of this ridiculous blackmail." She pulled herself up from the bed and wobbled to her dresser, limping on her sprained ankle.

Kai stopped her from opening the drawer. "Talking to Marco isn't going to solve anything. Marco is my problem, not yours."

"No," Ma said. "He's my problem. And I'm going to end this right here and right now."

"What are you talking about?" Kai said. "You're not making any sense."

"I thought his beef was with Pop," Noah said. "Not you."

Ma paced the floor, grabbing a new tissue every time she walked past the box. Tears streamed down her face as she mumbled words in German.

"Ma?" Noah stood up. "What's going on?"

Ma wandered aimlessly around the room, not looking up at her sons' concerned faces. Her lip trembled. "I can't say. I can't say," she repeated over and over again.

"What is it?" Kai marched to his mother, gently putting his hands on her shoulders until she finally came to a stop. "Look at me, Ma."

"I need to sit down," she said, hobbling back to the bed. "Marco and I..." Her words drifted into the stale bedroom air.

Kai's body tensed, not expecting the words *Marco and I* to stream out of his mother's mouth.

"Marco and I have a history," Ma said. "That's all you need to know."

Kai leveled his eyes with her. "What. Kind. Of. History?"

The room fell silent as their mother drifted away, her eyes vacant. Physically sitting there, she was less present than if she had been flying around in never-never land.

"You can tell us," Noah said.

"You know I loved your father very much," Ma said, "but there was a time we were going through a rough patch. He was working late."

Kai gripped the edge of the bed. "Please say you didn't have an affair."

Ma swallowed, unable to look Kai in the eyes.

"Ma... an *affair*? Really?" Kai perched his knuckles on his hips, unable to process the news.

She must be joking. Surely this was a ruse. Maybe she and

Marco had buried a body somewhere instead. For some reason a homicide seemed more bearable than the thought of Ma and Marco in bed together.

Ma nodded. "I'm so sorry, boys. I made a horrible mistake."

"You slept with Pothole Face?" Noah stuck out his tongue in disgust. "Yuck. How could you do that to Pop?"

"I know." Ma's voice was weak. "It was a horrible thing to do."

Kai had thought this whole time his parents had the perfect relationship. They never argued, not once, as far as he could remember. Ma and Pop loved each other more than anything in the world. She had supported him when he decided to quit his finance job, and he had slaved away hours and hours at the roastery, trying to create the best life for her. So that they could live like they were on vacation every single day, just like they wanted.

And she betrayed him.

"Did Pop know?" Kai said.

"Your father," she blubbered, "was so mad when he found out. He marched over to Marco's office and beat him within an inch of his life."

"Pop isn't the reason Marco has those scars on his face, is it?" Noah said.

Ma shook her head. "Your father may have left a mark or two, but Marco always had the scars."

"Then what happened?" Kai said.

"When your father came home, he got down on his knees and apologized for being an absent husband and father. He took the blame for something I did," Ma said. "I promised that I would never do anything like that to him again, and he promised he would be a better husband and father. And that's what happened. We were stronger for it. We overcame the whole ordeal together."

Kai wished he could say the same thing about him and Jolie overcoming their differences.

"After that, the war between him and Marco got vicious." Ma blew her nose. "Marco was hurt that I had chosen your father over him, and he found endless ways to make your father's life miserable."

"How so?" Kai said. He couldn't recall ever seeing a Marco and Pop quarrel in action. He had only heard of his father moaning about Marco blaring his music too loud as he drove into the office every morning.

"Marco would do small things here and there," Ma said. "Sometimes your father would find nails in the driveway. He was sure Marco had put them there."

"Did Pop do anything back?" Kai said.

Ma looked up at the ceiling as if she were asking their father's angel, right in front of them. "Your father may have let the air out of Marco's motorcycles from time to time. It was all childish stuff. But one time it was malicious."

"What happened?" Noah said.

Ma folded her hands in her lap. "Did you say Marco is still holding this blackmail over your head?"

Kai closed his eyes, letting the hissing air blow through his nose. "I'm not exactly sure. I need to talk to him tomorrow morning. Why do you ask?"

Ma shrugged her shoulders. "Because I may have something that could be useful."

Kai and Noah both stared at her, waiting for a follow-up.

"What?" Kai said impatiently.

Ma cowered on the bed, hunching her shoulders like a dog in trouble for getting in the trash.

"What is it?" Noah said.

Ma covered her face with her hands. "I can't..."

"Say it," Kai said. "Whatever it is, I could use all the help I could get. I don't know how I'm going to bargain my way out of the debt. He's ruthless."

Ma peeked through her fingers at her sons, before snapping her fingers closed again. "Marco sent a video of us to your father."

Kai's eyes grew wide as his mouth dropped.

"A video? What video?" Noah asked, confused.

Ma looked at Noah sheepishly.

That kind of video. Kai couldn't even muster the words to tell her to stop talking.

"I didn't know he was taking a video at the time! He's a weasel." Her face fell back into her hands. "That's not even the worst thing he pulled," she said.

"I don't want to hear it." Kai shot up, marching toward the door.

"He had played the audio over his parking lot speaker systems."

"Stop." Kai held his hand out. "I can't hear anymore."

No.

No.

No.

The thought of his mother sleeping with anyone was more than he could take. Pop was her world. How could she have done something like that to him?

"I'm sorry you had to find this out," Ma said tearfully. "It's the last thing I ever wanted you boys to know."

"Then why are you telling us this, Ma?" Kai said.

"What is even happening right now?" Noah said, bewildered.

Ma sniffed, rubbing her chafed nose with a tissue. "Because I still have the DVD."

"What the hell?" Noah said.

Ma smacked Noah in the chest. "Language!"

"Ma, no offense," Kai said, "but we don't want to see that."

"You said he blackmailed you, right?" Ma said.

"Yes, but what does your sex tape have to do with this?"

Ma looked down at her hands, studying them until she sniffed back her tears. "I happen to know his new wife. I see her at church sometimes."

Kai shook his head. "Oh no. No. No. *No*. We're not going to use your sex tape for blackmail. Now I know where Raffi gets his crazy ideas."

"Listen," Ma said. "I've been waiting for the day to use that tape against him. For what he did to your father with it. It was horrible. Let me help you."

"That's enough. I can't handle one more crazy idea from this family. Ma, I really wish you hadn't told me that. You need to destroy that DVD immediately."

"Kai, wait," Ma called out to him as he stormed out the bedroom.

"I can't handle you people!" Kai yelled, leaving his mother and brother in his wake.

If he ever even considered for one second using his mother's sex tape as a way to get Jolie's money back, then he would have officially lost his mind like the rest of his family.

CHAPTER TWENTY-ONE

Jolie tore down the note from her landlord and pulled her luggage over the threshold. It was probably her final reminder that her rent was overdue.

Crumpling it up, she tossed the note on her couch and zombied toward the kitchen, a little limp in her step still lingering.

She grabbed the kettle while Frido and Sneeker yipped at her feet.

"Give me treats!" they barked. It had become a ritual. Every time she came home, they would get a snack. Jolie tossed them each a bone and then stared at her teakettle until it hissed with steam.

Of all the reckless things she'd ever done, giving one hundred thousand away *for a guy* was by far the dumbest. Why couldn't she have just left it alone? Kai didn't want her help, and he didn't want her.

She was left with nothing, and she couldn't count on Kai to get her money back. He was probably already in jail by now. Jolie cursed herself for getting involved.

She glanced around the apartment she couldn't afford

anymore. Samuel and Franklin were nestled on the couch, their tails flipping side to side. She couldn't even afford to keep her little family of pets together.

Jolie sat down between her furry cats, her mug warming her hands. Their purrs vibrated through the couch fabric, which somehow made her even more sad.

The San Francisco fog rolled outside her window, casting a gray hue across her apartment. She spread a blanket over her legs, but it didn't help the chill that had settled in her bones.

It was the end of her dream. She had failed what she had set out to do in Costa Rica and departed with a broken heart as a bonus.

Kai had left a mark on her, one that she wouldn't forget for a long time. He was sweet and kind, yet so frustratingly righteous. What man in their right mind would shut her down while she was naked and straddling him?

A man who didn't feel the same way, she told herself. If he felt the same way she did, he wouldn't have stopped.

But then again, he *was* dealing with a lot of problems.

Jolie sighed. Maybe she was just too wild for him. He seemed like the type of guy who would want to take things slow. Not at all the type of guy she had dated in the past. She was in uncharted territory. Jolie didn't know how to handle a man like Kai, a walking contradiction. A criminal Goody Two-shoes.

And then she had to go ahead and try to control the situation with her money, just like her father would have done. She was only trying to help, but there should have been another way. Something other than throwing all her money at the problem when he said he'd been handling it.

Of course he was upset with her. He probably felt emasculated or embarrassed. Unworthy. Exactly how her father made her feel when he swooped in and solved all her problems.

What was she thinking? She had turned into the very person that had been making her own life miserable for years.

Jolie lingered on that thought, letting the steam of the green tea warm her nose.

She took inventory of all the beautiful pieces of furniture that her father had given her. The designer lamp. The framed artwork over her big-screen TV. The gold-plated vase on her coffee table.

He gave her those things to keep her close. It was a control tactic that made Jolie crazy. But he also spent money on her because he cared. It was his way of showing her his love. And it was exactly what she had tried to do for Kai.

Duchess moseyed her way to Jolie's feet and rested her snout on her shin. The pain still lingered from where she had been kicked, but it was tolerable. Duchess's corgi ears stood upright as she looked up at Jolie with her big goopy eyes.

Jolie grabbed a tissue from the Kleenex box on her coffee table and wiped the corners. "It's okay, old girl. We'll be fine," she said, patting her on the head.

A small whimper left Duchess's throat.

Tears streamed down Jolie's face as she set her mug down and took Duchess's face in her hands, giving her kisses on her nose. "I'm sorry," Jolie said. "I'm sorry I failed." Jolie sniffled, grabbing another tissue. "I'm sorry we have to move. I'm sorry I won't be home to play with you during the day. Mama needs to put on her big-girl pants now and get a real job."

Jolie stroked Duchess's back and head and behind her ears. Jolie petted her until the tears dried on her face. It was time to do what she needed to do.

Grabbing her phone, she called her father.

"Hello, Jolie."

"Dad?" Jolie swallowed. "I'm ready to work for your company now."

There was a long pause on the line. The longest, most agonizing two seconds of her life. Would he call her a failure? Would he berate her for losing the money he had only given her less than a couple of weeks ago? Jolie braced herself for his wrath.

"I'll have Cindy get the paperwork started. Come into the office on Monday."

Kai marched across the street, right into the lion's den, Marco's lot. It was a warm morning, the sun already breathing down Kai's neck. It was going to be a hot day in hell.

Motorcycles cluttered the open garage as men in coveralls and blackened hands worked on repairs. There was no sign of Marco yet. He was probably in an office somewhere, swindling some poor schmuck out of their money.

The lobby smelled of gasoline and sweat, despite Marco's attempts at making it appear to be a luxurious motorcycle dealership. White leather chairs had yellowed in spots where people had baked in the un-air-conditioned room. Posters of motorcycles from the nineties hung on the wall, and a little glass dish of mint-chocolate candies was perched next to stacks of motorcycle pamphlets.

A Costa Rican woman wearing a hot-pink jumpsuit and gold baubles around her neck and wrists sat at a desk behind a computer. Her jaw dropped as Kai barreled in through the front door.

"Can I help you?" the lady asked in Spanish. Kai hadn't

seen her around before, but by the looks of her golf-ball-sized diamond ring, she must be Marco's new wife.

"I'm here to talk to Marco," Kai said, looking around. He had to be around somewhere, but if he wasn't, Kai was prepared to drive to the ends of the earth to give him a piece of his mind.

If only he had a plan. That is, a better plan than to berate Marco for nearly breaking up his parents' marriage and for taking Jolie's money without consulting with him first.

"Marco's busy at the moment," she said. "Please take a seat, and I'll page him."

Kai's back teeth ground against each other as he thought about what he was going to say. How was he going to get Jolie's money back?

Kai looked at the stained leather seats and decided he'd rather stand. He paced instead while the lady in pink eyed him cautiously. He wondered how much she knew of the blackmail and if she realized she'd married a sniveling piece of shit.

Or maybe she didn't know a thing, and Marco had kept his dirty little secrets from his wife.

He pulled out his lighter from his pocket. Rubbing the grooves of the wheel, he stared at the red case. A little graphic in the shape of a jaguar sat just below the Clipper logo. How was this the first time he'd noticed that?

A smile reached his lips as he thought of his own wildcat. He wondered what Jolie would do if she were the one trying to get the money back.

He imagined her kicking and screaming until she finally got what she came for. She wouldn't take no for an answer, of that he could be sure.

She would be pleased to hear Raffi was in jail.

Then it hit Kai all at once, like a bag of bricks. Marco

didn't know Raffi was in jail either. And if he did, he wouldn't know what for.

Kai suddenly had a plan.

"I can't wait anymore," Kai said as he zoomed past Marco's wife toward the back door.

"You're not supposed to go back there," she called as Kai let the door slam behind him.

Kai stomped down the hallway past the bathrooms. His eyes landed on an office door, and he charged forward. Marco was standing behind his desk, pressing a button on his phone.

"Well, well. Look what we have here." Marco's mouth curled into a malevolent grin.

"You," Kai said, practically foaming at the mouth. "You slept with my mother."

Marco's face fell, and he ushered Kai in the room. "I see you spoke with Gretta."

"I ought to finish what my father started and kick your ass."

Marco pulled out a cigar from his pocket and lit it with a patience that made Kai's blood boil. Smoky cedarwood and nutmeg filled the room.

"Now, now. Let's not let threats be added to your list of criminal offenses, shall we? You've got enough on your plate to account for."

"I want the money back," Kai said.

Marco offered up a playful smile. "What money?"

"The money that Jolie gave you. I want it back now."

"Where are all these demands coming from, boy? I'm the one with the video of you hiding narcotics, remember?" Marco pounded on the table. "Now pay up before I send the video to the police."

"Marco, is everything okay?" the lady in pink said, popping her head into his office.

"Everything is fine, Camila," Marco said, blowing a puff of smoke from his mouth. "You can go back to your desk."

Camila raked her gaze up Kai's body before turning on her heel.

"Where were we?" Marco said.

"You were threatening to send the video to the police," Kai said, "but there's nothing to report. Raffi is already in jail. You've got nothing on us now."

Marco snarled before sitting down. He puffed on his cigar a few more times before locking his beady-eyed gaze onto Kai. "Well then, shall we say we just drop this whole thing?"

"I'm not finished with you," Kai growled. "I'm here to get Jolie's money back."

Marco cocked his head and laughed. "And why should I give it to you? I owe you nothing."

Kai gripped the lighter as if it would give him strength. He would not back down. "I want to strike a bargain with you. I'll give you the warehouse. The entire operation. It's yours, if you give me back Jolie's money. You'll have everything you wanted, and the best thing of all, we'll be gone. Forever. You'll never have to look at us again or be reminded of my mother."

"I see your negotiating tactics have improved since your last attempt," Marco said, tapping the ashes of his cigar into an ashtray. "There's only one problem."

"What?"

"I don't want your warehouse anymore. I've changed my mind. I'd rather keep the money."

"But you could expand your business and open up whatever you want in that thing. You could make twice as much as the one hundred thousand in just a couple of years."

"I've decided to retire instead. I have no use for the warehouse anymore."

"But…" Kai was at a loss for words. The warehouse was his only chance of getting Jolie's money back. That is, unless he sold it to another buyer. He wasn't sure he would be able to get one hundred thousand, but he would have to try.

Marco leaned back in his chair, a smug smile swept across his face. He had won. He got his one hundred thousand and his revenge on the Greene family. The cloud of smoke wafted around his head like an evil victory lap, slow and mean.

"I guess we're done here," Kai said, defeated. Before he pivoted to leave, something caught Marco's attention by the door. He shot up from his seat, stamping the cigar out into the ashtray.

Kai turned toward the door to find Camila standing next to Ma, both beaming and chatting as they barged in.

"Camila, why did—?" Marco started.

"Marco, I wanted you to meet my friend Gretta from church," Camila said.

Ma smiled graciously at Marco and then leveled her gaze at Kai with the same mischievous spark that Raffi had.

Kai would have sent laser beams through his eyes if he could. Ma better not be doing what he thought she was doing.

Then he saw the DVD case tucked under her arm.

Son of a—

"Gretta said she is this young man's mother and wanted to bring him something for your meeting."

Marco's nose flared when Gretta held the DVD in the air, an ominous smile firmly planted on her face. "I thought this video might be of use to my son as you were working out your… negotiations."

"Ma, this is not the time or place to—"

"Oh honey, I know you've got everything taken care of. But I think this information would be quite helpful as you two work through your business problem."

Kai could hear Marco growl under his breath. "Camila," he said firmly, "can you please go to your desk? I'm expecting a call any minute, and I'd hate to miss it." He practically spat out the word.

Camila tapped her manicured fingernail to her lower lip while her gaze shifted from Ma to Marco and back again to Ma. Knitting her brows together, she dashed away, her gold-plated baubles jangling down the hall.

"What are you doing here, Gretta?" Marco said, making a steeple with his fingers.

"Remember this?" Gretta waved the DVD in the air.

Marco coughed loudly, shifting in his chair. "That was a long time ago."

Ma strolled up to Kai like a lion who had just taken over the den. "Did he give you back your money?"

Kai shook his head. "Don't do this," he whispered. Leveraging his mother's sex tape was not how he wanted to get the money back. He would do it the proper way and just sell the business.

Ma waggled her eyebrows at Kai and turned toward Marco. "It would be a pity if Camila received a copy of this tape, would it not?"

Marco hissed. His hands gripped the arms of his chair so hard his knuckles looked like they would burst from his leathery skin. "You wouldn't dare," he said. "You were always so prim and proper. It was what I loved about you then."

"Ah yes, that was before you took one hundred thousand from my son. And I'd like you to give it back," Ma said.

Marco gritted his teeth, baring the yellowed Chiclets that remained stained from years of cigar smoke. "You're bluffing."

"Camila?" Ma called. "Camila, can you come here a second?"

What was she doing? Had his mother lost her mind?

A moment later, Camila had shuffled back into the office. "Yes?"

"Do you happen to have a TV or a computer that can play DVDs? I was hoping we could use this powerful video to help prove a point."

Camila looked at Marco. "Should I bring my laptop over?"

"No!" Marco shouted with such force, it stunned both women. Kai's mouth had gone dry. He swallowed, but his tongue felt clumsy in his mouth.

"There will be no need to play the video. Gretta has already proved her point."

Kai exchanged a surprised glance with his mother. Had he finally caved?

"I'd like some proof," Ma said. "This deal and all future deals are off, or this... *presentation...* gets unleashed."

"What presentation?" Camila asked, confused.

"There's no presentation needed," Marco said through clenched teeth. "Camila, please tend to the front desk."

Camila pouted and left in a huff.

Opening the top right drawer with a quick jolt, he pulled out a checkbook.

Kai stared in amazement while Marco scribbled a check for one hundred thousand. He peeled it off and handed it to Kai.

"Here," Marco growled. "It's settled. Now give me the DVD."

"Delete the video from your phone first," Kai said. "I want to see you do it."

Marco pulled out his phone and scrolled. He showed Kai his screen as he pressed Delete.

"Happy?" Marco growled.

"You don't have any other copies?"

Marco snarled, shaking his head.

"Wonderful," Ma said. "We'll keep this DVD just to be sure my boys are secure." She waved her hand through the thick smoke. "I look forward to seeing Camila at Sunday's service. We've become such good friends." Ma's eyes sparkled. "Come along, Kai. There is much to be done at the roastery with your brother gone."

Ma gave Marco one last piercing glare before she sauntered out the door. Kai quickly followed her, the check for one hundred thousand gripped tightly between his fingers.

CHAPTER TWENTY-TWO

The café hummed with espresso makers and Latin jazz music. Jolie had already chewed through three wooden stir sticks, which were now sitting in shards on the table. She had just finished briefing Nora on her trip to Costa Rica, who sat stunned.

"I don't even know where to begin," Nora said, dumbfounded. "I think you just gave me my next book idea."

Jolie chuckled. "Nah, it's too unbelievable. I mean, getting lost in the jungle with a handsome man. So cliché."

"Yeah, but the whole cocaine debacle is a fun twist." Nora smirked into her cup.

"Well, it didn't have a happy ending, because here I am. Broke and without the guy."

"Yeah, but the way you talk about Kai makes it sound like there was really something between you two."

"Nah," Jolie lied. "For a criminal, he was all too chaste for me." Jolie stuck out her tongue. "He was a walking contradiction. Kidnapping me one minute and being a complete gentleman the next."

Nora giggled as she pulled out her notepad and pen.

"Are you seriously taking notes?"

"This is just too good not to write down."

Jolie rolled her eyes. "Anyway." Big dramatic pause. "I could tell he was a sweet person. I was willing to overlook his baggage—"

"You mean the two hundred kilos of cocaine kind of baggage?"

"Yes, *that baggage*." Jolie smirked. "But he wasn't willing to let go of his problems for just a couple of minutes—maybe several minutes, if you know what I mean—for me."

"There's something you're not telling me," Nora said. "Chewing through three sticks is a lot for even a woodchuck like you." Nora took a sip of her foamy latte.

Jolie sighed, not knowing if she was more upset about how things ended with Kai or the fact that she was near homeless and had to ask her best friend if she could crash on her couch for a while, along with her herd of pets.

"I… um…" Jolie got up and picked another stir stick from the container and sat back down. "I need a place to stay." Jolie stumbled over her words with the stick in her teeth. She twisted her hands in her lap. "I don't have enough money to pay my rent."

"You don't need to explain," Nora said, putting one hand on top of Jolie's and pulling the stick out of Jolie's mouth with the other. "You know you'll always have a place at our house."

"And the pets?" Jolie asked tentatively.

"The pets too," Nora said.

Jolie leaped over the table, cupping Nora's face. "I freaking love you. Thank you."

"I love you too."

Was that so hard? Telling her best friend how she felt came so easily. Why couldn't she have just said the way she felt to Kai when she had the chance?

"I feel bad though. You and Kellen just got married, and—"

"Stop. Jolie, you let me live with you for years. For free. Remember? When I had no money, no career. I want to return the favor."

"Are you sure Kellen won't mind?" Jolie started gnawing on her stir stick again.

"Kellen will be fine. Plus he's constantly between here and New York. It'll be nice to have someone to keep me company while he's away."

Jolie fabricated a smile. "Thank you."

"Bring your stuff and the family over tonight. We'll drink wine and have a welcome party for our new roommates. I can't wait to see Kellen's face when you tell him your story."

"I'm more interested in the look on his face when he finds out I'm moving in with my little zoo."

"Stop worrying," Nora said, pulling the stick out of her mouth again. "We love you and your animals. It'll be fun to have you all around. As long as you don't chew up our furniture."

"My pets don't chew furniture."

"I wasn't talking about your pets."

They both giggled into their coffees.

Jolie showed up that night just as Nora and Kellen were finishing dinner. Kellen was washing the dishes when Jolie walked in with her luggage.

Nora gave her a hug. "Welcome, roomie."

Kellen walked over and opened his tattooed arms wide. "Get in here," he said, wrapping them around her. "Roomie."

Jolie filled to the brim with joy. "Thank you so much for letting me crash here until I can figure my shit out."

"We're happy to have you," Kellen said.

"Time for wine!" Nora said excitedly. "I haven't told

Kellen a thing about your trip to Costa Rica. I wanted you to tell the story."

Jolie raised her eyebrows.

"It sounds like it was eventful?" Kellen asked as he pulled a bottle from one of their racks.

"You could say that," Jolie said, smiling at Nora.

Jolie relayed her story while Kellen's eyes grew wider with each detail. The burglary, the kidnapping, the exit through the jungle. Everything except the fact that Jolie had fallen in love with Kai and stupidly gave him all her money in hopes that they could be together.

By the time Jolie finished her story, they were tipsy and slurring through purple-stained lips.

Nora paced around her living room, her arms flapping wildly in the air.

"Best story ever!" Nora squealed. She disappeared into the kitchen and reemerged with a jar of homemade pickles and set it on the coffee table.

"Want one?" she said, chomping on one over a napkin as she sat down in her love seat.

"Eww. How can you eat that with your glass of wine? My tongue is sweating at the thought of it," Jolie said.

"Pickles go with anything," she said, munching happily.

"Gross… Anyway," Jolie said. "So that's the story."

"What is the deal with this Kai guy?" Kellen said. "I mean, he risked his life for you. Ditched his brother and everything. Whatever happened to bros before hoes?"

Jolie and Nora rolled their eyes.

"I think he was just a nice guy trying to do the right thing," Jolie said.

"It sounds like it was more than that to me," Kellen said.

Jolie set down her wineglass. The room was spinning. "I don't know," she muttered. "He wasn't exactly open to the idea of showing his affection."

"So?" Kellen said. "It sounded like he had a lot of shit going on."

Jolie couldn't talk about it anymore. "It doesn't matter. Our lives are just too different. We both have our own messes to clean up. It wasn't meant to be."

"Do you have a picture of him?" Nora asked, bright-eyed.

Jolie shook her head. "No, he refused to let me take his picture, probably because he didn't want me to use it against him as evidence."

Nora pouted. "Is he on Facebook?"

"No, I've already tried looking him up. He's nowhere on social media. The guy carries a *flip phone*."

Both Nora's and Kellen's mouths formed little Os. "Holy cow. That's unusual," Nora said.

"No kidding," Jolie said. "I do have a picture of my little friend Buddy though." Jolie pulled out her phone and scrolled to the picture. "He saved our lives."

"Oh my gosh, he's so cute! That scar! What happened?" Nora said, cupping her mouth.

"I'm not sure."

"Poor guy," Kellen said, looking at Jolie's phone screen.

Jolie tilted her head drunkenly, staring at the picture. "If it wasn't for this furry little creature, we would have never found help." He really was magnificent.

"I have an idea," Jolie said.

"More wine?" Nora asked.

"Yes! And I'm going to post this little guy on Instagram and see if I can drive any traffic to the ARS—see if I can help them out even if it's just a little bit."

"That's an amazing idea!" Nora leaped off the couch. "Both the wine idea and your thing... about helping the monkeys."

"The wine was your idea," Jolie reminded her.

"Exactly!"

Kai stood in his office, his hands perched on his hips. The boxes of cocaine were still there, stacked three rows deep, with nowhere to go.

"It's time we get rid of this stuff," Kai said. He wiped the sweat from his forehead with the back of his hand. The office had become muggy now that they never left the garage door open. Air wasn't circulating through the building as it once did, and Kai was tired of sweating in the office.

"If someone was looking for it, you'd think they would have tracked it down by now," Noah said, standing beside him.

"Did the crew go home for the day?"

"Yeah, they're gone. Everyone's snickering about Raffi being gone though."

"I can't deal with that right now," Kai said. "I'm doing my best. You or I can't run the business without Raff."

"Let me help more," Noah said.

"I might take you up on that while I get this place ready to sell. Let's deal with the drugs first, and we can worry about the rest later."

Kai counted the boxes. Twenty-four. He didn't want to put Noah at risk, but getting rid of them would go a heck of a lot faster with his brother. "So where do we dump it?"

"Can't we just take it to the police?" Noah said.

"You mean dump it on their front porch like some unwanted baby?"

"Yeah."

"That won't work. They've got all kinds of cameras at the station. We'll have to dump it somewhere more discreet. Somewhere it won't look odd to have a bunch of boxes lying around." Kai rubbed his cleanly shaved chin while he listed the places that came to mind. "We could dump it behind a grocery store or one of the markets."

Noah mimicked Kai, rubbing his baby-smooth chin. The kid didn't have a lick of stubble to rub against, which meant he was probably mocking him.

"There would be cameras around the markets too. And people."

"How about the docks?" Kai said, shoving both hands in his jean pockets.

Noah, again mimicked Kai's gestures, a shit-eating grin on his face.

"Stop copying me," Kai said, popping him in the shoulder with a soft jab.

Noah pretended to give Kai an uppercut jab and then a hook, nudging Kai's shoulder with an elbow gently.

"Do you think they'll have video cameras in the parking lot at the docks?" Noah said.

"Probably."

"I don't know, it seems riskier than just leaving it here."

"We can't keep the stuff here. Sooner or later one of the staff will come sniffing around the office and find it."

"Yeah, but if we get caught dumping the cocaine, we're toast."

"We can put tape over the logo on the van and the license plate so they aren't on camera. We'll drop the loot and scram."

"Scram? What is this, the thirties?"

"Bite me," Kai said.

"Oh, you're right. It's the nineties."

"Screw you, Noah."

"I think you've just jumped a decade."

"Fuck off," Kai said, jabbing Noah in the arm.

"There it is! Welcome to the current century."

Kai shook his head at his younger brother. Without Raffi

around, Noah had nobody else to tease. Looks like Kai was the lucky one who got to take his place.

Setting his knuckles back on his hips, Kai continued to stare at the boxes, formulating his plan.

"You really think this'll work?" Noah asked. "If drug dealers actually show up looking for the stuff and find out we dumped it, you're not worried they're going to chop us up into tiny pieces?"

"I'm not sure we've got another option."

Noah mimicked Kai again, resting his knuckles on his hips. "I feel like Batman in this pose," he said.

"I'd say you look more like Robin to me."

"Oh really? You think *you're* Batman?" Noah said, jabbing Kai's arm.

"I never said that."

"But you implied it. You think you're Batman. I see how it is."

Kai grunted. "Shut up and help me put the cocaine back in the van."

"You sound like a bossy Batman with a drug problem."

"Go fuck yourself, Noah."

"There you go!" Noah said. A slow clap ensued. "You're so cute when you curse."

CHAPTER TWENTY-THREE

Jolie sat up in bed, huffing at the outfit hanging on the hook of the guest bedroom door. The button-down shirt mocked her. The pencil skirt sneered. The matching patent-leather flats were heel blisters just waiting to happen. The ensemble was a straitjacket, strapping her into her own failures.

Tomorrow was the first day of the end of her life. She decided she would still try to do the Instagram thing on the side, but it would be much harder without putting the proper amount of time and energy into it.

There was still no word from Kai, not that she was expecting it. He didn't have her phone number, but then again anyone could look her up and send her a direct message. Maybe not on his rusty phone, but a computer would suffice.

Even if he did get her money back, it didn't matter anymore. She had already committed to working for her father's company as a merchandising assistant, whatever that meant. She would soon find out. It was time to finally start acting like an adult.

She couldn't be trusted with large sums of money anyway. It just took one set of sad, puppy dog eyes and she'd give it all away in a heartbeat.

She was a sucker, and always would be.

An entry-level job at thirty-two was the swift kick she needed to grow up. She'd stay with Nora for a few more weeks before she could move into a place outside the city that she could afford. Somewhere practical. Somewhere Kai would approve of if he were there.

Not that she needed Kai's approval…

It was futile to even think of him. He was out of her life now, no matter how much it hurt.

Jolie sunk deeper in bed, wallowing in self-pity.

She needed to think about something else. Anything other than the man who still held her heart in Costa Rica.

Jolie opened her laptop to check in on her Instagram post of Buddy. His picture ended up being her most popular post ever. Her blog had never received so much traction. Link clicks were through the roof.

More people had commented about donating to the rescue center since she had looked at it that morning, which made Jolie's heart sing. She might not have been able to run a successful online business, but at least she was able to contribute to a greater cause than her own.

Jolie was wrapping up the final touches on another Instagram post when Nora poked her head through the bedroom door. "Kellen just ordered Burmese food. You want some?"

"That sounds great."

"Perfect," Nora said, closing the door. A second later her head popped back in. "Oh shoot, I just remembered you're on a vegan diet."

"I think I've given up on that one." Jolie sighed. "I can't afford to turn down a free meal these days."

Nora offered her a rueful smile.

"I'll be there in a minute," Jolie said.

"I asked for an extra pair of chopsticks," Nora said playfully. "For your chompers."

Jolie threw a pillow at the door, just missing her. Nora giggled all the way down the hallway.

"Biotch," Jolie said, resuming her work.

A green pop-up appeared on her computer screen. It was a call from a Costa Rican number. Jolie's heart fluttered in her chest. Could it be Kai? Could he have found her number?

Jolie's finger hovered over the touchpad of her laptop.

She accepted the call, and her body almost went up in flames. "Hello?"

"Hey, Jolie, it's Trip. From the ARS."

Jolie deflated like a great hot-air balloon that had just touched down.

"Hey, Trip. How's it going?"

"I hope you don't mind me calling out of the blue like this. I found your number online."

"No, not at all. How are you?"

"Amazing, actually. I wanted to talk about your post."

"Oh, the picture of Buddy?"

"Actually, his name is Jorge. When I saw the picture, I couldn't believe it. He was one of our rescues."

"No way!" Jolie slapped her knee.

"Yes way. I'll never forget that scar. He came in as a little baby."

"What a coincidence! That explains why he was so comfortable around people. It was like he expected me to give him food."

"That little stinker could eat," Trip said, chuckling.

"What happened to him? Do you know why he has that horrible scar?"

"He was one of our electrocution cases. Poor little guy was with his mother when it happened."

"Oh no."

"We think his mother died instantly, but she must have been carrying him."

Jolie shook her head. "I can't hear anymore. That's just awful."

"Yeah, sorry, but it had a happy ending. He survived, obviously, and he brought you to us."

"He is an incredible little creature," Jolie said, looking up at the framed picture of Buddy, or Jorge, whatever his name was.

"Anyway, that's not why I called."

"Oh?"

"That post seems to have driven more donations to our foundation than we know what to do with. The website has crashed two times."

Jolie's eyes grew wide, her hands flew up in the air. "Are you kidding? That's wonderful news! You know, except for the website crashing part."

"It's a good problem to have, don't get me wrong. We had to contract a tech guy to help us fix our website. The money has been flowing in."

"That's amazing."

"All thanks to you, Jolie. That post really made a difference."

"Oh, it was nothing." Jolie felt her face grow warm. "The animals deserve it. You deserve it too."

"About that." Trip's voice cracked. He cleared his throat. "It might be a silly thing to ask, but I'm going to do it anyway. We need more help in the marketing department. Well, actually, we need to revamp it entirely. Our marketing guy just retired. I thought since your post was so influential, you might want to consider interviewing for the job. We could set up a contract and flex the time based on how long you can stay down here."

"Oh" was all Jolie could muster. Work in Costa Rica? "I..."

"I'd just need you to fly back down for an interview. The board would want to meet you in person before we put in an actual offer. It doesn't pay much. But you'll have a free place to stay for a little while in one of our volunteer bunks."

"Wow." Running her own marketing department? For a company that was actually making a difference?

Trip continued, talking about the job, the culture, and what the people were like. He even mentioned he was super-flexible as a boss. "People just get things done on their time. I hope you don't like routine."

You've got to be kidding me. It was too good to be true. Jolie rubbed her sweaty palms on her knees. It was perfect, apart from the fact that she might have to give up her entire inheritance if her father didn't approve.

"Wow, I'm just stunned and flattered. Thank you."

"Think about it and let me know, okay? Let's talk soon."

Jolie clicked off the call, and the room fell silent except for the ringing in her ears.

It was the perfect job except for one thing. The one thing that had been dangling over her head this whole time.

Her inheritance. Her father wouldn't go for it, not after she agreed to work for his company. She'd have to prove to him it was a responsible choice even if it didn't pay much.

Jolie lumbered to the kitchen where Nora and Kellen were casually sitting around their kitchen table. The warm smell of cooked chicken and beef made her queasy.

One plate with two pairs of chopsticks awaited.

"I just got the strangest call," Jolie said. "Trip, the guy from ARS in Costa Rica, just offered to interview me for a job."

"No way!" Nora said with a mouthful of food.

"I can't go through with it, right? I'll lose my inheritance if I don't abide by my dad's contract."

"What do they want you to do?" Nora asked.

"They want me to revamp their marketing department."

"Oh my God, Jolie. What are you waiting for?" Nora said.

"I'd be walking away from millions of dollars."

"What good is an inheritance if you're not happy?" Kellen said. "You'd just be sitting around, waiting for your father to die."

Jolie slumped into her chair and promptly grabbed the extra pair of chopsticks. She yanked the two sticks apart, a satisfying crack of splitting wood in her hands.

"I'm surprised you guys are so encouraging of this idea. I'd be thousands of miles away from here and too poor to fly back to see you."

"Yes, but then we'd have an excuse to visit Costa Rica! I could come down and do more research for my next book."

Jolie chewed the end of the chopstick in her mouth. "Nonprofits aren't known for paying their employees well. I'm not sure I could survive. I failed as a blogger. I failed as a vegan. How could I possibly do this?"

In between the Styrofoam boxes of Burmese food was a bowl of bananas and apples. Nora grabbed a Red Delicious and placed it on Jolie's plate.

"That's just the thing. You survived," Nora said firmly. "You survived without money. You can do this."

Jolie stared at the apple on her plate.

She had to make a choice: eat the apple or eat the Burmese food.

Duchess appeared from under the table, her big goopy eyes looking up at Jolie.

"I can't leave my babies," Jolie said, rubbing Duchess's chin.

"We can watch them for you," Nora said. "I've loved having them here. Kellen?" Nora looked up through her lashes at her husband.

"If Nora wants the zoo, she can have the zoo," Kellen said.

"I don't know, guys," Jolie said. "Walking away from my pets, my inheritance, my life here? It's just a lot to sacrifice for a job."

"It's not just a job. It's your life." Nora took a sip of her wine. "It's the type of work you've been waiting for. Think of all the help you would be giving to those animals down there."

Jolie tapped her unchewed chopsticks on her plate. "I'll talk to my dad before I decide anything. He's expecting me in the office tomorrow. Maybe I can reason with him." Jolie laughed, knowing there was no way she could actually reason with her father.

Kellen held up the to-go box of noodles, and Jolie stared at it blankly.

"I'm sorry. I'm not hungry anymore. This decision is making me sick to my stomach." She stood up from the table, grabbing a pair of chopsticks to take with her.

"Just go easy on those chopsticks," Nora said. "They didn't do anything to you."

Kai and Noah arrived at the harbor, a giant concrete slab of buildings posted where the land dips into the silvery ocean. A giant cruise ship had arrived earlier that day. After some research, Kai had learned that it wouldn't be leaving for two days, and a plan was born.

Kai stepped out of the van to look around. A few cars were parked along the street but not a person in sight. The ocean moaned just beyond the warehouse they parked in front of and echoed against the metal sliding doors. If they hurried, they could drop off the boxes right here and not be seen.

Kai waved his hand, giving Noah the signal to get out.

"This is as good a place as any. Shipments are always coming and going from these warehouses. If anyone sees us, nobody will bat an eye," Kai said, more confidently than he felt. "Let's hurry."

Kai reached for a box, gripping it with his arms. Lifting it out of the van triggered the ache in his rib. He had been meaning to go to the doctor, but who had time for doctor visits when there was a business to run and cocaine to be dumped anonymously?

One by one, boxes were placed on the cement. The throbbing in Kai's side had turned into a sharp, staggering pain. Kai winced as he lifted up the next box.

"Are you okay?" Noah asked.

"I'm fine," Kai lied. "I may have cracked a rib while I was in the jungle."

"Dude. You need to get that checked out."

"*Dude.* I know, and I will. I just want to get this"—Kai flinched as he set the box down—"over with."

"Take a break. I can get the rest."

Ignoring his brother, Kai reached for the next box, only this time the pain was too excruciating to lift. He tried again, and it felt like his rib was about to snap in two.

Noah nudged past him. "Just relax for a second. I've got this." He picked up the next box as if it were nothing and waddled over to their stack.

There were still a dozen boxes to go, and they needed to get out of there as soon as possible. Kai looked over his shoulder to see if anyone was coming, but there wasn't a soul in sight.

"You know, you haven't talked much about what happened in the jungle," Noah said. "What ever happened to that hot chick?"

"She went back to San Francisco, as far as I know. And what's there to tell? We got lost in the jungle. I mean the *rainforest* that didn't have enough rain," Kai said snidely. "We came across a couple of wild animals on the way and then eventually got picked up by a group of high schoolers."

"I think there's more to you and Jolie than you're letting on."

"Nah," Kai said, wishing that were the case. The truth was she had left an imprint on his heart, and there wasn't a minute that went by where he wasn't thinking about her, wishing he hadn't messed things up.

"You've been brooding." Noah grunted as he lifted the next box.

Kai scoffed. "I have not."

"Yes, you have."

"Have not."

"Have."

"Have not."

"Have so."

"Stop it," Kai said. "I have not been brooding. Jolie is gone, and I don't want to talk about it."

"That sounds like something a brooding man would say."

Kai shoved Noah as he hobbled by with a box, almost tipping him over.

"She must have really gotten under your skin," Noah said, regaining his balance. He set the box on the ground and shot right back up.

He was right of course.

"Well it doesn't matter now, does it?" Kai said, attempting to lift another box. The shooting pain paralyzed him from making any progress. "I still need to give her back her money."

"Why haven't you sent it to her yet?"

"I don't know," Kai said, running his hands through his hair. "I think I was just waiting for the right moment, whenever that will be. I guess a part of me feels like when I give her the money, it's officially over—whatever it was."

"I *knew* it," Noah said. "I knew something had to be going on between you two. I couldn't make sense why she would loan us the money after all we put her through."

"Yeah, well. She's gone now, and we didn't really end on great terms."

"You can always win her back. You just have to turn on a little bit of that Greene charm somewhere underneath the stick-in-the-mud thing you have going on right now," Noah said with a grin.

Turning on the charm was easy for Noah. It came naturally. Like a God-given gift.

"Can't say I blame you for falling for her. She was hot."

"She's beautiful, all right. I'm sure every warm-blooded man on this planet would think so, but that's not what makes her… her."

Noah arched a brow, encouraging him to go on.

"I don't know." Kai paused. "I'm worried that if I start talking about her, I won't be able to shut up."

"Aw," Noah cooed. "That's so romantic."

"Shut up," Kai said. "Anything would sound romantic compared to the ladies you've been courting."

Noah laughed. "You are so old-fashioned. People don't court anymore," Noah said. "They're either in a texting relationship or not in a texting relationship."

"Then I guess I'm out of luck because my phone doesn't have text."

Noah shook his head. "You really need to update that thing, man. For the sake of you and your hot chick."

"That hot chick has a name," Kai said sternly. "It's Jolie Boulard."

"Easy. Easy. We're just talkin' here. No need to get all medieval on me."

Suddenly Kai got the feeling that they weren't alone. He turned his head to see if anyone was around, but nothing was there but the triangle glow of streetlamps on pavement.

"Hold still," Kai whispered. He heard something.

Noah froze in midgrip, turning his ear toward the faint echo of thumping footprints.

"Someone's here," Kai whispered. There were still two boxes left in the van. They needed to get out of there before they were seen. Kai lunged toward the van, attempting to pick up the last box again.

Fighting through the pain, he hoisted it up, but as he pivoted on his heel, he saw the figure underneath a streetlamp, walking their way.

A flashlight shone in Kai's eyes, and the next thing he knew, he had dropped the box on his feet, the weight of the cocaine crunching his toes. He grunted in pain.

"Who's there?" the voice called in Spanish.

Kai looked at Noah and then back at the man with the flashlight. A stocky old man in a security uniform charged forward with a glowing cell phone in his hand.

CHAPTER TWENTY-FOUR

Jolie stood in front of her father's office, staring at the door. Her blouse made her skin itch.

"He won't bite," Cindy said from behind the desk. "Just go on in. He'll be done with his call shortly."

Jolie exhaled. "Thanks, Cindy." She knocked twice, then entered.

Her father had white earbuds in his ears. He wore a cashmere sweater over a collared shirt and jingled his car keys in his pocket as he paced the office and barked orders on the phone. When he saw her, he gestured to the black leather chairs.

The office was sterile, cold and hard, adorned with silver finishings and dark wood. Even the potted plants were sharp and arrogant.

Clicking off his call, her father spread his arms out wide. "You made it."

Was that an invitation for a hug? Jolie unsteadily walked toward her father and let his arms wrap around her in an unfamiliar embrace. He smelled like the Hugo Boss cologne she bought him for his birthday a few years back.

"I trust Cindy set you up with the paperwork already?"

"I haven't signed anything yet. I wanted to talk to you first."

"What's wrong?" Her father's brow furrowed. He sat down in one of the black leather chairs.

Jolie sat across from him, squeezing her thighs together. Her slip had bunched up underneath her skirt, and she strained to pull the hem down toward her knees.

"I was offered an interview last night at a nonprofit organization. One that saves animals. I'd be running my own marketing department. It's a dream job really, even though I'd be working for someone else."

Her father crossed his arms and folded his leg over his knee. His silence was punishing in his own special way, but Jolie pressed on.

"Since it is a stable job, I was wondering if that would suffice to maintain our arrangement."

Her father shifted in his chair, although his facial expression didn't change. His eyes bore right through her as he let an uncomfortable amount of time pass between them.

"The contract states that if you can't turn your business around with the money I gave you, you would work *here*. And I don't even want to think about how you managed to waste one hundred thousand in less than a few weeks. It's sickening. You have a lot to learn about business. No better a place to learn than in the safety of your own family's company."

"The whole point of you setting up that contract was to help me secure a steady income on my own, right? I've found a way to do that."

"Where's the job?"

Jolie looked down at her hands. "It's in Costa Rica."

"That's ridiculous, Jolie. You can't move down there. It's too far and too dangerous."

If only he knew how dangerous it *could* be. Although her situation had been an extraordinary circumstance. Not many people could say they've been held hostage and lost in the jungle during their trip to the Caribbean.

"I would just be a flight away, and it'd only be for a few years."

"Out of the question," her father snapped. "You're not backing out of our deal for some part-time job on the beach so you can prance around like a bimbo in a bikini. You'll just be begging me for money when your job is up. I won't allow it."

"I'll be working for a good cause."

"You're supposed to be working for this company."

"I don't want to do that. I told you before. I wouldn't be happy working here."

"We can't keep running around in circles like this, you chasing your dreams and me cleaning up your messes. I'm tired of pissing my money away on your failed attempts at living on your own. It's time you need to earn your keep. On my terms."

"But Dad—"

"End of discussion. If you ever want to see a penny of your inheritance, then you'll march over to Cindy's desk and fill out the paperwork like a big girl."

She was cornered. Trapped. Her hands balled into fists on her lap. There was no reasoning with this man, this *tyrant*.

Her father's face softened. "I'm sorry, but this is for your own good. One day you'll understand and thank me."

Jolie rose to her feet, ignoring the sharp pain in her heel. She couldn't look her father in the eye for fear of losing her nerve. She had tried to prepare for this moment, knowing full well that her father would not budge, but it was much harder than she imagined.

Her father was worth millions. *Millions* of dollars. Money

that she could own one day if she followed her daddy's wishes.

She could travel anywhere or do anything with that kind of money. She could start up multiple businesses, including a nonprofit animal rescue agency of her own.

But taking the job at Boulard Jewelers and following her father's rules was like strapping an electric collar around her neck.

Slipping off her patent shoes, she let her bare feet touch the cold, concrete floor. Her heels could breathe, and so could she.

"Jolie, what are you doing? Put your shoes back on," her father said.

Jolie ignored him, padding her bare feet across his office until she reached the door.

"You're staying," he bellowed from the chair.

Jolie looked over her shoulder and stared directly into his eyes. "I can't stay and live by your rules. I'm going to Costa Rica."

"Don't be a fool, Jolie." He stood up.

"I'm sorry," she said and stormed out of his office, her father following her.

Cindy looked up from her desk, and her eyes grew wide as father and daughter approached her. "Is everything okay?"

"Cindy, I'm sorry, but I won't be working here after all."

"Don't listen to her," her father boomed over Jolie's shoulders. "Hand her the paperwork. She *will* fill it out."

Cindy's eyebrows shot up in surprise, darting between the two snarling Boulards.

She grabbed a manila folder and held it up for Jolie. Of course she would listen to her father first; she was his employee after all.

"Sign the paperwork. Make the right choice," her father snarled.

Jolie stared at the file in front of her. She grabbed it only because Cindy's arm looked like it might fall off her fragile sixty-year-old body. Jolie couldn't sign her life away like this. No amount of money was worth the agony of living under her father's rules.

A Post-it note stuck to the manila folder caught Jolie's eye. The word HAIKU SWIM was scrawled next to a phone number. Jolie stared at the sticky note as if it held the answers to all her questions.

"Why is one of my brand partners' names on this note?" Jolie peeled it off, showing it to Cindy.

Cindy's mouth dropped open, then shut again.

Underneath the sticky note was another one that said FRIZZANI, the other brand that had dropped Jolie that year.

Jolie sucked in a breath. "Did you have something to do with me losing my contracts?"

Cindy snapped her lips shut and shook her head violently, her eyes drifting to Jolie's father.

Jolie turned to face her father, who was breathing heavily. His face and neck had reddened.

"Dad? What did you do?"

Her father's throat bobbed up and down with a hard swallow.

"Are you the reason the brands backed out?" Jolie asked as everything clicked into place. This made so much more sense than them backing out on their own. She knew her numbers had been solid. There had been no logical reason why companies were pulling out from their contracts—unless someone had interfered. Someone who was willing to do anything to force Jolie to settle down.

"Jolie," he said, "it was for your own good. I was protecting you from continuing down this destructive path you were on."

"You were the reason my business failed? *You?*"

Tears pricked the back of Jolie's eyes, but she fought against them. Her lips were shaking as she held back her sob.

Of all the truly dark and scary things Jolie had seen in the past week, this was by far the worst. The lowest of all lows. Her own father's betrayal.

"How could you?" Jolie tossed the manila folder to Cindy. "I'm done here," Jolie said, rushing toward the elevator. Her toes pressed against the cold metal of the doorframe.

"Jolie, wait." Her father ran after her, catching the elevator door before it shut. "Don't leave."

"How dare you interfere with my life," Jolie growled. "You sabotaged me. You wanted me to fail so you could manipulate my every move. I've had enough. You don't own me. If I ever find out you've stuck your neck in my business again, I'm going to press charges."

"But—"

"Goodbye," Jolie said, letting the elevator doors shut between them.

"What are you doing there?" the security guard said in Spanish. The flashlight shone in Kai's eyes as the man charged toward them.

Kai stepped forward. "*Buenos noches*," Kai said, slapping on a large grin. "A fine evening tonight, isn't it?" Kai was surprised his own voice didn't shake as he was trembling inside.

The security guard slowed, moving the flashlight down, out of Kai's eyes. Bright yellow spots meandered across Kai's vision like big blobby amoebas. He tried blinking them away to get a better look at the security guard but kept the smile on his face regardless.

Just act casual.

"Who are you?" the security guard asked.

"I'm Kai Greene, and this is my brother Noah. He's helping me with this load here."

Kai looked at the boxes and then back up at Noah. Noah gave him a nod of understanding as he walked over to the stacks.

They had a plan if they had been seen by a passerby: Stuff the boxes back in the van and abort the mission. What Kai didn't know was if it would work. He continued with his lie.

"I was picking up these leftover boxes of coffee from the cruise ship."

"At one o'clock in the morning?" the old man said.

Kai chuckled nervously, running his hand through his hair. As part of their plan, they had an excuse for everything, except an excuse for the *time*. How could he have made such an oversight?

Why the hell would anyone be picking up a delivery in the middle of the night? Kai wiped his clammy hands on his shirt while he tried coming up with an explanation.

"Well… you see… it was meant to be picked up earlier…" Kai stalled, catching Noah's gaze for help.

"Kai hurt his back," Noah chimed in. "And he needed help. I couldn't get here until after I was done… studying."

Kai felt his body relax, relieved Noah could think on his toes better than Kai could. Kai was never good at lying, especially on the spot. He looked back at the security guard to see if he was buying it, but the man didn't back down. The jury must still be out.

The security guard shined his light on Noah's face, who squinted under the harsh glare, and then flashed it back at Kai.

Kai held up his arm to shield his eyes but kept the smile on his face. He caught the breeze under his sweaty armpits and waited for the verdict.

If the guard asked to see what was in the boxes, they'd have to shift to plan B: explain the whole story and pray he believed them. It was a pathetic plan but a reasonable one nevertheless.

Thank God Raffi wasn't there with them, or their whole plan would have blown up in their faces. Raffi would have done something rash like knock out the guard and hightail it out of there.

"Are you William Greene's boys by chance?" the man said.

Kai's mouth fell open. The last thing Kai expected was to hear his father's name slip from the security guard's mouth. "Yes. Did you know our father?"

"I used to see Willy over at Titto's bar from time to time. That man can drink."

Willy? Since when did their father go by Willy? Pop probably hated the nickname, but when it came to drinking, he might have been in a state of mind to let it go. Any other time, Pop would insist on being called William.

"How's the old bastard doing? I haven't seen him in a long time. Your mother must have tightened the reins."

Kai swallowed back the sorrow that bubbled up his throat. He hated to deliver the news of his father's death even if it would soften the guard up from calling the police.

"I'm sorry to tell you, but our father passed away a few weeks ago," Kai said. "I didn't know he was a regular at Titto's. We would have told the bartender."

The security guard frowned, turning off his flashlight. Darkness settled between the men as the air stilled.

"My condolences," the man said. "I'm really sorry to hear. I knew Willy wasn't in great health, but I didn't think..."

"It's okay. He didn't talk much about his health with people, but it had been failing him for quite a while."

"He was a good man."

The words echoed in Kai's head, bringing him back to the

funeral on that hot day. There were lots of people there. His father had made friends wherever he went. Of course he would make a buddy or two at the local bar. It was something he would do. And it might have just saved Kai and Noah from heading to jail.

"I'm Mauro," he said, holding out his hand.

"Nice to meet you, Mauro," Kai said, accepting the handshake.

"It's a big loss, losing your father. I'm going to miss seeing him around."

Kai nodded his head, looking down at his shoes. His toes still throbbed from dropping the box on them earlier. Perhaps it was a proper punishment for leveraging his father's own death to get out of a pickle. It wasn't intentional of course, but Kai still felt guilty.

"Your father talked a lot about you boys. I remember him saying how proud he was of all three of you."

And just like that, an extra dish of guilt was served.

"You must be the youngest," Mauro said with a friendly smile, reaching his hand out to shake Noah's.

"Sure am, sir," Noah said.

"I hear you've got a way with the ladies," Mauro said.

Noah smiled, looking away. "Pop told you that?"

Mauro nodded and looked back at Kai. "Are you the oldest or the middle son?"

"I'm the middle," Kai said. "Not so good with the ladies."

"Ah yes, the responsible one. Your father mentioned you took a good job in San José." He scanned the boxes. "I presume you're here to help out with Willy's business."

Kai offered a curt nod in response, although it wasn't too far from the truth. He had been trying to save Pop's business all along. He just happened to be there, in that moment, for a slightly different reason.

"Do you need a hand with putting these boxes in the van?" Mauro asked.

Kai's eyes bugged out. "Oh no. Thank you though. Noah's got this. He'll be quick."

"No, I insist. These night shifts can be so boring, and I could use a little exercise."

Kai and Noah exchanged nervous glances as Mauro shuffled toward the boxes.

"These boxes are heavier than they look. I insist that you let Noah handle it," Kai said. "I'm usually in pretty good shape, but—"

"Nonsense," Mauro said. "A little elbow grease is good for the soul." Mauro stretched his sixty-some-odd-year-old body, crouching down to pick up a box of cocaine. He teetered for a second, and both Kai and Noah darted to catch him from falling over. When he righted himself, he huffed through a smile and staggered to the van until the box thumped against the van bed.

So this is happening.

"You really don't have to help," Kai said, watching the security guard hoist another box of cocaine.

"I'm happy to. It's the least I can do for Willy and his boys." Mauro's cheeks reddened as he wobbled his way to the van. "That is some tightly packed coffee you have in here."

Kai's eyebrows shot up as he caught Noah's gaze. Noah shrugged before bending down to pick up another box. One by one, the boxes went back into the van while Mauro regaled them with stories of their father.

Kai stood by nervously as he watched the cocaine get packed away, back in the damned van.

CHAPTER TWENTY-FIVE

Jolie fumbled through her tote bag, her cell phone and passport in one hand while she frantically searched for her boarding pass with the other. She just had it a moment ago. Had she dropped it somewhere between the ticket console and the security line?

Normally Jolie would send her boarding pass to her phone, but she had been out of sorts, fretting over her interview, completely forgetting to check in before she arrived at the airport.

Everything was happening so fast. The day she walked out of her father's office, Trip had booked her flight for the next day. She was on her way back to Costa Rica before she had a chance to finish her laundry from her last trip. When Jolie asked why the rush, Trip mentioned there was a strong contender for the position she was interviewing for.

She needed to impress the board, with little time to prepare. Her head was spinning.

There was only one person left in line in front of her. Jolie stuffed her hand in a side pocket of her tote bag. When she felt the edges of her ticket, she yanked it out just as the TSA agent ushered her forward.

"Got it." Jolie beamed, handing over her documents.

The agent scanned her ticket, circling the date and name with a pink highlighter before giving it back to her.

"Next," he drawled.

Jolie let out a sigh of relief. She made it.

Her phone buzzed in her hand, and her mom's name flashed across the screen.

Not a good time, Mom. Jolie hit ignore.

Placing her boarding ticket back in her side pocket, she made a mental note this time where it was.

She watched as her phone flashed on again before disappearing through the scanner.

What could her mom possibly need so badly that it deserved a second ring? Could she be in *real* trouble?

Jolie shook off the thought, taking a deep breath before she walked up to the body scanner.

It was probably a waxing emergency. Maybe a chipped nail. Or a new gadget she saw on QVC that she had to have.

Not this time, Mom.

Jolie held her arms up as the scanner did its thing.

But what if something *was* wrong? Maybe she was in the hospital. She could have gotten in an accident. Her mom was never a good driver.

As soon as the airline security let her pass, she darted for her bin. Before she could get her hoodie back on, she was dialing her mother back.

"Mom? Is everything okay?"

"What is this I'm hearing about you moving to Costa Rica?"

"Oh, so you are okay." Jolie balanced her phone between her ear and shoulder while she stuffed her laptop in her tote bag. "Nothing is official yet. I'm just going to an interview. How did you hear about it?"

Her mother fell silent.

"Hello? Mom? Did I lose you?" Jolie checked her phone screen.

"I just don't know how you're going to make that work out there all by yourself. Won't you get lonely?"

"It'll be fine," Jolie said. "I don't even know if I got the job yet. Seriously, how did you find out?"

Jolie scanned her memory for how it would have slipped. She only made the decision a couple of days ago, and she'd only told Nora and Kellen, and they wouldn't have spoken to her mom.

"I heard it from your dad," her mother said.

"Whoa. You talked to Dad?" Jolie stopped in her tracks. People from behind her swarmed on either side as they pushed their way down the airport corridor.

"He called to tell me you had made the decision to walk away from your inheritance. This whole Costa Rica thing just doesn't seem like a practical decision. I think you should reconsider."

"I'm still stuck on the fact that Dad called you. What the hell?"

"Oh, don't get your panties in a twist. He said it was an emergency. We care about you, and we both think you're making a mistake."

Jolie scoffed. "That's rich, coming from you. I would think if anyone who could understand, it would be you."

"I know your father can be unbearable and controlling. I just don't want you to make the same mistakes as me."

"You mean walking out on Dad and me?" Jolie snapped. She immediately regretted it as soon as it left her mouth.

"You were the one who left *me*," her mother said. "You

could have come with me, but you chose to stay with your dad, remember? You abandoned me."

Jolie pressed her lips firmly together. It was not an argument she wanted to get into right now in the middle of the San Francisco airport while she was now running toward concourse C to catch her plane. It was a good thing her leg felt better, or she would have never made it.

"Mom, I can't talk right now," Jolie said.

"Wait. I just want you to know the amount of regret I've carried ever since I left. It was hard living life without the things I used to have, you know? I don't want you to make the same mistake."

Jolie pinched her eyebrows together at her mother's admission, regretting the *things* she used to have, not the life she could have had with her teenage daughter.

"Life is not about the things, Mom. It's about the experiences. It's about making an impact on people's lives."

"You sound like a millennial."

Jolie held her tongue from calling her mom a superficial brat. "I'm sick of the guilt trips. I felt bad for not coming with you when I was a teenager, so I gave you money. But I can't do that anymore. I have nothing to give. I'm broke."

"Doesn't that bother you? To be out of money? Think about what you would have waiting for you one day. You'll be able to do whatever you want. Whenever you want."

"Why would I spend a lifetime waiting to be happy when I have found something that could make me happy now?"

"Jolie, I'm telling you right now, that's shortsighted thinking. You will regret this decision one day. And your father won't be there to catch you when you fall," her mother said.

"Why can't my parents trust that I'm going to be fine? I can live on my own. I can survive without this codependent bullshit."

Jolie dodged a toddler that ran across the hallway, nearly

tripping her over. She smiled at the apologetic mother who had been hovering close behind.

"I know that, but—"

"But what? You're just upset that I don't have the money to give you anymore. My decision affects *you*. That's why you're calling. You couldn't care less if I were in Costa Rica or the middle of Russia."

"That's not true. Your father and I both just want you close."

"Did Dad tell you what he did to me? He interfered with my business. He somehow convinced my brands to pull out. I don't want to be anywhere near him."

"Your father feels really bad about that," her mother said. "He's willing to give you the money you could have made if you turn back now and work for him."

Jolie stared at the phone in disbelief. Was her mother really acting as the spokesperson for her father? What planet was Jolie on? "This doesn't make any sense to me. I don't understand why you're speaking on his behalf unless… Oh God, Mom. What did he offer you?"

"What?" Her mother's voice cracked.

"What did he offer you? To get me back?"

"Jolie…" Her mother's voice trailed off, confirming Jolie's worst fear. Her parents were in collusion together.

"I knew it. You are both sick. You know that? Well, I'm done. I'm finished with this manipulative stunt you two are pulling. It's over."

"You are going to regret it if you walk away. I know you will. I'm only trying to do the right thing for you."

Jolie belted out a one-note laugh as she scurried up to the flight attendant. She was the last to board.

"I'll believe that when you and Dad both stop trying to control me with money. If I can survive an escape through the jungle with nothing but the shirt on my back, you can survive without your Botox and your self-tanners. Stop asking me for anything, and tell Dad he can keep his money and shove it."

The flight attendant stared at Jolie with wide eyes, her hand frozen in midair, waiting to accept the boarding ticket that Jolie hadn't retrieved from her bag yet.

"Sorry, Mom. I have to go. I'm getting on the plane now."

"There's no turning back from this, Jolie," her mother snapped.

"I know." Jolie clicked off the phone. Perhaps she had been too harsh with her mother, but there was no time to dwell on that now. She pulled out the ticket and handed it to the lady before hurrying down the Jetway.

Now that she'd basically given the middle finger to both her parents, she *had* to get this job to prove them wrong. The last thing she could stomach was coming home with her tail between her legs, without the job of her dreams.

She needed to think of something big and flashy to impress the board, and she only had a seven-hour flight to figure it out.

CHAPTER TWENTY-SIX

Kai put his fork down, his stomach full. His mother looked happy for the first time since their father died. Noah hovered over his third plate of pasta, wiping his mouth with a napkin between spaghetti slurps.

Ma rambled on about politics, acting as if she hadn't just used her sex tape as blackmail against Marco Venega. Kai couldn't focus on anything, let alone his mother's musings over the judicial system.

Kai tuned it all out, visualizing the night ahead. They were going to attempt a drop-off again, only this time they would do it in the jungle. Tonight was the night they would get rid of the cocaine, once and for all.

A million nerve endings were tingling all over his body. They'd been lucky before. Getting caught by their father's friend was like a divine intervention, but they wouldn't be so lucky again.

Kai's leg jittered under the dinner table. It would be only a matter of time that he would be free from the obstacle that was preventing him from reaching out to Jolie. He had been torn between keeping his distance from her and flying out to

San Francisco to see her in person. He did have her money, after all, and soon this would all be over. She could get her money back, and they could try to be together—safely.

"What's wrong with you?" Ma asked. "You look like a dog who lost his bone."

"He's been like this for days," Noah said with a gurgling sound.

"Don't talk with food in your mouth!" Ma swatted Noah's arm.

Noah swallowed the large mouthful of meatball. "Sorry, Ma."

"It's nothing," Kai said, ignoring the pesky throb in his heart.

"It's a girl," Noah said with a mischievous grin.

"Who?" Ma perked up. Her spine straightened. "What girl? There's a girl?" She clasped her hands together. "I want to hear all about her. How did you meet her?" Ma's eyes twinkled.

Kai and Noah exchanged glances.

"There's no girl," Kai growled. "She's gone, so it doesn't matter."

"Oh, honey. What happened?" Ma asked.

He had messed up, letting Jolie slip through his fingertips like a fool, but Ma didn't need to know that. "That'll be a story for another time," Kai said, knowing he'd have to explain it without the whole kidnapping part.

"You're no fun," Ma grumbled, getting up from the kitchen table. "Although I don't know which is worse. You, who never tells me anything about your girlfriends, or your brother here, who flips through women like a deck of cards at a blackjack table."

Noah snickered into his food.

"One day I'd like to see my sweet Kai-baby settle down and get married."

Kai rolled his eyes. Not that again. She had been hounding him for years on the importance of taking a wife and having babies, extending the family line. "Why don't you ever say that about Raff or Noah? Why's the pressure all on me to get married?"

"Your older brother had his chance and blew it on a stripper, and now he's in jail. I think that ship has sailed. As for your little brother," she said, peering at Noah, "he's been planting his seed around enough. I'm sure I'll end up with a grandbaby at some point. What I want is a legitimate grandbaby." Ma turned on the faucet at the kitchen sink.

"Hey, I resent that," Noah said.

Kai stood up from the table. "We've got the dishes, Ma. Why don't you go relax and sit by the TV?"

Ma gave him a tired smile, patting his shoulder before lumbering her way toward the television.

Kai busied himself with a sticky pot. Eventually Noah joined him, swatting Kai with the kitchen towel before helping him dry the dishes.

"Are you ready for tonight?" Kai said, looking over his shoulder toward Ma. She had propped her feet up on the recliner where their father used to sit.

"Yeah, I'm ready. You ready?" Noah said.

"I guess so."

"Think someone is still out there looking for this stuff?"

Kai shook his head. "It's been a couple of weeks now. We've got to be in the clear, right? Unless Raffi opens his big fat mouth in jail."

"He won't," Noah said, putting the last dish in the cupboard.

Kai dried his hands. "All right, let's go."

"Thanks again for dinner, Ma," Kai said, giving her a kiss on the forehead.

"Holy shit," Noah said, gaping on the television.

"Language!"

"Sorry, Ma. Kai, check it out. It's that chick." He pointed to the screen.

"What chick?" Kai asked, whipping his head toward the TV.

"Your girl! Look!"

Kai squinted his eyes, taking a few steps forward. Jolie's smiling face was plastered in the corner.

White text stating "Thousands of colóns with just one post" was scrolling at the bottom of the video.

Kai felt his knees buckle as he watched the video image of Jolie take over the entire television screen. There was a brief flush in her face before she dazzled the camera with her smile.

It was her.

"Hello, and welcome to KGTB news. I am Nina Romero. Tonight's story is about a woman named Jolie Boulard from San Francisco. Less than a week ago, Jolie came home from a harrowing adventure where she and a friend got lost in the jungle just outside of Limón. While she was there, she discovered a heartbreaking truth for some of the animals in the wild. Raul has the details."

The screen cut to a young man with a microphone to his mouth. "Thanks, Nina. With me is Trip Rojas, one of the cofounders of the Animal Rescue Sanctuary, and the woman of the hour, Jolie Boulard," the news guy said in Spanish. He turned toward Jolie and switched to English.

"Jolie, tell us about what you saw in the jungle and what you did about it."

The camera shifted to the right, and Jolie's beautiful eyes pierced the screen. Her hair was pulled back into a simple ponytail, and she was wearing the same red T-shirt as Trip, with the bright white ARS logo in the center.

Kai's body tensed. What was Trip doing there? His hands balled into fists.

Jolie's smile glowed through the camera, and she sweetly put a loose strand of her hair behind her ear.

"A friend and I were hiking through the rainforest and got lost. After two days, we weren't sure if we were going to survive, but then I met this little monkey. I called him Buddy. He had these horrible scars along the side of his head and down his neck."

The Spanish translation scrolled across the bottom of the screen with a ten-second delay.

God, she looked beautiful. More gorgeous than ever. His heart clenched at the sight. He would have done anything to touch her.

"It turned out Buddy—whose name is actually Jorge—was a victim of electrocution and had been rescued by the ARS and brought back to health a while back."

A picture of Buddy was flashed across the television screen.

"Buddy followed us through the forest for miles, hooting and hollering at us. It was like he wanted us to follow him, so we did. That's when he brought us to the very same rescue group that saved his life as a baby."

"Wow, what a story," Raul said. "So you were rescued from the jungle, and then what happened?"

"Well." Jolie smiled at Trip. "I wanted to help the ARS, so I posted my story online, and the donations came flooding in."

Kai's spaghetti churned in his stomach at the sight of Trip's arm resting around Jolie's shoulders.

"What in the *fuck?*" Kai said.

"Language!"

How on earth did Jolie end up with Trip? That sniveling weasel. Kai knew that twerp had eyes for Jolie. He knew it. This was horrible.

Jolie must have never gone back home. Which means—Kai's heart clenched—she was staying with Trip?

Ma turned the television volume up, and Trip's voice pierced Kai's ears. "Because of that single post, we now have the funding to insulate more transformers to prevent some of the thousands of animal electrocutions that happen every year."

"That is wonderful," Raul said. "And what do you plan to do next?"

"Well, I'd love to stay here and help at the ARS, but it depends on how things work out," Jolie said, waggling her eyebrows at Trip.

What the hell was *that* look?

Trip laughed. "Needless to say, I hope Jolie is able to stay here for a looong time." He gave the camera a wink.

Kai balled his fists, ready to punch the first thing in front of him.

The camera had cut to Trip, who continued to move his mouth, but Kai could only hear the beating of his own heart.

When Trip's hand rubbed the top of Jolie's shoulder, it unearthed a rage so far deep inside he didn't even recognize his own voice as he yelled at the TV. "Get your hands off her!"

"We wish you the best of luck, Jolie," Raul said in English. "There we have it, Nina," Raul said, switching back to Spanish. "A near-death disaster turned into a happy ending for both Jolie and the animals here in Costa Rica. For more information on the ARS and where to donate, you can go to www.ARS.foundation. Back to you."

The video clip switched to Nina, who exchanged idle pleasantries with Raul before she changed topics to an oil spill off Nicaragua's coast.

Kai gaped at the TV. "She's here," he heard himself mutter.

"She's got another dude's arm around her shoulders," Noah said. "You going to do anything about that?"

Kai shoved Noah's shoulder, setting him off-kilter.

"Is that the girl you've been hung up on all this time?" Ma said from her chair. "She is very pretty, but Noah's right. It looked like she was being claimed by that twerp in a head-band. You're not going to just sit around and let him steal her away, are you?"

Kai got to his feet. His arms hung heavy at his sides.

"What are you going to do?" Ma said.

"I'm too late," Kai said, his throat constricting. Jolie had been in Costa Rica this whole time, for days, with *him.*

"That's it? You're going to give up and let that tree-hugging hippie take the girl of your dreams?" Ma said.

Kai couldn't fathom the thought of Jolie and Trip together. It tugged at his unhealed ulcer. "No," Kai snarled.

"Then what are you waiting for?"

What *was* he waiting for? A life that was unattainably perfect? Did everything need to fall in place before he could take a chance on Jolie?

Who was kidding? He was in love with her, and she had another man's arm around her shoulder.

Kai darted toward the door.

"Wait, what about the van?" Noah called out, his arms in the air.

"It can wait. I'm going to get the girl."

"Wow. I have to say, I'm impressed," Trip said. "We haven't even officially hired you yet, and we've already had more press in the past week than we've had all year." He pulled his hair back into a man bun.

Jolie beamed. "Do you think I'll get the job?"

Trip pulled out his cell phone as if he were checking on the answer to her question. "It's not official, but I think it's safe to say you crushed your interview. The press was just the cherry on top. I texted a few peeps on the board to make sure they turn on their TV tonight."

Jolie was relieved to hear. She had thought of the idea to call the local news on the flight to Limón. She figured her social media following and her jungle escape might be a good enough hook to get a journalist interested. She was also sure to mention she was only there for one night so they would show up that day, although technically she extended her stay for another night so she could help out at the center.

Even if she didn't get the job, which Jolie couldn't bear the thought of, she wanted to volunteer with the animals and learn about their operations. If ARS didn't work out, there would be other animal rescues she could try to work for—although none as good of an opportunity as this one.

If it weren't for Kai, she wouldn't have even considered a job like this. But he had opened her eyes to the possibility that there could be something out there for her and her supposed *high-maintenance* tendencies.

ARS sounded like a dream. If she got the job, she would make her own hours. She would get to hire a small team of two to help her with graphic design and communications. And she would be surrounded by the cutest, most adorable animals on the planet.

"Are you hungry?" Trip said. "I know it's been a long day for you, but I'd love to take you out to dinner."

Jolie's eyes darted up in surprise. Why did that sound like a date? It wasn't a date, right? She was hungry, but she didn't want to give him the wrong idea, and she certainly didn't want to get her dream job by flirting with the future boss.

"You know, I'm kind of beat. I'm thinking I might call it a night," Jolie said. "But thanks for offering."

"How about a tour instead? We can ride in my Jeep. I'll take the top down and show you around town, convertible-style. You won't even need to get out of the car."

Jolie tugged her lips to the side. That did sound less date-y. And she had been wanting to explore a bit before she left. If she were going to live there, it would be good to get the lay of the land from a local.

"That sounds lovely, actually," Jolie said.

"Great!" Trip said, his chocolate eyes sparkling. "I'll get the Jeep ready, and then we can go."

Jolie smiled, stuffing her hands in her pockets. "I'll get my purse out of the lobby."

Trip scuttled off to his parked Jeep while Jolie made her way to the main building entrance. Tourists were scattered along the premises, brochures and flashlights in hand, cameras draped around their necks. *There must be a night tour happening now*, Jolie thought. She had learned about them in her research.

The sun had fallen behind the canopy of trees. The surrounding forest had a purple-gray hue, like an Instagram filter that could only be used in the Costa Rican rainforest. It brought her back to the nights she spent in the jungle with Kai. It had been less than a week, but it felt like ages ago. Her memories of Kai and his sweet, gentlemanly tendencies had started to blend with the pain she felt when he left.

He was *a good man though*. The type of guy that she would be lucky to end up with one day, assuming the feeling was mutual.

She wanted to believe him when he said that now wasn't the right time. He did carry quite a lot of baggage, and trouble seemed to follow him around as if it were hitched to his wagon. But no man in his right mind would have peeled himself off her in the throes of passion even if they only felt a fraction of what Jolie felt for Kai. Right?

The whole thing wasn't real.

The teasing. The laughing. The intense curiosity of her life with question after question after question.

He was a nice guy, but he couldn't have possibly felt the same way about her.

She had been attempting to mend her broken heart ever since, but it was impossible not to think of him—especially here. The bird calls. The monkey howls. The bugs, buzzing and swarming around her head. Everything here reminded her of him, as if he were there with her in that very moment.

Jolie stepped in the lobby. She had tucked her purse underneath the receptionist desk when the news crew had gotten there. Bianca, the twentysomething receptionist, retrieved it for her, a sweet smile planted on her face.

"How did the interview go?" Bianca asked.

"I think it went pretty well," Jolie said, crossing both her fingers. "We shall see. I think I'll know in the next couple of days."

Bianca leaned forward, cupping her hand over her mouth. "I'm rooting for you," she whispered, her thick Spanish accent coming through.

Jolie smiled. "Thanks. I hope I get it too."

Jolie peered out the glass lobby doors to find Trip had just pulled up in his red Jeep.

"I gotta run. But maybe I'll catch you tomorrow? I'm planning on volunteering."

"I can't wait," Bianca said.

Jolie gave Bianca a wave before dashing out the door. Trip was grinning from ear to ear, his hair had been pulled back in an even tighter man bun than before. "You ready for Costa Rica's finest tour?"

"I'm ready," Jolie said, hopping in the passenger seat.

Trip peeled out of the gravel roundabout. The Caribbean

breeze kissed her cheeks as they drove down the winding path.

It was time to make new memories in Costa Rica. Memories that could help her forget the man who'd kidnapped her heart.

CHAPTER TWENTY-SEVEN

Kai tore down the highway, the cool evening air whipping him in the face. When he spotted the ARS sign, he pulled a sharp right onto the gravel path, rocks kicking up into the back gate of his truck.

Sweat dripped from his forehead as he raced down the gravel road. He hoped he wasn't too late.

Kai craned his neck from side to side, searching for a parking space among the stream of parked cars until he found one nestled in between two tour buses.

A middle-aged couple had just gotten out of their car ahead of him, and they trotted down the gravel road, their fanny packs bouncing along. Kai quickened his pace after them until they caught up to a small tour group circled around a toucan perched on top of a glass case, their phones held high in the air as they gawked at the brightly colored bird.

A young Costa Rican girl in a red ARS shirt was explaining how the toucan isn't good at flying when Kai interrupted her.

"Excuse me. Do you know where I might find Jolie Boulard?"

"I don't know her. Try checking the main office building," she replied.

Kai thanked her and ducked away, continuing down the path.

What would Jolie think of him, showing up out of nowhere? Would she be happy? Mad? Or would she be preoccupied in Trip's limp arms?

He grunted and charged toward the front door.

The air-conditioning nipped at his skin as he stepped into what looked like a medical office. The desk was vacant, but the fluorescent lights were on.

"*Hola?*" Kai called out, peeking his head over the receptionist desk.

The computer screen was in sleep mode with the ARS logo bouncing from one edge of the monitor to the next. "Anyone here?" Kai pressed the small metal bell on the desk.

Ding.

Ding.

Ding. Ding. Ding. Ding. Ding. Ding.

Kai paced. The floorboards creaked underfoot, and he scoured the room. Photographs of animals were hung on the wall with scribbled names and dates. Harry the black-haired monkey. Dominique the reptile. Jarvis the opossum.

Brochures and magazines were neatly displayed on a coffee table surrounded by a mismatched set of chairs. There was something about this room, a hint of sea salt and jasmine lingering in the air.

Jolie was there, she had to be.

Several minutes went by, and there was still no answer. The thought of searching the building crossed his mind, but the door was locked. Breaking and entering was not something he wanted to add to his list of felonies.

Kai bolted out the front door. A path, fenced in by cages and wooden pens, led him around the building. Walking through a symphony of bird calls, he approached a cage with a furry creature hanging upside down on a tree limb.

The sloth turned his head slowly until he fixed his round black eyes on Kai.

"Hey there, friend. Do you know where I can find Jolie?"

The sloth blinked.

"I shouldn't be here, should I?" Kai said, looking around.

The low murmur of a tour guide echoed up the path. Flashlights darted through the trees as they came near. He hadn't bought a ticket, Kai realized too late. He was probably trespassing.

Kai tiptoed through a patch of trees and stood behind a large trunk. He waited for the night tour to round the corner, blood thumping in his ears.

Ten or twelve people gathered around the sloth cage, none of whom were Jolie, while the tour guide explained how they found Mr. Pembrook after he'd fallen out of a tree, probably after fighting with another sloth over a mate.

Kai raised his eyebrows and listened intently as the girl continued.

Apparently sloths fell out of trees all the time and could plummet from over one hundred feet without injury.

How about that, Kai thought. The tour group oohed and aahed.

Another fun fact Kai learned while hiding in the trees; it was not a good idea to hide in the trees. A flashlight shone in his eyes as a kid shouted out, "There's a man in the trees! Over there, look!"

Then there were ten flashlights on him and no way out. Kai slinked from behind the tree, his hands in the air. "*Lo siento.* I'm sorry," he said. "I had gotten lost, and I didn't want to disturb the tour."

He was the worst liar ever. Kai didn't need to see the disapproving faces. He knew they were there.

Kai's cheeks burned. He stepped over a bush onto the pebble path with his hands up in surrender. He immediately put them down when he reminded himself he hadn't done anything wrong.

"You're supposed to pay for a ticket at the front desk," the tour guide said, pointing back at the main building. He looked like a younger version of Trip, only with short hair.

The Trip look-alike pulled out a Walkie Talkie and held it up. "Do I need to get someone to escort you?"

Kai's hands shot up again. "Oh no, sorry. I'll head back on my own. I'm sorry to intrude." He stepped backward, one foot at a time while the flashlights followed him up the path as he scampered back to the main building.

Of course this time a receptionist was at the desk. A young girl with a white name tag displaying Bianca on her shirt greeted Kai in Spanish.

"I'm looking for Jolie Boulard. Do you know where I can find her?" Kai said.

The receptionist perked up. "Oh yeah. She left with Trip a little while ago."

Kai saw red. "Do you know if she'll be back?"

The girl shrugged. "I'm not sure, but she mentioned that she was going to volunteer tomorrow. I can leave a message, or you can swing by later."

Kai silenced the growl at the back of his throat and mustered his next words as calmly as he could. "No, thank you."

He needed to see her tonight. It didn't matter where they went or what they were doing. She was out there with *him*. It needed to be stopped.

Kai stomped out the door with heavy feet and a sagging heart.

He was too late. She had already moved on to the next guy, and on a date no less. A luxury Kai didn't allow himself when he had the chance.

Stupid.

Stupid.

Stupid.

Kai trudged back down the gravel path, kicking a rock with every internal insult he could think of along the way.

The evening air had cooled, settled under a twinkling sky. He took a deep breath in and pushed it out, flicking his lighter on and off.

He would come back, he decided. Tonight he would dump the cocaine. Tomorrow he would win back Jolie.

No sooner than his hand latched onto the door handle of his truck, a red Jeep came tearing down the gravel road, music blaring from the car speakers. Behind the yellow headlights was a guy in a man bun and a girl with her hair pulled back, her ponytail whipping in the wind. As they zoomed past, Kai got a glimpse of the beautiful smile that had been haunting him for days.

It was her.

And it was now or never.

Kai took off running back up the gravel road, waving his arms, yelling at the Jeep to stop. He ran as fast as his legs could carry him, despite the pain in his side. He really needed to take care of that rib.

Rocks under his feet had him wobbling unsteadily, but he pressed on, his lungs burning as he raced to keep them in his view. Thundering up the road, Kai eventually caught up to the red brake lights of the Jeep, rolling to a stop.

"Jolie!" Kai cried out, closing the distance.

Only a couple hundred yards to go. Kai yelled again. "Jolie!"

Jolie had just stepped out of the Jeep when she turned her head, locking eyes on Kai as he barreled toward her.

"Kai?" Jolie said, her brows pinched together.

"Jolie," Kai huffed, struggling to catch his breath. He slowed to a walk, his hands on his hips as he gasped for air. His leg muscles quivered after the dead sprint he had just put them through.

He approached Jolie cautiously, still unsure if she would be mad to see him. Her beauty would have taken his breath away if he had any left. She was every bit as stunning as he remembered her to be, even though she looked confused. Or was she angry? Kai couldn't tell. He'd had so many bright lights shone in his eyes lately his vision probably had permanent damage.

All he needed was some time to talk to her, to convince her that his feelings for her were real even if he had to spill his guts in front of Mr. Cargo Shorts.

Were Jolie's eyes deceiving her, or was Kai Greene running straight toward her? What was he doing here?

"Hey, I know you," Trip said to Kai. "You all right, man?"

"I'm fine," Kai said, waving Trip off. "I need to talk to Jolie." He staggered closer, his chest rising in falling with big gasps of air.

Jolie's heart leaped up her throat at the sight of him. His eyes were wild as he approached her, his skin glistening, cheeks flushed. He looked good enough to lick from head to toe, until she quickly remembered the feelings were not mutual.

"What are you doing here?" Jolie said, perching her hands on her hips.

"Stopping you from making the biggest mistake of your life," Kai said.

Jolie stepped back in surprise. "What are you talking about?"

"Him!" Kai pointed to Trip, whose eyes were now bulging out of his skinny head. "I can't let some granola-eating, ass-kissing, sniveling cargo-pocket-wearing twerp swoop in and take you away from me. You're mine." Kai pointed to his chest.

Jolie's eyes grew wide at Kai, shocked by this new alpha side of him she had never seen before. Although she had been wanting him to fight for her this whole time, now was not the *best* time to play out her fantasies.

Trip puffed his chest. "Hey now. You can't talk to me like that."

"I wasn't talking to you," Kai growled. "Douche."

Jolie cupped her hands over her mouth. Did he just call her future boss a douche? Who is this version of Kai? She watched in horror as the two men advanced each other like two cavemen.

This is bad.

This is very, very bad.

"Kai, stop this," Jolie said.

"I suggest you settle down, man," Trip said.

"I suggest you keep your hands off Jolie," Kai said, shoving Trip in the chest. It looked like a small shove, but Trip still had to step back to catch himself.

"Kai, I said stop it!" Jolie said, but it was no use. The fire burned in Kai's eyes, and Trip had a target on his head.

"I think it's time you get off this property, dude," Trip said, shoving Kai in the chest.

Kai rammed his shoulder into Trip's middle, wrestling him to the ground.

"No!" Jolie yelled, rushing over to the brawling Neanderthals. Kai straddled Trip while attempting to control his flailing arms. Trip's hand smacked Kai's cheek, leaving four red fingerprints on his face.

"Ow," Kai said, grabbing Trip's free hand and pinning it to the ground. "You just *slapped* me."

Trip thrashed under Kai's weight, but it was no use. Kai had him pinned down like a bucking bull in a rodeo.

"Enough! Get off of him," Jolie yelled, shoving Kai with all her might.

Kai softened under her touch, although he didn't budge. Looking up at Jolie's glare, the fire behind his eyes fizzled out, and he let go of Trip's wrists. "I'm sorry."

Another smack cut across Kai's jawline, which appeared to have stunned him just before Trip kneed him in the groin.

"Oof." Kai keeled over, tumbling to his side, his hands cupping his man parts.

Trip grappled to his feet, dusting off the leaves and dirt that stuck to his tie-dye shirt.

"I'm so sorry," Jolie said. "I don't know what's gotten into him."

"I'll tell you what's gotten into me," Kai bit out.

"Kai, now is *not* the time," Jolie said, helping Trip pull out a leaf from his disheveled man bun. "Are you okay?"

"I'm fine," Trip said, catching his breath. "Do I need to call security?"

"No." Jolie shook her head, shooting daggers at Kai. "I will handle this. I am so, so sorry."

This was a complete *disaster*. Kai couldn't have picked a worse time to be jealous—and of Trip, of all people? She had thrown herself at Kai less than a week ago, and yet Kai seemed to think she had already moved on?

The nerve of this man!

Kai had gotten to his knees, still wincing in pain from the shot to the balls.

Serves him right, Jolie thought, folding her arms at her chest. He was a few days too late to be fighting for her now, and she would not let him ruin this. "Kai, get out of here."

"I'm sorry," he said, pulling himself up to stand. "I'm sorry for walking away from you before. I'm sorry I didn't take the chance when I did. I'm sorry I put my problems before you. I will never make that mistake again. Ever. No matter how dangerous it is, I want to be with you. I need to be with you."

Jolie's cheeks burned, his words piercing her heart. She had wanted him to say those words, but not like this. Not now.

"Kai," Jolie said, taking a calming breath. She needed to do damage control before it was too late. "Now is not the time to hash things out. You need to leave."

Kai's face softened, looking at her in confusion. "But... I love you."

Jolie flinched. He was not going to make this easy, but she needed to show Trip that she had things under control. He wouldn't want a hot mess working at the ARS, no matter how good she was at marketing.

"Apologize to Trip right now, and get out of here before we call security."

Kai let out a puff of air, his face dropped in defeat. The sheen in his eyes nearly shattered her resolve, but she held firm.

"I'm sorry," Kai muttered under his breath. He took one step back, and then another, holding on to her gaze.

Jolie fought back angry tears. Why hadn't he fought for her before? It was exactly what she needed to mend her aching heart, yet the absolute last thing she needed to get her life on track. It would be a miracle if Trip forgave her for this.

Kai backed away, never letting go of her gaze until he faded into the darkness.

"I am so sorry for that. He is never like that. I don't know what came over him. I promise that will never happen again."

Trip stepped closer to Jolie, putting his hands on her shoulders. "What did he mean by being too dangerous to be together? Are you in trouble? Is there something I need to know?"

Jolie's pulse quickened as she tried coming up with something that would make sense, but her mouth opened and shut again, unable to form an explanation that didn't involve drug dealers and cocaine.

"Does he beat you?"

"Oh God no. It's not that at all," Jolie stammered. Kai wouldn't hurt a fly, which was why it was so unlike him to tackle Trip to the ground, although it wasn't lost on her that he hadn't taken any swings himself. "It's nothing. I promise. Don't worry about me. I'm fine."

Trip nodded his head in understanding, taking her into a hug. "I just want to make sure you're safe. And if being with him is dangerous, I can't have him showing up here, making a scene like that."

"Kai and I are over. I swear."

Trip gave her a half smile, rubbing her shoulders before looking at his glow-in-the-dark watch. "It's getting late. Let me take you to your bunk."

"Are you okay? Did he hurt you?"

"I'm all right," Trip said. "But I got him pretty good, I think."

Jolie smiled weakly. *If you think a bitch slap and a cheap shot to the groin is "getting him pretty good," then yeah.* Jolie held her tongue.

"Did he just ruin my chance at getting the job?"

"Nah," Trip said, rubbing the back of his neck. "If you promise to keep him away from here, I'll let the whole thing slide."

Jolie let out a breath of relief. "Okay, I promise."

Even though everything Kai said was exactly what she had wanted to hear, she could finally see clearly now. It was time to start acting responsibly first. Her heart would need to take the back seat while she got her ducks in a row.

Trip switched on the light inside the musty bunk. The room was small. A twin-sized bed was placed along the back wall and another along the side wall. Two wooden desks and a small television with a rabbit ears antenna were propped between the two beds. Her suitcase was placed in the center of the room where they had dropped it off earlier that day.

"We've got Wi-Fi." Trip pointed to a sheet of paper with curled edges on one of the desks. The faded password was barely legible. "And if you need to take a shower, it's around back. Let me show you where the towels are."

Jolie followed Trip into the bathroom.

Stacks of white towels and bars of soap were neatly tucked away behind the cabinet door. Trip took her outside to the back of the building. One shower consisted of a square cement block and a printed shower curtain adorned with rubber ducks in pink shower caps strung around a metal frame.

At least it was better than washing up in a dirty lagoon.

"I recommend wearing flip-flops when you shower. Sometimes the bugs like to congregate around the drain."

Jolie shuddered at the thought of bugs around her feet in the shower. *It was only for one night,* she told herself.

"Thank you for letting me stay here tonight."

"*De nada.*"

Trip ushered her to the front of the bunk. "Oh yeah, I

almost forgot. The toilet handle is broken in there. You just have to wiggle it a bit until it catches and then pull."

"Okay." She could handle this. An outside shower. A wiggly toilet handle. It was only temporary.

The moon shone on Trip's smiling face. "I'm really glad you're here," Trip said. "I just hope that guy doesn't show up to give you any more trouble."

"He won't. I'll make sure of it. I'm so sorry again. I couldn't be more embarrassed."

"It's fine." Trip opened his arms for another hug, and Jolie obliged, wrapping her arms around his thin waist.

Trip really likes his hugs, she mused. *They must be a touchy-feely kind of group here.*

"Now get some rest. We have a fun day ahead."

Jolie picked up a flash of something in his eyes before he blinked it away. Was he having second thoughts about giving her the job? Maybe he regretted flying her there after that Jerry Springer episode out front. Her stomach churned at the thought.

Jolie waved goodbye as he hopped down the step.

"I'll see you *mañana*," he said, tripping over his own feet. He chuckled at himself, muttering something about being clumsy, and then galumphed down the pebble path toward the main building.

Jolie stifled her laugh. He was a goofball. And he probably would be a good boss if things worked out. She looked up at the stars, praying that her interview and press stunt were enough to win everyone over.

As soon as she was alone, she whipped out her phone, connecting to the ARS Wi-Fi.

Password: ARS.

How trusting. Everything seemed so laid-back here. The staff were super friendly, and the schedule was very flexible.

Even though Trip had threatened to call security on Kai, Jolie wasn't entirely sure they even had security.

The air in her bunk felt warm and stale. She opened a window, letting a breeze flow into the room. Taking a deep breath, she contemplated a shower. Although an outside shower was the last thing she wanted, the airport grime on her skin convinced her to open her luggage and strip off her clothes.

Wrapping a towel around herself, she slipped into her flip-flops and walked outside, her travel bottles of soap and shampoo clutched to her chest.

The monkeys and birds sounded louder than before. She wondered if Trip's clumsiness riled them up. Jolie smirked at the thought that animals might find him goofy too.

She grabbed the shower handle and pulled until cold water spurted at her face. Her body tensed under the blast. Then the water warmed to a pleasant temperature, just hot enough that her body relaxed under the Caribbean stars.

Her thoughts wandered to Kai and the helpless look on his face when she shooed him away.

He had shown up, unannounced, like a bull in a china shop. Where was that initiative when she was naked and straddling him at the resort?

Jolie's chest ached. Her heart wanted to hear him out, to understand why jealousy was what brought out his wild side. The side she had desperately wanted to mount merely days before.

But it was too late now. Kai had made his bed, and now he had to lie in it.

She would get over him eventually. It was time she led with her head, not her heart. And her head told her to steer clear of him. He would only bring her trouble.

Turning off the shower, she trudged back to her bunk, wondering if she still had Kai's business card in her purse. If so, she might be tempted to call him one day when she was feeling weak, losing the battle over her resolve. She didn't trust herself. She needed to destroy the card before she invited him back in her life.

Before putting on clothes, she rushed to her purse, rifling through it until she found it, bent at the edges and discolored. She ripped it in two, the tearing cardstock leaving a mark on her heart. Then she ripped it again, the sound more painful than the last. The shredded business card scattered across her desk when she heard a man clear his throat from the back of her room.

Jolie's body seized.

CHAPTER TWENTY-EIGHT

A darkened male figure stood by the door.

Jolie's heart beat so fast it nearly ran away without her.

Stepping into the lamplight, Kai was illuminated under the soft, warm glow.

"Jesus! You scared me," Jolie said, clutching her chest.

"Most people call me Kai," he said, approaching her with his hands in surrender. "But you can call me Jesus if you want."

Jolie straightened her lips into an unamused line. "You have some nerve coming here after what you did to Trip. You shouldn't be here, Kai."

"I'm so sorry. I don't know what got into me. I couldn't stand the idea of you and him together."

"Together?" Jolie said. "Trip and I are definitely not together. He might be my boss one day, no thanks to you, but absolutely not a boyfriend."

"Your *boss*?"

"I interviewed for a job here, but then you came barreling

in like a wild boar and tackled the one man who's trying to help me get my life in order."

Kai's face scrunched together. "I didn't know."

"Well, there you have it," Jolie said, crossing her arms over her towel. "And now you need to leave, because if Trip finds out you're here, I'm going to lose my chance at getting this job."

"I thought you only wanted to work for yourself? To revamp your business. What happened to that?"

"Obviously that didn't work out given that I gave all my money to you. And look how well that turned out."

"About that." Kai pulled out his wallet and opened it up. Sliding his fingers through the fold, he pulled out a slip of paper and handed it to her.

"What is this?"

"I was able to get your money back," Kai said.

Jolie sucked in a breath, not expecting she'd ever see that money again. "How?"

"It's a long a story."

Jolie accepted the check and gaped at it. One hundred thousand dollars neatly written in his handwriting. She studied his signature, noting the pretty loop he made with the G in his last name.

"Okay. You've given me my money back. You can go now. You're free from your burden."

"You were never my burden, Jolie."

Kai took a step closer. A dim light cast shadows on his chiseled features, and Jolie felt a flutter in her stomach. Her knees weakened as he drew near.

She needed to stand strong, to gather her wits.

When he reached for her shoulder, she twisted away from him and hovered over her luggage to get her clothes. "That's right, you had other burdens that you needed to take care before me." Jolie grabbed her pajama slip and twirled her finger in the air at Kai, signaling him to turn around.

"We are square, apart from you almost killing my chance at getting this job. But I'm willing to overlook that too since you brought me my money back. So go. Don't you have a thing to get to? Another one of your life's problems to take care before you can talk to me?"

Kai whipped around, a fire blazing in his eyes. It stunned Jolie, obliterating her train of thought.

"I should have never left you at the resort that day." Kai took a step closer, and Jolie could feel the heat radiating from his skin. "Don't you get it? I've been trying to protect you. To keep you safe. Not because I owed it to you, but because I wanted to. I cared about you, and I never stopped."

Jolie's mouth went dry; her chest rose and fell with heavy breaths.

"When I saw you on the news with Trip's arm around your shoulders, I snapped. I couldn't take it. I left the damn van full of cocaine unattended, for God's sake. I should be trying to protect you from the dangerous life I'm drowning in, but here I am," Kai said, his hands flopped to his sides. "I'm a damn fool with nothing to offer you but a life in shambles."

Jolie swallowed.

"I can't stand the idea of losing you again," Kai said. "Maybe I'm too late, and maybe that's for the best. But I'd be damned if I didn't try."

Jolie searched for lies in his body language, but nothing gave him away. His eyes stayed locked onto hers as he inched so close she could feel his breath on her nose.

Kai had taken a risk, leaving a problem behind that could expose him for a crime he didn't even commit. For her.

The ball was in her court now.

She could smell the icy mint on his breath. A little presumptuous, if you asked Jolie, to pop a mint before barging back into someone's life.

But he had made his case. If he didn't really care for her, he wouldn't have tackled Trip to the ground or appeared in her bunk out of the blue.

She studied his face and the freckle below his eye that she loved so much to stare at. She had missed his mouth and the way his face crinkled when it smiled.

She had missed him and had been too afraid to admit to herself how much, but she could clearly see now that she cared for this man with all her heart.

"You abandoned your van of cocaine… for me?" Jolie said, batting her eyes.

A small smile tugged at the corners of Kai's mouth. "I'd do anything for you."

Jolie moistened her lips as she tilted her face up to him. Her breath tickled his mouth.

"You took a big risk to be here."

Kai swallowed, his eyes dropping to Jolie's mouth. A breathless yes escaped his lips.

And she would be risking her job opportunity if she let him stay.

"Do you forgive me?" he whispered.

Jolie responded with a kiss. She wrapped her hands around his neck and pulled him in tight. His mouth was warm and wet and perfect.

He kissed her softly at first but quickly became ravenous for more, pressing his hard body against the thin fabric of her nightgown. Kai slid his arms around her, gripping her backside.

Like currents of energy flowing together, they entangled themselves, electricity building up to levels that could power the city of Limón.

Pulling and tugging and clawing at his back, Jolie couldn't get enough of him. Kai's muscles flexed under her fingers as she gripped him harder.

Her breath was his. His breath was hers. They had become one, writhing on their feet, in the middle of the bunk.

"Wait a second," Kai said. He pulled away from her, his mouth swollen and red. The absence of his lips left a gaping void.

Is he seriously stopping again?

"What is it?"

"I want to take this slow," Kai said, breathing heavily.

"Are you freaking kidding me right now?"

"I mean, I want to enjoy this for as long as possible," he said. "Which means I need to slow down."

Jolie tilted her eyebrow. "We have all night, unless you have somewhere you need to be. Again."

Kai bit his lip. Shaking his head slowly. "I'm supposed to be dumping two hundred kilos of cocaine in the jungle right now, but I suppose that can wait."

Jolie placed her fingers on his chest and guided him toward the bed. As he sat down, he looked up at her with voracious eyes.

Jolie took a step back to admire him. His strong jaw peppered with stubble. His thick lashes outlining his blazing espresso eyes.

"Take off your shirt," Jolie said in a faint whisper. She had to see him. All of him.

He pulled his shirt over his head and tossed it to the side. His body was chiseled like a Greek god.

Jolie's breath hitched, drinking in the sight of him. Her body urged her to touch him, but her mind forced her to wait.

Bringing her finger to her mouth, she lightly caressed the

tip with her tongue. She imagined her finger was his, drawing it down her lip, her chin, her neck. The slick trail evaporated into the air, creating tingles that shimmered on her skin.

Air escaped Kai's lips, giving Jolie the satisfaction that her technique was working.

She continued, drifting her fingernail across her collarbone until it slid under the thin strap of her nightgown. The string slipped over her shoulder, sending ripples of goose bumps down her arm.

A playful smirk spread across her face as her finger trailed across her chest to her other strap. She played with the thin fabric between her fingers and heard a soft moan escape Kai's lips.

"You said you wanted to go slow," Jolie said devilishly.

"Yes." He swallowed. "But this is torture."

"Sweet torture, I hope," Jolie said, tilting her head to the side.

Kai nodded, staring at Jolie's finger as if he were begging for her to complete her task and unwrap herself in front of him.

"What are the magic words?" Jolie said, pulling up the string, holding it hostage atop her shoulder.

"Oh God. Is it please? Pretty please. *Please.*"

Jolie bit her lip, shaking her head. "That's not it."

Kai grunted. "You're killing me. What is it?"

"Tell me you want me."

Kai's eyes darkened as he stood from the bed. "I want you," he growled. He stalked forward, only inches from her lips. "I want you more than you could ever know. I love you, Jolie."

Jolie shuddered under his words. She knew in her heart now that she felt the same, although the words were stuck deep down.

He placed his hand on hers, holding the nightgown in place, and pressed a soft kiss on her bare shoulder.

"Hey," Jolie said. "I'm in charge here."

"Oh, I know," Kai said, his fingers grazing her arm, leaving a trail of goose flesh in their wake. "I'm only here to serve you."

Jolie shivered under his touch, frozen in time, as he placed another light kiss on her shoulder blade. A ripple of pleasure went through her spine. She nearly liquefied into a puddle on the floor.

"Stay put," Kai said, placing another kiss by her neck. His trail of kisses led him to her back. One by one, he placed earth-shattering kisses down her spine. Jolie fought back the quaking in her legs when he reached the dimples just above her backside.

Kai's hands gripped her hips and twirled her around. Now on his knees, he looked up at her, his eyes glittering in the lamplight.

"It's your turn," he said, his breath tickling her belly button.

"What?" Jolie croaked.

A slow smile spread across his face. "Say the magic words."

"I want you," Jolie said, although it came out as a plea.

Kai shook his head, taunting her. "That's not it."

Jolie knelt in front of him, the wooden floorboards creaking under her knees, and cupped his face in her hands. She knew then that her body would never be enough for him. He wanted more. He wanted her heart and soul.

He had them.

Jolie inhaled deeply, gathering all the strength to pull the words out of her, to tell him how she really felt.

"I love you," Jolie whispered, unshed tears formed behind her eyes. "I love you so much."

Kai scanned her face, cradling the back of her head with his hands before crashing onto her mouth.

CHAPTER TWENTY-NINE

A monkey shrilled, stirring Jolie out of her sleepy fog. She fluttered her eyes open to find Kai smiling down at her, his dark hair in a swirl on top of his head. Fresh air pooled in from the window, and little dust particles danced in the sunbeams.

"How long have you been watching me sleep?" she grumbled.

"Long enough to know that it's become my new favorite hobby."

"Creeper," Jolie said, batting his shoulder.

Kai caught her hand and tugged her on top of him, his body warm and hard. Her hair dangled in his face, and as she swayed, she tickled Kai's nose with the ends of her wavy strands.

"Come here, you," Kai said.

She kissed him softly and then pulled back to look at him, not remembering ever being as happy as she was in that moment. Waking up next to Kai might just be *her* new favorite hobby.

He had become her home.

Jolie nipped at his lower lip. Then his chin. Her teeth lightly grazed the Adam's apple of his throat and his collarbone. She felt Kai shudder under her mouth, and her tongue trailed along his chest until it twirled around his nipple.

Kai flinched under the flick of her tongue.

"Whoa there," Kai said, gripping Jolie's hips.

"You are so ticklish." Her tongue grazed his little nub again, and Kai jolted, nearly springing off the bed.

"Don't go spreading it around though. I'd hate to get a reputation."

Jolie smirked, pulling herself up, her chest rubbing up his stomach until her mouth reached the soft spot just below Kai's ear.

Kai jumped slightly and jerked away.

"Here too?" Jolie smiled at him. "I'd hate to see what happens when I get to your feet."

"Not the feet. Oh God, not the feet," he begged.

Jolie cocked her eyebrow at him.

Kai rolled her over, pinning her underneath him. "Maybe it would be better if I was the one doing the tickling."

Jolie's eyes grew wide. "Don't you dare."

Kai's fingers drifted toward her rib cage.

"Kai, I'm warning you."

He pressed lightly, just enough to make her squirm under his hands.

"Kai!" Jolie said, laughing. "Stop!"

Kai smiled and let go, collapsing next to her on the twin-size bed. His head rested on the nook of his arm.

Jolie turned to him and shimmied closer, pressing into every groove of his body. Like two puzzle pieces, they fit perfectly together.

Kai moved a strand of hair from her face and placed it behind her ear. She closed her eyes, relishing in the wave of pleasure that came with the soft stroke of his hand.

She listened to him, breathing through his nose, like ocean waves, buoyant and powerful. She would have recorded it if she could, in hopes that she would never forget the sound of pure tranquility.

"I love you," Kai whispered, his hand drifting over her body and landing at the peak of her hip. "I loved you the moment you spat at my brother."

Jolie snorted. "That was the moment? When you kidnapped me?"

Kai grimaced. "It was not kidnapping."

"Yes, it absolutely was kidnapping."

"Can't we agree that it was simply a contentious bed-and-breakfast?"

"I don't recall ever receiving breakfast."

"Fair point," Kai said. "Either way, I knew I loved you then. You were like a wildcat. Fierce. Biting and scratching like you were," Kai said, his eyes sparkling.

"That's a twisted way to fall in love with someone."

"Our whole situation is twisted."

"Yes, but that certainly wasn't the moment I fell in love with you."

"When was it then?" His smile lit up the room.

Jolie bit her lip, trying to think. "Probably the moment you panicked when you thought I had sepsis and you tore through that jungle like a bat out of hell. You carried me as if you didn't have a crack in your rib. I can't imagine how much pain you were in."

"I was seriously worried about you."

Jolie nipped at his mouth. "You're cute when you're worried."

Kai's mood shifted suddenly, a frown appearing on his face.

"Will you ever forgive me and my brothers for what we did?"

Jolie cocked her head to the side. "Maybe you and Noah," she said eventually. "The jury is still out on the other one."

"Raffi? I don't blame you there, but he got what was coming to him because he's in jail now."

Jolie gasped. "He is?"

"For robbing a bank, the night we got out of the jungle. The schmuck was caught red-handed."

Jolie shook her head. "Really?"

"His hearing is in a month, so we'll see what happens."

She shuddered, remembering the wild look in his eyes. There was something wrong with that guy. She was sure he would have killed her if Kai hadn't helped her escape. "I can't say I'm too sorry that he is behind bars."

"I get it. You witnessed his darkest side. He always had a couple of screws loose, but throwing you into that van was by far the worst thing he'd ever done."

"That was pretty bad," Jolie said.

"It was. But if it weren't for my lunatic brother, I wouldn't have found you."

"And I wouldn't have had the chance to be rescued by the worst, sweetest kidnapper on the planet."

Kai laughed, kissing the top of her forehead. "Well said."

A knock on the bunk door startled them both.

"Jolie?" Trip's voice called from behind the door. "You there?"

Jolie's eyes bugged out of her head. If Trip found out Kai was there, her future was over. Kai needed to hide.

"Hold on one second," Jolie called.

Kai bolted out of bed and snatched his pants from the floor.

Jolie shooed him toward the bathroom while she rummaged through her luggage. She pulled the first items of clothing she could find and slipped on a maxi skirt and cotton T-shirt.

Kai closed the bathroom door while Jolie pulled her hair up into a bun and opened the door.

Trip stood on the stoop with a big smile and blue eyes glittering in the sunlight. He was wearing his ARS shirt and a necklace with a crystal at the end. His hair was pulled back with a headband today, and his face looked different. Jolie tilted her head to figure out why. Then she noticed he had shaved off his goatee.

Clean-shaven Trip looked like a whole new person, but he still smelled the same. Hemp and granola and maybe a little hint of aftershave.

"What brings you here so early?" Jolie said, trying not to sound annoyed. She looked at the alarm clock in the corner of the room. It was only seven o'clock.

"Oh, did you not get my text?" He pulled his phone out of one of his many cargo pockets and clicked the screen. "Crap. It never went through. Sorry about that." He stuffed the phone back in his pocket. "I was going to see if you wanted to grab breakfast before we started our day."

"Oh." Jolie sighed a breath of relief. "That is so nice of you." She looked toward the bathroom door.

Jolie needed to think. How would she get Kai out of there without being seen? It was like high school all over again, hiding a boy under the bed when her father would knock on her door unexpectedly.

Maybe leaving with Trip was the best way for Kai to sneak out on his own.

"I would love that, but I just woke up. Do you mind if I freshen up first?"

"You look refreshed. Did you get a good night of sleep? Your cheeks are rosy."

"Are they?" Jolie blushed, touching her face. "Yeah, I must have." Or truthfully not at all. Kai had kept her up most of the night, and she would pay for that later without copious amounts of coffee.

"Good. I'm glad to hear," Trip said, his eyes resting on something in her room. His face twisted into confusion.

Jolie looked back to see Kai's shoes splayed out on the floor.

Shit.

Her heart thumped in her ears. How could she possibly explain her way out of this one?

"Are those...?" Trip started.

Jolie's mouth dried up. Her tongue felt clumsy in her mouth. "Um, those?" Jolie squeaked. "Those are... um..."

Think, Jolie. Think.

Jolie's spine stiffened at the touch on her back. Kai's fingers pressed firmly as if it were a warning. He was going to speak up, but she had no way of stopping him.

Kai, don't.

"They're mine," he said, opening the door.

Trip shot back in surprise. "What the hell?" Trip stumbled over his own feet, tripping down the porch steps.

"I'm sorry." Jolie winced. "I should have told you."

"I thought we agreed he wouldn't come back here," Trip said.

Jolie glanced between Kai and Trip and back again. Both men's chests were puffed up like angry peacocks. Actually, a peacock and a chicken would be a fairer comparison.

"Listen, I don't want any trouble," Kai said. "I'm really sorry for tackling you last night. I was being a real idiot."

Trip pushed a rock with the edge of his sneaker as he rolled his lips to the side. "I'm sorry for kneeing you in the balls."

Jolie let out a breath of relief. At least apologies were out there in the open, but this was not over. She wasn't in the clear.

Jolie turned to Kai. "Do you mind giving me a minute?"

Kai nodded, and his jaw clicked as he stepped out of the way.

Jolie tread onto the stoop, closing the door behind her. "I know I promised you he wouldn't be back here, but he found me anyway. You guys really need a new security system," Jolie said, placing her hands on her hips. "But he won't cause any more scenes, I promise. I talked to him."

Trip kicked another rock with the toe of his shoe. "I still don't like him being here."

"Say no more. I'll tell him to leave, and if I get the job, I will find my own apartment." Now that she had money again, she could probably afford somewhere that had an indoor shower.

Trip pushed his tongue along the side of his cheek as he looked off into the trees.

"Please," Jolie said. "I really want this job."

When his gaze drifted back to Jolie's, she noticed he was holding back a smile.

"What is it?" Jolie said.

Trip looked down at his shoes, stuffing his hands in his pockets. "I heard from the board last night. It's unanimous. You got the job."

"I did?" Jolie squealed. "Are you serious?"

"Everyone was super impressed with your ideas and your ability to get a news crew on the day of your interview. The job is yours if you'll have it."

Jolie jumped down from the step to give him a hug. "Oh my God. Oh my God. Thank you!"

"Don't thank me. You earned it." Trip looked up at the window as if he might have caught Kai staring. "No thanks to your boyfriend though."

"Well, actually he was the one that got me thinking it was okay to work for someone else in the first place. I didn't even consider the fact that there would be organizations out there that would have an opportunity like this—doing what I love, working with animals. It's a dream come true."

"I'm glad he was good for something. Just be careful, okay?" Trip said, nodding back at the window. "Come find me at the main office when you're ready, and I can take you around to introduce you to everyone."

"Thank you so much," Jolie said, clapping her hands. "You're not going to regret it."

Trip bobbed his head once and smiled before he pivoted toward the main building. He took off in an awkward jog, kicking up sand and pebbles as his shoes swiped at the ground.

Jolie practically skipped up the steps, opening the door to find Kai standing with his arms crossed over his chest.

"I hate that guy," Kai said.

"*That guy* is officially my new boss." Jolie beamed. "I got the job."

"You got the job?" Kai said, releasing his arms.

"I got the job!" Jolie repeated again, leaping up into his arms only to crash to the ground with him.

"Ow," he said, holding his side.

"Oh, I'm so sorry. I already forgot about your rib."

"It's okay," he said, regaining his composure.

Jolie helped him up onto his feet.

"I can't believe you're going to be here," Kai said. "When I came here to win you back, I was prepared to book a one-way ticket to San Francisco if I needed to."

"You would have done that, really?"

"Yes," he said, rubbing her arms. "I would do anything for you."

"Well, I'm excited to live down here." Jolie reached in her bag and pulled out her ARS shirt. She draped it over her chest and twirled around. "What do you think?"

"Conformity looks good on you," Kai said, taking her into his arms. He planted a kiss on top of her head and looked in her eyes. "I should probably go."

Jolie's face fell into a frown. "I don't want you to."

Kai cupped her chin with his hands, tilting her head up. "I've got a van of cocaine to deal with. When do you leave for San Francisco?"

"My flight leaves late tonight," Jolie said, looking up at him through her lashes. "But I should be back in a couple of weeks."

"That's plenty of time for me to figure out what I'm doing. If everything goes smoothly with the drop-off."

"What is your plan? Are you going to go back to San José?"

Kai sighed. "I don't know. I need to get my father's business ready for sale. With Raffi in jail, we've got nobody to run it. And my sabbatical from work will be up soon. I've got to figure all that out."

"How far away is San José?" Jolie asked.

"About a three-hour drive from here."

Jolie stuck her lip out. "That's a long way away."

"I know," Kai said. "But people make long-distance relationships work all the time, right? It's better than from here to San Francisco."

"Could you ask your boss if you could work from Limón?" Jolie's shoulders shot up to her ears. "You said so yourself, companies are willing to be flexible."

The skin around Kai's eyes crinkled as he smiled down at her. "One thing at a time, wildcat." He took her into his arms, stroking her back until she hummed in his chest.

"What if everything doesn't go smoothly tonight? What if the police catch you and get the wrong idea? What if the drug dealers find out you dumped the cocaine?" There were still so many obstacles to overcome.

"You're starting to think too much like me. Don't fret. I've a plan. And it'll work this time."

"What do you mean it'll work *this time*?"

"Don't you worry about it. Everything is under control. Just focus on getting yourself settled in Limón. You'll be back in my arms before you know it."

"You promise?" Jolie said weakly.

Kai placed his lips on hers in response and pinned her against the bunk door. His hungry mouth wrapped around hers. He pressed his rock-solid body into her, weakening her legs until she became putty in his hands.

Rocking his hips into her, a little growl escaped his throat. "I can't wait to be with you again."

"Me too." Jolie's voice came out in a hoarse whisper as Kai gave her everything in his kiss. His hands, his breath, his heart.

Everything except the promise that things were going to be okay.

CHAPTER THIRTY

Visions of Jolie danced across his mind as Kai drove up the highway, palm trees on one side and the Caribbean coast on the other. The sun was shining, and the ocean glittered under the sun.

Pulling up to a stoplight in the city, reggae music blared from a convertible in the right lane. An older man in a straw fedora had his arm around a lady in her sixties with red lips and big sunglasses.

Kai imagined what it would be like to grow old with Jolie, driving up the coast on a sunny day like this, the wind blowing in her hair, not a care in the world. They'd buy a beach house on the water and spend lazy days lounging under sun umbrellas and tending to their herd of children—that is, if she wanted children. He'd have to ask her.

As he drove past the Limón police station, his mood darkened. The stressful task of dumping the cocaine was imminent, and it poked at his ulcer.

Tonight was the night. They would get rid of the drugs, once and for all.

Kai's phone buzzed, and he pulled the heavy chunk of

metal from his pocket. Jolie was right, he really needed a new phone. He smiled as he picked up Noah's call.

"Hey, Noah. I was just on my way over to—"

"Kai," Noah cut him off. "I may have done something really stupid." The sound of whooshing wind and cars blew through the speaker.

Kai snapped his eyebrows together. "What is it? What's wrong?"

"The cops came to the house, asking Ma questions. They had been tipped off about something in the warehouse."

"Tipped off? What do you mean, tipped off?"

"I don't know." Noah's voice rose an octave. "I didn't wait to see. I panicked and snuck out."

Kai took a deep inhale. "What did you do?"

"I took the van out of Limón, and I'm heading north. I'm not sure where I'm going, but I was going to find a place to stash this myself."

"Okay, where are you? I can meet up with you now to help."

"There's a problem." Noah's voice shook. Kai could hear more cars zooming in the background. It sounded like Noah was driving through a vortex.

"What is it?" Kai shouted into the phone, his heartbeat spiked.

"There's a car."

"What car?"

"A car that I saw parked outside the warehouse. A blue four-door sedan. I think it's a Mercury Sable. It's been following me."

"Are you sure?"

"I've been driving a hundred and forty kilometers per hour, and it's been behind me the whole time. Yes, I'm sure."

"Okay, just calm down. This obviously has gotten too

dangerous. I think we should call the police and let them know what's happening."

"No! We can't call the police now. After everything we've been through? Do you know how much trouble we'd get in if they don't believe it's not ours? I can't do it."

"This is not about getting in trouble anymore, Noah. We don't know who these people are, but we know what they did to Raffi's guys. I can't let anything happen to you."

"I'm not doing it. I'm not going to risk getting you or Ma in trouble."

"Then I'll take the fall for it," Kai said, swallowing the lump in the back of his throat. The dream of growing old with Jolie was drifting away like a bubble heading into a windstorm. "I'll call and tell them it was me. I was behind the whole thing. I'll spare you and Ma. Who knows, it could all work out. They could give me a pardon."

Maybe they'd believe that a van full of cocaine just magically showed up at their warehouse one day, and they'd be so appreciative they'd put him in some form of a witness-protection program as a thank-you. It could happen, Kai thought to himself.

"No," Noah said. "I can't let you take the fall either."

"Then what's the plan, Noah?"

"I don't know, but I do know one thing. You need to go check on Ma."

Ma. Kai drew in a breath.

"If these people knew where to track down the cocaine, they might know where she lives too," Noah said. "You need to get her out of there, now."

Kai's worst fears had realized. Noah was right. Kai needed to go to her and get her out of the house if they hadn't gotten there already.

"Fine," Kai growled. "I will take care of Ma, but then I'm coming to help you. Give me a time and place."

"I can't," Noah said. "I don't know where I'm going."

"Pick a town. Any town."

There was silence on the other line, apart from the flapping wind coming through the car window and Noah's jagged breath.

"I can't pick a town because I'm going to try to outrun them," Noah said finally.

Kai slammed on his brakes, nearly running a red light. "That is a terrible plan!" Kai shouted. "You'll get yourself killed. Just tell me where you are. I'll take care of it."

"I've got this, Kai," Noah said. "You deal with Ma."

"Noah, please," Kai said urgently. "Don't go—"

Click.

"Noah? Noah!" Kai shouted. He fumbled with his phone and pressed the Redial button, waiting for the phone to ring, only to hear the voice mail recording drone into his ear.

"Dammit!" Kai gripped the steering wheel until the skin on his palms burned. When the light flashed green, he made a hard U-turn and stepped on the gas.

He needed to get to Ma before it was too late.

The local news blared from the television set in Ma's living room. Wafts of onions and garlic drifted from the kitchen. Ma was hovering over her stove, sautéing her vegetables, speaking to herself in German, one of the many prayers she said when she was worried sick.

"Ma?" Kai said gently.

"Oh!" Ma jumped, dropping the kitchen spoon to the floor. "I'm so nervous I don't know what to do with myself. Have you talked to your brother?"

"Yes, he's got the van, and he's riding out of town. It's going to be okay," Kai lied. He didn't know if it *was* going to be okay, and his insides burned at the thought of something terrible happening to his little brother.

"Noah darted out of the house when the police got here. I told him to go. It was all my fault. I should have never said anything," Ma said.

"Why not? If he hadn't gotten the van, then we would have all gotten in big trouble."

"No! We wouldn't have." Ma's hands shook as she reached for Kai's face. The raw onion on her fingers bit at Kai's nose as she cupped his cheeks. "It would have been fine if we had just left it there. After Noah left, the police told me Raffi confessed."

Kai's muscles seized. "Raffi confessed?"

"He told the police that he was hiding the cocaine. He was trying to do us a favor. He also begged them to put surveillance on our house to keep us safe."

"He did that?"

"Raffi was trying to make amends for what he put you boys through. And now I don't know how to get ahold of Noah. He's not answering his phone."

Kai embraced his mother while her shoulders shook under his arms and smoothed her hair. He grabbed the box of tissues from the counter and set it in front of her.

Kai waited while his mother calmed down. He leaned forward on the kitchen table, resting his throbbing head in his hands. "So what you're saying is, Noah should've just left the van?" Kai said. "This whole thing would have been over?"

Ma nodded, wiping her eyes.

"Dammit, Noah," Kai said, pounding his fist on the table. He pulled his phone from his pocket and dialed Noah's number again, hoping and praying for a ring.

The voice mail recording picked up. "You have reached five—"

Kai slammed his phone on the table.

"Okay, I will deal with Noah and the van. Has the surveillance been set up yet?" Kai said, stalking toward the window, looking around for a police car or something to ease his mind.

"Not yet, I don't think," Ma said.

"Then we need to get you out of here." Kai stood up from his chair and reached for his mother. "I want to get you somewhere safe now."

"But… but…" Ma resisted Kai's grasp trying to pull her out of the chair. "Stop grabbing me!"

"Ma, I don't think you realize how dangerous of a situation we're in."

"What danger? The police know about the van. All we have to do is bring it to them, right?"

Kai ran his fingers through his hair, debating how much to tell her. She didn't know Noah was being followed or that cocaine dealers could be at her front step at any moment. He also didn't want to worry her if he could avoid it.

"This has been a very stressful time. I think it would be good for you to go away for a little while. Spend some time with Aunt Ida."

"In Berlin? Now?" Ma cried. "No, I need to be here for Noah. I need to make sure he's okay and everything is settled."

"I've got this, okay? You need a break."

"To hell with a break!" Ma stomped her foot. Her eyes were as wild as the flowing mane around her face. "I'm not going anywhere."

A low grunt escaped Kai's throat. He would have to tell her everything. He steadied his breath and crouched down in front of her, staring into her eyes.

"Listen to me carefully." He swallowed. "There was a car."

"What car?"

"A car at the warehouse. A blue Mercury Sable. It's following Noah right now."

Ma covered her mouth.

"I think those are people who are looking for their cocaine."

Ma gasped. "My baby," she moaned, signaling the sign of the cross at her chest. "My poor boy."

"If someone is following Noah, there's a chance that someone might come looking for you too."

"That's preposterous. That's inconceivable. That's—"

"A possibility," Kai said, his voice low.

Ma drew a sharp breath. "What am I supposed to do? Where am I supposed to go?" Her lip trembled as she pulled off her apron.

"Go as far away from here as you possibly can. At least for a little while."

"But... but..."

Kai lifted her up from the chair. She was less resistant that time. Her limbs trembled in his grasp. He led her toward her bedroom on unsteady legs.

Reaching into her closet, Kai pulled out her flower suitcase and plopped it on her bedspread.

Ma's lower lip quivered. "I can't just leave you here to deal with all this yourself."

"If you want to keep me safe, you'll stay away for a little while, okay? Until Noah or I tell you everything is clear." Kai tugged at her drawer handle and grabbed a handful of satin undergarments.

"Get out of my knicker drawer!" Ma scolded him, smacking his arm away. "I can do it." Her hands shook as she packed her luggage.

Kai placed his hands on her shoulders, bringing her into a hug. "It's going to be okay."

"I'm so worried about Noah."

"I'll make sure nothing happens to him."

Kai's mother sank into his arms and sobbed. Her tears soaked through the cotton fabric of his shirt, leaving wet spots on his chest underneath.

He held her for a long while, occasionally pulling out his phone to check if Noah had called him back.

Nothing.

Kai left his mother to finish packing while he dialed Noah one last time, leaving a voice mail message.

"Noah, listen, the police already know about the van. Raffi fessed up. I have a plan, but you need to call me, okay? Everything will be fine."

Kai hung up and hovered over his father's computer in the study. He booked the first flight out to Berlin with his credit card. When the confirmation page popped up on the screen, Kai blew out a breath of relief.

They had only a couple of hours until boarding time.

"Let's go, Ma," Kai said from the door.

His mother appeared from the bedroom, rolling her suitcase behind her. Her eyes were still puffy, but she had applied a little makeup, making her appear more like herself. She frowned at the messy kitchen, the chopped onions and burnt garlic still on the counter.

"I should probably clean this up."

"I'll come back and take care of it," Kai said, picking up a business card from the kitchen table. "Is this the number to the police officer who came here?"

"That's the detective, Clara. I was supposed to call her when I heard from Noah."

"I'll call her after I get you to the airport. Let's go. We don't want you to miss your flight."

Ma's lip trembled as she gripped a hand around Kai's bicep. "Promise me Noah will be safe and you'll call me as soon as you hear from him."

Kai draped his arm around his mother's frail shoulders, guiding her out the door. "I'll promise to do everything I can to get him home safe."

Ma sniffed, giving one last glance over her shoulder. "Nothing is going to be the same, is it?"

"Everything will be fine," Kai said, ushering her out, locking the door behind him.

CHAPTER THIRTY-ONE

Jolie held her phone steady, snapping a picture of Mr. Pembrook as he hung from a giant tree branch in the cage. It was feeding time, and Glenda, the sloth biologist, had just given Jolie a handful of leaves.

"He's so cute. You sure he won't bite me?"

"Well, maybe a little," Glenda said.

Jolie shot back in surprise. "He will? He seems so friendly."

"I'm just messin' with you. Sloths are pretty tame. This one is no exception."

"Whew." Jolie blew out a puff of air.

"Here's one for ya," Glenda said in her thick New Jersey accent. "What do sloths make when it snows?"

Jolie fought the urge to roll her eyes. Another joke, and Jolie was at the end of her nice stick. She could only fake laugh at so many of them in one day.

"Let me guess," Jolie said. "Slow balls?"

Glenda laughed. "That's pretty good, newbie. I was going to say slow angels, but I think I like yours better. Especially for Mr. Pembrook here. He's got a pretty large set of testicles for his kind."

Jolie laughed nervously, praying that Glenda didn't tell any more jokes.

"So what do I do here?" Jolie said. "Just hold out the leaves for him?"

"Yeah, just like that," Glenda said.

Jolie waited patiently as Mr. Pembrook moseyed up the tree limb, hanging upside down. He took a bite from the leaf held out in front of him and then wrapped his three claws around the rest of the bunch. They scraped at her hand just enough to tickle her skin.

"He eats upside down like that?" Jolie said.

"Not all the time, but it seems he doesn't care to move out of this position today."

Mr. Pembrook munched on his leaves, looking about as bored as any animal could look while eating their dinner.

"I'll be right back. I left my chart in the office," Glenda said. "Are you okay 'hanging out' for a second?" Glenda used air quotes with her fingers.

Jolie plastered on a smile. "Yep, I'll be fine."

Glenda stepped over the bucket of leaves and left the cage.

"Looks like it's just you and me, Mr. Pembrook." Jolie looked over her shoulder to make sure Glenda had gone. "But between us, I needed a break from her bad jokes."

She held out another bunch of leaves, and the sloth took a lazy bite.

"I've grown accustomed to a similar diet recently," Jolie said. "I only eat plants too. For you, it's normal, but for me, it's called being a vegan. It's a whole thing." Jolie waved her hand. "It was hard at first. I do love a good cheeseburger. However, the last time I craved one, it got me into a whole lot of trouble."

Mr. Pembrook blinked at her and reached for another leaf.

"It's a long story." Jolie shook her head. "But craving that cheeseburger was how I ended up here at ARS. Even though I never got a cheeseburger. At first I was just trying to prove to my father that I could be a vegan, but then it all kind of just stuck, I guess."

More munching ensued.

"I see you're not much of a talker. That's okay," Jolie said, sitting back in her chair. "I could really use a listener right now."

Jolie let out a sigh. She wasn't sure when she was going to be able to see Kai again, but she already missed him. It had only been twelve hours since he left, but Jolie ached for him.

She was having fun as a volunteer, and everyone on the team was super nice, which helped ease the pain of being away from Kai.

They were definitely a physically expressive group. Trip wasn't the only serial hugger. Bianca at the front desk gave her a hug the second she walked into the office that morning and again when seeing her at lunch.

Jolie decided she was going to like it there. She would just need to take one last trip to San Francisco to pack up her things, and she would be in Costa Rica for good.

Her heart fluttered at the thought.

And with the money that Kai had given back, she'd also try to grow her vegan Instagram account. Her father was letting her keep the money as retribution for the damage he had done. She might have earned one hundred thousand over the course of a year or two if her father hadn't meddled, so Jolie wasn't too hung up over keeping it.

Maybe one day she would even forgive the man. *Maybe.* For now, everything else was falling into place, except the unknown with Kai and the cocaine.

The sickening pit in her stomach had been a constant reminder all day that Kai might not ever come back if his plan failed and he got caught. What if he was in some kind of trouble already? The drug dealers could have gotten to him for all she knew. He could be in the middle of a drug bust this very moment.

Jolie frowned. "I'm sorry I'm not myself today. I'm just really worried about this guy." She paused. "He's the love of my life." Jolie mused at how easy those words rolled off her tongue now. "He could be in real trouble."

Mr. Pembrook continued to chew, watching Jolie blankly.

"We didn't establish when he was going to call me. Do I call him? Or just let things be?"

More chewing. More blank stares.

"He's probably fine. I'm overreacting." At least that was what she wanted to believe. "Worrying about it isn't going to do me any good."

Jolie handed Mr. Pembrook another bundle of leaves. Her heart was heavy, and she glumly sat back in her chair. Pulling up her Instagram account, she checked the likes and comments from earlier. Her latest post of her cleaning up bat dung had gone viral. Why that one had gone viral was beyond her. She wasn't even semi-nude. She had more follows today than she had since her post on Buddy.

People were loving her new posts, sharing with friends, encouraging everyone to visit the ARS website and donate. It was amazing to watch it unfold throughout the day.

Jolie looked up to find Mr. Pembrook reaching out with his claws toward the bunch of leaves in her hand.

"Oh, sorry. Here you go," Jolie said, handing him the bunch. "Do you mind if I take a picture of you, Mr. Pembrook? You just look so darn cute with that leaf hanging out of your mouth."

She pulled out her camera and snapped a picture and then another.

"So handsome," she cooed. "And a great listener."

Jolie flipped through the pictures, satisfied with at least two of them. "Would you mind if I took a selfie with you too?" Jolie said. "Don't worry, I won't get too close."

Crouching down next to him, she held out her phone and framed their faces on the screen. He sluggishly watched her iPhone while chomping on his leaf.

She pressed the button, but the picture came out blurry, so she tried again, tilting her phone the other way.

"Hmm, not my best angle."

A man cleared his voice outside the cage. "I can take the picture for you if you want."

Jolie started, dropping her phone on the ground.

"Kai? You're here?"

"I'm here."

Jolie raced out of the cage and wrapped her arms around his neck. "I didn't think I was going to see you for a couple of weeks. Is everything okay?"

"I'm fine," Kai said, lifting her up from the ground and then promptly setting her back down with a grimace. "Ow."

"Still hurts?" Jolie said, pointing to his rib.

Kai nodded silently, like a wounded animal. She pulled him down to her, planting a kiss she hoped would make him feel better.

"God, I've missed you," Kai said into her mouth.

"I've missed you too."

It had been less than a day, and she couldn't handle being away from him any longer. She breathed in hints of coffee and fire, kissing his cheeks and his nose, his eyelids, and back to his lips.

His tongue caressed hers, and she writhed in his arms in response.

He moaned as her fingernails trailed up his neck and through his hair.

"Ahem." Glenda coughed behind them, her eyebrows raised.

"Oh, sorry, Glenda." Jolie pulled away, wiping her mouth with the back of her hand. "This is Kai. Kai, this is Glenda, the sloth biologist."

Swollen-lipped and starry-eyed, Kai reached out to grab Glenda's hand. "It's nice to meet you."

"You too, handsome. I'll be out of your hair in a minute. I just have to write down a couple of Mr. Pembrook's vitals here, and I'll be on my way."

Jolie and Kai stood back while Glenda wrote in her chart.

Kai's hands inched toward Jolie's as he wove his fingers in between hers. He leaned down toward her ear and whispered, "You are the most beautiful creature in this sanctuary."

Jolie looked up at him, pinching her eyebrows together. "Are you comparing me to the sloths and monkeys?"

Kai nodded, grinning ear to ear.

"Then that is the most romantic thing you've ever said," Jolie said, kissing him again.

"All right, you two. I'm off," Glenda said, startling them both. "Jolie, do you think you could finish feeding Mr. Pembrook? He's starting to slow down, if that's even possible for a sloth. I'd give it another ten minutes or so."

"Sure, no problem."

"Very good then. I'm off. Before I go: How did the sloth become president of the tree?"

Kai put his hands on his hips, tilting his head as if he was really thinking about the answer.

He is too nice.

"How?" Jolie urged, wanting the joke to end quickly so she could be alone with Kai.

"He slept his way to the top." Glenda threw her head back

and laughed, chortling at her own joke all the way down the path.

Kai smiled nervously and looked back at Jolie.

She shrugged. "Glenda likes her sloth jokes."

"I noticed," Kai said.

"So what happened?" Jolie said, taking a seat next to Mr. Pembrook. She gestured toward the folding chair next to her. "Were you able to drop off the stuff?"

Kai slumped down into the chair and rubbed his hands together. "No. Things have escalated a bit since this morning."

"Is everything okay?"

Kai shook his head. "Yes and no. The cops showed up, and Noah panicked. He took the van out of town."

Jolie gasped. "Oh no."

"Oh yes. Turns out the cops were actually trying to help. Raffi had confessed to the whole thing."

"You've got to be kidding me."

"Raff was trying to do the right thing by telling the police the truth, but the message hadn't gotten to Noah in time."

"Oh my God. So why doesn't Noah just come home?"

"There was a car parked in front of the warehouse, and it had been following Noah ever since he took off. His phone died before I could tell him that the police were willing to help. He made it all the way across the country by the time I heard from him again. I've been on the phone with the police all day, telling them what I know."

"What happened to the car that was following him?"

"He thinks he lost them in San José."

"Is he sure?"

Kai shrugged. "I don't know. I guess you can never be too sure. Which is why I booked a flight for my mother to get out of Costa Rica. She's on her way to Berlin as we speak."

"This was a big day for you."

"No kidding. I'm exhausted. There's nothing more I can do now. The detective should be meeting up with Noah soon, and this whole nightmare will be over with."

"You're a hot mess," Jolie said, stroking the hair around his temple.

He closed his eyes at her touch. His thick lashes were like resting butterflies on his face.

"I can only imagine how stressful this has been for you."

Kai nodded, keeping his eyes closed as Jolie threaded her fingers through his hair, around the base of his neck.

"There's one other thing," Kai said, flicking his eyes open.

"There's more?"

A mischievous smile tugged at the corner of his mouth. "I called my office in San José. They're going to let me work remote here in Limón. I may have to go to the city from time to time, but I can be here. With you."

Jolie jumped up and down, clapping her hands. With all the excitement, she had forgotten about his responsibilities in San José. The long distance would have been a pain, although she would have endured it for him.

"You did that for me?"

Kai nodded with a toothy grin. "I hadn't even thought to ask until you brought it up this morning. Now we can be together."

He placed his hands on Jolie's hips, and she could have floated into heaven without even knowing it.

"However, there's one condition," Kai said.

Jolie stilled, holding in her breath. Her smile fell when she saw the grave look on Kai's face. "What is it?"

"If I'm going to be working remote," Kai said, "I need to upgrade my phone." He pulled out his old flip phone.

Jolie laughed. "Finally!" Jolie said. "It's about damn time you upgraded."

"If I have to." Kai gave her an exaggerated eye roll.

She hugged him, resting her head on his chest as he held her tight, rocking steadily from side to side.

"I am so happy right now," Jolie said into his shirt.

"Are you ever going to introduce me to your new friend here? He's been staring at me since I walked in."

Mr. Pembrook had his eyes locked on Kai.

"Oh! This is Mr. Pembrook. Mr. Pembrook, this is the guy I was talking about." Jolie giggled.

"We've actually met before."

Jolie dropped her head to the side, peering at him curiously. "You did?"

"It was a whole thing. Never mind." Kai waved his hand in the air. "You were talking about me?"

Jolie arched her brow but decided to let it go.

"I told Mr. Pembrook I was worried about you and how I missed you terribly."

"Is that right?" Kai said, leaning forward, his gaze fixated on Jolie's lips.

"Yep," Jolie said, biting her lip, watching his mouth draw near.

Kai claimed her mouth, caressing his tongue against hers, sucking gently. "I love you," he whispered on her lips.

Shivers rushed down her spine.

Jolie kissed him slowly, imagining all the delicious things she would do to him later. She couldn't wait to rip that shirt off his taut body and feel the smooth ripples of his muscles under her fingertips. Her hands drifted down his shirt, feeling the curve of his chest and the ridges of his stomach. Just as she reached the skin above his jeans, a slow whine came from Mr. Pembrook.

Jolie peeled her lips off Kai to see what was the matter.

Mr. Pembrook was out of leaves. "You need more?" Jolie reached into the bucket and grabbed another cluster. "Hey, wait." Jolie handed her phone to Kai and crouched next to Mr. Pembrook. "Do you mind taking a photo for me?"

Kai positioned the phone in front of his face, his eyebrows pinching together.

"You just press the small circle toward the bottom of the screen."

"Ah," Kai said, holding the phone up.

"I can't wait for you to get a smartphone like the rest of the world," Jolie said playfully.

Just as Mr. Pembrook took a lazy bite from his leaf, Jolie took a bite from a leaf too. It was bitter and fibrous, dry on her tongue.

With the leaf dangling from her mouth, Kai snapped a photo and laughed. "That's a great shot."

Jolie spit out the leaf. "Oh good, because I don't want to have to bite on that again."

Kai held out her phone, revealing the picture of the funny duo, leaves hanging out of their mouths. It was the perfect picture for her Instagram account. "I'll have to ask Glenda to help me with a sloth pun to use for the caption."

"Something tells me she's full of them."

"You have no idea," Jolie deadpanned. "Nice job, Mr. Pembrook. You did great."

Kai placed his hands on her shoulders. "I'm so proud of you." He gave her a kiss on her forehead, rubbing the length of his arms with his callused hands.

Jolie's heart swelled. She was proud of herself too. She had finally found something she loved doing. For the first time in her life, she felt like she was making a difference.

"What do you want to do now?" Jolie asked. "My flight doesn't leave until midnight. We've got a few hours to kill."

Kai slipped his fingers through hers and gently kissed the tip of her nose. "I'd like to take you out on a date."

"A little late for that, don't you think?"

"Nah," Kai said, following her out of the sloth cage. "It's never too late to take my girl out for a proper vegan dinner."

My girl, Jolie hummed to herself. She loved the sound of that.

Jolie felt warm and tingly inside, but she also knew she smelled like bat dung and opossum fur. "I'm going to need a shower first."

"Lead the way," Kai said.

Jolie guided him down the pebble path toward her bunk.

"Listen," Kai said, bringing a finger to his lips. Birds trilled and squawked in the trees as they walked hand in hand, quietly listening to the vibrant life of the rainforest.

Jolie cocked a smile. "This sound will always remind me of our great escape through the jungle."

"Ah yes, a harrowing tale, featuring yours truly—a dashing hero if I may add—rescuing the beautiful damsel in distress." He leaned over to whisper in her ear. "That's you."

Jolie playfully swatted him on the arm. "Can you be considered the hero when you got us lost in the jungle in the first place?"

Kai slipped his arms around her waist and pulled her tight. "A minor detail," he said, pressing his lips to hers. "It might behoove you to leave that out when telling our children one day."

Jolie's mouth dropped. "I never said I wanted chil—"

Kai silenced her with a kiss.

"Hush now. A topic for another day. Now where would you like to go on our first official date?"

Jolie decided to let his little diversion tactic win. She looked up toward the darkening sky and tapped her finger to her bottom lip. "I'd be fine with just camping out here, snuggling up in my bunk. With our clothes off."

Kai grinned. "You are a little wildcat, aren't you?"

"You better watch out. I scratch."

"And bite too," Kai said, nipping at her nose. "Are you sure you don't want to just take a brief jaunt through the jungle again? Relive the early days of our budding relationship?"

Jolie laughed. "You just gave me an idea." She whipped off her ARS shirt and threw it on the ground.

Kai's expression morphed from shock to awe in a matter of milliseconds.

"Your turn," Jolie said, tugging off his shirt.

"What are you doing?" Kai stood frozen in his spot, his eyes blazing hot.

"Come here and make up for leaving me hanging in the lagoon," Jolie said. She licked her lips as she unbuttoned his jeans.

Within seconds, they were naked and writhing in front of her bunk.

"I love it when I get to see your wild side," Jolie said, pressing her chest against his. She ran her fingers down his spine and savored the perfect curve of his backside.

"But all I can think about is how my clothes are on the muddy ground."

"You're thinking too much again. Just shut up and kiss me."

Jolie pulled him back down to her mouth until their tongues mingled and their limbs intertwined. She placed tiny bites on his jaw and down his neck.

A low growl escaped Kai's throat as she clawed at his back.

"You're mine," he husked, lifting her up toward the bunk's stoop. He pressed her against the wooden door, claiming what was his with his mouth.

"We should probably go inside," Jolie said, turning her

back to him. He molded himself against her backside while she reached for the doorknob.

It was locked.

Jolie looked at Kai in surprise. She hadn't remembered locking the door, but she must have turned the lock from the inside by accident. Not a second later, they saw beams of light from flashlights approaching. A night tour was coming around the bend.

"Grab my purse!" Jolie pointed toward it on the ground by her clothes.

He leaped off the stoop, grabbing it and the clothes around it.

Jolie swiped her bag from him and shoved her hand inside, still naked and shaking on her stoop.

The tour guide's voice was getting louder.

"Hurry!" Kai said. "I just got out of trouble. I can't get back into trouble for indecent exposure."

Jolie felt the small groove of the metal key at the bottom of her purse and she pulled it out. *Thank God!* The flashlight beams were starting to turn their way. Jolie jangled her key into the hole, shaking wildly from laughter as she tried to thrust it in.

Kai grabbed her hand to keep it steady, and together the key slid in. Jolie turned the knob, and the door opened just before the tour group made their way around the corner.

Slamming the door shut behind them, Jolie and Kai launched toward the floor, laughing and hugging each other, grateful they weren't seen.

Jolie came down from her fit of giggles and settled onto the wooden floor, basking in the warmth of her bunk as Kai lay down next to her. The tops of their heads touched as they both looked up at the blank ceiling.

"You're going to keep me in trouble for the rest of my life, aren't you?" Kai said.

Jolie turned her head toward him and smiled. "Sure am."

The End.

EPILOGUE

O*ne year later...*
   "Are you done chopping up that garlic?" Jolie said, sautéing the onions.

Kai pivoted from the kitchen island with the cutting board in hand. The little bits of garlic were chopped unevenly, but Jolie didn't care. He was so cute when he tried helping in the kitchen. A few big chunks of garlic in her sauce wasn't the end of the world.

Kai scraped the garlic with his fingers into the sizzling pan and planted a kiss on her cheek before returning to the salad.

The doorbell rang, and a frenzy of yips and barks erupted from the living room.

"Sneeker, hush," Jolie shouted.

"I'll get it," Nora said, getting up from the couch. She set down her laptop computer on the coffee table and gingerly stepped over the canine security.

"Hello, you must be Nora." Jolie heard Gretta's voice from behind the door.

"Come in," Nora said. "It is a pleasure to meet you. Jolie has told me all about you."

"Same goes for you, dear. You are just as cute as Jolie described."

"Here, let me help you with that," Nora said, taking a tray covered in plastic wrap from Gretta's hands.

"Oh, thank you. And who are these little guys?" Gretta cooed, bending over to pet the little rascals who had congregated at her feet.

"Those are Jolie's pets," Kai said. "Nora was kind enough to bring them all the way down from San Francisco."

"I'm going to miss them," Nora said. "But they belong with their mama." Nora crouched down, letting Sneeker and Frido jump up and kiss her face.

"What did you bring?" Jolie said, turning the heat of the stove down.

"Oh, just a few coconut balls. I found a vegan recipe on the interwebs," Gretta said in her adorable German accent. Jolie loved it when Kai's mother referred to the internet. She called YouTube "the YouTubes" and Facebook "the MyFace."

She dumped a can of coconut cream into the pan and gave it a swirl before rushing to greet Gretta. "You didn't have to do that."

Wrapping Kai's mother up in her arms, she squeezed her softly.

Hugging Gretta was like walking through a field of sunflowers on a sunny day, warm and inviting and perfect. She smelled of peonies and green tea and rocked Jolie gently from side to side, holding their embrace always a touch longer than normal hugs. Jolie loved every second of it.

"I'm so happy you could join us for dinner," Jolie said.

Gretta's eyes sparkled as she cupped Jolie's face. "You look radiant, my dear."

"As do you," Jolie said, noting the mascara and red lipstick Gretta used for fancy occasions.

Not that dinner at Jolie and Kai's house was a fancy occasion. They got together every week, trading off between Gretta's new condo and Jolie and Kai's house right down the street.

Nora was in town for research, and Jolie had planned a feast of all her favorite vegan dishes she had created over the past year. Black bean enchiladas with vegan cheese. Salad with avocado, mango, and macadamia nuts. Quinoa stuffed peppers in a decadent cream sauce made with a spiced coconut cream.

"It smells divine in here," Gretta said. "And how's my baby?"

Kai shuffled around the kitchen island to give his mother a kiss, and she squeezed his cheeks in return.

Jolie and Nora exchanged smiles. She must have been thinking the same thing, because Gretta and Kai were a mother-son duo too freaking cute not to gush over.

"Shall we eat?" Jolie said, unwrapping the apron she had tied around her waist.

The dinner table was set in their backyard. Tea lights in glass votives were placed next to miniature, potted succulents. Nora had made a pitcher of lemonade and poured it into the tall glass goblets Jolie had found at a flea market.

The food was set in large white platters, and everyone gathered around under the rows of string lights that Kai had hung for this very moment.

"Look at how domestic you've become," Nora said, her eyes wide. "It's beautiful."

Jolie rolled her eyes as she poured her friend a glass of wine. "I'd hardly call myself domestic, but you're right. It's pretty. I'm going to take a picture of it."

"You'd be impressed with Jolie's commitment to her new job too. She even has a schedule," Kai said.

Nora gasped. "A *schedule*? How... responsible."

Jolie flicked her hand at Kai and her snickering friend as she ran inside to grab her camera. She figured it was a matter of time before Nora and Kai would gang up and tease her.

They were right though. Jolie had created a schedule that seemed to work for both her job at the ARS as well as her online business. She spent her mornings taking pictures, her afternoons with her marketing team, and her evenings snuggled up on the couch with Kai and her laptop, tying up loose ends from the day. It turned out she liked having a routine after all.

While Noah and Gretta took their seats, Kai finished pouring the wine, praising Jolie's ability to manage her business and her marketing job.

"Trip and I didn't get along at first," Kai said, eyeing Jolie as he topped off her wine. "But we've become... acquaintances, if you could call us that. And he said she's got more talent than any other marketing person he'd ever worked with. And the board agrees."

Jolie felt the flush in her cheeks as she set up her tripod.

"Oh stop," Jolie said. "You're embarrassing me."

"It's true though," Kai continued. "She's killing it at her job, and she's even been approached to publish her very own vegan cookbook."

Nora and Gretta nearly jumped out of their chairs.

"That's amazing," Nora said.

"I'm so proud of you, honey," Gretta said.

"Thanks," Jolie said, then promptly gave Kai an admonishing glare. Her face must have been bright red as Kai cowered slightly.

"I'm just so impressed by you," Kai said, his eyes glittering. There was something he wasn't telling her. She ignored it for now and got back to her tripod.

Clicking the camera in place, she set the timer for ten seconds, hoping her skin would normalize for the picture in time. "You guys ready?"

"Ready," they said in unison.

Jolie sat down in her chair and leaned into Kai. She planted a smile on her face as she waited for the camera, then felt the soft tickle of Kai's breath at her neck as he turned in to her.

What was he doing? He was going to ruin the picture.

"Jolie?" he whispered.

"Kai, turn around. The picture is about to—"

"My little wildcat," he said.

"Kai, stop. Look at the camera. You're going to ruin the shot."

"I love you so much," he said huskily.

"Kai! Turn around. I'm serious. It's about to—"

"Will you marry me?"

Jolie sucked in a sharp breath, her mouth in the shape of a large O.

Both Nora's and Gretta's eyebrows shot up toward the string lights, waiting for Jolie's response, leaning in as they watched with wide eyes.

Click.

EXIT THROUGH TORTUGA BAY
ESCAPE IN PARADISE (BOOK 2)

CHAPTER 1

Noah rolled over in his bed, his muscles aching in protest. Tangled strands of brunette hair draped across the pillow reminded him he wasn't alone. The taste of the brunette's cigarette mouth lingered on his tongue.

Was it Bridgette? Brianna? He couldn't remember. Either way, it was a mistake. The last time he would let a cougar in his bed for a one-night stand, or so he told himself for the hundredth time.

It was as if Noah had a bull's-eye on his forehead for tourists looking for a good time, and the bar had been swarming with them last night. Brittney—or Blanca?—had been very handsy. He had cabbed home in a drunken stupor with her paws in his pants and a whispered list of all the things she planned to do to him. Fuzzy memories confirmed she had gotten to them all, only this time he shuddered at the thought.

He was done with these casual flings.

All he had wanted was a night out with friends, drinking

away his problems as if they didn't exist. That had been his plan anyway. But like all the plans he had tried to make, it failed the moment Bianca or Brenda showed her vulnerable side.

Brenda. That had to be her name. Recently divorced with two kids in high school. It was all coming back to him now. His drunken heart had been swallowed whole the moment her eyes had shimmered in unshed tears as she talked about the fifteen years she had given that *bastard.* Her words.

He shouldn't have taken her home, but that eighth shot of chiliguaro had taken charge at some point, abusing its responsibilities of helping him forget about his bigger problem. More specifically, the problem waiting for him at the warehouse.

It was no ordinary problem either. No broken faucet or running toilet. It was far more serious.

Two hundred kilos of cocaine had been stashed in their family's business. For weeks.

Two. Hundred. Kilos. The weight of a male tiger. Or a moose. And Noah wasn't even a drug dealer. Or a drug user. The blow had shown up one day out of the blue, compliments of his oldest brother, Raffi, who had accidentally involved himself with a cartel.

Who accidentally gets involved with a cartel? An idiot, that's who. That summed up his older brother in a nutshell.

Now a mountain of drugs worth at least thirty million dollars was currently stashed in their coffee delivery van, waiting for Noah and his more reasonable brother, Kai, to anonymously drop it off at the Limón police station.

Stress levels were high, to say the least.

Brenda moaned into the pillow, blinking a few times, and then pulled the hair off her face. Charcoal smudges blended in with dark circles under her eyes. Fine lines emerged across her forehead and around her mouth. Under the soft glow of the Costa Rican sun, Noah estimated she was at least fifteen years older than him.

Noah didn't understand how this kept happening. It was a curse really. He couldn't go anywhere without being approached by an older woman. He was a good-looking guy but not any better-looking than his brothers, and they never had the same problem.

He had been told before it was his charm that wooed the ladies. And if he were being honest, he always liked the attention from older women. They made him feel mature and respected—unlike how he was at home with the constant belittling he got from his two older brothers and the babying he got from his mother. Older women treated him like the adult he was.

He had been happy to go along with the cougar phenomenon for a while, but lately the one-night stands had left him feeling empty and alone. He would've probably been better off if he had just stayed home.

"Good morning," Brenda said, her voice scratchy.

"Morning."

"I had a really good time last night," she said, tracing Noah's shoulder with her finger. Her fingernail snaked up his neck and behind his ear. The gesture felt forced, her eyes not quite reaching his. He could almost see the escape plan forming in her mind.

She didn't need to pretend this was anything more than what it was. He had thought he'd made that clear last night, but then again, he had thought he'd taken off his shoes too, but he felt them tug against his cotton sheets.

Had he had sex with nothing on but his Air Maxes? He peeked under the covers to confirm. His dumb ass had been too drunk to take them off. At least he hadn't tracked too much sand into bed from the beach bar.

"I had fun too," Noah said, stopping her hand from

caressing him any further. He gently gave it back to her before pulling his fully laced shoes out from under the covers. "I've gotta head to work." He slipped his shoes through his boxers—not an easy task on the first try. Was he still drunk? "I can show you out before my mother wakes up."

"Your *mother*?" She shot up, covering herself with the bedsheet. "You still live with your mother?"

"Well, yeah. Did I not mention that?" Noah said, scratching the back of his head. "I've been helping with the family business and—"

The woman cocked her head to the side, narrowing her eyes. She zeroed in on his face. "How old are you?"

"Twenty-two."

She gasped. *"Twenty-two?"*

"Did I forget to mention that too?" Noah winced. "Sorry. I was so drunk and—"

"Oh my god, oh my god," she repeated, over and over again.

His charm had apparently worn off. The woman frantically gathered her clothes while holding the white sheet to her chest. Her hands shook as she reached for her bra, which was hanging over the edge of the bed. Noah grabbed the lacy fabric and handed it to her.

She snatched it, avoiding eye contact while she dressed. "This was a terrible mistake," she said, slipping on her tank top and grabbing her heels.

Yep. He couldn't have agreed more, but it was too late for that now. Regardless, he hated to see a woman in distress, and he stalked over to her, placing his hands on her shoulders to calm her down. "We had a good time. Don't sweat it." He smiled, coaxing a grin from her.

Brenda pulled her blouse over her head. "I should go," she

said, storming toward the door in a frenzy, reaching for the knob.

"Wait, hold on," Noah said, stopping her from heading out first. He nudged her aside and opened the bedroom door, sticking his head out into the hallway toward his mother's room.

Clanking plates and water running in the sink drew his attention toward the kitchen instead.

"Ma is up. We can either go through the window, or I can sneak you through the front door."

The woman's mouth dropped in horror. "I'm not climbing through *that*."

"All right, then you'll have to follow me. Don't get caught."

"Are you serious?" Brenda huffed.

"Just tiptoe behind me and you'll be fine."

"This is ridiculous."

"Shh," he whispered. He tiptoed down the hall and poked his head into the kitchen.

Ma's back was turned, her round hips jostling while she whisked a bowl of eggs. Bacon crackled on the stove.

"Now," he mouthed, ignoring Brenda's scowl.

Grabbing hold of her hand, they crept past the kitchen and dashed through the living room, out the front door. Noah pulled Brenda onto the front step, lightly closing the door behind him. He let out a breath of relief. "We did it," he said, beaming.

"I can't believe I just had to sneak out of your mother's house," she said, strapping on her heels.

"Yeah, but it was fun, right? Sneaking around like a teenager?"

Brenda's mouth tilted into a smile.

"There's that smile," Noah said, nudging her with his elbow.

"You are quite the charmer, aren't you, Noah?"

"And you are quite the woman, Brenda."

Brenda's face fell, and she turned to leave.

"Was it something I said?"

"I knew this was a mistake," Brenda huffed before turning back around to face him. "My name is *Belinda*."

"Shit." Noah cringed. "Sorry."

"Whatever." With a flick of her long, uncombed hair, she turned on her heel and thundered down the sidewalk.

"Can I at least call you a cab?" Noah shouted.

"I've got it," Belinda said, not bothering to turn around. She pulled out her cell phone while she marched down the sidewalk.

Noah crossed his arms at his chest, watching her take her post at the street corner. He waited to make sure she got into her ride safely. Of course she didn't look back to wave goodbye.

The emptiness was back, only this time it was worse. He had never, ever made a woman feel as insignificant as he felt after a one-night stand.

Never again, he told himself.

Noah lumbered toward the rolled-up newspaper at the end of the driveway. It was his best excuse for having gone outside in his underwear and his damn *shoes*. And he needed to prepare for the interrogation he was about to get from Ma.

Creeping back through the front door, he jumped at the sight of her in the kitchen, standing with a hand on her hip and a spoon raised in the air. Long strands of white hair had fallen out of her bun. "What did I tell you about bringing women over to my house?" Ma said in English with her thick German accent, waving her spoon at him.

"What are you talking about? I was just getting the newspaper."

"Don't you dare feed me those charming lies of yours, boy. I can see right through you."

Noah cowered. "Sorry, Ma," he said, plopping the newspaper in the basket by the door. He averted her icy glare as he slumped his shoulders.

"When are you going to stop fooling around and find yourself a nice college girl? Someone your own age?"

Noah leaned down to give her a kiss on the cheek. Although she fought it, her lips curled into a smile.

"I've already kissed my chances at college goodbye, remember? I've got responsibilities here." Noah had dropped out of his first semester of college when his father had become ill and his company was on the brink of bankruptcy.

"You're not tied to the business anymore. Kai is going to sell it."

"Yeah, but we still have that damn van of cocaine to deal with. If Kai hadn't run out of the house for some chick last night, this whole ordeal would be over by now."

Ma harrumphed. "Just let Kai handle the business stuff. You're my baby. I can't have anything happen to you."

There she goes again. Always putting his older brothers in charge. And now that Raffi, the oldest of the three, had royally messed up by getting involved with the cartel, it was up to Kai and Noah to clean up the mess.

"It's a lot of cocaine, Ma," Noah said. "It's too risky for Kai to handle it on his own."

Noah still hadn't gotten used to talking to his mother about the drugs. He and his brothers had tried keeping it a secret from her, but she had eventually found out. Now she was an accomplice, whether she wanted to be or not.

"Also, Ma, you gotta stop treating me like a kid. I'm an adult now."

Ma squeezed Noah's cheeks, giving them a tough yank. His pounding head felt like it would split in two. "You'll always be my baby," she said, returning to the stove. "Now get some clothes on and eat some food. I cooked this American breakfast for you, just how you like it."

After a quick rinse in the shower, he slipped on a pair of shorts and a shirt with the Greene Coffee Roastery logo printed on the front.

The surfboard in the corner of his bedroom called to him. He needed to clear his head.

Tomorrow. He would surf tomorrow after the cocaine was out of his life forever. He'd baptize himself in the holy ocean and pray to the surfing gods for forgiveness for missing a day.

Noah had just finished pulling on his sneakers again when a knock came from the front door. He looked out his window to find a police car parked in the middle of their driveway.

Noah's heart leaped in his chest. Muffled voices echoed from the living room. He opened his bedroom door a crack, pressing his ear against the edge of the doorframe.

"We have a warrant to check the warehouse," a male voice said in Spanish.

"The warehouse? For what?" Ma shrilled.

Fuck.

Fuck fuck fuck fuck. How did they know? Who could have tipped them off?

A voice came over the policeman's radio, and the air in his room stood thick and heavy. He had to do something. He had to get rid of the cocaine before the police got the wrong idea. They had never wanted the drugs in the first place, but the police wouldn't understand.

If Noah didn't do something now, his mother and his brothers would pay the price.

"I'm sorry, ma'am," the officer said. "I can't say."

"Officer, I...," Ma stammered. "I mean, I am shocked."

"We'd appreciate it if you'd come with us to the warehouse."

Noah's stomach sank. He had to go right now. Grabbing his keys and his cell phone, he opened his window and leaped out into the bushes. Tiny branches scratched his ankles.

He hunched down low, scurrying to his car parked on the street.

Luckily, the cops were still in the house while he slipped into the driver's seat.

Ma would eventually notice he was gone. Hopefully she could stall them while Noah got rid of the van with the cocaine.

Noah's blood pumped furiously through his veins as his shaky key scraped against the ignition.

Maybe this was his chance to prove to Ma and Kai that he could handle things himself. He was a man after all. Tired of being treated like a kid.

Okay, so he was scared shitless, but he'd be damned if he didn't save his family from going to jail for a crime they didn't commit.

CHAPTER 2

Noah tore through his father's office, or what used to be his father's office. Kai had taken over and reorganized everything. The keys to the van were normally on the hook by the garage door, but they weren't there this time. He checked all the drawers and cabinets before he had the idea to check the van itself.

Sprinting back to the garage, he climbed into the van's driver seat, frantically searching the glove compartment and console. He stuffed his fingers in the seat cushions and under the floor mats.

Nothing.

Noah didn't know how much time he had, but it couldn't be long until Ma and the policemen arrived at the warehouse. The cocaine had already been stuffed in cardboard boxes in the back of the van. All he needed to do was drive away before he was seen.

Noah pulled down the visor, and the small ring of keys fell into his lap. "Finally," he muttered as he turned on the engine and hit the garage door opener. He looked back at the cardboard boxes and cursed under his breath. What the hell was he going to do with two hundred kilos of cocaine? Where would he go?

Pulling out of the warehouse, he noticed a car parked across the street. A baby-blue Mercury Sable with two men sitting in the front seats.

That was unusual. Nobody ever parked there this early.

Noah's muscles tensed.

Paranoia settled into his bones as he pulled onto a main road, keeping an eye on the Sable in his rearview mirror.

It was probably nothing, Noah assured himself. If the cartel knew how to find the cocaine, they would have come for it days ago. Weeks ago, actually. It was impossible to think they would just show up today, of all days, while the police were on their way.

The Mercury Sable slipped out of view. Noah sighed, running a nervous hand through his damp hair. He wasn't sure where he was going, but he knew he needed to get out of Limón.

Noah pressed the gas and drove forward, nervously tapping on the steering wheel.

This was all his brother's fault. Raffi was a certified idiot.

Noah used to look up to Raffi as a kid, but that was a long time ago. It was hard to forgive him for dumping all his problems on the family. Granted, Raffi had tried handling things himself, but he only made matters worse, finding himself in jail for a completely unrelated crime.

Moron.

Noah pulled up to a stoplight as a prickle crawled up his neck. When he checked his rearview mirror again, his body seized.

It was the damn baby-blue Mercury Sable, pulling up right behind him.

Fuck.

This was just a coincidence, right? Maybe they were hanging out in front of the coffee warehouse to figure out their directions. Or maybe the driver got lost on their way to brunch. That's it. They were going out to brunch. Definitely. Probably meeting their mother at the diner down the street. The one with the really good churrasco and eggs.

When the stoplight turned green, Noah inched forward, expecting the Sable to make a left turn, but it drove straight through instead.

"The diner is that way," Noah said aloud, hoping that somehow they'd realize their error and make a sudden turn.

Nope. They tailgated him instead and followed his next turn, despite Noah's attempt at pulling the wheel last minute.

Okay, new plan. Noah reached for his cell phone and dialed his brother.

Kai's voice came on the other line. "Hey, Noah. I was just on my way over to—"

"Kai," Noah cut him off. "I may have done something really stupid."

"What is it? What's wrong?"

Noah proceeded to tell him about the cops showing up at Ma's house and the blue Mercury Sable on his tail. "You need to go check on Ma," Noah said. "She's with the police now, but if these guys knew where to track down the cocaine, they might show up at the house. You need to get there, now."

"Fine," Kai growled. "I will take care of Ma, but then I'm coming to help you. Give me a time and place."

A time and a place? Seriously? When could he have possibly come up with a plan? He was surviving by instinct. "I can't. I don't know where I'm going."

"Pick a town. Any town."

Noah looked in each mirror. The Sable was unrelenting in its pursuit. To keep his family safe and out of jail, he only had one option.

"I can't pick a town because I'm going to try to outrun them," Noah said.

"That is a terrible plan!" Kai shouted. "You'll get yourself killed."

"I've got this. You deal with Ma."

"Noah, please," Kai said urgently. "Don't go—"

Beep. The phone shut off. The battery icon appeared on the screen, mocking him for forgetting to charge his phone last night during his drunken escapade.

Noah threw the cell phone in the seat and pulled up to another light. He made a right turn, and sure enough the blue Mercury Sable tailed close behind.

The signs for the highway came into view, and he did the only thing he could think to do: he pressed on the gas.

He might not have had a plan, but he knew he had to get the hell out of Limón and get rid of this cocaine once and for all.

The van rattled down the highway. Noah wiped his forehead with the back of his hand, his eyes frantically shifting between the road ahead and the rearview mirror.

The men in the Sable had been driving for almost three hours, and Noah's pounding hangover headache had lingered the whole way. He had hoped that the men would eventually give up the chase or run out of gas, but they hadn't backed down.

The exit sign for San José zoomed overhead. The city might be his only chance of escape—that is, if he was able to lose them in the intense traffic clogging the streets.

Giant towers sprang into view, surrounded by a jungle of buildings atop rolling hills. The San José Mountains anchored the skyline with clouds settled around the peaks. The fresh, salty air was replaced by wafts of exhaust fumes and wet cement after the rain. The clouds had begun to part, and the sun shone down through the windshield, directly into Noah's eyes.

Noah yanked the steering wheel to the right, cutting off a truck full of chickens. A series of bawks and high-pitched clucks filled the air as he skidded over a median onto an exit ramp. Fixating on the rearview mirror, he prayed the Sable didn't see his exit off the highway.

He held his breath, pumping the brakes as he pulled up to a stoplight.

Just as a victorious smile reached his lips, the Sable snaked around a city bus and onto the exit ramp, picking up speed.

Shit.

Noah's heart pounded in his chest, and he gunned the van forward, driving over the sidewalk to pass the car ahead. He made a turn, cutting off a cab that slammed on its brakes with a loud screech. An angry horn quickly followed.

"Sorry!" Noah yelled out the van window.

He tore through the streets, dodging between cars and cutting corners.

It was beginning to look like he had lost the Sable between Avenue 16 and 18. He felt a wave of relief, and his breath began to normalize.

There was a brief opening in oncoming traffic, and Noah jerked the wheel to the left, nearly swiping a moped. More horns blared as Noah swerved around a businessman. He looked back in his rearview mirror as squealing tires were followed by crunching metal, the Sable colliding with a black SUV. All the cars in the intersection came to a halt. The Sable's headlight hung from its socket.

"Yes!" Noah yelled, adrenaline ringing in his ears. He pumped his fist in the air, tearing up the street before he made a hard-right turn. The wreck slipped out of view. This was his chance to make his big escape. But where would he go?

At the next stoplight, he could finally relax. Music from the shops and restaurants seeped into the van. A swarm of people crossed the sidewalk, ambling around with coffee cups and cell phones in their grips.

A billboard over the freeway featured a setting sun over the ocean. A silhouetted surfer held his board under neon-pink letters that read THIS WAY TO TORTUGA BAY.

That seemed as good of a place as any.

He checked to see if he had enough gas to get to the west coast and took the exit onto Highway 27.

Tortuga Bay, here I come.

ACKNOWLEDGMENTS

I came up with this book idea on a writer's retreat with my sister. Like both of my books before this one, my stories wouldn't be possible without my fabulous brainstorming partner, Kweek.

I remember that trip like it was yesterday. We sat on a glittering beach one morning after too many drinks the night before. Our bellies full of breakfast, our bodies relaxed under the golden sun. We lazily pitched ideas back and forth until the premise of a spoiled rich girl and a criminal began to form in our minds.

That weekend, I also happened to be finishing up my final draft of *To My Muse, With Love*, and decided that Jolie Boulard needed to redeem herself. And that, my friends, is how my story and main character were born.

I wanted to give Jolie a purpose, something beyond simply being a beautiful Instagram model. So I did some research. That's when I discovered the Jaguar Rescue Center, the inspiration behind the ARS (Animal Rescue Sanctuary) in the novel.

Hundreds, maybe thousands of animals are killed by

exposed power lines every year, and I knew Jolie had to do something about it. I thought, wouldn't it be great if she could use her social media influence to save the animals and help create awareness so people can donate to institutions like the JRC?

Shameless plug: Not only does the JRC rescue and rehabilitate animals, but they also created the Shock Free Zone Project and work with the Costa Rican Electricity Institute (ICE) to identify the most dangerous areas to insulate and prevent future tragedies. Check them out when you get a chance and hit the Donate button to support their amazing work.

Anyway, the original story (previously named *The Escapists*) took several wrong turns in its first draft. I won't go into detail to spare my embarrassment, but luckily my amazing book coach and development editor, Sarah Pesce, steered me down the right path. Thanks to Sarah, this book isn't the mortifying slop of words it once was. You can also thank her for the happily-ever-after ending. I was tempted to leave you all on a cliff-hanger, but she insisted I make this a standalone book. I'm glad I took her advice.

Special thanks to Anne Victory and her proofreading team for fine-tuning the manuscript. Every book needs a solid proofreader, and I've got the best in the biz.

This novel also wouldn't be possible without the Hubs. In addition to his general support and encouragement, he also played a huge role in its development, helping point out what a man would or wouldn't say in certain situations. He's a good sport, letting me read to him while he's busy doing a million other things, including designing my book cover. If you haven't seen the blooper reel of me reading this particular story to him, I highly recommend checking it out on my website, www.aliciacrofton.com.

Last but not least, I want to thank my friends, family, my

ARC team, and my Street Team for helping me spread the word about this novel, and for writing an honest review online. Your support means the world to me. Truly. I couldn't do this without you all. Thank you.

I hope you'll stick around for the next book in the series and follow the charming Noah Greene as he attempts to get rid of that damn van of cocaine, finding love along the way.

JRC
https://www.jaguarrescue.foundation/en-us/

Shock Free Zone Project
https://www.jaguarrescue.foundation/en-us/SupportUs/ShockFreeZone

Alicia Crofton writes contemporary action-adventure romance set in faraway places. When she's not fictionally escaping through the Caribbean, she's self publishing her work, mothering her two rascals, and promoting her husband's artwork on IG.

Alicia and her family live in Portland, nestled among Oregon's finest jungle of roses.

Visit www.aliciacrofton.com and sign up for her newsletter for sneak previews, freebies, and behind-the-scenes fun.

facebook.com/aliciacroftonauthor
instagram.com/aliciacroftonauthor